KILLING
INNOCENCE

A JACK FARIEL MYSTERY

KILLING INNOCENCE
Copyright © 2021 Merit Clark
eBook 978-1-7369198-0-4
Print 978-1-7369198-1-1

Cover Design & Interior Format by
The Killion Group, Inc.

into deadly "sex games." A web of deceit, murder, lost love, and regret, coupled with more than a few surprising twists, and sprinkled with a psycho killer or two, make for a better than average serial-killer thriller."

~Publishers Weekly

"A captivating, edgy, dark read. This is the first Jack Fariel book, and I'm looking forward to see where this author will take the second book."

~ Shana Gray, author of the *Girls' Weekend Away* series

"I had not read any books by this author before, but had been reading Michael Connelly and Robert Crais and thought this novel would be right up their alley.

Is it ever. And it's nice to read a novel set, not in L.A. or New York or Boston, but in Denver. It features fully developed characters and an original plot with more twists and turns than a Rocky Mountain mining road has switchbacks. In fact, the setting is one of the book's strengths. You get a real feel for the place, and its weather becomes, almost, another character. I like a good sense of place in a novel, and Killing Streak definitely has one."

~Amazon Reviewer

"Killing Streak is an exceptional first novel, better than many works put out by the major publishers. Clark's carefully plotted story flows smoothly from an opening scene that takes a lot of the tenderness out of sadomasochism to a conclusion that affirms the possibility of love, even for the jaded and guilty.

Killing Streak is not for readers with faint-hearts or weak-stomachs. Those who love cozies will be well-advised to add an extra dollop of warm milk to their tea and avert their eyes with a moue of genteel distaste. But for those who prefer their corpses bloody and their heroes troubled, Clark's first book provides an exceptionally

ACCLAIM FOR

KILLING STREAK

"I'm an avid reader and am continually drawn to murder mysteries. The characters are complex and intriguing...I found myself identifying with them one moment and pulling away from them the next. While I hesitate to use phrases like "a real page turner" and "I couldn't put it down", it's hard not to. I often reread books that I love but there's always a year or two between readings. Not this one...as soon as I finished it I started it all over again to pick up on things I missed the first time through. I'm anxiously awaiting the next book in the series."
~Amazon Reviewer

"Homicide detective Jack Fariel's first case after a bout with cancer involves his high school sweetheart, her rich, psychotic husband and a string of unsolved murders.
. . .
The Fariel chapters are confidently written, and Clark paints a convincing portrait of the Denver Police Department in action. Fariel doesn't have a futuristic crime lab or Sherlockian insights; he just does good police work that's fun to follow."
~ Kirkus Reviews

"Evan Markham has it all ~ beautiful wife, a new house in a "neighborhood of million-dollar homes," and a successful consulting business. Or is he a Jekyll and Hyde figure who, as his wife, Corie, may come to find out, is

satisfying entertainment."

~ Harlen Campbell, author of *Sea of Deception* and *Monkey on a Chain*

"Unpredictable, gripping. It took over my life, I couldn't put it down and leave it alone. Clark's writing is sophisticated and her characters come to life. Boundaries are crossed. Don't jump to conclusions too soon; you might be wrong, and wrong again. Kudos to Clark for a well-paced novel that draws the reader into a world where normal appearances, and perhaps your own instincts, can't be trusted."

~Amazon Reviewer

"If you enjoy Karin Slaughter you will enjoy Merit Clark's first novel, Killing Streak. I look forward to more books with these characters whom I found real and flawed and yet you still want to get to know them and root for them. There were definite surprises along the way which made for a quick read because you couldn't wait to see what would happen next."

~Amazon Reviewer

"I don't know why Merit Clark's book is not on the New York Times Best Seller List. It is much better than many that make the list, in both plot and the quality of writing. Many times I can figure out the ending, but this story has a twist I didn't see coming. Move over, J. A. Jance!"

~Amazon Reviewer

*To the real-life Jack Fariels of this
world who fight evil every single day.*

ACKNOWLEDGMENTS

I am more grateful than I can say for my law enforcement contacts who have been so generous with their time and done their best to educate me. Any procedural mistakes are mine, and mine alone.

Michael Bush, Criminalist II, Forensic Imaging Unit, Denver Police Crime Laboratory

Lieutenant (retired) Sam White, Bernalillo County Sheriff's Department

Brent Lounsbury, police firearms instructor and armorer

Dennis Beauvais, a retired officer with 31 years in law enforcement including 22 with the Federal government

Forensic pathologist Dr. Judy Melinek, co-author with T.J. Mitchell of Working Stiff and the Jessie Teska mystery series (First Cut and Aftershock).

Detective Elli Reid, Colorado Springs Police Department, for invaluable—and unsettling—information about human trafficking.

Lee Lofland and the Writers Police Academy, an amazing resource for authors.

My developmental editor, Kristi Yanta, and line editor

Kimberly Cannon. Their efforts to train me in the appropriate use of commas is bound to sink in someday. But probably not.

The incredibly talented Kimberly Killion for a cover that exceeded my expectations.

My Denver crew is still the best group of drinking buddies a girl could ever have: Lisa Birkhofer, Jodi Escalante, Cheryl Robinson, Connie Schafer, Ellie Petrini Skriletz. We lost one of our circle in 2020, but I'll never forget you, Anne Durrant, and you'll always be an inspiration.

Sally Kurtzman for infinite support, friendship, and use of your guest room, as well as being a great beta reader.

Ali Boehm and Wendy Ward for advance reading, feedback, and encouragement.

My Santa Fe writing group, Wendy Foster and Lorrie Bonds Lopez.

Fellow authors who have become dear friends Donnell Bell, Bonnie Biafore, Page Lambert, Mark Stevens and Janine Whalley. It's endlessly amazing to me how supportive writers are of each other.

I lost the last few years of my life to my own personal flavor of evil. It's not good when people hear about my real life and say, "Wow, that's like something out of your books." Minus the murder part.

To all of the people who've said, "When the hell is the next book going to be out?" Here you go.

KILLING
INNOCENCE

A JACK FARIEL MYSTERY

Merit Clark

CHAPTER ONE

———

THE BODY WAS found on Acoma Street by a man walking his dog in a blizzard. A young woman, wrapped in fabric next to a dumpster. Nothing to indicate who she was or where she'd come from.

First homicide detective on scene, Jack Fariel squinted into slanting blasts of snow and considered the dedication required to be a dog owner. His idea of a pet was one tall cactus that survived on very intermittent water.

Temperature that Sunday morning, according to his car, was a brisk twelve degrees. Weather that kept most sane people indoors. Weather that called for hitting snooze and burrowing under the covers. Nor was it a location conducive to walking. Light rail on one side of the street and three blocks of dirt on the other, scraped for new development. A few dull commercial businesses remained, waiting for the right offer to sell—a storage warehouse, a plumbing supplier, an auto parts franchise. This stretch of South Acoma was redeveloping fast, like most of Denver, so fast it was hard even for Jack, with his expansive mental map of the city, to remember what had been there a month ago.

On the far side of the empty lots to the east were shiny new multicolored condos that from a distance resembled L-shaped blocks fitted at neat angles. Maybe that's where the dog walker lived. Jack made a mental note to ask since he was loathe to remove his gloves and write an actual one.

Hands buried in pockets, shoulders hunched, he nodded to a uniformed officer guarding the perimeter of the crime scene. The officer wore a standard issue puffy blue winter jacket and looked as miserable as Jack felt.

He'd passed out on the couch what felt like minutes before he was awakened at seven by the call from homicide, and when he first got up his left arm was numb. Jack was thirty-six and a runner; it couldn't be a heart attack. Just stress, a bad mood, and another restless night.

Out of sight of the officer, he shook out his arm and followed footprints in the six inches of fresh powder to his victim on the ground next to a construction dumpster. Wrapped in white fabric and snowed on, she would've been hard to spot except for the fact that dogs seemed to love peeing on dumpsters and trash bins, a splotch of yellow stained the snow a mere two feet from the body.

Officers scrambled to erect a tent over the scene for protection and Jack learned the devoted dog owner, a man named Luis Gregson, sixty-two, no record, had been taken to sit with his beagle in a nice warm patrol car.

Tempting as that sounded, Jack liked to get a feel for the scene before the usual cast of dozens trampled everything, although there wasn't much to feel this morning other than cold. And hungover. As he watched officers fight with the tent, Mike Delgado, the homicide detective who'd be assisting, arrived along with Tiffany Quintana from the crime lab.

"About time you showed up." Jack offered Mike a gloved fist bump.

"Thought Scalamandre was on call," Mike said by way of greeting, referring to a detective neither of them liked very much.

"Sorry to disappoint you."

"Doesn't the homicide rate go down in the winter?"

Mike was the same age as Jack, a big, solid guy, with a shaved head and a goatee. They'd gone through the Academy and risen through the ranks virtually in tandem.

Jack offered a brief summary. "Caucasian or Hispanic female, maybe late teens, no obvious signs of trauma, found by a man walking his dog who's been cooperative."

"Any ID on the vic?" Mike asked.

"Nope. We'll have to let Tiffany go dumpster diving, see if she can find a purse or a phone. With all the snow it's unclear what she's wrapped in, or if she's wearing anything at all underneath it."

Tiffany grimaced. "Brrr. Just the thought of being naked."

Jack paced, squinted, impatient for them to get the tent in place so he could process this and move back indoors. Noticed what appeared to be rope looped over the white cloth wrapping the body. "I've been informed it might be a while before the medical examiner gets here."

There'd been a six-car pileup with fatalities on I-25. Motorists in Denver reacted to anything other than dry pavement like it was a shocking insult on the order of a zombie apocalypse. The way people drove in the winter you'd think it was a state full of recent immigrants from more tropical climates.

"Snow."

In one disgusted word Mike summed up what they both knew, how much snow screwed with forensics, body temps, tire tracks, response times, everything.

"Those guys in LA," Jack said. "All they have to worry about is palm fronds contaminating their scenes."

"It does rain," Tiffany said. "And they have fires."

"Tiff why don't you help them put that tent up?" Jack said. "Way they're going the whole thing's gonna be airborne like a giant sail."

"I'd flip you off but I don't want to take my hands out of my pockets until I absolutely have to."

Erecting tents was below her pay grade and after several near catastrophes officers managed to secure it over the body and the dumpster. Next came work lights, so bright they were scalding, like illumination for a photo shoot in hell. Once she was shielded inside the room-sized tent Jack could see the young woman's arms were exposed, close to her sides with palms facing up, and her feet were bare. Brr, indeed. The white fabric wound in a spiral around her torso and legs; one narrow strip bound her ankles together, another looped under her chin and over the top of her head, where it was secured with a precise knot. Long brown hair snarled around her shoulders.

"Mike." Jack indicated her hands. "Check this out."

A dark object, what appeared to be a black stone, was tucked in each hand and rigor curled her fingers around them like talons. A third stone lodged just below her chin in the notch at the center of her collarbone.

"Interesting." Mike nodded, the homicide sage who'd have the whole case solved by lunch.

Jack couldn't help but laugh at the understatement, releasing a cloud of fog. "Yep."

"And what's with the makeup?"

The girl's head was tilted at an odd angle to the right and a garish swipe of red approximated her mouth, so messy Jack wondered if it had been applied by someone other than the victim, for some as-yet-unknown reason, post-mortem.

"Tiffany, what are your thoughts?" Jack asked. "Doesn't look like she put that lipstick on herself but what do I know."

"Maybe we have a new serial killer." Tiffany's mouth twitched with a smile. "The lipstick lunatic."

"Oh, that has a ring to it."

Wind snapped and tore at the sides of the tent like hands eager to snatch it away. Jack's headache mutated into an unseen band that felt like his skull was in a vise grip and he forced himself to think. Preparation this elaborate would have been difficult in the middle of the night during a storm. Snow had started before midnight with temps plunging to the single digits leading him to speculate the girl had been killed and—for the most part—staged elsewhere.

"You thinking what I am?" Mike asked.

"If you're thinking she was killed somewhere else."

"No blood," Mike said. "No castoff on the dumpster, no obvious injuries, no sign of a struggle, although it'd be hard to tell in all this white shit. So yeah, that's where my mind went. The other thing I thought was an OD but she looks healthy and I don't see any track marks."

Mike was right. Even in her current condition the young woman looked too good to be a junkie. Perfect white skin on her arms, not emaciated, manicured, unbroken nails.

"Could be natural causes."

Jack managed to deliver the line with a straight face and Mike snorted. "Then what would we do for fun? Be interesting for sure to find out how she died. You think that rope is some kind of bondage?"

"Nope." Jack's instincts said the presentation was symbolic. If a deceased was covered—for example, tucked into a comforter—it could be an indication the killer cared for the victim. This was different. Someone played with this girl, wanted more from her than her life.

Memory clicked into delayed awareness. "It's a burial ritual."

Whenever Jack pulled some random fact out of his ass it seemed to entertain Mike, and this morning was no exception. "They also make the gals look pretty and give them rocks to carry to Mecca or wherever?"

Jack pointed his index finger in Mike's direction. "You're not as dumb as you look."

"That would be difficult," Tiffany said.

"The Mecca reference. Muslims wrap bodies in white

cloth." While it had been screwed with by the elements, the scene still held an air of ritual. Jack was glad his brain had decided to make an appearance and gestured with a gloved hand. "The way her eyes are closed and her head is turned to the right? That's part of Muslim funeral tradition, and they wash corpses too, an odd number of times."

"Oh, special," Tiffany said. "That'll be fun for getting trace."

Mike frowned. "Your theory is we're looking for a Muslim killer?"

"I don't have theories."

"But you're an expert on funeral custom?"

"Everyone needs a hobby." Jack matched Tiffany's ironic tone but it was because of his family history. His mother was from Iran, a piece of information he didn't broadcast. Although, being a detective who spoke some Farsi along with a high-profile case he'd closed had made him catnip to the FBI, another fact he hadn't shared with his co-workers.

"Whole thing's bizarre," Mike said. "At least, I haven't heard of homicides where they played with stones and makeup."

"Where did you come from?" Jack stared down at his latest victim. No visible piercings, tattoos, or apparent wounds. A young girl left like an offering in a snowstorm, like a very perverse gift waiting to be unwrapped.

CHAPTER TWO

———

KEN HARROWSMITH KNEW it would be an insult to check his watch. Across the table, his wife Ruth spread jam on a sliver of wheat toast with a silver knife. She always insisted they eat together before he left on a trip but this morning she hadn't said more than the bare minimum required for civil cohabitation. Ruth had silences the way others had moods and over the ten years of their marriage he'd learned to interpret most of them, like reading emotional braille.

They hadn't had an argument—in fact, last night they'd had sex for the first time in months. But now she was back to her habitual cold, stoic self and he was back in his familiar position of tiptoeing around for fear of pissing her off.

Maybe her sour mood was because of her upcoming birthday. Ruth was turning forty in two weeks and Ken was working hard to make it perfect—dinner reservations at Denver's finest restaurant, elaborate (and expensive) bouquets of flowers for every room, a private tour at the art museum. He decided to shop for an extravagant piece of jewelry; that always worked on women.

Divorce was abhorrent in their culture but sometimes Ken needed a break and anticipated his business trip with a longing bordering on pornographic. Crappy food, unlimited TV, conversations with strangers in bars—

heaven. In an act of optimism he'd been ready to leave much earlier than necessary and his suitcase waited by the front door for a quick exit. He wondered how long before his car service arrived to drive him to DIA, and his wrist twitched with the repressed urge to check the time again.

Ruth presented breakfast the same way she'd sprung a black-tie benefit on him last night—as a fait accompli. He wasn't asked, rather informed, and it never seemed to occur to her that he might have other plans. He'd seethed, at least until her hand slid like a snake onto his lap during the symphony.

She gazed at him across the table, impossible to read. "Remind me, what time is your flight?"

"Noon."

"And you're connecting through Chicago? You should be able to get something decent to eat there."

"They'll have food on the flight." Ken's routine was to gorge on wings or a cheesesteak hoagie at O'Hare but knew she'd be horrified.

Ruth was thin as a rail and tracked her weight with an app as well as a wristband. She never ate much in his presence and he wondered if she ate at all when he was gone. For his last birthday she got him one of the bands, too, which he wore for a month and then stashed in a drawer.

"You're upgraded to business class, yes?" She asked.

"First, actually."

"How nice." Ruth recrossed her long legs and dinged her knee on the edge of the table. A frown shadowed her features, but she didn't exclaim or whimper.

"Are you all right? Do you need some ice?"

Ken used to find Ruth's stoicism arousing. Her wall of composure crumbled when she was alone with him and it made him feel like he'd done something extraordinary.

"I don't know why they call it a funny bone when it hurts so much."

She rewarded his inaccurate, lame attempt at humor with a closed-lip smile. "I'm fine."

"I enjoyed the symphony yesterday evening." Ken remembered how careful she'd been, moving her hand so no one would see. She'd tormented him through most of the third and fourth movements of Mahler's sixth.

"Did you? I thought you didn't want to go."

"I quite enjoy Mahler."

"When I reminded you yesterday evening you were indignant, even though it had been on our calendar for months."

Was that why she was giving him the silent treatment? "I wasn't upset at all."

"No?" Ruth took a sip of espresso. "I know you made a very frenzied phone call."

"I don't remember."

"I'm glad you wound up enjoying yourself at any rate." Ruth rearranged her white napkin on her lap and sighed. "This is stained and so is the tablecloth. Disappointing."

Ruth's exacting standards drove their maid Lucia to distraction. Bed sheets, bath towels, table linens—all white and all required to be pristine.

"Are you sure your knee is all right?" Ken asked.

"It's nothing, I told you."

He tried to imagine Ruth in sweats, eating pizza with her hands, and drinking soda from a can. Couldn't do it. On the road he observed other families like an anthropologist. They laughed too loud, had no manners, were sloppy and disheveled; yet he ached with envy.

"I think I hear the car." Ken shoved his chair back. "I'll let you get on with the things you need to do this morning."

"Won't the driver text?"

"Will you be going to church?" That was a stupid question. She was dressed to go out, high-heeled boots, perfect makeup. He knew full well where she was going.

"Yes, the late service. I have plenty of time, let me pour

you more coffee."

Was it his imagination or did she sound plaintive? Ken picked up his plate and carried it to the sink while his mind raced for a change of subject. "As a matter of fact, I was just thinking of Heather and Dustin."

"Were you?"

Dustin was the minister at Ruth's church and Ken didn't know him well at all. "Yes, of course, I remember you commenting that they were having difficulties. Please give them my best regards."

"How kind of you." Ruth continued to stare at the spot where he'd been sitting. "Do you regret not having children?"

It had to be turning forty that was putting her in such a strange mood. "What on earth makes you ask that now?"

"We never discussed the decision at length and I was curious."

"To be honest, I don't give it any thought."

"That's because men don't have to." Ruth turned in her chair and faced him. "Tell me, what did Lucia have planned for her free day?"

"I wouldn't know." Ken answered without hesitation but he felt her question in his stomach, as if he'd dropped twenty stories. "The tablecloth is nothing, I'm sure you'll get it sorted."

"I will."

Combined with her observation regarding his "frenzied" call this whole conversation was anything but civil. "I must be off. Security lines are dreadful these days. Are you going to be all right here on your own?"

"Yes, of course, and besides I'm not alone, I have Bibi."

"Good, good, that's good, okay then, I'll go look for that driver." Ken forced himself to stop muttering like an idiot. "I hope your week is productive."

"Yours as well."

She raised her face as he passed and he grazed her lips, eager to make his escape.

CHAPTER THREE

A UNIFORMED OFFICER WHISTLED low. "Oh, good, we got the cute one."

Jack stood outside the crime scene tent clutching a cup of coffee with both hands, willing the warmth into his fingers and the caffeine to chase away the last of his brain fog. He followed the young male patrol officer's leer and watched Cecelia—or Cece—Bennett, a young investigator from the medical examiner's office, approach. An assistant accompanied her, a young man carrying a case with supplies and a clipboard. It had taken them almost two hours to get there and despite the coffee Jack's team was pretty much frozen.

Cece's petite curves were packed into jeans which she'd tucked into knee-high black leather boots. Her purple down coat was belted around a small waist and her hair color was different every time Jack saw her. Today the top was flame-orange, striking against a base layer of jet black. Not quite Broncos colors; maybe the Bengals?

"Car accidents." Cece made a face. "I hate them. All that metal impaling things. Why can't people wear seatbelts?"

"Because people are idiots." Jack handed his coffee to an officer and held open the tent flap.

Before she went inside, Cece crossed herself, and then noticed his expression. "I always do that. I figure it can't hurt."

"Whatever works."

She tugged on multiple layers of purple nitrile gloves, brisk, professional, and then her gaze registered the body. "This is unusual."

One way of putting it.

"What does she have in her hands?"

"Black stones," Jack said. "So far as we can tell."

"Way more interesting than a car crash. After we're done you guys can bag those."

The stones would go to the Denver crime lab for analysis. Unlike TV, they often used paper bags and cardboard containers not cute little clear Ziplocs. The white cloth the victim was wrapped in would go to the lab too, but it wouldn't be removed until she was at the morgue.

Jack watched as Cece and her assistant took photographs and measurements. At one point she touched the victim's jaw and attempted to bend an arm. "Do you know when she was last seen alive?"

"I don't even know who she is."

"There's not much I can do here because she's frozen."

"Her, me, and everyone else."

"Ambient temp is eighteen degrees," Cece's assistant said.

"Hey, it's warmed up." The cold didn't seem to bother Mike, who wore his habitual winter gear including the world's ugliest hat with fur-lined earflaps.

"I don't believe that hat's regulation. I should confiscate it."

Mike grinned. "You're too vain, that's your problem."

"Nah, man, I have standards." But at that moment Jack would have traded appearance for comfort.

Cece gave the girl's hands a cursory look. Black stones were extracted from her bent fingers and brown paper bags went over the hands themselves to preserve any trace evidence.

Tiffany took one of the stones and turned it over. "No markings on it."

"Would've been helpful to have a name and address stamped on the back," Mike said.

"We can't get that lucky." Jack tipped his head from side to side and felt small bones in his neck crack. "I guess there's no point in discussing time of death."

"I guess that'll depend on the last time anyone saw her alive."

Cece said it sweetly and Jack got the message. "Same for cause, right?"

"She needs some time in the refrigerator to thaw before I can do anything."

"Like a Thanksgiving turkey," Jack said.

"Remind me not to come to your house for the holidays. Look, this cold throws everything off. It can make it appear they haven't been dead very long. They've found bodies from over a hundred years ago in permafrost that are still recognizable. What was that arctic ship?" Cece looked at her assistant.

"The Franklin Expedition."

"Those bodies are creepy." She gave an exaggerated shiver. "Poor guys died of lead poisoning. Anyway, point is, I won't have much in the way of answers until autopsy."

"Plus there's cell damage when you get below twenty-three degrees for an extended period," the assistant said.

Jack held up his hands in a gesture of surrender. "Got it. I'm on my own."

"Seriously, you should look up pictures of those old sailors online. Their clothes, their skin, all intact. Oh, look, there's two more of those things."

Cece talked while she and her assistant rolled the body onto its side revealing a stone on the ground under the girl's head and another beneath her shoulder.

"You know," Tiffany said, "smooth rocks like those are

consistent with the ones spas use for massages."

"Spas." Mike gave Jack a morose look. "Good thing there's not a lot of them in Denver."

"We need to find a spa that does hot stone massage that's missing five of them. Easy."

"Five so far." Cece watched Jack. "We might find additional objects inside a cavity."

"Instead of stuffing."

Cece flashed him a quick smile and then grew serious. "Lividity is consistent with her found position, more pronounced on her back."

"Meaning she was killed here?" Jack asked.

"That, or she was moved soon after death." Cece's purple gloved fingers moved the dead girl's hair aside. "Interesting tattoo here."

On the nape of the victim's neck were two bold, swooping black characters in a foreign alphabet. The letters were dotted with squares set at an angle in a contrasting crimson color.

لذت

"Is that Russian or something?" Tiffany asked.

"No. Farsi." Jack snapped a picture with his phone and texted it to his mother for a translation. The spoken bits he'd picked up from relatives amounted to "hello," "good to see you," "nice weather." While he recognized the characters, he'd never learned to write using the Arabic alphabet.

"And you know that how?" Cece's voice rose with curiosity.

He hesitated and Tiffany answered. "Jack's a walking search engine of random bits and pieces."

"He should be on one of those game shows," Mike said.

"Huh." Cece gazed at the victim. "Either way, the tattoo's certainly different."

"All of this is different." Jack saw the next few days of his life evaporating like the mist from his exhaled breath. "Spas and tattoo parlors. Should keep us busy for a good long while."

CHAPTER FOUR

HEATHER RATTENBERRY'S JOB as the pastor's wife was to sit up front, so she'd made an effort with her appearance—flat ironed her long wavy blonde hair into submission, applied eyeliner with a shaky hand, and put on a floral dress she knew her husband, Dustin, liked. It was one of her fat dresses, but there was nothing she could do about losing fifteen pounds in a morning.

She chose the eleven o'clock service hoping the snowstorm would thin out the crowd, and panicked when Ruth Harrowsmith approached her pew. Heather liked to sit with her friends, but hadn't seen any of them when she arrived.

"Morning." Heather glanced at her black riding-style boots that made her feel stylish until she saw that Ruth wore suede stilettos despite the crappy weather.

"I'm here by myself so I thought I'd sit with you." Ruth settled onto the wooden pew and somehow, as if by magic, her tight skirt didn't ride up.

"Um, where's Lucia?" It was unusual for Ruth's housekeeper to miss a service.

"She had a prior commitment." Ruth almost-smiled. "How kind of you to inquire."

"Sure."

"My husband chose to head off on a business trip despite this dreadful weather."

"Maybe his flight'll be canceled."

Heather felt stupid but Ruth leaned in an inch, agreeing. "I told him that very thing but men can be quite stubborn, as I'm sure you're aware."

Heather held her smile until it felt like a grimace. "I hope he'll be okay."

"I'm sure of it. How are you and the children?"

"Fine."

"Do they enjoy Sunday school?"

"Uh-huh." Heather racked her brain for something else to say. *Okaaaayyy.* But what?

At the sight of Ruth's jewelry she realized with a start that she'd forgotten to put on her engagement ring or anything other than her plain wedding band, which she never took off. She dug around in her purse for her phone, and checked the time. Five minutes until the service started.

Ruth continued her easy stream of small talk. "You're quite dedicated, coming out in this weather to support your husband. I'm sure he appreciates it."

"Yeah. You, too. Well, I mean, not the husband part." *Oh God, I'm such an idiot.* Heather's foot bobbed up and down a hundred times a minute which made her notice water stains in stark contrast to the perfect, unmarked black suede Ruth wore. It was hard not to feel sloppy sitting right next to her in her perfect dress and hair that looked like she'd just come from the salon. Somehow, without being obvious, Ruth let you know she was rich.

An old man Heather didn't know lowered himself into the empty spot on her right and she offered up a hesitant smile.

"How are you dear?" His knobby hands clenched the top of a cane.

"Fine thanks, and you?"

He launched into a lengthy complaint about the hazards of walking on ice and how the church needed to shovel better.

Heather hated it when she was cornered by an old person, but she was so relieved she no longer had to think of things to say to Ruth that she listened to him with abnormal interest until Dustin started, right on time. That was one of his things, he couldn't stand people who were late.

While he talked he walked around on the stage, or whatever it was called, Heather could never remember. A cordless mic clipped to his suit jacket kept his square hands free and his larger-than-life gorgeous image was simulcast on screens mounted from the ceiling. His hair cropped close, his square jaw free of stubble. No tats or piercings anywhere to interfere with his sculpted muscles. When she caught his eye he winked and Heather felt her face warm and her body soften.

He was gorgeous enough to star in the movie of his own life while she—hell, Heather didn't have to take a poll to know everyone thought she was inferior. When they'd met she was nineteen and she'd already been with lots of men but no one like him. Desire had warred with horror; no way in hell she could be a pastor's wife, no way in hell she could resist him. Then she got pregnant, he asked her to marry him, and that was that.

During the service, Heather's masochistic pastime was watching everyone else watch Dustin. Or, rather, the women. One row back and to her right was Cherie Allmond, who stared with pale moony eyes; if he gave her the least bit of invitation she'd go blow him right there in front of the entire congregation. Cherie's husband, Jordon, sat next to her with his cheap suit jacket open and his fat stomach bulging.

To Heather's left, also in the front row, she saw a new Sunday school teacher—Angie? Angel? She was twenty-two, blonde, and yet another crush-on-minister groupie. Angie/Angel wore a really short skirt, really high heels, and followed Dustin's every move with big mascaraed eyes. She kept crossing and recrossing her legs to draw his gaze as her skirt inched higher and higher. And then of course there was Lucia, Ruth's absent housekeeper, who volunteered for everything to spend time with Dustin.

All around Heather people listened as if her husband had answers in addition to charisma. Even the ancient dude clutching his cane watched with rapt attention, his eyes sad and watery.

Heather snuck a sideways look at Ruth with her perfect posture and immobile expression. It was rude to stare, and to be envious, and Heather knew disliking Ruth meant she was a bad Christian. Dustin told her she lacked confidence and insecurity was the root of her problems. Deep down, he said, she was a good, kind woman but Heather found it impossible to feel much compassion when she burned with jealousy. She lived on borrowed time before Dustin ditched her, before he went and found the perfect wife to match his beautiful church, one who didn't visit rehab the way other people did the dentist.

He was preaching that morning from Corinthians and Heather recognized the verses she'd helped him select. Over the years she'd become the world's most reluctant Bible expert and he often practiced sermons on her. No one would believe Dustin, the perfect man, the kind minister, relied on his sloppy, unpredictable wife. It was ironic, though, that he was preaching about love, because lately loving him had become more and more of a challenge.

CHAPTER FIVE

———◆———

JACK DUCKED OUT of the crime scene tent and Mike
followed.

It was still snowing and as icy flakes accumulated on his
head he seriously regretted his aversion to hats. "When's
this shit supposed to stop?"

Mike looked all snug in his fur-lined monstrosity.
"According to the news it's tapering off by nine."

"Right." Since it was now after eleven a.m. that was a
typical meaningless forecast. Jack would've preferred
wet, heavy snow, at least from an evidence perspective,
to the light, downy flakes drifting under his collar. They
could use snow wax and get decent castings of tire and
shoe impressions from packable snow with a higher
water content. The stuff coming down this morning was
what the ski areas bragged about, powder that floated and
fluffed, that refused to clump and fucked forensics.

"Don't think we're gonna have luck with HALOs around
here," Mike said.

Police had become dependent on the high-tech remote
control security cameras used, as the acronym for their
name implied, for observation in high activity locations.
This transitional construction zone wasn't likely to have
them.

"We'll do a survey of the few businesses," Mike
continued. "Look for video surveillance, talk to people

who'll deny seeing anything."

"You mean do it the old-fashioned way."

"What'd cops do in the old days? No DNA, no databases—"

"No bodycams."

"Okay, so it wasn't all bad. Which way you want to walk first?"

Only so he'd have the wind at his back Jack chose south, finding, as he feared, closed businesses and no one to talk to. Or any place to go inside and warm up.

They reached the corner and Mike stopped. "You look like ass."

Jack made another ineffectual tug at his collar. "It's snowing. How am I supposed to look?"

"Snow responsible for the mopey look on your face?"

"We've got a Jane Doe in the middle of a blizzard. It's a laugh riot."

Mike regarded him shrewdly. "I'm guessing you left work Friday, crashed on the couch, and proceeded to drink yourself into a stupor until the phone rang this morning."

"You don't know shit."

"Did you ever even leave the house?"

"For Christ's sake." Jack stalked across the street. He hadn't intended to survey another block in a southerly direction but wanted to end the conversation.

Didn't work. "Corie's been gone two months, more than enough time for this self-pity garbage. Next time, you're going out with us."

It had been a long time since Jack hung out with the guys like he used to, back when things were normal. Back before...had she been gone that long? He did the math.

"Why are you even here?" Mike asked.

"Last time I checked it was my job."

"No. On call today instead of Scala-fucking-mandre. Like that waste of space needs more time off. How much are you gonna punish yourself?"

Jack had taken extra shifts thinking work would be good for him. Keep his mind off Corie, move life forward, distract him until the promised day when he'd be able to think about her without feeling like a giant Sumo wrestler had twirled him end-over-end and slammed him to the ground. Fail.

"Could we do the psych eval another time? Preferably indoors with heat?"

"Dude." Mike drew out the word. "After we close this you're going out and I'm not taking any bullshit excuses."

"We're never gonna solve this if you keep jawing at me." Jack's phone buzzed with an incoming text. "Oh, thank God, something work related."

"You need to find a way to put Corie behind you and move on."

Mike wasn't moving on from this conversation and Jack scoffed. "Like you? Your way of getting over a woman is getting on top of another one."

"That might be your best option right now, man."

An image of empty liquor bottles overflowing his recycling bin flashed through Jack's mind. "I got an answer on the tattoo, if you're done with your therapy session. Those characters spell the word 'joy.'"

Mike huffed out a cloudy breath. "Now there's irony for you."

Jack started to retrace their steps north toward the dumpster but Mike didn't follow. "You coming?"

"I have an idea."

"Great. I love your ideas."

There was a long, beige cement building on the southwest corner and Mike walked toward the back where a narrow no-man's-land of brush and trash ran between the building and the train tracks. In this section of town the light rail wasn't at grade. It sat on top of a cement wall about fifteen feet high, and in front of that meager shelter homeless camped in the weeds and broken glass. Denver, in the midst of its economic boom, had a significant—and stubborn—homeless population.

With a disgusted sigh, Jack followed as Mike approached a snow-covered pile of trash and nudged it with his foot, dislodging a slide of snow and revealing what appeared to be a tattered gray moving blanket. "There's someone under here."

"Swell. Like we don't have enough to do? You gotta find another DB?" A dead body seemed a very real possibility, considering the cold.

Mike gave another push with his boot and incoherent curses came from under the grimy blanket, a male voice. The mound heaved and shifted, revealing sub-strata of cardboard and newspaper.

Even in the cold the man smelled bad. Not like decomp, like urine and other things Jack didn't want to think about.

"Hey." Mike toed in the general direction of the man's midsection, although it was hard to tell under the layers of filth. "Wake up."

"What are you doing?" Jack asked.

"He could be a witness. Probably out here all night and the body dump was less than a block away."

"I suppose if he was conscious and sober. Let's say I don't have high hopes."

"We can at least get him to a shelter."

That did the trick. "I ain't going to no goddamned shelter." A strong bellow from below the newspaper, furious thrashing, and a ravaged male face appeared with bloodshot eyes and white beard stubble, wearing a filthy knit watch cap. His right hand waved an empty bottle of Kentucky Deluxe.

"Sir." Mike used his best no bullshit command voice. "We're the police. You can't stay here."

"I ain't going to a shelter. They drug your food and steal your stuff."

"Then we'll get you a room," Mike said. "We need to talk to you first though."

"There was a very serious incident last night and we need to know what you saw." Jack went along even though he was sure this was a waste of time. Whether this man had real information or not, homeless were terrible witnesses. Most of them had serious substance abuse and mental health issues.

"Hold on, I need to take a piss." Which entailed homeless guy hoisting himself onto unsteady legs, stumbling a mere step away, and turning around.

"Let's hope there's no one else under there." Jack watched a bourbon-colored stream stain the snow. "We need to talk to you about last night, sir."

"What about last night?" Wobbling from side to side the man tucked parts away and squinted at the two detectives. "I didn't do nothin'. Who told you I did somethin'? If they did they's lying."

"We need to know if you saw anyone around here late last night or very early this morning," Mike said.

The man swiped at a runny nose with his hand and stared at Jack. "Your friend doesn't like me."

"We're the police, sir," Jack said. "We're investigating a homicide. A murder. We need to know what you saw."

"I was asleep."

"That's bullshit," Jack said. "You fall asleep in this kind of cold and you die. Lucky you already didn't freeze to death. We're going to get you someplace to thaw out and talk to you."

"I could use some coffee." Bloodshot eyes regarded them with surprising shrewdness. "The Queen has a good special. Two eggs, toast and coffee."

"We buy you breakfast, you have something for us?" Mike asked.

The man screwed up his face like he was going to be sick and Jack took a couple of quick steps back. "Mike, I don't think—" He was interrupted by a very loud, messy sneeze.

Homeless guy took another swipe at his nose then regarded the back of his hand. "Yeah. Saw someone by the dumpster." He wiped his hand on his pants and then pointed in the right direction. "Down there."

Reflexively, Jack pushed at his own nose. "You sure, sir? Last night?"

"Like you said, gotta stay awake."

"What's your name?" Mike asked.

"Dwight." He pronounced it dee-white. No last name. No date of birth or other identifying information. But he seemed certain about what he saw. "Car drove up. Nice one. Couldn't see what the guy put out there but he made a couple of trips to get things. He was there a few minutes which is why I noticed."

"One man? By himself?" Jack asked.

"Didn't see no one else."

"Where'd you park?" Mike asked Jack.

To save time with the snow and snarled traffic, Jack had driven his own car instead of detouring miles out of his way to headquarters downtown and checking out one of the usual detective rides. "Uh-uh. Hell no. I drove my personal vehicle. He's not going in that."

Mistake. Mike grinned and slapped Dwight on the back, setting off a round of moist, productive coughing. "Hey, you ever ridden in an Audi?"

CHAPTER SIX

———

B IBI'Z WAS PART dance club, part Hookah bar, part
Middle Eastern restaurant—serving Americanized
versions of what Denver locals "knew" to be authentic;
hummus dosed with sugar and ingredients you'd never
find in the actual Middle East—corn syrup, salsa, MSG.
Sahir never ate the food, thought it was shit, and
epitomized everything he hated about America: cheap,
quick, phony.

In fact, Sahir tried not to eat much, period. Liked being
lean and alert, took perverse pride in seeing how little
food he could survive on. A habit he shared with Ruth.
Sahir took it further, though, practiced abstention like a
fetish, whether from alcohol, drugs or physical comfort.
Wished there were more religious fast days because they
added structure and discipline to an out-of-control world.
Sahir's beliefs were few but immutable; life wasn't for
pleasure but for earning future reward. Indulgence now
meant eternal deprivation, and whatever he was missing
would be given back to him a thousandfold in the afterlife.
Sahir's fixation on rules made him the polar opposite of
Bibi who had no self-restraint and wanted none. Would
eat, snort, or fuck anything in sight.

Offer him Oxy and a blow job and Bibi'd let you have
his own sister which would be no great loss. Bibi's father,
Mohamed, had died six years ago and his widow was

a useless cunt who had some kind of breakdown and was paid off to go into seclusion and not embarrass the family. Sahir heard she never left her gated compound in a Tehran suburb where she wandered around naked and had gotten hooked on benzos.

Ruth became Bibi's guardian after her brother died, controlled Bibi's property, money, and assets, which included the restaurant business named after him. When the young man achieved the age of majority, if not the maturity to go along with it, Ruth saw no need to change the arrangement. But Sahir knew they lived on borrowed time before even idiot Bibi figured things out and asserted his authority. The scope of the impending disaster seemed lost on Ruth, who loved Bibi and believed with enough patience he'd grow up.

Sahir harbored no such illusions and sought a more permanent solution to the Bibi problem. Once they were rid of him Ruth would come around and see it was for the best.

Down a waitress on a busy Sunday, Sahir was at the restaurant with Avi, the manager, in a futile attempt to motivate Bibi into something approaching work. Avi scowled at the unset tables and unmopped floor while Bibi paced behind the service bar chattering on his cell phone.

He should have been in a drawer at the morgue, no longer breathing and causing disappointment. Sahir had given him enough coke laced with carfentanyl to put down ten elephants yet here he was, fat, oily, and somehow alive. Bibi wore the restaurant uniform they all did, a black polyester golf shirt embroidered with bright green palm trees and a Bibi'z logo. The shiny fabric emphasized his stomach and he held up a finger indicating they shouldn't interrupt his call.

Sahir extracted the smartphone from Bibi's pudgy hand and dropped it into a pitcher of water, eliciting high-pitched yelps and squeals.

"You asshole. That's my new phone."

"I'm surprised to see you at work," Sahir said. "You feeling okay?"

"Give it back," Bibi wailed in soprano and lunged for the pitcher, which Sahir held out of reach.

"Ugh," Avi grunted, bored, then noticed a waitress watching them. Snapped his fingers at her. "Yo. Bitch. I want flowers and silverware on these tables in the next ten minutes. Go."

Sahir might not be able to leave visible marks because of Ruth, but he could punch Bibi in his gut, which sank under Sahir's sharp, fast knuckles like dough that had been left to rise.

Avi put a strong hand on Sahir's shoulder and pulled him away as Bibi doubled up over the bar sink.

"We open in ten," Avi said. "With Val MIA I need him."

Sahir settled for dumping the pitcher of water on Bibi's head. The ruined phone clattered into the stainless sink.

"I'm telling my aunt," Bibi managed, through gasps.

Sahir made no effort to disguise his hatred when Ruth wasn't there to see. "Your hair needed to be washed, you filthy pig."

Val, the missing waitress, was Bibi's girlfriend. Sahir wondered if he'd shared the tainted drugs with her and there was a body out there somewhere to find. If so, it was imperative Sahir got to it before the cops.

He grabbed the collar of Bibi's soaking wet shirt and hauled him away from the sink. "Where is she?"

"Who?"

He got in a couple more quick jabs before Avi interfered again.

"He's not much, but he needs to be able to function."

"He needs to tell us where Val is."

"She didn't show up for work last night, either," Avi said. "You check her apartment?"

In fact, Sahir had let himself in for a look around. "All her stuff's there but no sign of her."

"She never ignores me," Avi said. "Something must have happened."

What happened was Sahir miscalculated. Maybe because he found it hard to believe any girl in her right mind would be attracted to Bibi. Val as collateral damage would be a shame, one of the few in their employ who didn't cause problems, who showed up for work on time, didn't steal, didn't drink alcohol. If her weakness—in addition to Bibi—was drugs, she'd kept it under the radar.

"You have a fight with Val?" Sahir asked.

Bibi found a towel and scrubbed his face. "No."

"You saw Val last night before work, right? You party?"

Bibi's eyes shifted. He shrugged.

"Ah, shit." Sahir regarded Avi, not sure how much he wanted to let the other man in on. "Maybe Val got smart and dumped his ass."

Avi grunted, scratched his buzz cut with thick fingers. "Bad timing. Can you get me a couple of new girls?"

"I have some packages fresh off the boat, they don't know anything."

"As long as they have tits and arms to carry a tray," Avi said. "Bibi, from now on, find pussy somewhere else and lay off our employees."

"You can't tell me who to date."

Sahir considered timing. He knew Ruth had ordered a Porsche for this lump of camel dung, planned to surprise Bibi at home later, a reward for nothing and a touching moment Sahir planned to miss. But it also meant he couldn't make another attempt on Bibi's life right away.

A crash from the dining room interrupted his thoughts. In a rush to set tables, the waitress had dropped a tub of silverware.

Avi reacted. "Is everyone who works here fucking useless?" He left to supervise and to play jovial host to customers lining up by the door.

Sahir focused on Bibi. "Where can I find Val?"

"How would I know?"

"Where'd you meet her to get high?"

"I don't have to tell you."

Sahir extended his fingers and clenched them into fists. He ached to hit Bibi for real, to strangle him, to give vent to his rage. This was denial Sahir didn't find pleasurable.

"I gave you drugs. Didn't you share them with her?"

It wasn't possible, was it, that Bibi had such high tolerance the lethal dose didn't kill him?

Bibi's eyes looked anywhere but at Sahir. "I don't remember."

"You don't remember last night?"

Customers were sitting down, talking in their loud American voices. Sahir had to let it go for the moment. Avi returned and ordered Bibi to fill glasses with tea and water.

Sahir said, "I'll go get those girls," and started to push through the swinging door to the kitchen.

From behind him, Bibi's voice rose with complaint. "I wanna know who's gonna pay for my phone."

"You want your phone?" Sahir spun with enough energy that Bibi flinched. Fished the ruined smartphone out of the sink and tucked it into the chest pocket of Bibi's shirt. Sickened to see a man blink back tears.

Smiled as he patted the phone into place and slapped Bibi on the back. Anyone watching would think they were friends. "Where you're going, you're not gonna need a phone."

CHAPTER SEVEN

———

" SORRY, EMMA."

The owner of the Breakfast Queen tossed her waist-length black hair and batted false eyelashes. "Only for you, Jack."

She led them to a booth near the kitchen, swaying on high heels. A lacy purple bra strap peeked out from underneath her sleeveless top.

Dwight's eyes bulged and he gave Jack a conspiratorial nudge.

"Don't even."

The Queen was a quintessential greasy spoon with some eclectic updates including purple vinyl booths and stools at the counter with backs shaped vaguely like crowns. Emma and her most recent husband used to own a place called the Prince of Breakfast, but after they divorced she opened her own, competing place and put him out of business by undercutting his prices—which she could afford to do since he was paying her a nice alimony.

Cheap, fast, and open twenty-four hours, the Queen was popular with law enforcement and Emma always took care of cops, bringing free coffee and extra stuff like sides of bacon and hash browns on the house. She didn't leave menus because she knew Jack and Mike didn't need them. A server appeared in under a minute with a plate of pastries and poured three coffees without asking.

"Was the dude she put out of business her fourth husband?" Mike asked.

"Fifth, I think." Jack reached for a small dish of half-and-half creamers and cringed when Dwight folded a cheese Danish and stuffed it into his mouth.

Mike, naturally, had maneuvered himself so that Dwight sat directly opposite Jack. "I don't know how old she is, but I'd hit that."

"Me, too." Dwight talked with his mouth full.

Jack breathed through his nose. "You don't have enough money."

"Aw look," Mike pointed at the plate. "She gave you a croissant. She's sweet on you. I'll bet you could be lucky contestant number six."

"I'll pass."

"Oh." Dwight ignored the paper napkins and used his hand to smear powdered sugar across his stubble. "Can I have it?"

After they ordered Jack pulled out his notebook. "So, Dwight, tell me about last night."

"Cold as shit, man."

"Right. Were you out there all night?"

"Uh-huh."

"What time did you, uh, go to bed?"

"Time, man," Dwight said. "I don't do good with time."

Jack looked daggers at Mike who he could tell was fighting a smile.

"You said you saw a car by the dumpster, correct?"

"Nice ride, one a them black SUVs, maybe a Jeep."

"Maybe?"

"One a them nice ones."

Jack sighed. "See a license plate?"

"Uh-uh."

"Maybe Colorado? You at least see the state?"

Dwight shrugged and started decimating Jack's croissant.

"Okay. Tell me about the man you saw."

"He was medium."

"What's that mean?"

Dwight's face torqued like he was thinking hard. "Not tall. And he wasn't a brother."

"That's it? Do you think you would recognize him if you saw him again?"

A sly look entered Dwight's eyes. "Ah, you know, I was pretty wasted."

"Was this man by himself?"

"I'm almost a hundred percent on that."

Jack contemplated ways to get back at Mike as Dwight poured coffee from the cup into the saucer and blew on it. "Okay. What did this medium-sized man do?"

"He backed up to the dumpster and opened the SUV, you know, the hatch thingy? People are always dumping shit. Usually I go see what it is in case I can get some bank for it but it was too fuckin' cold and besides, I had me a nice bottle to keep me company."

Jack didn't think there was anything nice about Kentucky Deluxe or any of the other cheap shit these guys drank.

"Seemed like whatever he had was heavy, from the way he moved. I got the special, sweetie."

Dwight's eyes lit up at the sight of the waitress delivering breakfast and yolks ran on his plate as he shoveled with his fork.

Jack cleared his throat. "Did you hear the man say anything?"

Dwight shook his head, focused on eating.

"Did you hear any other voices?"

Another shake.

"Someone calling for help, shouting, screaming?"

"Nah, it was quiet on account a the snow." Dwight's chin was shiny with grease.

Jack could manage bodies burnt to a crisp in a fire,

decomp on a hot day, and a woman who'd basically turned herself into soup by dying in a Jacuzzi. But watching Dwight eat was beyond his capacity.

Mike, of course, enjoyed Jack's discomfort. He nudged with an elbow in case Dwight's poor table manners had gone unnoticed.

"I'll get you back," Jack muttered. "Next time we have a code 10."

Mike's deal was he couldn't stand needles. An OD with a syringe in their arm, EMTs starting an IV—or even a simple flu shot—made Mike go weak at the knees.

"You gonna eat all your bacon?" Dwight asked.

"Take it." Jack wasn't going to eat much of anything. He shoved his plate across the table. "In fact, take the whole thing."

Dwight smiled like it was Christmas, revealing half-chewed food.

Jack cleared his throat again. "So, when did you see this big, black maybe-Jeep?"

"Between two thirty and four a.m."

"If you don't do well with time how do you know that?" Jack asked.

"The trains. I count 'em."

"You do?"

"Man, I like trains, people goin' somewhere. During the day there's one every few minutes. Ten forty-five, ten fifty-one, ten fifty-seven." Dwight made a conducting motion with his hand. "Whoosh, whoosh, whoosh."

Except his lack of teeth caused it to come out "wooth."

"At midnight it switches to every half hour. One thirty-five a.m. northbound, *wooth*. One fifty-three a.m. southbound, *wooth*. There's a two twenty-three and then nothing until four a.m. He was there during the gap."

Mike gave Jack an I-told-you-so look. Middle of the night there wouldn't have been much traffic in the area. Now that they'd narrowed down the time they might get lucky with cameras on nearby streets.

"He used his phone," Dwight said. "I saw a flash."

That surprised Jack out of his revulsion. "Like he was taking pictures?"

"Uh-huh. I wanted to see what he was looking at but it was too frickin' cold."

Jack turned to Mike. "She was a work of art."

"Piece of shit wanted a souvenir."

"Maybe he posted the pictures online," Jack said. "He needs an audience."

"That would be stupid." Mike seemed as pleased as Jack about a potential lead. "I like it when criminals are stupid."

"Dwight, you're sure about that train schedule?" Jack reached for a piece of bacon. Useful information restored his appetite and, besides, Dwight's messy hoovering had slowed. "If I check with RTD those times'll be right?"

Dwight nodded emphatically. "I know my trains, man. I'm out there every night and it ain't like I got a lot else to do."

CHAPTER EIGHT

"**H**EATHER!"

"Nicki. Oh my God, I'm so glad to see you."

Her friend stood in the open driver's door of her car and Heather jumped in. She'd been hoping to grab the kids from Sunday school in the conference center without feigning any more polite interest in business trips or bunions.

Nicki offered a cigarette and Heather sighed with relief. "You're a saint. Where were you earlier? I didn't see anyone and I had to sit with Ruth."

"Poor you. Were you down front?"

Heather wrinkled her nose. "First row. Why were you late? Big Saturday night?"

Nicki smirked. "I might have had a date. Or two."

"What? Spill."

"Remember that Bumble guy?"

Nicki was a few years younger, twenty-seven, and Heather listened to her adventures in online dating with a mixture of horror and envy. "You mean the professor you've been having the long conversations with?"

"Uh-huh. I met him for dinner last night." Nicki wrinkled her nose. "Turned out to be like forty-five."

"Ugh."

"But while I was at the restaurant I met another dude who's the same age as me and, get this, a personal trainer.

He's cut."

"You picked up a different man while you were already on a date? Seriously?"

"I didn't do anything." Nicki opened her green eyes wide, all innocent. "My date went to the bathroom and this other dude came over and started chatting me up. I always drive myself when I meet someone for the first time so after dinner, I walked outside with professor dude, said goodnight, all polite. Kissed me on the cheek, adorable. Then went back and did shots with Rob. The trainer. I'm supposed to hook up with him again later."

That all sounded like a lot of fun and Heather forgot all of Nicki's sad stories. "I so wanna be you."

"I don't know why. Is it—are you still suspicious of Dustin?"

"Am I paranoid?"

"Maybe a little."

Heather took a deep drag, slowly blew it out. "Enough people—women—throw themselves at him that he's bound to weaken. How am I supposed to hold on to someone like him?"

"He knew who you were when he married you and he's totally devoted. In addition to drop dead gorgeous. Why would you want to be me?"

Heather reminded herself she had everything— handsome husband, kids, her own house. She repeated the list like a...what were they called? Affirmations? "You don't know what it's like being married to Dustin."

"What does that mean? He loves you."

"What about Lucia?"

"What about her? You have no proof."

No, Heather didn't. *A wife knows these things*, she thought. Nicki'd never been married so she didn't get it.

"I wonder where Lucia was this morning," Heather said. "She never misses a chance to creep on Dustin."

"Why do you torture yourself?"

Heather needed her friend to simply believe her. "You've seen the way she stands there staring at him. Besides, it's kind of my job to be concerned that Lucia missed church."

"Right. So, Mrs. concerned pastor, did you ask Ruth? You said you sat next to her."

"Ya, she didn't say. A typical Ruth non-answer answer. I wish I could be that reserved."

"Icy cold is more like it."

Ken being on a business trip made sense, he did that a lot. There were rumors about Lucia and Ken, too. Girl got around for someone who never went anywhere on her own. "Where do you think Lucia is?"

Nicki sighed, bored with the conversation. "Maybe she's sick. C'mon, let's talk about something else."

But Heather couldn't. "What do you think it's like to work for Ruth?"

"All the jewelry in the world couldn't make me work for that bitch."

Lucia had shown up at church a couple of weeks ago wearing a necklace that looked like real diamonds. "Church is probably the only place she gets to wear that stuff although I still can't feel sorry for her. Does that make me a bad Christian?"

"Heather, puh-lease, give it a rest."

"Dustin says jealousy is a sin."

Nicki put a hand on Heather's arm and repeated, "He loves *you*. He married *you*."

"You're right." Heather wasn't the least bit reassured. She ground out her cigarette in the ashtray and wanted another but she had to get the kids and meet Dustin to go to brunch. It was a regular Sunday thing after the late service and anyone in the congregation was welcome to join. At his request, it was alcohol-free and afterwards they'd go home, where she'd hound the kids about homework, start on the mountains of laundry, and if she was really lucky, squeeze in some vacuuming.

"Have any gum?"

Nicki reached in her purse. "Altoids."

"He can always tell." Dustin might have known who Heather was when he married her but he couldn't stand the smell of cigarettes. She popped three mints and opened the door. "I'll just say I was sitting in your car and that's why I smell like smoke."

"You think Cherie'll go to brunch?" Nicki asked.

"She always does, along with that nasty husband of hers. At least Ruth never goes." Which meant Lucia never went either, much to Heather's guilty relief. "Hey, you're going, right? I need all the moral support I can get."

"Sure. I'm starving, I need some hangover food. And maybe I'll order a drink just to piss Dustin off."

CHAPTER NINE

———◆———

JACK AND MIKE dropped Dwight, with much protest, at the hospital. It was a fair bet he had pneumonia and he'd have a warm place to sleep, at least for a few hours. Mike made him promise to go to one of the motels that participated in Denver's voucher program providing free rooms when temps dropped below forty, and said he'd follow up with him later. Mike had a soft spot for the old homeless guys, although, while he looked sixty, Dwight was probably younger than them.

Cece Bennett called with an ID. She'd scanned Jane Doe's fingers and got a hit from the DMV database. Lucia Santiago's address turned out to be a church on south University named Stoney Gate.

Jack called a different homicide detective, Serena Owen, and tasked her with finding Lucia's death photos online and starting background checks. Mike was on his way back to the area near the alley looking for cameras and Jack was going to church. He wanted to go straight to a car wash and eradicate the old-man's-crotch-meets-stale-feces aroma of Dwight from his vehicle, but it would have to wait. The snow was tapering off so even though it was still cold, he rode with the windows down and the heat blasting.

He'd noticed the modern structure on South University before. It was a sharp origami bird of a building, white and low slung, not a spire or flying buttress in sight. A tasteful sign at the curb identified it as a church and there were no pithy marquee quotations some houses of worship favored, like *Sin For Breakfast, Salvation For Lunch*. The parking lot was empty and the main church sanctuary locked up tight. A blonde-brick, one-story building at the back of the property had a glass door and Jack peeked inside. Folding chairs were stacked against one wall and there was a whiteboard at the front, possibly a classroom space. He took a quick tour of the grounds, thinking Lucia could've lived in a caretaker's apartment or rectory, but saw no sign of a residence and no one responded to his pounding on doors.

The posted emergency number reached the pastor, Dustin Rattenberry, who told Jack he was at brunch with his wife and agreed to talk.

They sat in Jack's car outside the restaurant and Dustin's deep voice was solemn as his demeanor. "Heartbreaking. Such a beautiful young woman."

Dustin was about forty, tall, caucasian, clean shaven. Dressed in a dark suit. Ministers and homicide detectives, Jack thought, only men who wore suits anymore.

"Lucia's ID lists Stoney Gate Church as her address," Jack said. "Can you explain that?"

Dustin rubbed his face. "How odd. Lucia works as— worked as—a housekeeper for parishioners named Ruth and Ken Harrowsmith. They provide room and board."

"I'll need their contact information."

"Of course." Dustin took the pad Jack offered and wrote in neat block printing.

"What else can you tell me? Lucia's friends, her activities, her usual routine?"

"Man, oh man." Dustin had the thousand-yard-stare of a person parsing bad news. "Lucia wouldn't harm anyone. Eighteen years old she hadn't had time to make a lot of friends, let alone enemies. Why did this happen?"

Might be an innocent slip, but according to her ID Lucia was only sixteen.

"Did Lucia have a car?" Jack asked.

"No. The Harrowsmiths were kind enough to drive her anywhere she needed to go."

"Do you mind telling me about your activities last night and earlier this morning?"

Dustin stared out the window for a few seconds before answering.

"Last night Heather and I had dinner, watched videos with the kids, went to bed early. We're kind of boring. I got to the church this morning at six-thirty to practice my sermon."

"When was the last time you saw Lucia?"

"At the Wednesday night service."

"How was her state of mind?" Jack asked.

"What do you mean?"

"Her mood. Was Lucia agitated, worried, did she seem off?"

"No. She was friendly and pleasant like always."

"Did Lucia confide in you?"

Dustin's smile was sad. "Sure. Work, crushes, getting her GED. Which she'll never do now."

"Do you know the last time Heather saw Lucia?"

A hint of a frown creased Dustin's forehead. "I'm not sure. My wife wasn't at church Wednesday. But she's in the restaurant now and I saw her sitting with Ruth Harrowsmith this morning. Do Ruth and Ken know yet? I'd like to call on them."

"I'm going to talk to them next so hold off for a bit. You mentioned crushes. Did Lucia have a boyfriend?"

"No, it was just talk." Dustin rubbed his face again. "I am devastated by this news. Devastated."

"What else about Lucia?"

"Such as?"

"Where she's from, does she have family here, did she

drink or do drugs?"

"Lucia? Never. And she was from El Salvador."

Now that was hardcore irony, Lucia murdered in Denver, when she came from a country with the highest murder rate in the world.

Jack nodded at the notepad where Dustin had written the Harrowsmiths' information. "I also need contact numbers for Lucia's family."

"I wish I could give that to you. You know how it is. People in those countries move constantly to stay one step ahead of the gangs."

"Are the Harrowsmiths wealthy?" It was pure instinct on Jack's part to ask and he was rewarded with a defensive response.

"Why would their income be relevant?"

Devastated pastor or not, Jack wasn't fond of interviews where the interviewee attempted to turn the tables by answering every question with another question.

"Determining relevance is in my job description. I'll assume they're affluent. A more interesting question is why it would bother you that I asked."

Dustin shrugged, shook his head. "No reason. I'm just upset. I've had parishioners die, of course, but not like this."

"How did Lucia get hired by the Harrowsmiths?"

"My church. We have a charity called Shores of Hope that teaches English and helps immigrants through the cruel bureaucratic maze of immigration. It's a passion of mine. Our parishioners often hire individuals from the charity. That was the case with Ruth and Ken."

"Lucia was here illegally, wasn't she?"

"No one has to provide documentation to attend my church." Dustin stiffened. "Do you think this could be a hate crime?"

Jack had to consider every possibility but wasn't about to brainstorm.

The minister, however, was off on a tangent. "It's beyond tragic. People risk their lives to come here, leave everything and everyone behind, are willing to work hard and in return they get beaten, harassed, deported, or worse."

"I'm homicide, not ICE. Has the charity or the church received any threats?"

"No, but that doesn't mean—"

"Let's get back to the Harrowsmiths, please. Did Ruth or Ken ever complain to you about Lucia?"

"Can you tell me where you found her?"

Another question-answered-by-a-question. Jack chose to answer. "Near the light rail tracks, off South Acoma."

"What was Lucia doing there?"

"I was hoping you could tell me."

"I have no idea. She led a rather circumscribed life." Dustin crossed himself. "Lord rest her soul."

"What do you mean by that statement?"

"The Harrowsmiths were kind to Lucia. They drove her to church and to doctor's appointments but she didn't come and go as she pleased. She never got to live her life and now she never will."

"You're making her sound like a prisoner."

"No, no, Ruth and Ken kept a close eye on her, that's all, like she was their own daughter. And you can't dismiss the possibility of a hate crime."

Bad pictures developed in Jack's mind, featuring a young vulnerable girl slaving away for a rich couple. Or perhaps a young desperate girl shaking her employers down for money. Could have gone wrong multiple ways.

It was an occupational hazard of being a cop to think the worst about everyone, including God-fearing churchgoers, and Jack reminded himself to get a grip on his assumptions.

And then Dustin said, "I guess I'm going to have to tell you about Ken."

CHAPTER TEN

K EN LOUNGED IN his hotel room, an open pizza
box on the bed, a bottle of wine on the nightstand,
and porn on the television. It made him chortle imagining
Ruth's reaction. His noon flight was canceled and his
rescheduled flight was also in jeopardy. He regretted not
leaving a day earlier and, while he needed to stay near the
airport, that didn't mean he couldn't enjoy himself.

He'd live in hotels forever, although this one wasn't as
nice as where he took Lucia. He enjoyed spoiling her and
it was sad how she'd changed. Maybe it was because of
Ruth. Lucia saw his wife in furs and designer clothes and
wanted that for herself. At first, she had no expectations,
was amazed and delighted by any gift. Quite at odds with
the shrill bitch on the phone last night during the call
his wife had categorized as "frenzied"—not that he'd give
Ruth the satisfaction of confirming her hunch.

She was right to fear turning forty; women got old faster
than men and that wasn't his fault. Ken decided he'd speak
to Dustin himself about their next housekeeper instead
of leaving it to Ruth. Really, his needs were quite simple.
Ken knew the women on the TV screen were fantasies,
he wasn't a twit, but a young girl who hadn't been ruined
yet, with a pretty smile and a little gratitude shouldn't be
that hard to find.

His large "mountain man" pizza was occluded arteries

on a plate, a thick, rubbery layer of cheese and extra hamburger that left a slimy residue inside the box. A cheap, salty antidote to the hushed five-star food temples where his wife worshipped. He ate the whole thing, polished off one bottle of wine and unscrewed the top on a second.

Before this one, his last pizza was in Italy with Ruth, a typical overpriced experience with an artistically charred crust and organic tomatoes no doubt crushed by the hands of virgins. Ruth had stared critically over her salad and reminded him he was prone to heartburn. In her honor he let out a loud, satisfied belch and then lifted his plastic cup and toasted the absent women; *To bitch number one. To bitch number two.*

Although. Lucia couldn't help being the way she was. His wife worked her until she was ragged and exhausted, too tired to be any fun. *This tablecloth is stained.* Ruth's haughty voice played in his head. Like they couldn't afford to use each tablecloth once and throw it out.

Ken channel-surfed when his pay-per-view ended, debated getting candy or a bag of crisps from the vending machine, but felt too logy to move. The local news flashed by, and he'd already passed the station before the face on the screen registered.

Lucia's Colorado ID photo.

His Lucia.

Police are asking for anyone who knew this woman and what might have happened to her to come forward.

He shoved the pizza box onto the floor, oblivious to the streak of oil on the bedspread, and groped with slippery fingers for the volume button.

The body was found early this morning in a Denver alley and anyone with information is asked to call Crime Stoppers.

Cause of death was unclear from the condition of the body and there would be an autopsy. They kept using those words: the body.

Her body.

His body.

Ken's first call wasn't to Crime Stoppers but to the special airline number for elite flyers demanding to be put on the first plane leaving Denver no matter where it was headed. Wasn't DIA supposed to be some high-tech masterpiece designed to handle weather? Didn't Denver have snow every single year? Why was it impossible?

All of the cancellations meant thousands of stranded passengers—that had been on the news too—and even being in first class wouldn't get him anywhere fast. The agent was smarmy and condescending: "I'm sure you understand, sir, we've got a lot of unhappy customers to reroute, and we want everyone to be safe." Ken hung up on her.

The extent of the disaster penetrated his alcohol- and fat-addled brain. He'd been pissed at Lucia last night. She'd been insulting and rude and he'd had to point out how things worked. She was an uneducated housekeeper and he was an important man. They exchanged angry texts, which he'd deleted, but Ken knew nothing was ever really erased. If—when—the police found those messages, he'd be screwed.

He wondered if his wife had heard and then, with a surge of panic, realized the police must have already talked to her. *Thanks, bitch number one, for giving me a heads-up.* Ruth didn't do anything she didn't want to do. The question wasn't whether his wife was capable of protecting him, but if she was willing.

Instead of a different country in another hemisphere with no extradition he was stuck on the ground in Denver. Ken paced to the window and felt the cold through the glass. He couldn't stay trapped in a hotel room, like a meek, ignorant deer waiting for the hunters. He couldn't go home and he couldn't fly but he had to do something.

CHAPTER ELEVEN

"I'M A MAN of God, not a man of gossip," Dustin said. That was cute. "You're the one who brought Ken up."

In a demonstration of reluctance, Dustin sighed and exhaled theatrically, checked his watch, and stared out the window. That, or he was hoping for a Golden Globe.

"You have to understand, I'm betraying a trust."

"Whose?"

"There were rumors about Ken and Lucia."

"Can you be more specific?" Was Jack going to have to drag it out of him one word at a time?

"I tried my best to shut it down, but at the same time, it was plain Ken was..."

His voice trailed off. Jack waited. It became apparent the information was going to have to be extracted in tedious pieces. "Ken was what?"

Dustin sighed dramatically again. "Fond of Lucia. He bought her gifts."

"What kind of gifts?"

"Clothes, jewelry. He's very kind."

"How did Mrs. Harrowsmith react to Lucia and Ken's, ah, friendship?" Jack asked.

"If Ruth shared personal concerns with me that would be confidential."

"If she made or knew of an explicit threat toward Lucia

you'd be encouraged by law to violate that confidence."

"Spoken like a true cop."

"Thanks. Now please answer my question: were you aware of threats against Lucia originating from Ruth or anyone else?"

"No."

"That's a nice watch."

"Excuse me?" Dustin glanced from his wrist to Jack.

"You've checked it several times which is why I noticed. You have some place you need to be?"

"No, uh, I just—I'm upset—I've never been inter—in a situation like this."

"Besides Ken, who else was Lucia physically intimate with?"

"I didn't say that." Talk about a nerve—Dustin sat up so abruptly he almost hit his head on the ceiling of the car. "I'm extremely uncomfortable with the direction this conversation is taking."

Jack wasn't aware it had been a "conversation" exactly. "So Lucia was involved with another man. Who is he?"

"No, that's not what I meant. You're twisting my words. I need to go inside and be with my family now."

"Of course. I need to talk to them as well."

Dustin opened the car door. "It's not possible anyone in my congregation hurt Lucia, not Ken, not anyone. You're looking in the wrong direction."

Jack loved it when people told him that because it usually indicated exactly where he needed to look.

———————

Inside the restaurant, a woman who easily weighed in north of two hundred pounds named Cherie Allmond started crying.

Her husband, Jordon, folded his arms across his chest and glared at Jack. "What makes you think we have anything to do with Lucia's unfortunate demise?"

"Did you?" They weren't witnesses or suspects so the overreaction was interesting, and Jack repressed a smirk at the odd humor of Jordon's name.

"No." Cherie had wispy blond bangs and pale blue eyes dwarfed by the volume of her face. "Tell him, Jordon. We loved Lucia."

Another parishioner at the table, a slim, pretty brunette named Nicole—or Nicki—Erskine chimed in. "Well, we liked her a lot, but loved is a little strong, don't you think?"

"That's a terrible thing to say." Heather Rattenberry sounded appalled. Dustin's wife was about thirty, blonde, wearing a conservative dress that reminded Jack of wallpaper, pink flowers on a pale green background.

Nicki stammered an apology. "I'm sorry—I just meant—I just thought—I don't know what I was thinking. We all cared about Lucia. I'm stunned." She reached for the margarita in front of her and took a healthy swallow. Nicki was the only one, Jack noticed, with what appeared to be an alcoholic beverage.

Dustin was in character as solemn, compassionate pastor. "It's all right, Nicki. We're all in shock. I told the detective—Jack—that we'd help any way we can."

"Of course." Heather put a protective arm around her daughter's shoulders. Ten-year-old Trysta had brown curly hair and her mother's blue eyes. She watched everyone with a serious expression through glasses. Ryan, their son, was oblivious in the way of six-year-old boys. He blew bubbles into his soda with his straw and asked to see Jack's gun.

Jack turned to Cherie. "Were you and Lucia close?"

She used her paper napkin to blow her nose and spoke in a breathless rush. "We didn't, like, hang out or anything, but she was nice. Always said hi and gave me a hug. She helped clean the conference center—there's a bunch of us who take turns. I can show you the sign-up sheet if you want."

"I'd appreciate that," Jack said.

"Remember that." Jordon was still suspicious. "We're cooperating."

"Can all of you tell me the last time you saw Lucia?" Jack asked.

Nicki looked at Heather. "I saw her last Sunday. How about you?"

"Me, too."

Trysta chimed in and said, "Me three," earning an indulgent smile from her mother.

Nicki tucked a piece of hair behind her ear. "Lucia's always at church, either for services or volunteering. It was weird for her not to be there this morning."

Heather shot Nicki a sharp look.

Cherie said, "We saw her last Sunday, too. There's a Wednesday night Bible study but we don't get to that as often as we'd like."

"We're very faithful about Sunday," Jordon said.

Dustin exhaled sharply. "Honey, you sat next to Ruth. Did she say anything about Lucia?"

Heather shook her head and Jack was tired of Dustin commandeering interviews. "Was Ken with Ruth?"

"No," Heather said. "He's, um, another religion I think."

"Did Ruth happen to say where he was?"

"A business trip."

Jack persisted. "Did she say where?"

"No, we, uh, didn't talk that much." Heather stood. "I should take the kids outside."

"Ken travels a lot for work," Nicki said. "All over, even some international trips. He's from England, I think, and Ruth is from the Middle East."

Heather shot her friend another look that seemed to mean *shut up* and Jack made a mental note to follow up and talk to Nicki alone first chance he got. Locating Ken also moved to the top of his priorities.

"Mommy, what'd they do to Lucia?" Trysta asked.

Ryan played mock battles with his silverware, muttering, "boom" and "pow" under his breath.

Heather steered her daughter by the shoulder with one hand and grabbed Ryan with the other. "I'll tell you at home. Come on, let's go, you too, Ryan."

Nicki waited until Heather and the kids were out of earshot. "What I said about not loving her—I didn't mean anything. She worked long hours, like really long. Plus extra stuff for Ken. Maybe it was a cultural thing. You know?"

"I'm not sure I follow," Jack said.

She started to answer and Dustin interrupted. "I've spoken to Ruth several times about the laws here, that an eight-hour work day is typical. She's from another country and no malice was intended. Once I explained she was very understanding."

Nicki's mouth hung open in disbelief. "Understanding? Are we talking about the same Ruth?"

"Gossip isn't helpful," Dustin said. "We need to pray for her as well as Lucia."

"It's true though," Cherie said. "Ruth acts like she's too good for us."

Dustin raised the volume a notch. "Seriously, this isn't helpful or Christian."

Nicki said, "Would it be *helpful* to tell Jack about the expensive gifts Lucia received? And the true nature of her relationship with Ken?"

The look Dustin gave Nicki could have stripped paint. "Leave it to you to go straight to the gutter."

"That's not fair." Nicki's cheeks flushed. "You know even better than I do what was happening."

"I know Ken gave Lucia gifts," Dustin said. "Interpretation beyond that I'll leave to your vivid imagination."

Nicki shot right back. "Who gives diamond necklaces to their housekeeper unless she's performing services above and beyond the ordinary? Or should I say, way below?"

"Why does everything with you have to be filthy?"

Jack intercepted Dustin's outrage by asking Cherie and Jordon what they knew about Ken and Lucia.

Cherie's pale eyes darted between Dustin and Jack. "I don't want to say anything un-Christian."

"It's hard to think that someone you know could've done something bad," Jack said. "But I'm asking because it's important."

"Lucia did have lots of expensive things." Cherie's voice faded.

"I don't see what that has to do with anything," Jordon said.

"Last Sunday she had a new necklace." Nicki's hand went to her own throat. "A key made with diamonds."

"Uh-huh." Cherie agreed. "That one was *really* nice and she wore it everywhere. And do you remember her purse? The one she said cost a thousand dollars?"

"And those Louboutins," Nicki said.

"Laboo what?" Jack asked.

"Super expensive shoes. They're gorgeous but I could never afford them."

Dustin said, "Perhaps Ken didn't use the best judgment in regard to Lucia."

Nicki's voice rose. "Seriously? Not the best judgment? Are you kidding?"

Cherie sobbed. "That poor thing. She'll never get to wear her pretty necklaces again."

"Yeah." Nicki glared at Dustin. "Where *is* your Christian compassion?"

"How dare you."

Dustin started in on Nicki again which made Cherie cry harder and all four of them talked at once.

"I'm sorry, Dustin," Cherie said. "Don't be mad at us, please, but she's dead."

Jordon shoved his chair back with a scrape. "My wife is hysterical and I'm going to take her home now. For the record, I fail to see the importance of Lucia's jewelry. So Mr. Harrowsmith was nice to her, so what? Are you saying it might have been stolen by whoever killed her?"

He pronounced it "stolden," a mistake that always made Jack wince.

CHAPTER TWELVE

---

*W*E *CAN STILL try, we can still try, we can still try.*
Words repeated in Raven's mind, trying to convince herself. So close. All the planning, scheming, stashing jewelry. Then Lucia forgets her purse. How could she? Although Raven couldn't hate her friend, she hadn't meant to.

All night Raven begged her phone to chirp, willed it, pleaded with it. Lucia said she'd text as soon as she found the purse, Raven waited, ready to bounce into action, but nothing.

She finally fell asleep, clutching the phone, stared at it now, all of her unanswered texts. *Where are you?????* A dozen times. Something was very wrong.

Denver news.

Shaky fingers typed on the keyboard. She was in the restaurant office, a place she wasn't supposed to be, like Was Not, like, she'd earn a beating was not, but there wasn't anyone she could ask. Not as if she could call Ruth or Ken, like, hey, how's it goin', Lucia still alive?

Then her friend's face was on the screen, featured story, major news. Raven figured some serious shit had gone down—but murdered? Her body in an alley?

Dead, over, screwed, all because of a stupid purse. If that was why. Was that why? Didn't make sense but nothing did. And what about her? Fuck. Had they found out, somehow, about the two of them planning to run? Maybe beat it out of Lucia before they—

No mention of injuries in the articles online for what that was worth. *Read, you can cry later.* Raven pressed her nails into her palm, hard, to make herself think. Fucking cops didn't say anything, body found, anyone with information, blah, blah, blah. Hell, she was the one who needed information. Last Raven knew Lucia was headed home to look for the purse then nothing, nada, crickets.

"You fucking bitch, you can't be in here."

Avi stood in the doorway and Raven stared back. Did he know? Would he act different?

"Get away from the computer. Now." He reached across the desk and hauled her up out of the chair by her arm.

"Lucia's dead. Look at the screen."

He threw her aside and Raven caught herself against the wall with a grunt. Fucking pig.

"I'm serious. Look."

He worked the mouse with clumsy fingers and after an eternity said, "No shit," but he didn't sound upset or even surprised.

"You knew."

"Whatever."

"Not whatever, she was my friend."

"Boo fucking hoo."

He stared at the screen, moved the mouse in circles, then banged it on the top of the desk as if it had misbehaved.

"Have the cops been here?" Raven asked.

"Why would they come here?"

Anger cut through desperation. Avi was such a moron. "Because they're fucking cops. It says they're going everywhere and Lucia and I were both here right before she—"

Raven couldn't say the words. Died. Was killed.

Avi sniffled loudly. "Why was that? I thought she spent Saturdays with Ken."

"Yeah but he blew her off. Some fancy thing for the Ice Queen."

"Okay. But I don't get from there to cops."

"They're gonna talk to everyone." She pointed at the laptop. "Didn't you read? I'm gonna be deported. The cops'll find out I'm undocumented and send me back."

"Sahir won't let cops anywhere near you."

Oh, fuck. *Sahir.* She was dead, too. Worse than dead. He couldn't find out about any of it. "How can he stop them from talking to me?"

"You kidding me?" The chair groaned under the load as Avi leaned back. "He owns you. Won't let anyone near you doesn't have his approval."

That was true although it shouldn't be. She should've been long gone by now but here she was facing everything alone. Raven shivered, suddenly freezing. Either way. Deportation or beatings. Sex with strangers, hungry, tired, cold all the time. Even now her stomach growled in response to smells from the restaurant kitchen—garlic, onions, grilled meat—food she was never allowed to eat. Which was worse? Being shipped back to die or dying here, with no one at home ever knowing?

"Who do you think killed her?" she asked.

"The fuck would I know. I hate this drama shit. Girls are a pain in the ass."

"You don't care about us at all, do you?"

He stared with flat brown eyes. "I care that you brought her here last night and now I have to worry about Denver homicide crawling up my ass."

She wanted to say boo fucking hoo back but knew better, longed for the day when she could tell a man like Avi to fuck himself. A day this one was supposed to be. It wouldn't do any good to ask him not to tell Sahir. It would only plant the idea in his stupid mind.

"It's not drama if it's real. And you know way more than me, like you knew she was already dead and you probably know who did it." Raven fought to keep her teeth from chattering while Avi sat there fat, warm and smug.

"Like I'd tell you so you could tell the cops."

"Why would I do that? So they give me to ICE?"

"You thought there was an angle, you'd spill. I never understood why Sahir puts up with your shit."

"Oh, yeah, I've got it fucking made." She tugged at her skirt. Said, with as much dignity as she could muster, "Sorry to have bothered you with the death of my best friend."

He grinned, never a good sign. "Hold on, before you go."

Pushed the chair back from the desk and thrust his hips so she could see his hard on.

"Ugh. You gotta be kidding me."

"Price for keepin' my mouth shut."

"I'm not supposed to give anyone freebies."

He laughed. "You're not supposed to do a lot of things."

CHAPTER THIRTEEN

———

THE MAIN ENTRY of the Harrowsmith house was
something Jack imagined you'd find in Morocco. He
walked through a large courtyard, heated paving stones
free of ice, and made his way to a towering mahogany
door recessed into an opening shaped like a keyhole. Even
in the dead of winter water gurgled from the mouths of
giant carved fish in a fountain.

He introduced himself to Ruth Harrowsmith and the
words "Denver Homicide" might as well have been "good
morning" or "I'm here to aerate your lawn."

"What is this in reference to?" Ruth asked.

"It would be better if we talked inside."

Her lips pressed into a line of displeasure, but she
opened the ten-foot-high monolith of a door and took a
step back.

No offer to sit. No further inquiries. Certainly no
dismay. Did this woman have homicide detectives show
up regularly on her doorstep? Jack had no intention of
standing awkwardly in the foyer like he was a Scout
selling cookies.

"Where can we sit down?" He straightened his spine
to its full six foot two and, while he kept his expression
neutral, his posture conveyed *don't fuck with me lady*.

Ruth didn't receive the unspoken memo. "Will that be
necessary?"

"I'm afraid so." Jack stared down at her with the pleasant, concerned demeanor he'd had lots of practice maintaining under much worse pressure than whatever Ruth could inflict. He'd stand there and watch her for an hour if he needed to and it might prove more revealing than any words she spoke.

Her eyes narrowed slightly in defeat when she turned and led him deeper into the house. Maybe she gave in because her feet hurt—her boots had skinny high heels and a red sole. Heels or not Ruth walked fast, a sharp staccato on gleaming marble, and stopped in a living room where she perched on the edge of a leather sectional sofa large enough to seat twenty.

Ruth's posture was the stuff elite girls' schools used to brag on, and her hands were folded quietly in her lap like small, dead white birds. He pegged her at forty, with smooth black hair as opaque and shiny as water-slicked asphalt. She wore a well-tailored gray dress and gobs of jewelry. Interesting, considering the churchies—Jack decided that should be a word—and their disapproval of Lucia's diamonds.

He described finding Lucia's body in an alley, no identification, no obvious cause of death, and she watched him with doleful brown eyes as if to say, "This is what we had to sit down for?"

He finished with his customary, "I'm sorry for your loss."

"Thank you. What a terrible tragedy." Her words were right but they were completely contradicted by her demeanor.

"Is Ken at home? I need to speak to him, too."

"I'm afraid that's impossible, he's on his way out of the country, flying to Amman for business."

Wow. Way to bury the lede, Ruth. "When was his flight supposed to leave? There's a chance it was canceled due to the weather." Jack could hope.

"That's in Jordan," Ruth added.

"Yes, I know. I like that soft cheese they have there topped with pistachio and syrup. Have you had it? It's delicious. Now, about Ken's flight?"

If Ruth was surprised by Jack's familiarity with Middle Eastern cuisine it didn't show. "I did receive a text that there were flight changes."

According to her travel app, Ken's new flight was scheduled for eight p.m. Jack stepped away for a minute and called Mike, delegating tasks including alerting the airlines and dispatching officers at the airport. Ken had left the house seven hours earlier. Even with snow, that was one hell of a head start.

It was standard procedure to get a date of birth from individuals the police contacted, and Ruth was even less enthusiastic than she'd been about inviting Jack inside. Background checks on Ken and Ruth were added to the quickly growing homicide to-do list.

At Jack's prompting, Ruth called Ken several times but it went straight to voice mail. Motionless, other than white hands working the phone, she barely blinked and it was hard to tell for sure that she was breathing.

Jack found her economy of motion grating. "You and Ken haven't spoken since he left this morning?"

Ruth cocked her head slightly. "Why would we?"

"Married people often talk to each other about the weather, or flight cancellations, or perhaps discuss changing plans and trying again another day."

"I have no indication from Ken that he's considering such a thing. He was quite eager to travel."

"Ken seems exceptionally determined for his trip to proceed even with a blizzard wreaking havoc and scores of canceled flights." Her odd formality was rubbing off; Jack never said things like "scores" or "wreaking havoc." He sounded like Heathcliff. "Why was Ken going to Jordan, and please don't say for business. What kind of business? And why Amman?"

Ruth nodded, a veritable earthquake of animation. "He's an executive with Monument Oil which is headquartered there. He was planning to combine high-level meetings with visiting my family."

"From your comment I can assume you're from Jordan? Yes? What about Ken?"

"What about him?"

This woman-slash-iceberg was irritating as hell. Jack took a deep breath and still mostly failed keeping sarcasm at bay. "In which country did Ken originate?"

"He's British originally, and now has dual citizenship. I'm here on a green card."

"And Lucia?"

Ruth hesitated. Up until now, while she hadn't been verbose she'd been answering promptly. That pause was what those in the detecting business called a "tell."

"She's from Central America."

"El Salvador." He saw Ruth frown. Or try to; her forehead had apparently been Botoxed into porcelain oblivion. "Do you have contact information for her family? We need to let them know what happened."

"Unfortunately, I don't," Ruth said. "Our church runs a charity that helps people like her, you should ask the pastor."

"You mean people here illegally."

"I support the work Stoney Gate does. There, she learned English, and I trained her to do light housework."

If Lucia had been responsible for polishing the seeming acres of marble around them there was nothing "light" about it.

"When did Lucia come to live and work here?"

"Nineteen months ago."

"And the last time you saw her?"

"Yesterday at breakfast, which is served at 8:30 on Saturdays."

That was all very precise. "Did Lucia tell you her plans for the rest of the day?"

Ruth tipped her head a micron to the side again, as if miming confusion. "Our employees don't take meals with us. After she served our breakfast it was her free time and, frankly, none of my concern. I believe in healthy boundaries, therefore we didn't socialize or have lengthy conversations."

"How would you describe Ken's interactions with Lucia?"

"My husband was quite generous. In fact, I thought he went over the top, giving her expensive jewelry. She could have run into a bad sort who saw diamonds and tried to rob her. Is that what happened?"

Another fan of the Lucia-was-killed-for-her-jewelry theory. "How many gifts has Ken given her?"

"He spent far too much money on the—on her."

"Were you going to say the help?"

Ruth grew animated. "My husband wasn't involved in the day-to-day running of the house. It was easy for him to act the benevolent sugar daddy, easy to see the pretty face and overlook the stained linens."

"Ken had a sexual relationship with Lucia, didn't he?"

Ordinarily, Jack would have eased into a question like that. He would have prefaced it with a disclaimer: "I'm sorry to have to ask you this, but..."

Ruth simply said, "Yes."

"How long had they been intimate?"

"At least six months, perhaps longer." Ruth consulted the dead birds in her lap. "Yes, I'm certain it was longer."

"How did that make you feel?" Jack asked.

"Is this a therapy session now?"

If Jack was married to Ruth he'd cheat, too. Scratch that. If he found himself married to someone like Ruth he'd bash his head against the marble. Repeatedly. Not to mention—not to mention—

"Ruth, I can sit here for hours and go minute-by-minute through the last couple of days of your life. Does that sound fun? No, I don't think so either. So how about telling me what you know about Ken and Lucia, their routines, what changed recently and why? You know, some exposition, since neither one of us is getting any younger."

Ruth's full mouth curved into an illusion of smile. "You want to hear about *them*."

Jack had the distinct feeling she'd been waiting for him to ask the right question, stress the perfect line of inquiry before she erupted.

"Ken took *her* to hotels because I asked him, to preserve a shred of my dignity, not to fornicate under my roof. I asked him to honor social engagements we had as an important couple. I'm on the boards of several prominent charities, I won't bore you with the details. Last night I co-hosted a benefit and when I reminded my husband of his obligation he made a call. From his body language and hand gestures, it appeared heated, and since it was Saturday I assumed he was calling the—her—to cancel. While it would be a luxury for me to believe they were growing tired of each other, I long ago stopped soothing myself with fairy tales."

Jack figured his eyebrows must be up around his hairline. "What hotels?"

"The Rose Terrace was his favorite."

"What time did your benefit start?"

"Eight. We drove together and were home by eleven."

"What happened after you got home and overnight?"

Ruth's exhale through her nose put Jack in mind of a bull. "My husband and I went to bed. Together. I took an Ambien because I have trouble sleeping. He was still in bed when I awoke and, to my knowledge, never got up during the night."

"Other than for prayers."

Ruth froze. For someone who moved so little to begin with, Jack wouldn't have thought it was possible. But she did. Froze so solid he suspected if he touched her she'd shatter like an ice sculpture.

"If you're from Jordan odds are you're Muslim and you don't marry outside your faith." Jack's realization from a minute ago. Rich older man screwing young, vulnerable, undocumented girl. Same man headed to a country with no extradition agreement mere hours after said girl turned up dead. In his head, Jack was already finishing the paperwork.

Ruth was on her feet, ready to show him the door. "If there's nothing else, I have an engagement."

"You have a lot of engagements."

She tried it louder. "*If* there's nothing else."

"But there is." Jack stood too, not to leave, to show her the electronic version of the search warrant on his phone.

Rage made her words come out so clipped he could almost see their sharp edges. "I insist my attorney be present for any search."

"You can have the Broncos offensive line present as long as they don't interfere."

CHAPTER FOURTEEN

———➤———

B IBI HELD RAVEN'S arms from behind. Sahir sent
her next appointment to a different girl and said they
needed to talk. Sahir's talks were torture in the literal
sense and Avi told her it went worse for her because she
presented Sahir with a challenge. Fucking Avi, blew him,
swallowed cum that tasted like pickled dogshit, and he
still narced.

The quote-unquote spa was in an old house owned
by an even older bitch named Dottie who was upstairs
watching TV. Not once had Dottie ever come downstairs
in response to a girl's screams.

"She was my friend aren't I allowed to be upset?" Raven
fought tears and then wondered if it'd be better if she
cried. Never could tell with Sahir.

"Why'd you do it?" Sahir asked.

"Do what?"

The punch to her stomach blinded her with pain. Bibi's
grip tightened, held her upright, kept her vulnerable.
Vomit ran down her chin and Raven coughed, trying not
to choke, Avi's spunk even more vile on the way back up.

Sahir's eyes scanned the finished basement and Raven
followed his gaze, wondered what he was thinking, knew
better than to ask.

Along one wall was a counter and cabinets where they
kept supplies: washcloths, a microwave, lotion, a Crock-

Pot for heating stones. Like a real spa, or so she was told, they played soft music and had flavored water for the customers.

"I treat you better than anyone," Sahir said. "You know why I buy you nice things? Why I take you out for steak dinners?"

Was she supposed to answer?

"I keep you safe but you still don't trust me. Lucia, Lucia, Lucia. What about your other friends? The ones you work with? You wanna get them killed too?"

He unplugged her curling iron, the one she'd just been using on the highest setting, primping for her next customer who was a good tipper.

"No." On a sob of despair.

"Can I have her when you're done?" Bibi asked.

She felt his hard-on against her lower back.

Sahir said, "Sure, why not," and held the curling iron close to her face to show her, like she didn't know what it was. He pressed the lever. *Click, click, click.*

"I can't let you get everyone killed."

"No." Over and over. "No." She saw her own hairs stuck to the red-hot barrel and waited for the sting of pain on her ear or her neck.

Sahir played it out, gave her time to imagine the pain, when it would come, where it would be, how bad it would feel.

"You're too smart for this shit, Raven." He ran his index finger under the hem of her dress.

"No." All she seemed able to say. Wildly, blindly, shook her head.

He pulled her dress up to her waist. "The more you fight the worse it'll hurt. If you cooperate I'll be quick."

She'd been punished enough to know he kept his word but who said, sure, go ahead, burn me? His fingers brushed the spot on her hip he was going to mark. Bibi's grip tightened until it felt like her arms were being pulled out of their sockets. It only lasted a few seconds and Raven hated herself for screaming.

"Can I do one?" Bibi asked. "For practice?"

"She's valuable property," Sahir said, "and you're not disciplined enough."

"No one ever lets me do anything. She's just a ho."

Through a haze of agony Raven listened to them talk about her like she was a piece of trash—like she was nothing.

"Let her go," Sahir said. "Get some ointment from Dottie."

"You said I'd get a turn."

Sahir jabbed at him with the iron. "You want a turn? I'll burn the hair off your balls, if you've got any."

Bibi released his grip and Raven fell to the floor. She heard a door slam shut. Dottie's hearing was bad but she had to have heard that scream. She wondered why the old woman let this go on in her house, wondered how much Sahir knew, and then was overcome with a wave of nausea that obliterated thought.

Sahir got mad if they threw up or had accidents. Lack of self-respect, he said. The burn felt enormous and she imagined her flesh was blackened like charcoal, didn't know how she'd bear to cover the spot with clothes or let anyone touch her. After what felt like a long time she saw that Sahir was holding out a washcloth.

"Clean yourself. You know you can't come and go as you please."

Come and go. She wiped at her mouth, her ruined dress.

"You don't move, you don't speak, you don't so much as look at a man unless I tell you to. Even Avi. Understood?"

She managed to nod.

"What's up with you lately?"

"I can't— I'm going to be deported." Maybe this was only for blowing Avi.

"You're worried about the police? That's my job."

"I know. I'm just—you know what it's like where I come from."

"See? Smart."

Despite everything, Raven felt a rush of pleasure at his compliment. *Stupid, stupid, weak girl.*

"Tell me about last night."

Fuck. She wanted to puke again but had nothing left. He held out his hand and she had to take it, had to let him lead her to the couch where she sat carefully, trying to keep fabric away from her hip.

"Wh-wha-what about last night?"

"Why'd you go get Lucia from the hotel?"

"She-she was bored." Raven dug her nails into her palms in an effort not to stammer. Even Sahir couldn't read minds. Right? He couldn't know what they planned, only that Raven took a car without permission and brought Lucia to the club. Bad enough.

"You know better than to interfere with Ken and Lucia," Sahir said. "I have reasons for my rules. See what happens when you disobey?"

It wasn't her fault Lucia was dead. It couldn't be.

Sahir *tsked.* "This was fair punishment, light punishment, for your behavior and you know it."

Raven felt dizzy. She risked looking at her hip where an angry red welt was beginning to blister. "She can't be dead."

"Unless you want more of your friends to die you need to be honest."

She squeezed her eyes shut. How honest? Her mind spun and she told him what actually happened, all he could possibly know, right? Taking the car, getting Lucia from the hotel, hanging out for an hour at the club.

"One hour and I went right back to work. You know that's true 'cause you spy on us with those cameras."

Sahir glanced at his phone where he watched video feeds then smiled at her in a scary way. "Sometimes you're too smart." He got up and brought her a cup of water.

"You need to sound casual and not make mistakes if the police talk to you. We're gonna rehearse until you get it right."

He made her start again. Interrupted to add a detail or told her to leave something out. By the third repetition he seemed satisfied.

Raven's stomach hurt. "You think the cops are gonna talk to me?"

"Not if I can help it. This mean you're still my girl?"

"Please don't let them deport me."

"Not what I asked."

"I'm your girl." Words more bitter than vomit.

"I trusted you."

"I'm sorry." Why was she apologizing?

"You pull shit like that again you know where you'll wind up." He stroked her cheek and it took every bit of willpower she had not to flinch or pull away. His fingernails, like his teeth, stained yellow from smoking. She was sick and scared, but something else, too, a reaction she didn't want to think about.

He raised her chin like he was going to kiss her, which he never had, his breath sour. "You're lucky. This face is too valuable for me to mark."

Lucky. Right. That was a bunch of shit. At the same time she wanted to lean into him and cry like a little girl. Wanted him to make it better when he was the man who hurt her.

She heard the door open and Bibi's voice. "That old bitch freaks me out."

Sahir wouldn't let him come down. He took the small tube from Bibi, ordered him to get a machine to clean the carpet, and then knelt in front of her. Raven was so surprised she forgot for a second about the burn then bit her lip to keep from crying out. But Sahir was gentle. He smiled at the spot and looked up at her. "It's not so bad."

As he stood his fingers grazed her inner thigh and she realized, with horror, that if he touched her right now he'd find out she was wet.

CHAPTER FIFTEEN

―――――

" THERE'S NO REQUIREMENT for you to be here so please, don't let me keep you from your engagement." Jack would infinitely prefer to execute his search without Ruth's gloomy presence.

Predictably, she was having none of it. "I will not have strangers going through my home unsupervised."

"Funny thing about that, I have a judge who says otherwise."

Four uniformed officers assisted, considering Jack was dealing with something like ten thousand square feet. Ruth shadowed Jack—lucky him—her skinny heels tip-tapping. Invisible speakers played soft classical music. Layers of heavy, fringed drapes smothered windows. Not a TV or magazine or family photo in sight. Candles, though, lots and lots of candles, and dark oil paintings in ornate frames. A large sculpture of a horse was mounted on a pillar in a corner of the living room. Jack couldn't imagine how many hours Lucia worked, buffing marble and dusting relics from pillaged tombs. Light housekeeping indeed.

Even the bathrooms were expanses of cold marble, counters clear of clutter. The powder room—correction, *a* powder room—had a notch chiseled into the thick stone through which a white tissue poked, folded into a fan.

Unable to resist the sudden need for a tissue, Jack wondered if Ruth would rush right in and refold the next one into a swan as soon as he left.

A guest room on the second floor violated Ruth's rules of order. Men's clothes were strewn everywhere, the bed was unmade, and plates of half-eaten food were stacked on the dresser. A cartoon played on a flat screen, young girls with enormous eyes, vaguely Asian boys with open shirts as ninjas. In the bathroom a comprehensive array of opioids—from Ativan to Xanax—along with an unflushed toilet and empty wine bottles in the trash. Jack pulled open drawers and looked under furniture.

"This is excessive," Ruth said from the doorway.

"Who's allowed to smoke in the house?" Burns scarred the nightstand and the familiar bite of skunkweed lingered.

"My nephew and he had nothing to do with Lucia. As you can see, this room hasn't been cleaned."

"Good thing you own the place, you'd never get your security deposit back."

"He's a grown man and I respect his privacy."

From what he saw, Jack wasn't so sure about the "grown" part. "I need the nephew's contact information."

"As I said, he had no interaction with Lucia."

"Make me do it the hard way, huh?" Jack retrieved a prescription bottle from the bathroom and read it aloud. "Nishaat Alzeshi."

"He's a bit untidy."

"I thought I was good at understatement."

After Nishaat's man cesspool the master bedroom was serene. A neatly made king-sized bed, no doubt hospital corners, covered with a fur blanket. His and hers reading lamps mounted on the wall under a giant oil painting of what might have been a scene from Revelation—roiling clouds, licking flames, faces contorted in agony. Not what Jack would have found conducive to a restful night's sleep. All surfaces polished and free of clutter which made the Ambien bottle stand out as if it had been put on purposeful display.

In the master bath, Jack loaded about forty tubes of lipstick into evidence bags and Ruth yelped in horror. "Do you know what those cost?"

"Nope." His thought process was to have the crime lab attempt to match the color found painted on Lucia's body. Making Ruth squirm was a bonus.

Closets were full of women's clothes. "Does Ken have a cubby where he's allowed to keep his things?"

Ruth led him to a different bedroom next door. Ken's wardrobe consisted of multiple bespoke suits in shades of gray hung on wooden hangers. A desk under the window held a stack of receipts under a heavy cut glass paperweight. Several of them were from jewelry stores.

"Ken have a computer? And, if yes, what kind and where is it?"

"A laptop and he took it with him on his trip," Ruth said.

An officer found several USB memory sticks in a drawer which were taken along with the receipts.

Ruth's office was on the main level. She stood silent as her laptop and tablet were confiscated, not visibly worried about them taking the electronics which was, in itself, worrying. From the wall, an anguished Jesus in a guilt frame watched the proceedings.

"No portrait of Muhammad?"

"Excuse me?"

"Why is there so much Christian iconography in a house where a Muslim couple live?"

"That's the kind of question you don't need to answer." A man spoke from the doorway then walked forward and extended a hand to Jack. "Tarek Domani, Mrs. Harrowsmith's attorney."

Tarek was in his forties, dressed in slacks and a sweater, with cropped black hair shot with gray. He did the kiss on each cheek thing with his client, very European, and

Jack remembered his relatives from Iran did that, too, but usually with someone of the same gender.

"I don't mind answering," Ruth said. "I want to help."

Tarek took one of her hands in both of his. "It's best not to have a conversation outside of a formal interview scenario. You're distressed about Lucia but you haven't had adequate time to process the information."

Spoken like a true lawyer. And since when was Ruth either distressed or helpful?

In the lawyer's presence she turned gracious hostess, extending an invitation to see Lucia's room as if it was up to her. Tarek extended his hand too, miming false congeniality.

Jack resisted an eyeroll. "Did you know Lucia?"

"Only by name," Tarek said. "Usually Ruth and I meet at my office or speak on the phone."

"I explained that Lucia was never part of our social life," Ruth said.

"Detective—Jack—I hope you don't jump to conclusions. Ruth's attitude might strike you as odd but it's because she's from a different culture."

"No problem." Jack matched Tarek's faux-friendly tone. "In fact, my mother's from Iran so I'm pretty familiar with that culture."

Ruth stopped walking for a moment. "She is? Why didn't you say so?"

"Why would I?"

"It may sound foolish but I *am* upset and I'm relieved to be working with someone familiar with the context."

Context? This conversation was so bizarre it should have subtitles.

They passed through an enormous professional kitchen with dishes stacked in the sink—neatly, by size—and long-stemmed wineglasses on the, yes marble, counter. All of the china was white—plates, bowls, coffee cups.

"You see?" Ruth motioned toward the sink. "Those were

waiting for Lucia to tend to in the morning."

Dirty dishes as defense theory? "Because no one else in the house knows how to use a sponge?"

They ignored Jack's sarcasm and continued down a back staircase to an actual servant's wing, or, more accurately, servant's basement. No marble here, although the floors were polished hardwood and the hallway was well lit— the better to admire more dark oils of Biblical torment.

Ruth opened the second door on the right tapping a code into a fancy electronic lock. The inside of the door had a blank metal plate above the lever.

"You locked her in?" Jack asked.

"No, that's left over from when we used this room to store artwork and other valuables,"

Lucia's room was bright, light, and very pink. What Jack imagined was a young girl's fantasy room. Paintings of flowers, sunlit meadows, horses. Lucia's tidy bed was covered with a rose satin comforter and at least a dozen decorative pillows.

It was so normal Jack almost sighed audibly. "Your nephew could take a lesson from Lucia."

"As an employee she was expected to keep her room clean," Ruth said.

"It seems she was also allowed to decorate."

"My husband..." Ruth's voice trailed off.

"Was quite generous, yes." Jack noted an intercom panel with a small screen mounted on the wall. Perhaps the modern-day equivalent of bells to summon the servants. Or keep an eye on them.

More lipstick was retrieved from Lucia's bathroom, which was spotless. No medication or evidence of drugs.

An upholstered white circle sofa sat in the center of another walk-in closet most Manhattan apartment dwellers would be proud to call home. Lucia's few dresses and blouses on satin hangars looked lonely. Colorful purses in shades of pink on one shelf and on another, high-heels with a red sole, like the boots Ruth wore.

What had Nicki called Lucia's shoes? La boo something? Jack checked the name on the insole; last thing he figured he'd ever have to do on this job—familiarize himself with designer brands.

"I used to use this closet to store my furs," Ruth said.

Jack brandished a shoe and resisted snarky speculation on whether or not she skinned the animals herself. "Even a lowly detective such as myself knows these are expensive. More of Ken's generosity?"

"I'd advise against answering," Tarek said.

"We can pull credit card statements."

"Then do that."

Smug lawyer. Shock. The sole of the shoe was pristine as if it had never been worn and Jack figured five-inch heels were impractical for scrubbing toilets. Maybe Lucia put on fashion shows in private for her benefactor. "Speaking of credit cards, did Lucia have any?"

"How would she know that?" Tarek asked.

"Right, Lucia didn't get her mail here because it wasn't her legal address."

Tarek managed to grow even more self-righteous. "Ruth and Ken felt since Lucia's stay here was temporary the church was a better long-term solution for her official address."

"Turns out they were right, Lucia's stay on earth was very temporary." Jack opened dresser drawers and found velvet jewelry boxes—all empty. A framed photo of Lucia with another young girl and an older woman sat on top.

"Please, feel free to take that." Ruth, still acting like she had a say.

Inside the nightstand, Jack found a packet of tissues, lotion, a Bible, and a stack of notecards tied with a pink ribbon. On one side of the cards was a picture of Stoney Gate Church and on the other notes written in a neat, block hand.

"Who wrote these to Lucia?"

Ruth's dark eyes flicked to the lawyer but he stayed silent. "The pastor at our church writes them out for everyone. They're verses to study for specific issues one might be experiencing."

"Lucia must have had a lot of issues."

He noticed the windows were covered with decorative iron bars and didn't believe Ruth for a second about the lock. To test his theory, Jack walked to the door and closed it. Turned the lever. Nothing.

"Uh oh, Ruth. Appears we're locked in together."

"I don't know how that could have happened, the locking mechanism is disabled." She tapped on her phone. "There's an app, I'll have it open in a moment."

"I don't understand why you felt the need to lock Lucia in. Where was she going to go without a car or any money?"

"That kind of speculation is out of line," Tarek said.

Jack was absurdly relieved when he heard the lock whir in response to Ruth's typing. "Who else had the password to free Lucia from her cell?"

"Detective, really," Tarek said.

"Did the app keep track of the times Lucia's door was opened?"

Ruth answered. "This door is standalone and not connected to the main system, but the house alarm does record when exterior doors are opened and closed."

"I need those records and footage from any video cameras."

"I'll put you in touch with their monitoring company," Tarek said. "You can subpoena the records from them."

"Did Lucia have a computer?"

"No," Ruth said.

"Let me be more specific. A smartphone, a tablet, an MP3 player. Any electronic device that turns on and off."

"Oh, yes, an iPad in a pink leather case."

"Her favorite color." Ruth looked blank and Jack gestured at the bedspread. "Pink. Not hard to figure out."

Ruth's eyes slitted in the way Jack was beginning to recognize as muted rage. "My knowing her favorite color wouldn't have helped her do her job better."

"I imagine Lucia was on your data plan. Do you use that find my phone app? An iPad's expensive, I'm sure you want it back."

Ruth checked in with the lawyer, then worked her phone. Lucia's iPad was in the vicinity of the Rose Terrace Hotel.

"Isn't technology wonderful?" Jack said.

CHAPTER SIXTEEN

———◆———

B ACK AT HOMICIDE, Jack brought Mike up to speed. It was after five on a Sunday and Serena had gone home, but Mike was working late and they pretty much had the place to themselves. Jack's desk was piled high with paper, notebooks, folders, binders. He moved a stack out of the way to set down a tray of Starbucks he'd brought as a thank you.

"We haven't found photos of Lucia's body anywhere online," Mike said. "We'll keep looking. I confirmed the light rail schedule and Dwight was spot on. And Serena emailed you an article about Dustin's church."

"My number one priority is Ken." Those empty jewelry boxes. Maybe Lucia pawned it, preferring cash, and Ken found that unappreciative.

"We're checking hotels near the airport and talking to all the rental car companies and—"

Jack finished the sentence. "And taxi drivers, and Ubers, and he's a rich fuck with a passport who could've chartered a plane or bought himself a car. He's probably not even in Colorado anymore."

"We'll put out a BOLO, everyone'll be aware." At least Mike didn't hit him with the usual "we'll figure it out" line. They both knew from experience that if someone wanted to disappear it wasn't hard if you had half a brain. Lucky for them, most criminals didn't.

While they talked Mike worked on database searches. Jack described Ruth's strange formality, her lawyer, Lucia's well-appointed prison of a room. "She wasn't exactly torn up."

Mike wasn't impressed. "Her husband lavished expensive gifts on the vic. That couldn't have made Ruth happy."

"Gifts I didn't find, at least not jewelry. And Ruth never said Lucia's name, it was always 'she' or 'her' or 'the,' like the maid or something."

"Sounds like a tough interview."

Jack leaned back in his chair. "Ruth's the queen of one-word answers except once or twice when I hit a nerve and got full, nasty sentences."

"Man, if you couldn't charm information out of her, who can?"

"I'm not taking that bait but Ruth might be impervious to charm. This is more than your garden variety cheated-on spouse."

Mike pointed at his computer. "She's clean."

Ruth Kilani Harrowsmith had a current license, several vehicle registrations, and had lived at her current address ten years, coinciding with her marriage to Geoffrey Kenneth Harrowsmythe. Ken held both American and British passports each spelling his last name differently.

"Make sure all the alerts show both versions of his name," Jack said.

"You got it."

Ruth's nephew, on the other hand, had led a busy twenty-three years. Nishaat Alzeshi's history included two DUIs, felony theft, possession of narcotics, receiving stolen property, and one charge of animal cruelty. It also listed an alias, Bibi.

"I'm surprised there's no vandalism or destruction of property. You should've seen what he did to that room."

"He never served a day in jail," Mike said. "For some

of this he was a juvenile and he got probation or did community service."

"Let's hope that wasn't at an animal shelter. I'll add him to the list of people to talk to." Jack failed at stifling a big yawn. "Bibi is slang for baby in Arabic."

"How do you know this shit?"

Jack smiled. "What else have you found out about Ken's last twenty-four hours?"

"I talked to Ken's driver from this morning. They discussed the snow and whether it would mess up his flight, and the interesting thing is Ken knew. His flight was canceled at three a.m. Driver said Ken told him he wanted to be at the airport so he could get on the first flight that did leave."

While Mike talked, Jack stood and wrote tasks on a whiteboard near their desks:

Harrowsmiths' security company
Find / Talk to "Bibi"
Rose Terrace
Where's the jewelry?
F/U up interview with Nicki Erskine
Confirm / deny Harrowsmiths' alibi @ benefit

Jack sat at his computer again and clicked on the link from Serena. "I couldn't tell if Ruth was covering for Ken or trying to make him look guilty."

"Maybe he is guilty," Mike said.

"Hey, this is interesting."

Mike scooted his chair closer and read over Jack's shoulder. Stoney Gate Church had been in the news a couple of weeks earlier for providing shelter to a woman who was an undocumented immigrant. The article described a makeshift bedroom in the church's basement. Or "sanctuary" as Dustin Rattenberry was quoted.

"This isn't an immigration issue, it's a religious freedom

issue," Dustin said in the article. "It's a Biblical precept to help those less fortunate. People ask what would Jesus do and that's where I take my direction, from sacred prophecy."

"Didn't you go to the church?" Mike asked.

"If anyone was there they didn't answer the door and I've got enough headaches without breaking into a church."

Dustin's background check was clean but his wife, Heather, had more in common with Bibi. Several arrests for possession and an apparent fondness for heroin. Her most recent charge pled down in exchange for attending mandatory drug treatment.

Jack mused out loud. "What's up with this minister? He hides illegal immigrants in a brand new, multi-million-dollar sanctuary. His wife's an addict which generates a need for cash. He wrote Lucia lots of notes, which I can't wait to read, and said all the right things to me about talking to Ruth about working conditions. He had to know Lucia was basically a prisoner coerced into a sexual relationship, don't you think?"

Mike feigned mock surprise. "What? You don't think Ken and Lucia were in love?"

Jack did the math. "Ruth said Lucia had been with them almost two years. How consensual can sex be between a fourteen-year-old and a fifty-two-year-old?"

"Nice." Mike offered a fist bump. "We can charge Ken when we find him."

"Statutory rape, sexual assault on a child, and false imprisonment. It's a start."

CHAPTER SEVENTEEN

———◆———

HEATHER SAT AT the kitchen table with Trysta and Ryan trying to eat and act normal, whatever that was. Macaroni and cheese and hamburgers, a quick kid-friendly meal.

Heather was paranoid about the abrupt way she left the restaurant and convinced the cops'd want to talk to her again. She didn't deal with police. Did. Not. Deal. There'd been a murder and Dustin couldn't protect her this time, like he had when she got busted for possession. Bullshit charge that was, too, when dispensaries were on every corner like freakin' Starbucks. All day she waited for a call or for a patrol car to show up at the house.

Trysta noticed. "Mommy, why do you keep looking at your phone?"

"I'm just wondering when Daddy's going to get home."

Alarm widened Trysta's eyes. "I hope he's okay."

"Of course he's okay. You know he's—gotta help everybody at church."

But not Lucia. Heather shoved down a prickle of happiness. It was so, so wrong to feel relieved that Lucia wouldn't be an issue anymore. So wrong. But a smile tugged at the corners of her mouth. Maybe she'd have Dustin to herself for a while.

"Why are you laughing?" Trysta asked.

"I'm not. But I'm happy to have my two snugglemuffins."

No lie. Heather would have eight kids if Dustin let her, a motivation to stay clean. She used to joke with Nicki, "If I could stay pregnant all the time I'd have no substance abuse problems."

Was Nicki talking to that cop? He was cute and she was flirting her ass off at brunch, making up shit to say to impress him. SOP for Nicki. But this was serious. Heather had been texting all afternoon but not gotten any conclusive intel. Maybe after Dustin came home she could meet up with Nicki, find out for real what was going on.

Trysta, at the table on Heather's right, seemed to pick up on moods and ate mostly in silence. Ryan was oblivious.

"Don't play with your food."

"What?" He had a piece of hamburger speared on his fork ready to launch.

"You know what."

Trysta stared with her enormous, solemn blue eyes, and Heather snapped at her. "Oh, come on, hon, not the look. Give me one of those pretty smiles."

"Sorry, Mom."

"You know your dad won't let anything bad happen." Was Heather trying to convince her daughter or herself? She wondered what Nicki was saying to the detective.

"The look." Ryan parroted. "Trysta's got the look."

"Listen you." Heather reached over and gave him a playful pinch. "Don't you dare tease her."

Then turned to Trysta. "Do you have much homework?"

Trysta's mouth twisted. "Um, a little?"

"Are you asking or telling?" Maybe, though, the unusual circumstances got her daughter a pass for one day. Heather imagined writing that note. *Please excuse Trysta from school today on account of homicide.*

Motion out of the corner of her eye. Heather blocked the piece of meat Ryan had launched and flicked the contents of her own fork flying his direction. Ryan shrieked and even despite her crappy mood, Heather dissolved into giggles.

"No fair." Ryan prepped another chunk of hamburger for counterattack.

Trysta gasped. "He can't do that can he?"

"Do what?" Heather kept an eye on Ryan and sent a forkful of macaroni headed her daughter's direction.

"You did not!"

Outrage melted into laughter. Trysta ducked and missed Ryan's next volley. Instead, a piece of meat landed in the sink.

"Nice one," Heather said. "See if you can catch this."

And like with a dog she pitched pieces of macaroni for him to catch with his mouth, laughing so hard her stomach hurt. Sometimes her kids were the only fun that she had.

"Let me try." Trysta's attempt didn't make it halfway across the table.

"Lame." Ryan sent more food flying her direction, joined by Heather.

Soon it was complete chaos, mess, and happy shouting. So loud they didn't hear the front door and then Dustin stood in the doorway.

"What's going on in here?"

"Daddy!" Ryan ran to him, followed by Trysta.

Heather covered her mouth with her hand. "Nothing." She sounded like a kid, too.

"Food fight." Ryan shouted. "And I won."

"You did not," Trysta said.

"I got meat into the sink from all the way over there," Ryan yelled.

"Remember what I've said about inside voice?" Dustin asked.

"Give it up, he doesn't have one." Behind her hand, Heather was still laughing. She grabbed a clump of mac and cheese off the table; God, that stuff was slimy.

"Did you guys manage to *eat* any of your dinner?" Dustin

asked.

He was answered by uh-huhs and sures.

Heather got up and started making him a plate.

"You guys," Dustin said, "I want to talk to your mom alone for a minute."

"Daddy, I'm so sorry about Lucia," Trysta said.

"Thanks, cupcake."

Their sanitized version of events: Lucia had an accident and wouldn't be coming back to church.

Trysta persisted. "But I'm scared."

"There's no reason to be," Dustin said. "It's very sad but it doesn't affect us."

Heather resisted an eyeroll; Trysta the drama queen. "We've covered this. Multiple times."

"I know…but…what if someone comes here?" Trysta blinked up at her dad with those eyes which nearly always worked. He picked her up and swung her around, eliciting screams and complaints that she was too big.

When he put her down she was breathless, flushed, and instantly happy again. Daddy's girl.

Dustin quoted Deuteronomy. "Do not be afraid; do not be discouraged."

Heather pulled two chocolate covered ice cream sandwiches from a box in the freezer, and wrapped each one in a paper towel. "Take these in the family room, please."

Ryan snatched and ran.

Trysta hesitated. "Are you sure it's okay?"

"Of course. Go."

"Man, that was a long day." Dustin leaned down to kiss her. "How were they?"

"I let them get a little bit crazy. Helped my mood, too."

"I can see that." He used a paper napkin to wipe off a chair. Gave her a look.

Heather stifled a giggle. "I'll clean it up." Then grew serious. "Tell me what else happened."

Dustin pulled off his tie, rolled it up, and stuffed it in his jacket pocket. "No one knows what to make of it and your friend didn't help."

"I know." Heather exhaled. "I need to talk to her."

"I thought you did great."

"You think the cops're gonna try to talk to me again?"

Dustin took a bite, grimaced, and got up to nuke his food. "I'll see what I can do about shutting it down. Fine line between being cooperative and stupid."

"So no lawyers?"

"Not yet."

"I need to ask you something but it's hard." Heather stalled, picked up dirty plates, got a sponge to wipe the table. "She told me."

"What? Who?"

"Lucia. She told me about the two of you." Heather was lying but Dustin deflated in on himself, like a kid's wading pool when you pull the plug.

"She never did that."

Heather wanted to cry. "How many times?"

Dustin leaned against the counter. "You're guessing and you're jealous but you're wrong."

"A wife knows these things." The line she tried with Nicki. Up against him it didn't sound as convincing.

"Can you find a shred of Christian compassion in your heart? Lucia's dead and you know what Ken did to her. How can you put me in the same category with him?"

"Don't preach at me." Heather threw the sponge, which he caught. "And don't act all innocent like you have no idea what happens to *all* of them. Do you even care how I feel?"

"Don't throw things at me."

"I was aiming for the sink."

"It wasn't sex."

"How stupid do you think I am?"

Dustin pitched his voice for the back pew. "She wanted

a cut."

In the silence that followed the microwave beeped.

Heather said, "The kids will hear."

He lowered his voice. "She said she helped train the girls, she should get a percentage."

"Did you give it to her?"

"No." He pulled the tie out of his pocket and re-rolled it. "She knew numbers, she was way too specific. My guess is she overheard a conversation at Ruth's. Ken gave her too much access."

"Is that what they're calling it these days?"

"Don't be a smartass, not now." He got his plate and sat down. "I need you to help me think this through. Please."

Heather slumped into a chair. "When did Lucia ask you for money?"

"Wednesday night, in the dorm, after the service. She told Ruth I needed her help calming one of the new girls and Ruth gave her fifteen minutes, no doubt timed her with a stopwatch."

Heather couldn't care less at that moment how hard life had been for Lucia. "She asked you in front of the other girls? Oh, my God. The police can't find them. If they talk to them— Dustin that was just a few days ago."

"I know."

"You didn't do anything to her, did you?"

"How can you ask me that?"

Of all the things Heather ever suspected him of, hurting a girl had never, ever crossed her mind before. "I need to know."

He took her hands and looked straight into her eyes. "As God is my witness. I'd never hurt a living thing. I have trouble killing a spider. You have to believe me."

Heather swallowed. "Okay."

"Lucia threatened me, like blackmail. She said she would go to the authorities, that she wasn't afraid. She'd read something online that said if you're a witness to a crime you can't be deported."

"Is that true?"

"I don't know. She gave me until today to decide."

"And instead she wound up dead." Her dinner formed a lump in Heather's throat and she ran to the sink. Drank water straight from the tap. Couldn't even process what it all meant and what they had to do. An idea came to her and she hated it.

"Maybe." Her hands gripped the edge of the sink and she squeezed her eyes against tears. "Maybe we should send the kids away for a few days."

Her kids. Her lifeline. Her happiness.

Dustin, surprisingly, didn't argue. "Where?"

She took a gasping breath, struggled to say the words. "Your brother called. He and Ayisha are in town. They wanted to—to have dinner but I put them off, you know, considering. I'm s-sure they wouldn't mind taking Trysta and Ryan with them for a few days."

Dustin sounded like he was going to be sick, too. "That'll make me look guilty."

"We've got to protect the kids. Trysta's already scared."

"She plays it up, you know that."

"I know but—you always say they're the most important thing and you're right. It's why you get so mad at me when I—" She hesitated. "Backslide."

"I'm afraid of that, too."

"You don't trust me, do you?"

"As much as you trust me." He walked to where she stood by the sink and pushed at the sleeve of her sweater. "Show me your arms. If I go in the bathroom am I going to find a fresh supply of eye drops?"

"That's not fair."

"None of this is fair. I agree with your plan, though, as much as I hate it. I'm surprised you thought of it."

"You really do think I'm stupid."

"No." He shook his head. He looked sad. "I know how

much you'll miss them."

He shoved the sleeve of her sweater higher. The inside of her arm had no fresh marks. He made a surprised, satisfied sound, leaned down and kissed it, checked the other arm, and kissed it, too.

Heather shivered. "What now?"

"I'll call my brother, you tell the kids. They'll be excited."

He wiped tears off her cheeks and leaned into her. Kissed her neck, her hair, her ear. His menacing words were a sexy whisper.

"But if you start using again, I have to be done."

CHAPTER EIGHTEEN

———◆———

JACK STOPPED HOME for a shower and change of clothes, had a hard time believing it was still Sunday, and the day wasn't over yet. He noticed the untouched expanse of snow in front of his elderly neighbor, Ginger Bowen's, house, grabbed a shovel and worked his way down his walk and then hers. Cold and exercise felt good, scrubbed away mental cobwebs, although he paused for a second to check the weather in Princeville, on the north shore of Kauai, Corie's alleged location where it was a balmy eighty-three degrees. Then he remembered Mike's stinging criticism that morning when they walked the crime scene and tucked his phone away, disgusted at how his mind veered back to Corie's abandonment like an old pickup truck skittering into the grooves on a well-worn dirt road.

He'd lived alone since his first marriage ended and thought he liked it until Corie moved in for ten weeks while she recuperated from gunshot wounds. Jack was weirdly thrilled to have someone to take care of and made the mental mistake of allowing their arrangement to feel permanent. He waited, as she got stronger, for the moment she'd be well enough for them to do things together. *When she's better I'll take her out for a nice dinner. When she's better we'll go skiing. When she's better we'll have sex with abandon.*

None of those things happened. When she was better she left and he hadn't seen or heard from her—as Mike helpfully pointed out—in two months. She'd been gone almost as long as she'd stayed with him.

Forcing himself out of self-pity mode, Jack rapped on Ginger's old-school metal storm door to say a quick hello. She was one of the last holdouts in the neighborhood who still lived in an original brick bungalow that hadn't had its top popped or its footprint supersized. He knew realtors regularly bombarded Ginger with cash offers to "redevelop" her home of forty years and she told them to get lost. She was fiercely self-sufficient and despite her age she'd retained a sharp intelligence as well as a finely honed sarcastic wit, one of Jack's favorite qualities.

Ginger answered the door wearing a yellow chenille robe and running shoes. The shoes were Jack's idea. He told her she'd kill herself shuffling around in the slippers she used to wear and, besides, they made her look like an old lady.

"I caught you getting ready for bed." Although it was only seven.

She peered over his shoulder at the clean sidewalk. "I was just gonna wait for it to melt."

"Wouldn't want you to get a citation." Theoretically, the city could fine you for not clearing your walk within 24 hours.

"Come in the house, I'll make coffee, it'll be a nice distraction from the TV." She clutched the robe closed with one veiny hand and started to unlatch the storm door with the other.

"Can't. I'm on my way out but wanted to see if you needed anything. Caught a new case so I'm not gonna be around much the next few days."

In return, Ginger said what she often did. "You're too nice to be a cop."

And Jack answered with his habitual response. "Glad I

still got someone fooled."

———◆———

Jack's mother, Maryam, ate dinner at what he considered a more appropriate hour, a throwback to her years living in the Middle East and Europe. She had old family photos lining the hallway that Jack had run by a thousand times as a kid without paying attention.

Tonight, he focused on an aunt's pre-wedding portrait taken in Tehran, one of the last images of the family intact, ignorant that their world was about to be blown apart. Adult women wore their long hair wound up into wide, flat buns Jack used to say looked like pancakes. Children, both boys and girls, had severe bangs cut ruler-straight across their foreheads.

All of the men wore suits, including Jack's teenage uncles who appeared awkward and surly with their shoulders hunched and narrow ties askew. No one in the old photos smiled or acted goofy or made faces. It was all deadly serious, eyes forward, sit up straight. Everyone said Jack resembled his grandfather, a man whose gaze even from an old photo was like a dark laser beam. Jack never met him but was sure his grandfather never took any crap from anyone.

His parents' wedding picture was harder to look at. Jack was nineteen when his father was killed and it was not only a catalyst leading him to his current profession but an ongoing background sense of guilt—*if I can solve all those other murders why can't I solve the most important one?*

His mother never remarried although Jack wouldn't have minded if she had. At least, he liked to believe he wouldn't have minded.

"You never look at those."

Maryam walked up next to him and Jack put his arm around her shoulders. He pointed to the portrait. "I know where I got my eyebrows. Or, I should say, eyebrow."

"They were handsome men, my brothers."

Two of those brothers were dead, along with Jack's grandfather. Family legend had it that when he lost his business and his fortune in the Iranian revolution he didn't have the heart to rebuild. That fierce Persian pride was one of the things Jack wanted to talk over with his mother and he turned away from the photos and followed her to the dining room. "This new case I'm working, I have a suspect from Jordan."

"I thought you had the weekend off?"

"Caught it this morning, you know how it goes."

"And I know it's pointless to express any concern about the hours you work. At least you'll have something decent to eat."

She started to pour wine into his glass and Jack stopped her. "Better not. I'm headed back to work as soon as I finish."

"Tell me about your Jordanian suspect. It's fun helping you solve cases."

She said it lightly and usually he told her carefully edited versions. This time, though, he needed her insight and he described how they found Lucia's body, the search, and Ruth's weird stoicism.

"She needs to be seen as beyond reproach," Maryam said.

"Doesn't everyone want to be right?"

"I've known women like Ruth. They're brought up believing it's their job to be the moral center and they take their role seriously. If they fall apart then everyone around them will, too. There's no"—Maryam hesitated, searched for the right word—"lightness. They're never silly or very much fun although they make excellent wives, at least culturally."

Jack couldn't picture Ruth being any fun at all. "I've seen a lot of people deal with grief and she was off the charts cold."

He felt like he was struggling to describe Ruth but Maryam got it.

"Keeping yourself in order is the most important thing."

What an odd way to put it. And then he remembered Ruth said something similar.

Maryam took a sip of her Bordeaux. "That photo you texted earlier. Was the dead woman Iranian?"

"We have evidence she's from El Salvador, possibly an illegal immigrant."

"And she worked for Ruth?"

"As a housekeeper. But there's way more to this. A fancy automatic lock on her bedroom door, cameras everywhere." Jack wondered how much to say. "The husband was buying Lucia expensive jewelry. And from witness statements she made a point of showing it off."

Maryam nodded thoughtfully. "The more Ruth suffered the more she believed she was being a proper wife."

"Would being a proper wife include killing her competition?"

"I doubt Ruth saw the girl as human, let alone equal." Maryam made her scarily accurate comment then broke off a small piece of homemade flatbread.

For his part, Jack was trying not to wolf his food. She'd made one of his favorite meals, a rice pilaf with chicken, onions, and pine nuts seasoned with saffron and fresh herbs. Eating on the run was a bad habit he'd developed as an adult. As a boy he'd been trained to slow down, make intelligent conversation, and to use the correct fork. Stuff that he used to dismiss as old-fashioned had turned out to be useful on dates.

Oh, right, those again.

It was downright annoying how Corie was never far from his consciousness. Anything could trigger a memory, even dinner at his mom's house. At least she knew better than to ask about it.

"How do I pretend to develop a rapport with Ruth?"

Jack asked.

"Flatter her but be subtle."

"How?"

Maryam laughed. "I don't really need to teach you how to flatter a beautiful woman, do I?"

In light of recent events, Jack could probably do with a refresher course. "What makes you think Ruth is beautiful?"

"A guess."

"Excellent guess." Jack high-fived her and reached for his third piece of bread.

"Although she won't let it show, her husband's indiscretion will have wounded her pride. She'll try to convince herself it's due to her insistence on inhabiting the moral high ground. You could use that, too."

"Maybe you should've been a detective."

Maryam's smile faded and she looked away for a moment. "That's right, there's someone dead in the midst of this. Why would a Hispanic girl have Arabic characters as a tattoo? Are you certain none of them are from Iran?"

Jack forced himself to stop shoveling food and set down his fork. "Especially the word 'joy.' It's really strange."

"Wound in white fabric as you described is consistent with a Muslim burial. Have you found yet how many pieces of cloth she was wrapped in?"

"How many—" Jack remembered the medical investigator saying Lucia's body would have to thaw before autopsy. He'd have to let them know to be extra careful when they unwrapped her. "There might be more than one?"

"Yes, don't you remember? For women, it's five pieces. Was she perpendicular to Mecca?"

Apparently, if Jack was on a game show he wouldn't have done so hot in the "Muslim Burial" category after all. He thought about the direction of the alley and Mike's unwittingly accurate comment. "As a matter of fact she was."

Maryam stared into her wine. "It's almost as if they were intending, in some demented way, to show respect."

"Demented" was the perfect word. "Her head was turned to the right and there was a strip of cloth running under her chin."

"Poor thing. If you don't think she was Muslim, you think the killer is?"

Jack had been trying all day to keep a lid on that piece of information, knowing the field day the media would have with the concept of a Muslim killer on the loose in Denver.

"It's way too soon to have solid theories." He showed her another photo from the crime scene, Lucia's face creepily clownish with a bright red mouth and a black stone under her chin.

His mother's expression shifted, distaste or, more likely, horror.

"Sorry." Jack darkened his phone.

"No, no." She made a brushing motion with her hand, sweeping away his concern. "I was wondering if the stones were a substitute."

"For what?"

"Three hard-packed balls of soil, about the size of a fist, are traditionally prepared." She mimed forming a ball. "They're put in with the body, one under the head, one under the chin, and one by the shoulder."

"That can't be a coincidence."

"We created you from soil and return you into it. It's a prayer from the Quran."

"From dust to dust."

Maryam shook her head. "A young woman comes here hoping for a chance and someone does this bizarre, cruel thing."

Even though he was born in the U.S., Jack knew from watching his parents what life was like for immigrants.

He remembered as a boy the constant mental calculations and adjustments in his own behavior—between the way he was required to act at home and the "American" behavior he needed to use everywhere else. Moving between different worlds was great training to be a detective but at the time had made him awkward and self-conscious.

"You're writing a whole backstory and we don't know much more than her name," Jack said.

"Is that how you do it?" Maryam asked.

"Do what?"

"Keep your imagination in check, don't allow yourself to fill in too many blanks about your victims. Is that how you preserve your humanity?"

Ouch. "More like my sanity. And some of my victims"—Jack stopped himself from making quote marks with his fingers—"are pretty culpable."

"There are times I wish you were an accountant."

"Ugh." His Aunt Fatima's husband was an accountant. "No offense to my uncle but I'd die of boredom."

"How did I fail?" Maryam spoke with mock sorrow and then her face broke into a smile. "You always did crave excitement."

"Ah, my job's maybe one percent excitement. The rest is paperwork."

CHAPTER NINETEEN

A T DINNER AUNT Ruth wouldn't stop nagging. How were things at the restaurant? What had he learned from helping Sahir? Had Val caused him any more trouble?

That was a sore subject. Bibi hadn't meant to disrespect her and seriously regretted it because Val's apartment was his escape. He'd sent flowers but she was still ignoring him.

Ruth asked about his day like he'd gone to work writing computer software instead of torturing girls and getting beaten up.

"I'm very proud of you," she said.

"Yeah, whatever."

His knee bobbed up and down and he knew he sounded surly but he hated everything about the restaurant. The stupid customers, dirty plates, smelling like grease all the time. He never got time off while his aunt never got off her bony ass. If they were rich why didn't he get to enjoy it?

Most of all, he hated Sahir, wasn't sure which was worse, being on the receiving end of Sahir's "discipline" or helping dish it out. Bibi knew all too well what it felt like to get hit and it freaked him out that he got turned on earlier with Raven. He wanted to know if it was normal to get a hard-on watching a girl get burned, but it wasn't like he had anyone to ask. Maybe it was the way Raven had writhed against him, her ass against his cock, simply a physical response.

"We have high expectations of you which is why we're so demanding." She was going on and on. "Sahir is an excellent teacher."

"He's an excellent asshole."

"Don't ruin my celebration. You're taking on responsibility and I'm proud."

She'd had cheeseburgers and fries delivered; she must really be trying to get on his good side. And of course no one was there to cook because of what happened to Lucia. He noticed Ruth had a small green salad and that, as usual, she didn't eat more than a couple of bites.

"I need a new phone," Bibi said. "Sahir ruined mine."

"I'm sure he had his reasons."

"His reasons are he's an asshole."

His aunt stood. "If you're finished, I have a nice surprise for you, a reward."

"Is it a phone?"

"Come. You'll see." She folded her hands into a praying motion and touched them to her lips.

He followed her out to one of the seven garage bays. Inside was a brand new, shiny, red Porsche. His favorite car in the world. His dream car.

"Do you want to get in?"

"That's okay." His stomach cramped and he suddenly needed a bathroom.

Her face changed. "Isn't this the right model?"

It made no sense. Punishment for doing the right thing, rewards for doing the wrong. It'd been like this for ten years. Jet skis, a pool, cars, trips, drugs, whatever he desired—just not when he desired it. But Bibi had no way to put that into words, any more than he could ask how he was supposed to feel when he helped hurt someone.

"The girls at the spa—you know what happens there—I

mean, I was wondering…"

Ruth cut him off, her tone brisk, her hand ready to pull open the door of the car. "Yes? What about them?"

"Do they like it?"

"What a ridiculous question." Her hand dropped. "What's the matter with you tonight?"

Bibi's cramps intensified and the sooner he said thank you, the sooner he could escape.

Did his aunt ever have sex? Did she like it? He thought Val liked it but now he wasn't sure. He wanted to go home but that wasn't an option, and having the thought made him feel like a child.

"This *is* the car you wanted?" He knew she was pissed. When Aunt Ruth gave a gift she expected lavish thanks.

Bibi forced himself to nod.

"Do with it as you wish."

She walked away briskly and he yelled after her. "I'm sorry, I don't feel well."

But it was too late.

He ran to the bathroom, barely made it, then washed down a couple of Oxy with vodka directly from the bottle. What he wanted was to shut his brain off, but his mind outraced the drugs.

Bibi was thirteen the first time he was raped. He accidentally bumped a boy in the hall at school, hardly touched him, hadn't meant to. Bibi tried to blow it off. His family was rich. He had the nicest clothes, the latest electronics, gave the best parties; everyone liked him.

Not this boy. He had a rep for being a bully and was a real turd, didn't smile, didn't laugh, didn't say it was okay.

Later, one of the bully's friends found Bibi alone in the washroom and locked the door. Bibi pulled all the money out of his pockets—which was a lot—but it didn't matter. He was forced onto his knees in front of a toilet and when he struggled the other boy calmly explained his choice: be a bitch or get dunked. How would Bibi explain being wet and smelling like piss when he returned to class?

After it was over, the boy instructed Bibi to meet the bully after school at a local park.

He zipped up and checked his hair in the mirror. "If you don't show, I'll make sure everyone knows you're a homo."

"What about you?" Bibi's lame defiance. "You're the one who buggered me."

"Who do you think they'll believe? Everyone already has doubts about you."

That couldn't be true. In the Middle East, where Bibi grew up, "sodomites" were the lowest of the low. People beat them, spit on them, hung them. Bibi's family would disown him and his life would be over. It wouldn't matter that it wasn't his fault. It would only matter that he hadn't been strong enough to defend himself.

The park featured a vertical metal rocket in a grassy clearing, painted red, and that's where three boys waited at the appointed time. Bibi realized his failure too late; the bully had brought reinforcements, including the boy from the bathroom.

The rapist greeted Bibi with a sneer: "Hello, sweetheart."

Then to his friends: "He's a tasty morsel, you should all try him."

"No!" Bibi hadn't meant to speak.

The boys smiled like they were his friends. They laughed and told him he was pretty like a girl.

"His skin is so soft, he uses lotion."

"He smells good because he uses his mother's perfume."

Bibi lunged at them, tried to land a punch, but it was no good. They were all bigger and stronger—and more willing to get hurt.

He wore glasses then because his parents said he was too young for contacts. The rapist took them and ground them under his heel. Then he helped the second boy hold Bibi's arms. The bully beat him until he tasted blood, punched him in the stomach like Sahir had hit Raven, until he threw up.

Only then, with vomit running down the front of his white shirt, did they let him go. The bully seemed bored in much the same way as Sahir, as if he had a job to do and was simply getting on with it. Bibi called them every curse word he could think of, words he'd heard his father use, but it made them laugh harder. As they walked off, Bibi screamed with impotent rage.

Come back you cocksucking balls of camel shit! Come back and I'll show you not to fuck with me! My father will kill you assholes!

He didn't mean a word of it.

Home was worse. His parents had no sympathy and he was sure his father knew everything. Even the servants were rude. Only his Aunt Ruth, who'd been visiting at the time with her new husband, showed kindness. She bathed his cuts, got him ice, and helped him into bed. She told him he was a fine boy and it wasn't his fault. With the right guidance, she said, he'd be a success.

Which meant her guidance. Bibi was never sure if Ruth asked or his father wanted him gone, but he was soon sent to the U.S. to live with her and Ken and he finished high school in Denver. He thought America would be like on TV and that living with his aunt would be easy and luxurious. He didn't know that even worse things waited for him across the ocean.

He really was a moron.

CHAPTER TWENTY

THE ROSE TERRACE was an iconic Denver hotel built in the late 19th century when Colorado's mountains created fortunes from gold and silver. The red sandstone building sat on a triangular plot of land downtown like a living museum illustrating everything people found opulent a hundred odd years ago: stained glass, gold leaf, griffins. A baby grand piano anchored the lobby where they served high tea in the afternoon and Jack wondered what a teenager from El Salvador had thought about all of it.

Jack was told that Ken had weekend holds for a suite on the seventh floor. A front desk clerk named Brian referred to Ken as Lucia's husband.

"You get a last name from Lucia? Or see her ID?" Jack asked.

"No, there was no reason to."

"Did her—" Jack almost choked on the word. "Her husband handle all the paperwork?"

"Yes," Brian said. "They were really into each other, ordered a lot of room service. Can't blame him, she was smokin'. Had this new sable coat he gave her, said she felt guilty about it, but she was always cold."

Into each other? Didn't he find a teenager rocking fur coats and sleeping with a fifty-something man even slightly suspicious? Jack kept his voice level as he asked his next question.

"Does the Rose Terrace participate in any of those human trafficking awareness programs? They're all the rage in the hospitality industry these days."

"Yes, we've had training." Brian stiffened. "But they seemed affectionate."

"You said Mr. Harrowsmith was the one who took care of registration and handled all of the money?"

"He had a standing reservation."

Which was a defense for what, exactly?

"Room service," Jack said. "Was the 'do not disturb' sign always out? Was Mr. Harrowsmith the only one who ever came to the door or answered the phone in the room?"

"I'm usually at reception," Brian said.

"And while you were, did you often see Lucia by herself in the lobby or going out on her own?"

"No." Brian's voice faded. "Last night was unusual."

"Any of that ring a bell from your training?"

"Thank you for bringing this to my attention," Brian said. "I'll make sure the rest of the staff is aware so we can improve our procedures."

"Swell. Can I see their room now or has it already been given to someone else?"

"Mr. Harrowsmith reserved it through Monday. Are we going to be in trouble?"

Everyone always wanted to know that and Jack didn't credit it with an answer. A bellman accompanied him to the seventh floor where, sure enough, the privacy sign hung from the polished brass lever on suite 719.

The bed was neatly made and several women's outfits hung in the closet. Toiletries and makeup were spread out on the bathroom counter along with a bottle of little blue pills. All of the liquor was still in the mini bar, although based on the wrappers in the trash Lucia had gorged on candy. A large bouquet of predominately pink flowers sat on the dresser next to an iPad in a pink leather case. At least Ken knew her favorite color. Jack found no black stones, no cell phone, no diamond necklaces.

When he returned to the lobby, he was informed that a hotel security staff member had cued up video from when Lucia left the hotel. Everyone was suddenly all sorts of speedy and cooperative after Jack's suggestion that one of Denver's finest hotels had overlooked signs of trafficking in their midst.

A manager, who introduced himself as Brian's boss, accompanied Jack to a back office where they watched video. Hotel security, at least, didn't disappoint, with one camera in particular providing an HD view of the door to Lucia and Ken's love nest. A whole lot of nothing relevant until 20:57 when Lucia got room service. At 22:21 she exited the room in a dress and fur coat, heavy makeup, hair styled, and what appeared to be a diamond-studded key on a chain around her neck. Neither coat nor jewelry had been found.

An exterior camera mounted above the main hotel entrance captured Lucia's back as she crossed the sidewalk and climbed into the front passenger seat of a black SUV. It would have been the perfect angle to see the vehicle's license plate if it hadn't been snowing like a son of a bitch. The lens had iced over, leaving the image blurry and obscured.

"Damn it." Jack muttered under his breath. No amount of squinting, rewinding, or zooming was going to bring that plate into focus. He'd get the video to the crime lab forensic imaging guys but didn't have high hopes.

No signage on the SUV, no decals, no neon logo in the front window. Heavily tinted windows made it impossible to see the driver. Lucia jumped in with no hesitation, a flash of long legs, and then she was gone.

As they watched, Brian's boss elaborated for Jack's benefit all of the mandatory courses and training provided to the staff, the many ways their security was cutting edge, and how the Rose had a sterling reputation for working with law enforcement. He actually used the word "sterling."

"I need to speak to the doormen working that night," Jack said. "Valets, bellmen, anyone out front."

"Of course," Brian's boss said. "I'm here to help." He offered Jack a card with his personal cell number written on it. "Call me any time, day or night."

"Appreciate it."

Then the manager asked the question that was apparently uppermost on his mind:

"This isn't going to be on the news, is it?"

———

Nicki Erskine was only a few blocks from the Rose Terrace and agreed to meet. Jack didn't quite have the will to follow strict by-the-book procedures and drag himself back to headquarters, which would be deserted and forbidding late on a Sunday night. Hell, that gloomy fortress of a building was intimidating in the daytime. Nicki's information might not be anything more than gossip. If she did have something substantive he'd bring her in for a formal videotaped interview; in the meantime, he could still record audio.

Jack recognized her easily. Long brown hair fell in soft waves around her shoulders and she squinted a little, scanning the lobby until she saw him and waved. She'd mentioned she was at a bar and he was concerned she might be drunk but Nicki seemed composed and sober. She wore leggings and boots under a short, tight skirt.

"You look nice. I hope I didn't drag you away from a date." Out of habit he stood and pulled out a chair for her.

"Actually, you gave me a great excuse, it wasn't that much fun." A flash of smile then she immediately grew serious. "Not that I—I mean—I realize this isn't a social thing."

"It doesn't hurt my feelings to have a drink with a pretty girl, even if it is work-related." What the hell. Charm never hurt and it wasn't like he couldn't use the practice.

A server arrived and Nicki looked a question at Jack before ordering a white wine. He was about to order a second club soda, or maybe coffee, then decided screw it, and ordered a Scotch. Along with being exceptionally stuffy the hotel had an outrageous selection of single malts.

"I want to help," Nicki said, as soon as the server left. "And I know how serious this is, but thanks for the compliment."

"It's true. You look great." She flushed with pleasure and Jack felt a twinge of guilt at using flattery to his advantage. But it wasn't a lot of flattery and it wasn't a big twinge.

Nicki jumped in with no prompting. "I'm actually glad you called. I've been feeling bad all day for what I said about Lucia. I didn't mean it. That was for Heather's benefit."

"How so?"

"Heather's kind of insecure."

"Does she have anything to be insecure about?" Jack asked.

"No." Nicki sounded emphatic and then backpedaled. "At least I don't think so."

"No one seems to know much about Lucia's family, or if she had a boyfriend, or what she liked to do. Any background you can provide would be helpful."

Nicki thought for a few seconds. "She was from El Salvador, had seven or nine or thirteen brothers and sisters, some unimaginable number. To me, anyway. There was a younger sister she was really close to who was twelve when Lucia left, and she wanted to bring her here. Even tried to talk to Ruth, which took courage, as you can imagine. Oh. Have you talked to Ruth?"

"Yes. And I can imagine."

"That witch wouldn't help a wounded puppy out of the road."

"She'd probably eat it," Jack said. "Or make it into a coat."

Nicki laughed and touched his arm for a second. "You're funny."

A pretty girl who liked sarcastic detectives. Noted. "What else, about Lucia?"

"She loved dresses and anything sparkly and pink, all the usual girlie stuff, I guess. TV when they let her watch, cheesy romances, her English was surprisingly good. No boyfriend, unless you count Ken, which I don't. He made Lucia so unhappy she even asked my advice."

"She did?"

"Uh-huh. How to get him to back off. But she was scared he'd kick her out and she had nowhere to go. At first, she was nice to Ken hoping he'd help her, but he didn't."

"How was Ken supposed her help her?"

"Bringing her family here, especially her sister."

Drinks arrived. The server placed crystal glasses on coasters along with a silver bowl of mixed nuts. "On the house."

Jack saw Brian's boss standing by the front desk. "No, please bring a check."

"Wow." Nicki's eyes widened. "You're important."

Jack took a sip and thought that instead of being noble he should have ordered a second round. "Sounds as if you liked Lucia."

"I did." Nicki nodded enthusiastically. "Don't tell Heather."

"Why not?"

"Heather thinks half the women at church are sleeping with Dustin."

"Are they?"

Nicki snorted. "As if. Heather has nothing to worry about. On that front anyway."

"What front does she have to be worried about?"

"It isn't a good time to be helping illegal immigrants. I probably shouldn't even be talking to you."

"I know Lucia was undocumented." Jack tried to sound reassuring. "I'm investigating her murder. That's my focus. I'm not an ICE agent."

"Still. You're the police."

"Deportation is hardly a concern for Lucia anymore."

"I know, but—"

Nicki displayed hesitation by chewing her bottom lip which was either very sexy or Jack really was very lonely. Or both. He also noticed she hadn't touched her wine but played with her glass, turning it around and around by the stem.

Jack remembered the article Serena sent him. "There are more aren't there? Illegal immigrants staying at the church, like a sanctuary. I've heard about that happening."

Nicki's voice faded. "Dustin's trying to do a good thing...I think."

"You think?"

Her phone chirped. "Oh, crap, it's Heather. She's been texting nonstop." To illustrate she showed him the screen. "She wants to talk to me."

"Ask her to meet you here," Jack said. Nicki hesitated and he added, "Is that a problem?"

"No, um." More lip chewing. "Heather doesn't usually go out this late and this isn't a place we'd go anyway."

"Is Heather a prisoner too?"

"What?"

"Nothing." Jack leaned forward, forearms on thighs. If he had his way both Nicki and Heather would tell him lots of things. "Say you're on a date and need her to rescue you. It's not even a lie. Tell her you'll buy the first round."

"She really won't believe *that*." But Nicki's slim fingers worked the phone. "Huh."

"What?"

"She's getting an Uber and'll be here in fifteen. She'll be

pissed when she sees you, though."

"Then you've got fifteen minutes to tell me what you wanted to say. You can start with why Heather's so suspicious of the police. I wouldn't expect that from a minister's wife."

"She's not a typical pastor's wife. Probably why I like her."

"In what way?" Jack already knew but was curious what Nicki would say.

"Liked to party, did some drugs back in the day. Definitely past tense. I don't know if I should be telling you that, either."

"What else don't you want to tell me?"

She finally took a sip of wine. "I think Heather's in trouble. I think she'll cover for Dustin no matter what."

"What's she covering for?"

"It's something Lucia said."

Maybe it was the Scotch but Jack was feeling flirtatious. He leaned in close enough to catch a whiff of her perfume. "Are you going to make me drag it out of you? I can be very persuasive."

Her smile meant she caught his meaning perfectly. "I bet you can." Then she grew serious. "Lucia told me that when Dustin places girls he gets a fee. I asked Heather about it and she said it was no different from an employment agency. They get paid when a client is hired. Sounded like a line Dustin fed her."

"How big a fee?"

"According to Lucia, a lot. But to her a hundred dollars would've been a lot. It made her mad. The way she saw it, two rich guys and neither one willing to help."

Interesting that Nicki would categorize the minister as rich. "Everyone, including Dustin, claims they have no idea how to reach Lucia's family. They don't know what happened to her yet because I haven't had a way to contact them."

Nicki looked appropriately horrified. "That jerk. Of course he knows how to get in touch with them."

"And yet you still attend Dustin's church."

She shrugged self-consciously. "I go because of Heather and because—this will probably sound dumb, but I didn't know Dustin was profiting from the charity and when Lucia told me at first I didn't believe her."

"What about now?"

A swig of wine, as if for courage. "The people Dustin places, the ones from the charity? The jobs he finds for them aren't like eight to five in an office. And I feel so stupid because he only ever helps girls and I should've figured it out."

"Why only young women do you think?"

"There doesn't seem to be much demand for male domestic help. Sorry. I shouldn't be sarcastic."

Jack couldn't fault anyone for that. He wasn't sure what to ask next. How many? How long had this been happening? "Do you know where some of these young women are?"

"A couple." Another nibble of her lower lip. "And woman is stretching it. Some of them were still children."

"What else did Lucia tell you about life at the Harrowsmiths'?"

"Life? Hardly. When she wasn't cleaning the floors she was cleaning Ken's—" Nicki broke off, angry and embarrassed. "I asked her why, you know? If it was so bad why'd she stay, why'd she want to bring her sister here? Lucia said it was a way out of her country, which was certain death, and she figured she could survive for a couple of years while she figured out her next move. So yeah, she might've gotten a diamond necklace but she worked a gazillion hours and had to sleep with Ken. And yeah, Heather might be mad at me for talking but, God."

"How much of this was Dustin aware of?"

Nicki took another gulp of wine. "To be generous, he

may not know about the sex. That's not the kind of thing you're gonna tell your pastor. But the hours? Hell, yeah. Dustin claims he talked to Ruth about the law—he literally did it this morning with you."

"I remember." Jack thought of the pretty pink prison, no car, all of that marble. "Lucia's life sounds like it was really hard."

"It makes me want to slap Heather because she should know better than anyone, and maybe I'm a terrible friend but Heather's only interested in whether or not Dustin's cheating and how hard she thinks her own life is."

"I think you're a good friend. To both Lucia and Heather."

Nicki's expression changed as she stared at something over Jack's shoulder. "Maybe not anymore. That was a quick fifteen minutes."

He turned and saw Heather approaching their table.

She recognized him at the same time and froze. "You bitch!"

Jack stood and took a step toward her. "Heather, it's important that we talk."

Heather ignored him. "You lying bitch."

Nicki stood too, her tone pleading. "It's not what you think."

"You'll do anything to get laid, even rat out your friend."

"No. I'm not. Let me explain."

Heather turned and ran.

Jack followed, shouting her name, but Heather had no intention of stopping. She was out the front door by the time he caught up, pushing past surprised pedestrians on the sidewalk, headed for the busy corner at Broadway. The last thing Jack needed was for her to get hit by a car evading him. He had no warrant, no legal justification for pursuit. As frustrating as it was, she didn't have to talk to him and he had no reason to detain her. He stopped short on the sidewalk outside the hotel and watched

Heather dodge and weave her way down the block until she disappeared from view.

"Please tell me I did the right thing."

He turned to see Nicki behind him, her face shiny.

It wasn't often a guy made one woman run into traffic, another one cry, and accused a five-star hotel of facilitating human trafficking, all within the span of a couple of hours. Not that Jack cared but he was probably going to be banned from the Rose Terrace for life.

CHAPTER TWENTY-ONE

A HAND REACHED AND snatched her drink off the
bar.

"Hey!" Heather spun.

"What are you doing here?" Sahir asked.

"Nice to see you, too."

Sahir motioned the bartender over. "You're new."

"Cole."

Sahir ignored his outstretched hand. "This her first?"

"Uh-huh."

Cole jumped as Sahir dumped the glass out behind the
bar. "Heather doesn't get served, ever. You want to keep
your job, you notify one of us any time you see her."

"It's not his fault." Heather tried to interrupt.

"Time to go, Princess. I can't hear shit and I'm the only
one working spa security."

"Everyone fucking like they should be?"

He slammed the empty glass on the wooden counter.
"Keep your voice down."

The bartender slid away. Heather glanced around self-
consciously but no one seemed to notice anything amiss.
Right. She was just a girl, invisible, pointless.

"Come on."

She resisted Sahir's pincer-like fingers on her arm. "No."

He tightened his grip. "Why'd you come here of all
places?"

Truth was, she hadn't known where else to go. If she went home Dustin would ask her how it went with Nicki and it hadn't gone anywhere at all.

She knew from past experience the way Sahir vice-gripped her arm she'd have bruises and he wouldn't let go until she complied. Might as well get it over with. Whatever it was. So she let him lift her from the stool and then followed him like one of those meek Biblical lambs. One part embarrassment, one part habit, one part the passivity Dustin worked hard to pray out of her. When her husband prayed he expected to be answered. She tried to imagine being as certain as Dustin, looked up to, respected, and couldn't manage it for an instant.

In the alley Sahir unlocked a car, the familiar whiny chirp, and got in the driver's seat, her entry—and cooperation—an assumed fact. She couldn't blame him because they had history. Her whole life was a back alley, no answers, no control. Her default existence shaped by what other people—other men—did to her, as if she had no existence or animation without them. As if she'd never been born which, as she often thought, might have been best, but which now brought her to tears because she had kids of her own.

"Bishop texted Queen." Sahir used their dumb code names; Dustin was the Bishop and Ruth the Ice Queen. "You were supposed to go meet the whore and go straight home."

"I don't need this right now. And don't call Nicki that, she's my friend."

Sahir fished a lighter out of his pocket. "Bitch is drinking at a fancy hotel with a detective, ratting us all out. What else should I call her?"

The sight of Nicki laughing, tossing her hair, touching the cop's arm, made her want to cry.

"Ugh." Sahir made a disgusted sound, grabbed a pipe from the overflowing ashtray, banged out the contents.

"No."

"Whaddya mean, no?" He tamped some weed from a baggie into the bowl.

"Rehab was hard. I don't want it."

"You need to calm down. You're under a lot of stress right now."

"I shouldn't have come here."

"You came to where you had friends."

Friends? Was he joking? "You're not my friend."

It was all a game, her acting a good pastor's wife, Sahir pretending he wanted her to clean up her act when he was the one who got her hooked and kept her hooked, everyone claiming it wasn't simply prostitution, no matter how many warm towels and cups of flavored water provided to "spa customers." No different from the old days—her old days—in the motel on Colfax, lights from the used-car dealership next door blinking on and off, casting the dingy wall an alternating pink. She liked the lights, only spot of color.

"What'd the whore tell you?" Sahir asked.

"Nothing. When I saw the two of them I booked."

"Completely useless. If you were gonna go you should've at least gotten intel."

From his phone, where he watched video feeds, a pornographic soundtrack accompanied their conversation.

I can feel your teeth bitch, what are you playing at? Oh, yeah, that's better. Nice and slow, I wanna get my money's worth.

Didn't faze Sahir, who only cared if a girl used their safe word, but it made Heather's stomach turn over. The vodka she'd managed before he arrived had gone straight to her head.

"Bishop told me the detective was good looking and your whore friend seemed interested. And the Rose Terrace? You didn't think you were walking into a trap?"

"Can we stop with the nicknames?" Heather said. "It's

so stupid."

"Let me connect the dots, as they say. You spied on Lucia because you thought she was screwing your husband. What was the hotel Ken took her to?"

His favorite hotel was the Rose Terrace. Heather knew that and went anyway.

Sahir continued. "Tell me what happened and what you said to the cop."

"Nothing."

"I don't believe you." Sahir held out the pipe and a lighter, not an invitation; threat and necessity. He locked the car doors.

Didn't Dustin know this would happen? Ruth would tell Sahir, Sahir would find her, and he never had "conversations."

"If I start again he's gonna leave this time for real," Heather said.

"He tell you that?"

"Yeah, tonight. He checked my arms."

"No needles so nothing to worry about. It's just weed."

There was no "just" anything for her but she couldn't see a way out. Was a klutz with the lighter, fumbled with her right thumb, odd for a girl who used to light her mother's cigarettes, who smoked anything handed to her from the age of thirteen. Used to think, *at least it wasn't until my teens*, like that was some kind of accomplishment to be proud of. Her earlier childhood unsullied by bad choices; at least, those of her own. Always, a blank piece of paper for others to screw up on. A non-entity. Nameless, faceless, impossible to hurt, like a cunt with no irritating personality.

"You're so young," men used to say, as if that was something special she'd done on purpose. Then she'd hang with dudes her own age and complain about the old guys, and the young guys wanted to bang her, too. No different. No one any different until Dustin, who looked

at her as if he actually saw her and cared how she felt. Asked questions and listened.

A string of stepfathers, as her mother insisted she call them, starting when she was three years old. Heather didn't remember or know her real father which made him his own variety of blank canvas for her to draw on. She made him good. If only he hadn't left, if only he came back for her. When she imagined him now she saw Dustin's face.

During her middle years, her tweens as she thought of them, she read books out of the school library and imagined finding her dad, his shock at learning her condition, her certainty that he'd rescue her. Heather started hating her mother then, for driving her real father, the good man, away.

Stepfucker number two, the one who introduced Heather to beer. A girl of single digits. He found it funny the way she acted drunk, told her she was his favorite drinking buddy. Why'd they always choose Heather? In her teens it made her feel powerful; chosen over her mother. Until a pregnancy days into fourteen, aborted. An awful clinic, her mother mad, telling everyone her daughter was a slut. Forced birth control after that. What was the reasoning there? If her men were going to fuck Heather they couldn't leave evidence?

When she was fourteen-and-a-half her mother turned a problem into an opportunity and started taking Heather to bars. Wingman. Original bait and switch. Put makeup on Heather, made her look older, got her a fake ID. Men banked them at pool games in different bars that might as well be the same one, pressed hard-ons into Heather as she bent over the table pretending they were teaching and she was learning while her mother bummed a light and laughed the other way. Men liked Heather's ass, her blonde hair, her lack of reaction. *"Thirteen or thirty,"* her mother used to say, *"who can tell?"*

Sixteen. Met Sahir on the street. Biggest cliché of all. Took her for a meal. Pretended to listen. When he got her in the motel room and laid out the rules she wasn't even surprised. He said, *"Going to be a slut you might as well get paid for it."* None of the crap about how it was what you'd do with your boyfriend anyway. Heather never had a boyfriend. No one had ever organized her fucking before. To her it was a relief, a predictability about nights that blended into half-days and the next night, and the next. Sahir told her he was impressed by her stamina. That she never complained. And the really, really sick thing was, at the time, Heather wanted to ask, complain about what?

He kept her high, fed her a little, and her body, the thing on the bed or the floor or against the wall had value. No more giving it away for free; made perfect sense at the time. She got thin. Sahir called her his lean, mean fucking machine which thrilled her and made her want to try harder. He kept most of the money but that seemed fair since he provided her room, food, clothes, drugs. He beat up customers who took more than they paid for. No one had ever come to Heather's defense and she loved him, right up until Dustin came to the motel. Heather was never sure what Sahir hated most; losing a product or losing her adoration.

Immolation, she thought, as the lighter caught the bowl in a short, mean sunrise of despair. A word she only knew from studying the Bible with Dustin. Sahir was burning her up with temptation, except it wasn't, not anymore. She must pretend to be what she used to be. For what reason? Unknown. Her kids flashed in her mind. *I can't. I don't even want to.*

The head rush was insane. It wasn't regular weed.

"You prick." Heather grabbed the door handle to steady herself.

"My special blend." Sahir watched her. "Why'd you hate Lucia so much? She had nothing to envy."

"She had my husband."

"Well," Sahir said, "now she has nothing."

And neither do I.

CHAPTER TWENTY-TWO

—◆—

"**D**ETECTIVE FARIEL?"

"Yep." Why did Jack even attempt sleep?

The voice on the phone identified itself as Colorado State Patrol Trooper Gray. Jack rubbed his eyes with one hand and checked the time on his phone with the other—three ten a.m. His suit was draped over a chair in the corner of the bedroom where he'd stepped out of it and fallen into bed what felt like fifteen minutes ago.

"We pulled Ken Harrowsmith out of a ditch. The alert said to notify you."

Jack swung his legs over the side of the bed, suddenly alert. "Where'd you find him?"

"Washington County. Near the intersection of V and 19."

"Where the hell is that?"

Trooper Gray chuckled. "A dirt road east of Woodrow and west of Yuma. Not a place as much as GPS coordinates. All agricultural around there and it was a hell of a blizzard last night. He's lucky anyone came along. Not to mention alive—his blood alcohol was .18 by the time they could get a sample and he'd been in that car for a while. Found a couple of empty wine bottles in there with him."

DUI, statutory rape, murder. The list kept growing. "Where is he?"

"At the hospital in Yuma, that's where they did the blood draw. He's pretty banged up and they're keeping him overnight for observation and to let him detox. He'll recover, but I'm not so sure about his rental car."

So Ken *had* been able to get one. "What company?"

Trooper Gray named a major chain. "I-70 was closed last night east of the airport. My guess is he was trying to get out of state on country roads."

"Fail."

And damn, if this guy wasn't guilty he was doing everything in his power to look that way.

According to the hospital, Ken would be well enough to be released into police custody and interviewed in the morning—or, rather, later that morning. Jack texted Mike and then made calls arranging his suspect's transport. Yuma was a good two-and-a-half hours east of Denver so, ever the optimist, Jack attempted a few more minutes of sleep.

The coffee shop was on a corner, decked out in steampunk décor including plasma cut metal and part of an airplane fuselage in the patio. Jack tolerated the precious atmosphere because their Americanos were good and there was a pretty blonde barista who worked mornings and always smiled at him like he was the only guy she ever made coffee for. The little things that made life tolerable.

It was turning into a beautiful day, snow gone, bright sunshine, and Jack walked the five blocks from his house, thinking about how to prioritize his activities with Lucia's autopsy and Ken's interview leading a long list. He decided it would be better to know how Lucia died first and that the alcoholic lying sleaze could sit in a holding cell until Jack was good and ready for him.

Lost in thought, he absentmindedly swiped his credit card in the iPad on a stand, selected a tip and drew a facsimile of a signature with his index finger. A familiar flash of hair drew his attention but it couldn't be, she wasn't in Denver she was in Hawaii, maybe she was back—confused thoughts tumbled like rocks sliding down a steep hillside. Even from a bad angle, even without fully seeing her he knew it was Corie. Thank God she had her back to him and then he wondered why he didn't want her to see him—it wasn't like *he* was the one hiding—and it took his sleep-addled brain a millisecond to register the relevant question: Who the hell was the guy sitting across from her?

She wore a pale turquoise sweater, shifted in her chair, and something about the delicate way she moved made it hard to breathe. Her slim, white hand held a china cup, raised it to lips he'd kissed. Her hair was growing back, reddish gold curls brushed her shoulders. He was sure she was smiling.

Walk over. Say hello. "Good to see you, Corie, you look well." Be the bigger man or take the higher road or whatever cliché bullshit the situation called for. She was the one who should feel bad. She was the one having coffee with some other dude when she hadn't called him or texted or in any way communicated she was in Denver or alive on planet Earth.

An old girlfriend once told him he had a kind of rolling mask that came down over his face, like a metal security shutter on a city storefront at closing time. She said he could be scared shitless, but it never showed.

Not this morning. While his thoughts scrambled for a foothold his actual feet froze to the ground and he wasn't sure but he might have been audibly whimpering. He stood rooted by the espresso machine so long the barista's expression of friendliness changed to wariness. Maybe fear.

With one abrupt motion—people waiting for their drinks were piling up behind him like a human log jam— he picked up his coffee and turned away from Corie's end of the room. He found out the top of the cup wasn't on securely when espresso scalded his hand. Maybe the barista left it that way on purpose so he could doctor it with the non-GMO cream and assorted raw sugars on display. Maybe she'd simply been in a hurry. Hot liquid ran up his arm, soaked the front of his shirt, and spattered his jacket.

Jack barely recognized a blur of the blonde barista apologizing and what he experienced as horrified stares of onlookers. He needed to get out the door as quickly as possible and declined proffered napkins and the offer of a new drink. All the while thinking, *Please don't turn around, please don't see me, not now, not like this.*

At home, he threw the soiled clothes into a corner like an insult, flopped onto the bed and thought about absolutely nothing. The light fixture in the middle of the ceiling was suddenly alien, more unfamiliar the longer he stared at it, swirls of metal and poorly soldered joints. He held himself perfectly still the way he did when he was a child and afraid he was going to throw up, as if to will himself into another dimension where the bad thing wasn't happening.

Over and over the flash of golden hair, the briefest glimpse of a smile. At another guy. For another guy. How long had she been in Denver? Why hadn't she told him she was here? Where was she staying? All unknown. And really, how good a detective was he if he couldn't decipher the meaning in her lack of communication?

She went out for coffee like nothing had ever happened to her in her life beyond maybe a mean boss and a fight with her high school boyfriend.

Bad analogy. Her high school boyfriend had been, briefly, him.

Even in his diminished capacity, Jack's brain wouldn't stop making relevant connections with surgical precision, homing in on the painful bullseye of whatever situation presented itself as the target. Normally, this was a good thing about how his mind worked, his preternatural ability to draw a picture by connecting scarce dots, the dark space between clues ripe for interpretation. In this case, any guess he made about the Corie sighting would only serve as a weapon for a self-inflicted wound.

In the shower he stood under hot water, in an unfocused state, like shock. Not showering, a verb, as much as presenting an object to the spray, like a rock interrupting the flow of a mountain stream.

A run might make him feel better, but he'd just showered. Plus, he didn't have time for this shit. He needed coffee but was out of filters and he needed to pick out a clean suit but hadn't managed to stop at the dry cleaners. He should call her, end the suspense, but she'd asked when she left that he specifically not call because she needed time. His brain tendered options and just as quickly defeated them, a sadistic mental target practice where all he could do was shoot imaginary clay pigeons and wait to see what his psyche would hurl into the air for destruction next.

Mostly he needed to get his sorry ass moving. His phone was blowing up but Jack couldn't quite make himself care.

Choices, decisions, simple next steps like *put some clothes on, moron*, sputtered on the screen of his brain and died. He was on the bed again, naked, and found it nice to lie there and resume examining the shoddy manufacturing quality of the ceiling fixture. Probably made in China like everything else. One light bulb was burned out and the rest were really dirty. He should do something about that.

Mike's words returned to him, from one of their nights out at Mike's favorite strip club, home of surprisingly philosophical conversations in sight of anatomically imaginative girls waxed within an inch of their lives.

"You don't have to be pure or noble or whatever the hell it is you think you're being."

Stupid. How about stupid?

Corie hadn't spent the last two months in suspended animation meeting no one, seeing no one, speaking to no one. Obviously, she had conversations and consumed beverages with people—men—who were not Jack. With a groan he rolled onto his side and put his feet on the floor. In the bathroom, he re-wet his hair and used his fingers and some gel in an attempt to get rid of the big flat spot in the back from lying down. Maybe Mike and a lot of the other officers were onto something with their shaved heads. Maybe Jack should grow a beard and become a hipster, wear flannel shirts and invent artisan cocktails.

He put on a gray DPD logoed golf shirt and black BDUs, decided he'd stop at the dry cleaners on the way to headquarters. Maybe get a coffee, too, and pour it into a sippy cup so he didn't hurt himself, or subject the populace to any further traumatizing scenes of self-destruction (lethal self-caffeination?).

His phone buzzed and he was going to ignore it again when he recognized the number for the Coroner's office. Among other things, Jack was late for an autopsy.

CHAPTER TWENTY-THREE

———◆———

"**WHATEVER I WANT?**" Willow's eyes were huge over the top of the laminated menu.

"Why not." Sahir sat across from her in the booth at a busy chain restaurant. Mostly, the promise of a steak dinner—or in this case a hot breakfast—was more than enough to gain cooperation. It was rare for him to have to take more severe steps with a girl, as he had with Raven, but she was a special case.

"Willow, I need to talk to you about—"

"That's not my name."

Sahir took a deep breath through his nose and let it out. She was very pretty, which was why he was bothering. Thick blonde hair, large almond-shaped eyes, and unblemished skin. She still had a childish body, slim hips, long legs, no chest to speak of, and was proving to be popular with customers.

"Do you want to be found by immigration? They're worse than ever. In those deportation camps you'll be raped without a dime to show for it. There are rats in those camps, you'll starve, and they'll take all of your pretty new outfits."

Sahir didn't need to exaggerate the horrors of ICE. The immigration crackdown had boosted his supply; no one, even a child like Willow, trusted the government anymore.

A waitress arrived and Willow ordered an omelet, a side of bacon, French toast, then looked at Sahir for permission. "Can I, Daddy?"

He demanded all the girls call him that, especially in public. "Are you gonna finish it?"

The waitress seemed amused. "My daughter's the same. Always with her eyes bigger than her stomach. How old are you?"

Sahir answered, "Fourteen. How old's your daughter?"

"Same."

"I'm really hungry," Willow said.

The waitress smirked. "What's your name, hon?"

Sahir was mildly curious what she'd say. Nothing at stake for him but the answer determined her future. Plenty more Willows in the pipeline. Or whatever her real name was. They changed girls' names to hide them and to mentally prepare them for a different life. If a girl went to work in a private home her new employer chose the name, and Middle Eastern families usually went with something American like Jane or Christine. For the spa, he liked exotic names, something to intrigue the customers.

Topaz eyes flicked between Sahir, the waitress, the menu.

"Willow."

"That's pretty." The waitress's voice was bright and phony.

"If she wants all of that food who am I to say no?" Sahir made the universal sheepish father gesture, palms up and sappy smile.

After the waitress left he said, "Tell me what happened at work yesterday."

Willow gnawed at the edge of her thumb.

"I provide food, clothes, keep you safe but you're stealing from me if you don't work."

She'd worn one of the new outfits to breakfast, purple sweater with a lacy collar and leggings covered in flowers.

Her stubs of nails were painted alternating pink and yellow. Sahir made a *tsking* sound.

"You bite your nails? That's a terrible habit."

Big eyes watched him.

"If you applied yourself you could be my favorite. You're younger and prettier than Raven."

"I am?"

"But I don't like you when you pull shit like you did yesterday."

She nibbled her thumb, saw his frown, and stopped. "I hate it."

"What?"

"Touching people. Men."

"But they like it when you do and it's completely safe."

Mostly. Customers were prescreened and read the rules before they got near a toy. That was his code word—he hated the term "bottom bitch." Sahir had high standards which made his product stand out in the crowded world of adult services.

Willow's complaints continued. "They're all so old. I was at the house with Raven and this one man came in and I started, you know, giving a massage like she showed me but he was moaning and he was fat and it was awful."

"You do realize that's your job, that's how you get to stay here?" Coffee arrived and Sahir sucked in a large mouthful.

"Raven said I was being a baby and to go back and finish but I couldn't."

Score one for Raven. "Let me ask you something. Do you have an ID?"

"You said you had it."

"Do you want to go to the police? I'll drive you to the station right now."

She slumped against the vinyl booth and stared.

He slurped more black coffee, reached in his pocket for a roll of antacids. "What do you think the police'll do with you, an undocumented girl in the country illegally?"

"I don't know."

"Yes you do. I thought you were smart. You'll go to one of those centers with the rats. People don't like immigrants here, Willow. Think about it, what were the *policia* like at home?"

"Bad."

"They're even worse here. Cops'll rape you first, though, because you're pretty. But if that's what you want, I won't stop you."

Fear and confusion were clear in those enormous eyes and he let her think until her order arrived.

"Wow, that's a lot of food." He gave the waitress a conspiratorial wink and saw her cheeks flush.

"Let me know if you two need anything else, like a box for the leftovers."

Willow poured a lake of maple syrup onto her plate and started in on the French toast.

"After this I was gonna take you to the mall," Sahir said.

"You were?"

"If you're not gonna work though…" He shook his head. "Then you have to leave. I can't afford to buy you shit or give you a nice room to live in. On your own, that what you want?"

Her eyes brimmed with tears. All of the toys could cry on a moment's notice but this one was a real pro.

"Do you even like giving massages?" he asked.

"The right way."

Sahir found that funny. "Shit. You don't even know what the right way is. Go on, finish your breakfast. I don't want to waste any more money on you."

"I can't."

"You can't work, you can't eat. If you don't want to be my girl then why are you here?"

He made sure no one was watching and peeled off five twenties from a roll in his pocket. "I was gonna give you this to buy whatever you wanted at the mall. Or you could send it home to your family. I'll help you wire it."

When she saw the cash her tears stopped as if by command. "They wouldn't want me to do anything bad."

"What you did to me yesterday was bad. Lying and stealing. Would they want you to do that?"

"You know what I mean."

But the way she watched the money he knew he had her and added two twenties. "This is for you extra if you're sweet and work hard but you have to prove you wanna be my girl, because right now I don't believe you."

"Do I have to do that crazy stuff?"

"Yes. Plus stuff you haven't learned yet. If you're good I'll take care of you and keep you safe. If not, you're with the rats, and you'll never see your family again."

Eyes fringed with long lashes followed the cash as he tucked it back in his pocket. She picked up a fork, poked, prodded, dragged a piece of toast through syrup.

"I'll be good."

CHAPTER TWENTY-FOUR

———

A T THE MORGUE, Mike gave Jack a once over. "Is it casual Friday or something?"

Jack offered his friend a very brief synopsis of coffeegeddon.

Mike's mouth pressed into a thin line and Jack reacted. "I don't need your disapproval right now."

"Wasn't disapproving of you."

"I'll grab a suit from the cleaner on my way back to headquarters." Why was he explaining? Who cared? They wore protective gear over their clothes anyway, including masks and face shields. If only there was a way to make his inner dialogue stop.

What remained of Lucia Santiago lay on a metal autopsy table. Part of her skull had been removed and, drained of blood, she more resembled a horror movie prop than a human being. No effort was put into making things pleasant or palatable for detectives and, under ordinary circumstances, they wouldn't have even been there in person. But they were going to make a somewhat unorthodox attempt to unlock Lucia's iPad.

Dr. Greer Spahr was the forensic pathologist who'd removed Lucia's brain for examination. The doctor was in her mid-forties with long red hair pulled into a ponytail.

"Morning, gentlemen. At least I think it's still morning. I assume you want the headline first. Your case died from blunt trauma of the head with an acute subdural hematoma."

"Like she was struck with an object?" Jack asked.

"Possibly. Defect was on the back of her head and I observed evidence of posterior subgaleal hemorrhage consistent with the base of her skull striking, or being struck with a hard object. Either a blow or she fell onto something."

Healthy teenagers didn't usually fall unassisted and Jack doubted Lucia would have hurled herself, base of the skull first, onto a blunt object.

"Is the hematoma a fatal injury?" Jack asked. "Or could she have survived if she'd gotten to a hospital?"

"Highly doubtful."

"What about defensive wounds?" Jack asked.

"Didn't observe any." Dr. Spahr continued her clinical report. "Appears to be a well-nourished, normally developed sixteen-year-old. No foam in her lungs or any indication of opioid intoxication. We swabbed obvious touch points, her anus and around her genitals for DNA. And of course we're running toxicology tests. She was naked under the cloth wrapping. There's only the one tattoo on the nape of her neck and one piece of jewelry, a labial piercing. I removed that ring for evidence and was surprised to find an inscription because ordinarily genital piercings are too narrow."

Jack wasn't sure he wanted to know what it said but the doctor told him anyway, thoroughly professional and detached: "Love Ken."

He repressed a completely unprofessional shudder, both at the concept and the content of the inscription. Tattoos were one thing, Jack had a few of those, but so far was unimpaled and planned to stay that way.

"Did you find any other stones?"

"Negative. No foreign objects inside her rectum, vagina or mouth. We took a sample of the lipstick. There are studies underway to determine reliable methods of forensic analysis of lipstick since it's so often present in trace evidence. But no databases yet."

"How many pieces of cloth was she wrapped in?" Jack asked.

"Three."

"Are you still pursuing the Muslim angle?" Mike asked.

Jack explained. "In Muslim burials women are traditionally wrapped in five pieces of cloth, one of them being a head scarf."

"This wasn't an actual funeral," Mike said. "Leaving her next to a dumpster."

Dr. Spahr's forehead creased. "Interesting. Her body was very clean, almost like it'd been washed. That's also part of Islamic burial rituals, done as soon as possible after death, within hours."

A lead was a lead and Jack felt grimly triumphant. "You have a better idea of time of death?" Rose Terrace at 22:30, alley at 07:00. Jack was hoping for evidence to at least narrow that gap other than a homeless dude's fascination with trains.

"Considering temperature and exposure my estimate is death occurred six to eight hours prior to her body being found. And there's one more thing I want to note before we try the iPad experiment. She was approximately eight weeks pregnant."

"Ah, shit." Jack was glad he'd waited to interview homicidal pedophile loser Ken—now very possibly baby daddy Ken—until after the autopsy.

Dr. Spahr and an assistant carefully raised Lucia to a seated position and adjusted her head. Jack powered on the iPad in the pink case, aimed it at her face and held his breath. Come on, facial recognition. He'd heard stories of this working. Fingerprint readers didn't react to dead fingers because there was no longer a slight electrical charge running through the skin, but devices that read faces had been fooled in some cases by photographs. It seemed like a long time but in reality only a second. The small padlock icon opened. A smiling selfie taken with Ken lit the home page. Text messages popped.

Mike whistled. "Got him."

CHAPTER TWENTY-FIVE

⬩———

DUSTIN WAS IN the conference center, practicing his Spanish talking to four young women currently in sanctuary, trying his best to explain that they were being transferred to another church, not deported. What was the word? He consulted his phone: deportado. Simple enough. *No deportado.*

When Ruth appeared he was relieved, at first.

"Your secretary told me you were out here." She airily kissed near both of his cheeks, and was dressed casually, for her, in slacks and a gray sweater. "Are these all the remaining packages?"

Dustin winced internally. "Package" was one of their code words but there was no reason to use it in front of the women. "I need to talk to you but I have to be careful because of, you know, all the cops. Coming here was smart."

"Yes, but." She hesitated. "I'm here to pick out a new housekeeper."

Was she insane? Lucia hadn't been dead a day. He spoke to the girls, told them to wait downstairs in the dormitory. *Abajo por favor.* Made a shooing motion with his hands.

"Why'd you send them away?" Ruth asked.

"Are you crazy?"

"I don't think so."

Now he had her attention but didn't know where to

begin and blurted his question. "What really happened to Lucia?"

"Nothing that concerns you."

"Nothing—me—what?" He sputtered with confusion. "It is my concern. It's very much specifically, personally my concern."

"As I told the detective, it's a tragedy, but it has nothing to do with you or the church and the further you distance yourself the better."

He felt a needle of panic. "You spoke to the police? What did you say?"

Ruth smiled quizzically as if surprised by his alarm. "They searched my residence and her room. It was to be expected. Do I have to explain this to you?"

"I was her pastor."

"Please, perform your pastoral duties. I would never suggest otherwise. What's wrong with you this morning?"

"Why do you look like you want to laugh? What's wrong with *you*?"

"I'm entertained by your show of naivete, I must admit." She walked to a row of metal folding chairs, straightened one of them. "However, it's best to play it straight with the police."

Anger blurred the edges of his vision and Dustin struggled for control. How was Ruth so instantly enraging? Was it the way she reacted to the most sordid facts as if discussing lunch? Her placid demeanor completely at odds with reality? "Don't tell me how to act. And why aren't you more upset? Why are you here if not to discuss Lucia's murder?"

"I told you," Ruth said. "I'm quite transparent. Life goes on and I can't be expected to scrub my own toilets."

He exploded. Couldn't help it. "That—you—are so far outside the realm of normal human behavior I can't even—you assured me Lucia was safe. Housekeeping only, you said. You worked her hard but he was no longer—you gave me your word."

"And I have kept it."

"Then why is she fucking dead?" Dustin tried not to curse—dignified minister and all that—but the way Ruth stood there, smugly curious, as if she couldn't imagine why he was upset, made him crazy.

But Ruth wasn't as calm as she appeared. "Everyone wants me to weep and exclaim. For what? For a girl whom my husband lavished gifts upon, who fornicated with him under my roof after I asked—no, begged, them not to?"

"As if she had a choice. He forced her. He forced himself on all of them. As your minister—"

"Don't be a cliché."

"And don't you be a psychotic monster." Dustin blindly reached for a folding chair and hurled it across the room.

"My. Are you this passionate with Heather or was it only Lucia?" She tapped her hand on the back of a chair. "I'd consider it a personal courtesy if you didn't throw any more of these."

He forced air into his lungs. "Please tell me what happened."

"It's best if I don't, you know that. Besides, I wasn't there."

"You have everyone under surveillance," Dustin said. "Lucia told me about the cameras."

"Did she? That was for her safety."

"Didn't work."

"You're assuming she was killed under my roof. Do you have information I don't?"

"What does Ken have to say?"

She reacted to the mention of her husband's name, made a muted snarling sound. "That worthless trash. If I have my way, not only won't I see him again, he'll never see daylight."

A pyrrhic victory, provoking emotion from Ruth. "Outlived his usefulness, has he?"

"I appreciate plain speaking with you because it takes too much energy to make up stories."

"It's too much energy to pretend you're human." But for the first time, he realized she was. "I knew when Lucia didn't come to church with you."

"Yes, she never missed a chance to make eyes at you. Yet even though you were alarmed, you didn't notify the authorities."

"Because she didn't live with me."

"Everyone thinks that because I wasn't Lucia's bff I must have killed her." Ruth extended her arms, slim wrists together. "Lock me up."

Dustin grimaced. "Now you're overacting. And why the sudden display of disgust? You procured for your warped excuse of a husband for years and never seemed to care."

"I know."

"Here's plain speaking. Are Ken's needs so outrageous that a nice, pretty girl doesn't keep him entertained for more than a year or two?"

"I agree. I share your revulsion."

"And yet you want me to let you go downstairs and pick out another one."

Ruth took a step toward him. "Don't you see? It won't happen again. I'm cooperating with the police. Ken won't be a factor going forward. Do I need to spell it out for you?"

"He has outlived his usefulness."

"By a far stretch."

"I'm still not letting you take another girl. They're going to a church on the west side and I'm going out of business."

Dustin went to the double glass doors and pushed one open to show her out.

Ruth didn't move. "Her baby was yours, wasn't it?"

He let go of the door.

"The girl was a slut so it's a fair question." Ruth tapped her phone. "I'm calling Heather and inviting her to lunch, she should be aware of all the developments and I'm sure she could use a friend."

"Shit. No." Dustin lunged and then stopped. What was he going to do? Grab the phone from Ruth's hand? He heard his wife's voice.

"Heather? Oh, I'm so sorry. It's Ruth. I must have dialed you by accident. As long as I've got you though, how are you doing after hearing the terrible news about Lucia?"

She listened to Heather and asked him a question with her eyes. Not much of a decision, really. A forty-two-year-old man, a husband, a minister; he was much worse than a cliché. Slowly, purposefully, he nodded and she gracefully ended the call.

"I have to tell Heather myself."

"And I need a new housekeeper. It's a win-win."

"How'd you know Lucia was pregnant?"

Ruth waved a dismissive hand. "Ah, women back home could always tell."

"And of course you knew it couldn't be Ken."

"That narrowed it down but I wasn't quite sure until I saw your reaction. It may surprise you, but I was kind to her. I prepared herbal remedies for nausea and made her tea."

Talk about things that were hard to believe. Lucia had told Dustin about the baby after church Wednesday night, the real reason she asked him for money. Ken claimed he couldn't father children, she said, same way he didn't worry about condoms or STDs because he preferred virgins. That was some plain speaking Ruth might enjoy. Is it true your husband only screwed virgins? Left you out, didn't it?

He said none of that. "What happened to Manuela?"

"Who?" Ruth tipped her head to the side, puzzled.

"The girl who worked for you before Lucia."

"Oh. You mean Abigail. I have no idea."

"You don't keep in touch with her?" Dustin asked.

"How? Send a holiday card? Maybe Facebook friends?"

"I don't know. It wouldn't be that strange to keep up with a young woman who worked for you for two years."

Confusion changed to annoyance. "You're as bad as that Iranian detective. No, I don't become friends with my employees, but that doesn't mean that I mistreat them. We gave Abigail a nice severance payment when she left."

"An uneducated teenager. How was she going to manage on her own?"

Ruth didn't blink. "She had family, or so she said. I didn't pry. Either way, she wound up much better off than if she'd never worked for us."

"If you count being abused by Ken the whole time as a bonus."

"He's a pig. I'll agree on that point all day long. But he's no longer an issue and I still need a housekeeper. Can we go downstairs now or should I call Heather back?"

"Ken's gone? The new girl will be safe?"

New girl. He'd already agreed.

Ruth sighed. "Give it a rest, Dustin. Separation of church and state; isn't that what you always say?"

CHAPTER TWENTY-SIX

———————

JACK FOUND THREE pertinent sets of texts on Lucia's iPad sent Saturday night. The first from someone who sounded like a friend saying they were on their way. Maybe the car Lucia jumped into? She'd responded with lots of smile emojis, rainbows, and blowing kisses.

Then the same number after midnight: *Where r u? Did you find it???*

Again and again all night: *Where are you? Answer me girl! I'm scared. R U OK?????*

Clearly worried about Lucia. And what was she supposed to find?

Jack called the unknown texter and no one picked up; the voice mail message was an automated mechanical repetition of the number. He texted and got no response or indication his message had been read. He'd try a reverse lookup but his instincts and experience told him it was probably a burner.

The second string of texts was from Bibi of the unkempt room.

Bibi: *Your pretty* ♥♥♥🌿🌿🌿
Bibi: *Why Won't you talk to me?*
Lucia: *Your aunt wouldn't like*
Bibi: *She don't matter*
Lucia: *you know that's not true*

Bibi: *Meet me later? Please?* Praying hands emoji.
Please? jUst want to talk

And so on, until 22:08 when she stopped answering.

The third set, from Ken, was more hostile:

21:34 Ken: *Stop calling me*
Lucia: *Well pick up*
Ken: *You know I can't*
Lucia: *You can if you want to*
Ken: *@ symphony w/wife Stop calling you Can't talk to
    me like that*
Lucia: *I don't wanna be in this stupid room alone*
Ken: *Stop I mean it she's already suspicious & don't you
    dare leave hotel*
Lucia: *Why? You don't care about me*

Jack knew from the Rose Terrace security video she
did leave at 22:21 headed perhaps for the aforementioned
"club" in the mysterious black SUV.
    Ken resumed texting, presumably after he and Ruth got
home from the benefit.

22:58 Ken: *You in the room? Can't get there sry*
23:01 Ken: *You mad?*
23:02 Ken: *Answer me please*
23:03 Ken: *Do NOT ignore me*

But she did and his texts grew angrier.

23:30 Ken: *you cunt I own you*
23:31 Ken: *I OWN you*
23:40 Ken: *Where are you!! I called the hotel*
23:43 Ken: *Fucking tell me Who you're with?*

Ken sent the best text, at least from Jack's perspective, at 23:57:

If you're with another man I'll kill you. I'll take my jewelry back & strangle that pretty neck

Maybe, despite her concern, Lucia gave in to Bibi's sexting. He was much younger and better looking than Ken if you liked surly wife-beater types. They came home together, Ken caught them, things got out of hand, and then Ken felt remorse and attempted a facsimile of a Muslim burial.

Or not.

Ken bought his plane ticket for the Jordan trip weeks ago and it was round trip, not one way. He reserved the car service to the airport a week before the murder. Mike had talked to one of Ken's colleagues at the oil company and confirmed the meetings in Amman had been planned for months. His bizarre determination to go on his trip despite a blizzard either spoke to dedication, premeditation—he planned to kill Lucia right before he left—or simply a man reacting to bad news in shock and panic.

Or a man who knew his jail bait was pregnant and had to tell his wife. Faced with the prospect of delivering that news to Ruth, Jack would have fled the country, too.

Lucia's iPad connected to the cloud and the last photo was a selfie of her and another girl with dark curly hair on what looked like a dance floor at 23:17 Saturday night. Possibly the mystery friend who texted about meeting. Nothing in the picture gave Jack a clue as to their location and the crime lab was at work processing metadata.

The obvious thing—that someone in the Harrowsmith household drove a black SUV—was quickly ruled out. Ken and Ruth were registered owners of a pair of sporty, late model, his-and-hers silver CLS Mercedes Coupes. Starting MSRP seventy grand. They also owned a blue

Prius, perhaps for church, and a hunter green Range Rover. Bibi had a brand new Porsche with a temporary tag, a car worth six figures. Whatever Ken did for that oil company, it paid well.

Jack had put both Bibi and Ruth under surveillance; she'd driven off at 8:30 that morning in the Range Rover headed to Stoney Gate, and Bibi hadn't yet left the residence.

Mike and Serena had analyzed the information from the Harrowsmiths' security company. All exterior doors, including the seven garage bays, were equipped with sensors and activity overnight Saturday into Sunday was sparse but intriguing.

At 19:35 and then again at 22:57 a garage door—"garage bay 2"—opened and closed. That more or less fit the timeframe Ken and Ruth left for and returned from the benefit. Serena had spoken to several individuals who saw the couple at dinner and the symphony afterward. For the rest of the night—and the rest of their alibi—they only had each other and possibly Bibi.

At 02:08 Sunday an exterior door—"gazebo1"—opened and closed. An arrival or departure? Nothing after that until the monolithic front door opened at six fifteen a.m. No video surveillance at the back of the house or the garages, and a camera outside the main entrance had been, conveniently, disabled. Ken had to have known how his own security system worked.

Jack Googled Muslim prayer times and found that Fajr was five fifty-five a.m. Rote recitations from the Quran comprised a ritual that didn't take more than ten or fifteen minutes, especially at home on your own instead of at a mosque. Pretty chill of Ken to arrange-bury Lucia next to a dumpster and say his prayers a few hours later. And extremely stupid of him not to call or text after his threat at midnight, as if he knew there was no point.

———◆———

"You shopping for me?" Tiffany Quintana said, from behind him.

Jack's searches for "key shaped diamond pendant" led him to the website of a high-end jewelry store. A paused image of Lucia in the Rose Terrace hallway was on one of his computer monitors and the store on the other. Because seemingly everyone, up to and including Ken, couldn't stop texting or talking about it, the jewelry felt important.

"Take a look. I think I found Lucia's necklace—it's from the 'rapture' collection." Jack read from the screen. "All of the pieces feature a small pink butterfly that unlocks 'one's joyful poetic spirit.'"

"And how much does this poetic thingy cost?" Tiffany peered over his shoulder and her voice rose an octave. "Nine thousand dollars?"

"More if you include the matching chain."

"You'd think a pawn shop would sit up and take notice of that."

Jack snorted. "Probably give someone fifty bucks for it."

"I'd kill my husband if he spent that much on a necklace for me, let alone his teenaged squeeze."

"Oh, c'mon. Don't tell me you wouldn't have multiple *raptures* if a guy spent that kind of bank on you."

Tiffany wrinkled her nose. "You don't understand women at all."

"You're telling me."

"Speaking of women."

"No, we're not."

"I have a friend that you'd really—"

"No, I wouldn't."

Tiffany put her hand on her hip and cocked her head to the side. "If you're not careful you're going to wind up growing old alone."

"Shuffling around in a stained bathrobe swilling cheap bourbon straight from the bottle, I know. You come by for some other reason than to give me grief?"

Jack was used to Tiffany's half-flirtations and fix up attempts. They'd dated a couple of times a few years ago and then had the friends talk, which was fine by him. He tried to steer clear of poaching dates at work even though virtually everyone did it—where else was a poor detective supposed to meet women? The morgue? The ER? Speaking of which, cops and nurses should have its own cable channel.

Tiffany grew serious. "There was fecal matter on the stones in Lucia's hands and under her body. Someone wiped them off but it was visible under the microscope."

"This killer is starting to piss me off."

"Don't they all?"

"I don't know, every now and then it seems they perform a public service. Any hope of fingerprints from the stones?"

"Did you catch the part about them being wiped off?"

"Why can life never be simple?"

"But wait, there's more," Tiffany said. "I analyzed the cloth Lucia was wrapped in. Some edges were hemmed and others were raw, indicating the material was cut from a larger piece."

"Like a curtain?"

"Tablecloth. The length of the strips were all 141.7 inches long. Why that odd number you ask? It's equivalent to 360 centimeters which is a fairly common size in Europe. I have even better news about the fabric and I will now pause to give you an opportunity to demonstrate your appreciation."

Jack mimed a bow. "Do I not seem appropriately awed at your skill?"

She grinned. "The jacquard pattern is unique to a store

brand sold at Harrods."

"In London."

"That's good, right?"

"Considering my leading suspect is a British citizen? It's not bad."

CHAPTER TWENTY-SEVEN

L IGHT SLASHED AT Bibi's face. Rough hands pulled his arm off his eyes and the covers off the bed. He cursed and fought but the hands were too strong; they yanked him up into a seated position. Sahir of course.

Through strobing sunlight he made out a figure on the other side of the room, a girl, dressed in the clothes they wore back home. "Lucia? You're not supposed to clean in here." Bibi didn't remember, for a second.

"Get up."

Bibi squinted at the girl. "Who are you?"

Sahir pulled open the second set of drapes with vindictive glee and said something intended for the girl in Spanish, which Bibi didn't understand.

With his hangover the bright sunlight might as well have been a switchblade. "Everyone get the fuck out of my room."

"Now, of all times, when your aunt's beside herself with worry." Sahir hauled him up and hurled him in the direction of the open bathroom door.

Bibi's shoulder hit the door jamb with a sickening thud but it broke his fall. He landed facing the filthy toilet and vomit erupted. He stayed there what felt like a long time, tile hard against his knees, heaving.

Through a haze of misery, he heard Sahir droning in Spanish. The girl appeared in the doorway and recoiled with a high-pitched cry. A crack like a shot as Sahir slapped her.

What was happening? Why couldn't he sleep? Was the new girl, whoever she was, supposed to clean the... disaster in his bathroom? Bibi's stomach had been upset last night and his vomit sprayed with a will of its own. Besides, it was his aunt's fault for not ever letting anyone clean.

"Don't make her." Bibi stared an apology at the girl who looked like a child in the baggy coat that hung to her knees. He didn't dare say he was sorry to a girl, that was one of the rules.

"You gonna do it?"

Sahir's voice held so much condescension Bibi groped for a towel on the floor, wiped his mouth, and started on the area around the toilet.

Sahir pincered his arm again lifting him to his feet. "We don't have time for this shit. You should have been at work an hour ago and you need a shower, you're disgusting."

Bibi stepped into the shower himself before Sahir threw him and then screamed at needles of cold water while Sahir held the lever and laughed.

———◆———

"Good morning, dear one." His aunt sat at the head of the dining room table, a white napkin on her lap, feet flat on the floor, knees tight.

"Don't say anything to upset her." Sahir hissed in his ear and shoved him toward a chair.

A silver coffee service was on the table, china cups, fruit like an abstract painting on a square dish, toast, salmon, cream cheese. Acid boiled up and Bibi couldn't imagine what Sahir would do to him if he puked in the dining room.

Yes, he could.

"You must eat something." His aunt's expression, like

her voice, pleasant and calm.

"No thanks." Bibi flinched when Sahir stepped close behind him, braced for a blow. Although, Sahir didn't usually hit him in front of her.

"You're right." Sahir addressed his aunt and put food on a plate. "That new girl is much more compliant. I don't think she's going to give you the same sort of trouble."

"I don't feel good," Bibi said. "I need to lie down."

Sahir set the plate in front of him. "Eat and sober up. Lucky I don't shove your face in it like a dog."

"I'm so glad you agree about Esther. Although, I'm going to have to teach her how to cook. She burnt the first two batches of toast and didn't even know what salmon was." Ruth speared a slimy pink piece and let it hang off a fork, oblivious to Bibi's distress.

"I'm sure under your guidance she'll learn fast," Sahir said.

"I was advised to wait a decent interval but it's important to maintain routine. In light of past issues, I'm ensuring Esther covers herself and behaves. That means you don't speak to her, Bibi. You've seen firsthand what happens when you become too familiar."

Esther. Bibi needed to remember because if he screwed up and used the wrong name he was punished. And as if any of what happened in that house was his fault.

"You forget how to use a fork?" Sahir picked one up and made Bibi take it.

"I had four packages to choose from and hope you approve of my selection since the other three will be working for you."

"I trust your judgment, *joonam*." Sahir addressed her with an endearment.

Bibi's lips were cracked and he gnawed at a loose piece of skin. "You should've let Lucia clean my room. It'll be hard for the new girl."

"And her name is?" Ruth prompted.

"Esther."

"Not that it's any of your concern how I run the house." Ruth took a sip of coffee.

Sahir reached for a piece of toast. "Do I need to shove this down your throat?"

Bibi knew he meant it. Forced himself to chew.

"I blame myself." Ruth sighed. "I've grown lax."

"Not your fault," Sahir said.

"At any rate." Ruth tapped the back of Bibi's hand. "The three of us need to have an important conversation."

"Not three." Sahir leaned down and kissed her. "You know I can't stay."

"Gotta go burn another one?"

"Bibi, why can't you for once keep a civil tongue?"

"Joonam, don't let him provoke you. He's not worth it." Sahir's small hard eyes bore into Bibi. "I was afraid you found disciplining Raven arousing."

Oh shit, oh shit, oh shit. Sahir knew about his hard-on when he held Raven. Would he tell Aunt Ruth?

"Raven?" Ruth's chin lifted and her gaze sharpened. "What's she done now?"

"It's dealt with." Sahir shrugged.

"That girl causes far too much disturbance. I'd never dream of interfering in how you run your business but you know my opinion of her."

Sahir's dark stare locked on Bibi. "Asserting our authority over the girls is necessary but it's not supposed to be fun. If you feel no pleasure you won't lose control."

His aunt chimed in, "They're property, not to have relationships with. Good for both of you to remember that."

"Finish that plate, then drive your fancy new car to work. See you in a half hour." Sahir left.

"It might be hard to follow, but we give you good advice." Ruth shook out her napkin and stared at it.

Bibi wondered which part she meant—food, torture,

driving his Porsche? "Esther is Lucia's replacement?"

"The police are going to speak to you."

"So?"

"What are you going to tell them?"

"Nothing. I'll ask for a lawyer."

"No." She scrunched the napkin into a ball. "We have nothing to hide and asking for a lawyer right away sends the wrong impression."

"What impression is Ken sending?"

"Don't worry about him. Everything will be fine as long as you stick to the script."

"Script?"

Ruth dropped the napkin on her plate and sighed. "You're still learning and have healthy appetites, like all boys."

"I'm not a boy."

She talked over him. "You had a few drinks, got high, and passed out. Pot's legal here. You didn't hear anything or see anything. Sunday you slept in like usual and, when you heard the terrible news about Lucia, you were shocked." She snapped slim fingers. "Simple."

"Whatever." Bibi stared at his plate, fidgeted with his fork, stifled a burp. All he wanted was to get away.

She shifted in the chair, crossed her legs, then set her feet flat on the floor again. "Are you worried they won't like you?"

"Who?" His gut clenched. What was she going to say? Was she going to lecture him about getting turned on with Raven? About Val? The bit of toast he'd managed lodged in this throat.

"There will be plenty of girls in your future," Ruth said. "Much more desirable ones. Remember, our employees are property. It's unfair to mislead them."

That's what everyone said. *Help them know their place.* But Bibi was sick and tired of being told what to do. How else was he going to meet someone? Maybe Val would answer calls from his burner since she wouldn't know who it was.

"Avi gets a taste whenever he wants."

"Don't be crude." Ruth clapped her hands. Shouted, "Esther."

"She's cleaning my room."

"That's—have you heard one word I said?"

"Why don't you want me to be happy?"

"When the police speak to you," Ruth droned on, "it's extremely important that you don't go anywhere with them. Be a gentleman, but be firm."

"Ever since I came here all you do is mess with me."

Ruth's hand cocked as if she'd slap him and at the last second she gripped the edge of the table instead. "I need you to listen. Unless the police place you under arrest you're not required to speak to them and you don't go anywhere in their custody. If they become too insistent tell them you want your attorney. That's when you mention a lawyer, not before. Can you remember that one simple fact?"

Bibi shoved his chair back so that the legs squealed against the marble, a sound he knew she hated. "What I remember is my life sucks and I wish I'd never come here."

"Sit down." Ruth used the tone no one disobeyed, not even Sahir. "Up until now I've gone easy because you're family, but I've had enough. You will listen and obey. Finish that plate or I'll call Sahir and have him come back and force feed you."

CHAPTER TWENTY-EIGHT

THE NOTECARDS FROM Lucia's nightstand all contained Bible verses—Romans 12:9, 1 Peter 4:8, 1 Corinthians 13:4-8—except for one. Jack wondered what spiritual concern this was meant to address:

I could say your lips are like a thread of scarlet

Thou hast ravished my heart, my sister, my spouse; thou hast ravished my heart with one of thine eyes, with one chain of thy neck (funny, isn't it?)

Ken means well and soon enough you'll be free. You say you can't bear it, but there's more kindness in you than any ten people I know.

I never got the pomegranate reference either until I met you.

"Found something."

Mike looked up and Jack put the card in front of him.

"Pomegranate? Not to mention 'scarlet lips'?"

"Yeah. 'Soon you'll be free'? That could be taken several ways. I now have another candidate for murder."

"And for baby daddy."

Jack put his hand to his chest with mock drama. "'Thou hast ravished my heart.' I might have to use that line."

"Couldn't do worse with women than you already are."

Jack offered a congenial, "Fuck you," and walked to the big whiteboard where they listed pertinent information about victims including leading suspects. Ken was already written and Jack added:

Bibi.

Dustin.

And on a whim, *Ruth.* He stepped back and stared for a few seconds. "I need to ask her if she knew Lucia was pregnant."

"And she needs to tell you the truth."

"Spoilsport." Jack sat down at his desk and opened a browser. The verse was from Solomon's Song but the adorable commentary was all Dustin's. He read from the screen. "Pomegranate was believed by the Israelites to be the original forbidden fruit. They're a symbol of fertility where good seed is planted."

"Subtle. And gross."

"Dustin's already got a family. Maybe he wasn't thrilled about adding to it."

"His alibi is home with his wife, right?" Mike's eyebrows went up and down. "The addict."

"Yep. The same woman who ran into traffic to avoid talking to me. And if you make one more crack about my having a way with women, I swear I'll punch you."

Mike grinned for a quick second but he gave Jack a reprieve. "Any other coded messages in the verses on the cards?"

With a heavy sigh, Jack turned to his computer. "Resisting the ungodly and the glories of love. Even I recognize this one from Corinthians, 'love is patient, love is kind.'"

"Are you two discussing the Bible?" Serena joined them carrying a cardboard tray holding several Starbucks coffees and some sandwiches. "That's very disturbing."

"We're going through the prayer cards from Lucia's room," Mike explained.

"Want me to translate? Jack's probably confused by all that Godly stuff."

"Nah. I'm finding the Bible is like a giant get out of jail

free card. Take this one from first Peter about how love covers multiple sins, how convenient."

"You are so cynical," Serena said. "Many people get comfort from religion."

"Yeah." Mike caught Jack's eye. "Comfort. That's what Dustin was offering."

"Well, of a more temporal sort."

Serena shook her head in disgust. "Are you going to Stoney Gate to talk to the minister again?"

"Headed there in a few minutes." Jack grabbed his coffee and out of habit removed the lid to see if he needed to add creamer.

"Are you actually checking to see if it's right? Do you think after all this time I don't know you're the exception to the rule around here who doesn't drink his coffee black?"

"This from the woman whose drink is half whipped cream." Sheepishly, Jack replaced the lid. "That article you found was really helpful. I have a witness that corroborates Dustin offering sanctuary to immigrants."

"Don't try to suck up."

"Female immigrants," Mike added. "Men are on their own I guess."

"Women need more comforting," Jack said.

Serena ignored them. "I haven't found any calls for service at the church. No protests, vandalism, anything along those lines. Other than that one article they have a low profile. I'll keep digging."

"While I'm at the church I'll try to take a look around but I can't do much without a warrant."

"Getting a search warrant for a church." Mike whistled. "I'll let you write that one. Have we found out what Dustin drives yet?"

"A seven-year-old silver Nissan and Heather has an even older minivan. Why?"

"Got another video from the forensic imaging guys.

Check it out."

Three fifteen a.m. Sunday, a camera at a convenience store on Broadway several blocks from the body dump site. A black SUV stopped at a light, driver's window rolled down a few inches, a hand tossed a cigarette.

"Good thing for us people still smoke," Mike said.

Looked like a man's hand, but impossible to be sure. And no clear image through the glass. At least they could now determine the vehicle make and model—Jeep Grand Cherokee—if not the identity of the driver.

"Law abiding to stop for a red in the middle of the night," Mike said. "After he's dumped a body."

"Careful," Serena said. "Not taking any risks."

"If that is in fact the individual who disposed of Lucia," Jack said. "And not some random citizen."

"Driving the same model car," Serena said.

"We'll find that Jeep," Mike said. "And I'm sure there's more video out there."

Ever the optimist, he was.

———◆———

The first words out of Dustin's mouth were: "Lucia wasn't supposed to keep that."

Jack found him in the main sanctuary kneeling in a pew in the front row. It was otherworldly quiet inside the church, and dark, which made the stained glass band running horizontally around the top of the walls especially vivid.

"She kept all of your cards," Jack said. "Tied with a pink ribbon. That one was the most intriguing."

Dustin pushed up from his knees and sat in the pew. "Solomon's Song with some paraphrasing. Usually I'm pretty old school when it comes to interpreting the Bible.

"Do you know what my first thought was when I heard about Lucia? Not now. Not when the church is moving in the right direction, when the charity is thriving. A man plans his course but the Lord determines his steps."

Jack wondered what exactly the Lord had in mind when it came to murder. "It's clear your relationship with Lucia went well beyond pastoral care."

Dustin took the copy of the prayer card Jack had brought. "I'm in this deep whether I want to be or not."

"Do you want to change your statement about the last time you saw Lucia?"

"She was more dear to my heart than I cared to admit. But my story hasn't changed."

Interesting that he called it a story. "I met your daughter yesterday. Trysta, right? Would it be okay to talk to her?"

"Of course. But the kids left this morning for a visit with my brother in Michigan. It's been planned for a while."

That was a bit convenient. "I still need to talk to Heather, too. Can she come down to headquarters and give her statement?"

"I'm sure that won't be a problem."

Either Heather hadn't told her husband about running away from the hotel or he was a very good liar. "Do you know where Lucia would've gone Saturday night? Maybe to her favorite club?"

"Like I told you, Lucia didn't go out on her own."

"You did tell me that. When you talked to Ruth about working hours did you also talk to her about locking employees in their rooms?"

Dustin sighed. "Ruth. Like Cerberus guarding the gates of hell."

An interesting choice of allegory as well as a jarringly casual response. "I don't think Ruth would appreciate you calling her monstrous, and when we talked yesterday you said Lucia wasn't a prisoner. In fact, you said Ruth and Ken treated her like a daughter."

"Their intentions are good."

Jack fought hard against an eyeroll. He showed the selfie of Lucia with the black-haired girl on the dance floor.

"Yesterday you told me Lucia didn't have friends, but that sure looks like a friend to me. Can you identify her?"

"I'm sorry." Dustin stared at Jack's phone. "At least she looks happy."

"Lucia was very beautiful. I can understand why you gave in to temptation."

Dustin stood abruptly and took the three shallow steps onto the chancel in one stride. A square marble table rose from the floor, most likely the altar, although there were none of the usual relics—no chalices, embroidered banners, or thuribles for burning incense. The minister leaned his forearms on the stone and bowed his head.

After a minute, Jack stepped up next to him. It might be sacrilegious but he wasn't about to gaze up at Dustin from the cheap seats like an adoring parishioner.

"We need to talk to the woman in the picture. We need to find that club."

Dustin raised his head. "Why do you think I'd know any of that?"

"Because I don't think, with as *close* as you were to Lucia, that you don't know her friends or where she went on the rare occasions she evaded her jailers."

Dustin didn't argue with the categorization this time. "I wasn't aware she went out at all on her own. Saturday nights she usually had to be with Ken."

"Earning her diamond necklaces."

"It disgusted me. I'm happy Lucia had a friend and if I knew who she was not only would I tell you, I'd want to thank her."

Jack motioned with his arm at the sanctuary. "The Harrowsmiths are Muslim yet they attend a non-denominational Christian church."

"Ruth does, Ken doesn't normally come with her. In fact, as far as I know, he's still a practicing Muslim."

"I didn't see a Quran when I searched their home."

"I can't explain that," Dustin said.

"Maybe you can explain why Ruth ignored the relationship, for lack of a better word, between Ken and Lucia? Not to mention, you and Lucia?"

"It must look strange."

"Wow, I thought understatement was my thing." Jack savored "gotcha" moments like the one he was about to have. "Here's a fact to take into consideration. Clergy are legally required to report child abuse. I'm sure you're familiar with the definition of a child under Colorado statute? Anyone under eighteen. Remind me, how old was Lucia when you began your sexual relationship? Because you got her age wrong yesterday. She didn't live to be eighteen."

Dustin's hands curled around the edge of the white stone. "I need to be crystal clear. My notes to her were flirtatious and inappropriate but our relationship was not sexual."

Luckily for him Jack was after more than a class three misdemeanor. "Ruth hired Lucia, and she hired whoever worked there before Lucia. All underage, undocumented girls from your charity."

"The very fact they were undocumented meant I didn't know how old they were. Those claims are unsubstantiated."

Jack remembered Nicki's statement about a finder's fee. "I think you know exactly how many girls you've sent to the Harrowsmiths because you made a lot of money off of them. I'm going to substantiate that Ken slept with all of them and you were complicit."

"You can't prove any of that."

"I can and I will. Same way I'll prove your involvement in Lucia's death."

"What are you implying?"

"I think I'm abundantly clear." Jack leaned closer and forced eye contact. "You knew what was going to happen to Lucia. I have her iPad with the photos and the love notes and her pleas for help that went unanswered. You have an opportunity to be honest and yet you keep lying. Why?"

"Because I was hoping my friendship with Lucia wouldn't become public knowledge. Look at this place. Do you think I want to lose all of this? I'm not proud of everything I've done but I'm not a criminal. I cared for Lucia. I never knew she was in that kind of danger and I certainly didn't know she was going to be murdered. Nothing like this has ever happened to me before and I'm off balance as well as grief stricken."

Jack went for the low hanging fruit; in this case, pomegranate. "How about getting an underage parishioner pregnant. Has *that* ever happened to you before?"

A range of emotions played across Dustin's face. He started to deny, stopped. Started to ask a question, stopped.

"When did Lucia tell you she was pregnant?" Jack asked.

"Wednesday night."

"Want to amend your statement that Lucia's demeanor hadn't seemed different lately?"

"Have there been DNA tests?" Dustin asked.

"Really? With the charges you're facing, with an emotionally fragile wife, with us digging into your finances, that's your number one question?"

"I'm telling you, on the record, it's not mine."

You had to give the man credit for one thing. He sure committed to his lies. "It would be so much better for you if you came clean now."

Dustin had the gall to shrug. "Not one speck of blood on my hands."

"What did Lucia want from you Wednesday night?"

"Money. Isn't that what everyone wants? Root of all evil."

A twist on Jack's theory that Lucia was extorting her employers. Instead, it was her minister. "You're not going to give me a sermon on greed are you?"

Dustin clung to the ever-shrinking moral high ground. "I'll accept your censure although I don't think you're being very professional. Love does not delight in evil. If you love others, you will never do them wrong. Lucia touched my heart and I fell for her."

Fell for her? Was he fucking kidding? Professional or not, someone had to be outraged on this girl's behalf. "What you had with Lucia was many things, illegal for one, but it wasn't love. You sold her and then you used her, the same as Ken."

"Put away falsehood and speak the truth." Dustin's shout echoed off the rafters. "I'm nothing like him."

"Watch it." The more riled up Dustin became the more confident Jack felt. "You're risking a dip in that lake of sulfur. Neither you nor Ken cared about Lucia but what I need to know is which one of you killed her?"

"Do not defile the temple of God. Look at my records, put together your case, but whether you believe me or not I never hurt anyone."

"In your records will I also find contact information for Lucia's family?"

Dustin took a ragged breath and his voice fell from the ecclesiastical to a more defeated human register. "I have an old number for her mother but I didn't tell you because I truly don't know if it's any good."

It wasn't worth mentioning that this Bible-spouting prick had wasted twenty-four hours. "What about the others?"

"Who?"

"The girls sitting right now in your conference center under the deluded belief that you offer sanctuary."

"There's no one here."

Jack was beyond fed up with this. "Do I need to get a warrant for that as well?"

"No." Dustin jumped off the chancel and stalked up the aisle. "Come on, I'll show you. I have no one and nothing to hide."

CHAPTER TWENTY-NINE

EATHER HAD BEEN afraid to talk to Dustin last
night, had snuck into the house like a teenager
pushing curfew and taken a shower in the kid's bathroom,
then gone into each of their rooms in turn and held them
while they slept.

This morning she packed bags, made sure to include
snacks, pillows, favorite toys. Trysta and Ryan shrieked,
talked over each other, jumped off the walls with
excitement; *we're riding in an RV, RV, RV!* Heather choked
back tears so she wouldn't ruin their fun. Said to Ayisha
when she and Dennis came to pick them up, *"You sure
you know what you're getting into?"* Dustin had gone to the
church as usual and left the crap to her.

All the while wondering what Sahir had given her and
how bad it was going to screw up her recovery. So far, she
didn't feel much, at least physically, although she would
love a drink. Not a day passed that she didn't want to
drink, though, so that was normal. Mostly her emotions
were out of whack, a little more jittery than normal, a
little weepier. When Dustin came home for lunch she
was slumped on the couch in the living room with the
TV on, abandoned coffee on the table, crumpled tissues
on the floor.

"Man, I had the worst morning, cops were all over the
church." Dustin leaned down to kiss her and she turned

her head. "What's going on? Are you mad at me?"

"What do you think? You're the smart one." She reached for the remote and cranked up the volume. He grabbed it and turned the TV off.

"I hope you didn't act like this in front of the kids and upset them."

"You weren't worried about whether the kids were upset earlier when you hid at church."

"I wasn't hiding. Quite the opposite."

She got the remote and he took it away again. They fought over it like children themselves, TV on, TV off, until Heather gave up in frustration and threw it across the room. Seemed she was always throwing things around him.

"How could you use me like that?" Heather shrieked, not having to be careful without the kids there. "How could you put me in that situation?"

"I thought it was best to go to work as usual and the kids were happy to be going on a trip with their cousins. I'm sorry it was hard for you, if I'd known I would have stayed."

"Not this morning, last night."

"Last night?" He parroted back.

"What'd you think was gonna happen? You tell Ruth where I am, she tells Sahir. He came and found me and literally dragged me out of Bibi'z, locked me in his filthy car and shoved a pipe in my face."

Dustin's expression changed. "He made you do drugs? Why didn't you tell me?"

"Oh, please, don't do the fake concerned thing."

"I am concerned. How much? What was it?"

"Some kind of pot. It wasn't even that good." She remembered the way the car felt like it had been rocked by an earthquake.

Dustin picked up a bottle from the coffee table. Curing pills, a Chinese herbal remedy, supposed to help you detox. "These helping? How do you feel?"

"I'm feeling used. What'd you think he was gonna do? Make me a cup of tea?"

"Do you feel like"—he hesitated—"like you want something?"

"I always want something."

"Sahir really, really shouldn't have done that." Dustin's voice got all tight and snarly, all gangster, eyes narrowed, hands fisted, like if you let him loose he'd go right after Sahir. As if. That prick'd eat her clean-cut husband for lunch.

She started to push off the couch. "If you won't leave me alone I might as well go to a meeting."

"I can't let you."

"You can't let me go to a narc anon?"

"The cops." Dustin motioned with his hand. "They're watching you."

"Me?"

"They're watching everyone, even Ruth and Sahir. That's what I'm trying to tell you. That Detective Fariel ambushed me at church."

Fucking cops. And fucking Lucia. In that moment Heather hated Lucia, blamed it all on her—adding a mental *Lord rest her soul*; if Lucia hadn't died they wouldn't be in this mess.

"And I hate to cast aspersions," Dustin said, "but we can't trust Nicki, either."

"I don't want to talk about her."

"We can't be sure who it's safe to talk to right now. And, speaking of conversations, aren't you a little curious what the detective asked me?"

She was dying to know, but didn't want to give him the satisfaction. Dustin was so good at steering conversations and hogging all the attention. In no mood to play concerned wife, Heather crossed her arms across her chest and stared at the dark television.

He gave up after a minute. "What'd you tell Nicki?"

"Nothing. I saw her with the cop and I booked. End of story."

Dustin sounded like he was giving a sermon, all knowing and wise. "I think it's best if you stay put in the house, at least until I get things get sorted out."

Heather grabbed a sofa cushion and screamed into it. "Ugh! I can't hide out in this shitty house for the rest of my life because your slut girlfriend got herself killed."

"Don't say things like that."

"God, Dustin, for once just tell me—"

He started to interrupt. "Don't use—"

"Were you actually going to lecture me about using the Lord's name in vain when you were fucking a teenager?"

"No." Loud pulpit voice. "No, no, and no."

"No it wasn't just her? No you didn't like it?"

"Honey, stop. You need to listen to me."

"What else could there be to tell me? How many times? Her favorite position? Probably missionary—ha ha."

He sat down next to her tried to take her hand. "Stop, please. I got her killed. I got that beautiful girl killed."

"What?"

"It's because of me." His eyes got red like he might cry. "I asked her to snoop, you know, at Ruth's. I wanted to stop working with them—you know I did—and I thought maybe Lucia could get information, something I could use as leverage. That's why we met so often. It's my fault and I can't send any more girls there and Ruth is pissed at me. There were four in the dorm and I was about to send them to that Baptist church and then she kidnapped one of them and I don't know what to do."

"Kidnapped?" His story was all over the place. Ruth hadn't seemed angry at church but then, Heather wasn't sure she'd be able to tell. Plus, nice of him to spin it so everything was about him.

"I told Ruth," Dustin said. "I was as clear as I could be

about getting out of the business and she ignored me. Took Ascencion anyway and it wasn't like I could call the cops same way I can't tell them who killed Lucia."

"Wait—what? You know who killed Lucia?"

"Isn't it obvious?"

"Not to me."

He got up and paced to the living room window. Closed the blinds, opened them again. Closed. Open.

"Are you gonna tell me who killed the bitch?" Heather added another silent, *Lord rest her soul.*

"Please don't call her that. It wasn't her fault. Why are you behaving this way?"

"You're just trying to take the blame off yourself."

None of it made sense, Lucia wanting the cut, then Lucia spying for Dustin, then Dustin knowing who killed her but not being able to tell. It was all coming at Heather too fast.

"The kids going on that trip is a stroke of good fortune," Dustin said. "The Lord always provides. We have a couple of days now to prepare but we've got to be quick and you've got to trust me. And you can't talk to the police."

Was he crazy for real? "Not like I want to."

"And you can't have any contact with Ruth or Sahir."

"Ditto. But I don't find Sahir, he finds me. You need to protect me from him—you need to protect me better in general. Staying clean is hard and now you're asking me—I'm not even sure what you're asking."

"For you to be my wife," Dustin said. "To start over somewhere new where we'll be safe. We've got enough money. I can't believe you don't think I put you first."

Heather looked around at the house she hated and suddenly couldn't bear the thought of leaving. Curtains they'd bought together at Bed, Bath & Beyond; the light fixture Dustin installed himself; the gas insert they pretended was a real fire at Christmas.

"Where would we go?"

He took that as cooperation. "That's what I'm working on right now. Passports for all of us, countries with no extradition agreements."

Countries? They were leaving the States? Heather didn't speak any language other than English. "I don't know."

"I'll handle everything. You trust me, right?"

She really didn't. "If I'm going to go along I have to know everything about you and her."

"No more accusations, please." He made a praying motion with his hands. "There was nothing untoward between me and poor Lucia. What have I ever done to make you think so poorly of me?"

"Don't make this my fault and don't give me that 'poor Lucia' crap." *Lord rest her soul.* "You want me and the kids to run away with you and hide like criminals for how long? Forever? They have to leave their school, their friends, the church. Oh my gosh, the church, after all the work we've done? Can't you just be honest?"

He got down on one knee, like when he proposed. Clasped her hands and stared into her eyes; that sapphire blue had always been her undoing.

"Give me a Bible and I'll swear on it. Whatever you hear, whoever you hear it from, the truth—God's truth—is that Lucia was helping me and she paid the ultimate price. But it's you I love with all my heart and soul. I yield to you and we are one flesh. Maybe, instead of asking if you trust me, I need to ask if you have enough discernment to recognize lies and those attempting to destroy the Godly?"

That was a little preachy and probably a trick. On the other hand, his suggestion she was too stupid to know truth from make believe pissed her off. "Yes, I can tell the difference."

CHAPTER THIRTY

———

JACK WAS CONVINCED if he put his hand on the
beds in the makeshift dormitory they'd still be warm.
Perfume lingered in the air. Photos were taped to the wall.
A bottle of nail polish sat abandoned on a maple dresser.
Dustin admitted "people" had sometimes stayed there but
none recently. Jack didn't believe him. Stalemate.

He'd have to talk to other parishioners, go through the
Shores of Hope records, see if there were any cameras near
the church that might have picked up girls going in and
out. His suspicions about the fate of Lucia's predecessors
went from hunch to conviction when he and Mike
reviewed the videos found on the memory sticks taken
from Ken's office.

At first Jack feared they were in for a viewing of pirated
movies or Ken and Ruth's wedding.

No such luck.

Nothing could prepare even a hardened detective for
the sight of Ken naked on the plush white circle sofa in
Lucia's walk-in closet. Ken's breasts sagged and enormous
belly yawed, his sparse chest hair was gray. Lucia wore a
tight pink T-shirt, tiny denim shorts, and stilettos. She
wobbled slightly as Ken put her through a rudimentary
stripping routine.

He asked questions. "Tell me about the first time you
saw me."

"My goodness." Lucia smiled with artificial cheer. "It was that hot day last week. You were mowing the lawn and you took your shirt off. I couldn't stop staring."

"You liked what you saw?"

"Seeing you without a shirt drove me wild," Lucia purred. "I wanted to see more."

Jack almost sprayed coffee out his nose. "Oh, shit, don't tell me Ken wrote dialogue for her to say?"

Mike's expression was a cross between disbelief and nausea. "Lucia being in the same room with him should be a felony."

It soon became apparent the two detectives were in for lots of creepy, awkward, amateur porn.

"Come closer so you can get a good look." Ken helped Lucia onto her knees and watched their reflections in the full-length mirror on the wall behind her. He guided her head under his mountain of flab and gave orders, all growly and fierce.

"He sure as hell doesn't get to tell his wife what to do." All Jack could think was that Lucia had been nothing more than an appliance to these people. That and Ken really needed to consider joining his wife at the gym.

Lucia was quite the actress, though; definitely earned her diamonds. She was eager, affectionate, and faked it convincingly. If you didn't know better—or have eyes— you could almost believe she was into him. Ken seemed transfixed by his own image in the mirror and turned the phone on himself for a climax-selfie.

What they didn't hear or see were threats or acts of overt violence. Or any application of black stones, therapeutic or otherwise. After over an hour of school uniforms, girls next door, and cheerleaders someone new appeared.

Mike leaned forward. "Hello, who is this?"

Timestamp twenty months ago, a girl with a childish face and breasts that looked real, a more exaggerated curve to her hip. Ken slouched on the same circular sofa to receive oral worship and they heard much of the same repetitive dialogue. Lucia 1.0 had been allowed to keep her pubic hair. And she wore a key-shaped diamond necklace.

"That looks the same as Lucia's." Jack stood and stretched in an effort to work some of the tension out of his shoulders. "Think Ken recycled the jewelry?"

"If it cost as much bank as you said he's not gonna let it go to waste," Mike said. "And watching his doughy ass may have turned me off permanently."

"Yeah. Not that it was ever really my thing, but this has ruined porn for me."

Lucia 1.0 next appeared in a Girl Scout uniform. She wore stripper high heels that sank into the carpet when she bent over so Ken could "inspect" her.

"Take it off, bitch." Ken growled and zoomed in on her ass.

"Why can't you use my name?" Her voice was girlish and high.

"Yes, Ken." Jack spoke to the screen. "Please tell us her name."

Pay dirt: "I don't like the name Abigail."

"I mean my real name, not the one your wife gave me."

"Don't talk about her," Ken shouted and the screen went dark as if he'd dropped his phone. "You fat slag. Don't ever talk about her."

"I'm sorry. Ow."

"Get dressed. You might as well go back to work."

Like servicing Ken wasn't work. Jack willed the girl to say more as the video ended. "Ruth named her?"

"If her name's not Abigail, who is she?" Mike asked, rhetorically.

"And where is she? And is she alive? This is like an archeological dig through hell with bad cell phone video."

Mike frowned. "You sure Lucia was her real name?"

"I confirmed it." With Serena translating, Jack had

made the notification earlier to Lucia's mother. He'd been astonished Dustin gave him a working phone number. Lupe Santiago had been hysterical but managed to tell an anecdote about a family tradition for naming girls all starting with "L."

In the next video, a naked Abigail in riding boots crawled around the room whimpering. An unseen Ken wielded a crop with enthusiasm, marked angry red stripes on Abigail's swaying rear end, called her fat and slow.

"Lucky for us Ken can't get an actual horse into that room," Mike said.

"What's next? Hot nurse? Waitress? Sexy pirate?"

"And how come Ken never dresses up?"

Jack couldn't help laughing. At least goofing with Mike helped save his sanity. "This a-hole has absolutely no imagination."

And then.

"Your time is up. I'm going to have to replace you."

"No, I'll be good. I promise." Abigail grabbed at his legs like a little girl, which she was.

"No matter how good you are you still get old. Dinah got old before you, and Sarah, and the other before her, and so on."

"Please don't do the same thing to me."

Her crying was messy and hard to listen to; Ken's voice was callous and careless. He zoomed in on her tear-streaked face. "Stop, stop, it's not so bad. I promise it won't hurt."

Any sense of absurdity Jack felt vanished. "What won't hurt?"

"And who the hell are Dinah and Sarah?" Mike wrote the new names down.

Ken's hand framed Abigail's round cheek. "I know you're all going to be mine for a very short time so I try to make it as pleasant as possible."

"This shit is pleasant?" Jack said.

Abigail begged through sobs. "Please, I'll do anything."

"But you'll never be any good after me. Men want virgins to marry and I couldn't bear the thought of another's hands on you regardless."

Jack started to say, "Yes," then stopped, realized if they were interpreting the dialogue correctly they were watching a snuff film. "Give us something we can use you piece of shit."

"Your life was short but full and undoubtedly I've given you beautiful memories to take with you to paradise." Ken's plummy voice could have been ordering a cocktail.

"Sounds to me like he was telling her she was gonna die," Jack said.

"Would it be wrong to high five you?" Mike did it anyway.

Jack couldn't quite drag his eyes away from the screen, from Abigail, still on her knees and Ken standing over her. Then Ken turned the camera on himself and the sick fuck was crying, acting like something terrible had happened to him. He wiped his eyes, walked into the bathroom, and Jack saw a glimpse of tile floor and heard the sound of water mixed with Abigail's pathetic whimpers before the video ended. Another started to play and Jack hit pause, only so much cheesy torment he could process in one sitting.

"Ken literally washed his hands of her," Mike said.

"She was clearly terrified, as if she'd been told what happened to the others before her. A threat to keep her in line."

"Seems to have worked."

"It's possible we're misinterpreting and these other girls are alive." Jack's skepticism was reflected on Mike's face. "Yeah, I don't think so either. Why was Lucia treated differently? She didn't disappear, she got expensive gifts, she kept her real name."

Mike did his almost-mind-reading thing. "Don't get

hung up on how he treated Lucia's body. Maybe he had to change it up because the ground was frozen and he couldn't dig a hole. Murderers refine their techniques all the time. Either way, he's a sadistic asshole."

"We need to identify these girls. Put together a timeline and go through the records from the charity. Run the names against missing persons databases."

"Quicker way might be to talk to Mrs. Minister."

"Yeah." Jack nodded. "Heather doesn't know who you are. Or, better yet, have Serena talk to her. I need to brief the El-Tee that the scope of our simple, yet exotic homicide seems to have expanded."

CHAPTER THIRTY-ONE

NICKI WAS LEAVING her office building dressed as if for a date in a short, tight pencil skirt and heels. Her blouse, under an open jacket, was unbuttoned to the edge of decency. Or maybe that was how she went to work every day.

Dustin intercepted her on the sidewalk and smiled. "Looks like I just caught you. Glen know you're cutting out early?"

Glen was a friend of Dustin's from high school and Nicki's boss. Dustin had, in fact, been instrumental in helping her get her job, all in service to Heather.

"Dustin. Hi. Are you here to see him?" Nicki squinted in the bright afternoon sunlight, shaded her eyes with her hand.

"You actually. Is there a place we could talk for a few minutes?"

"Me? Why?"

"You never reached out for any pastoral counseling." He wondered if that sounded accusatory. "It won't take long."

"I'm on my way to an appointment but you can walk me to my car."

She rooted in a large purse for sunglasses and he fell into step beside her on the sidewalk.

"You're not on your way to talk further with that detective, are you?"

"What? Why would you ask me that?"

He wasn't sure himself. He thought they'd sit down in an office somewhere, or in coffee shop, and he'd be able to ease into his questions. This rushed, public, moving confrontation had him off balance.

"I'm concerned about Heather, about what happened to Lucia, my church, my kids, everything."

"You drove downtown and hunted for parking to tell me that? You could have texted." As if for emphasis she waved her phone.

"This is serious."

"I know, but still."

Nicki had been a lot of things in the time he'd known her—flippant, flirtatious, irreverent—but never difficult to talk to. Had the cop planted suspicions in her mind?

He took a deep breath. "You were out with that detective last night when Heather joined you and consumed alcohol. That concerns me. I'm her husband, I have a right to ask."

They stopped at the busy intersection where 19th, Welton, and Broadway converged and waited for the light.

"Do you follow her?" Nicki asked. "That's not very trusting."

It was following Heather that had also put Nicki on Sahir's radar. Another reason for Dustin's visit, to somehow warn her. Although, her careless attitude was making him feel less benevolent by the second. "Where's your car?"

"The usual." She pointed vaguely in the direction of a surface lot on the east side of Broadway.

"Can you at least tell me the kinds of questions the police asked you?"

Nicki smirked. "That would be confidential, I believe."

"And I more than anyone appreciates confidentiality. But these are not ordinary times."

Her tone became defiant. "Fine. Jack asked me if I knew

how to get in touch with Lucia's family so he could notify them because apparently you wouldn't give him their contact information."

"But I did provide it. He was playing you and I'm afraid he'll exploit your weakness to get at me."

"Weakness? What weakness?"

The light changed and she plunged ahead with a crowd of pedestrians.

Dustin grasped her arm and pulled her past the parking lot, across 20th, into the long shadow cast by the narrow building on the corner. Screw discretion and correctness.

"Hey! Where are we going? My car's that way."

"Slight detour." She didn't offer nearly as much resistance as Dustin expected. *You should fight, Nicki, if a man accosts you on the street. You should scream.*

He didn't say that and had the presence of mind to glance up and check for cameras. Didn't see one. Let go of her anyway.

"You're too compliant," Dustin said. "Too easily swayed."

She rubbed her arm. "What are you talking about? Why are you acting like this?"

"I apologize for being—" Being what? A brute? A bully? Dustin wasn't sure himself what he was anymore. "Five minutes and I'll be out of your hair, I promise."

"I don't know." But again, she didn't argue or run.

"You don't realize how dangerous this whole situation is. Be careful who you talk to, watch your back. Whether it's a detective or—or someone else. You've been a good friend to Heather which is why I'm here. Lucia's murder threatens all of us in ways you don't understand and if I'm acting a little—untoward—that's why. Think about the church, if you don't care about me. Think about the immigrants we help. But please be careful."

Nicki tipped her head to the side. "How did screwing one of the immigrants help her?"

Dustin realized how foolish he'd been to try and warn

Nicki—not to mention thinking his affair with Lucia had been any kind of secret. This bitch—there really was no other word—hadn't listened to a word he'd said.

"You know," Nicki continued in the same acid voice, "Heather suspected all along and I defended you. Told her over and over how much you loved her and that she didn't have a thing to worry about. How much of an idiot am I?"

Dustin held up his hands in mock surrender. "I'm done, Nicki. I'm sorry to have bothered you. Why do you even go to my church if you have so little respect for me?"

"That's the second time I've been asked that question in as many days. I didn't have a good answer last night and I don't have one now."

"So I was a topic of discussion for you and your new police conquest. I may have slipped up with Lucia but you sleep with everyone. I'm trying to protect you and you're too brazen and foolish to see it."

All the while they argued, people flowed past taking no interest whatsoever. Verses about the fate of harlots ran through his mind.

Nicki pressed into the wall, her body language contradicting her tough words. "You are the most vile, deceitful, corrupt person I've ever known. And you call yourself a pastor."

"Remember this conversation when the time comes." A tortured verse came to him from Job. "Your wicked eyes will fail, Nicki, and there will be no escape when you breathe your last. By then it'll be too late to tell anyone, including your new cop fuck buddy."

He sensed her fear in his gut as he walked away, like you feel more than hear the thump of a marching band. Reminded himself that, for those who loved God, all things worked together for good; even his clumsy, profane behavior, somehow.

CHAPTER THIRTY-TWO

———◆———

"I'LL DEDICATE THE large corner conference room,"
Dani said. "I've already made some calls."

They were in Dani's office and the El-Tee was
organizing a task force, throwing resources at a problem
like command always did. In theory it was a good thing,
support from officers with specific expertise in trafficking,
missing persons, and sex crimes.

But Jack didn't want to be managing a bunch of other
detectives all wanting to take the investigation off in their
own direction. He wanted to be out on the street himself,
executing the warrant for the linens, talking to Bibi,
planning his interview-slash-evisceration of pedophile
Ken, finding the mystery selfie girl, identifying the driver
of the Jeep, digging into Dustin's alleged charity, and—
damn it. No way he could do it all.

"Control freak," Mike muttered so only Jack heard.

"Would you stop doing that?"

"I can see it on your face."

"Problem, Jack?" Dani asked.

"No, Lieutenant."

"Any ID on the other girls?"

"Negative. Dialogue in the video leads us to conclude
they were using assumed names."

Jack noticed command was good at stating the obvious.
If Abigail had been murdered in Denver there'd have been

an investigation but so far they hadn't found unsolved cases that matched. Searching ten years of investigations was another resource-intensive task.

"What about the minister?" Dani asked. "Maybe he'll know who these girls are, especially if they hid at his church."

"Dustin was uncooperative when I asked about the girls he'd placed with the Harrowsmiths. Anything you can do to fast-track the warrant for the charity would be great."

"How could four young women simply disappear?" Dani lobbed another obvious, rhetorical observation.

Lucia, Abigail, Dinah, Sarah. There were short gaps between each young woman's film debut, no doubt time for Ken to groom them.

"Undocumented immigrants from poor families," Jack said. "Illegal, possibly trafficked, don't speak the language, plus these a-holes changed at least some of their names. Even if families had the means to look they weren't going to be found."

"Hell," Mike said. "It's going to be hard for us."

All teenagers when they disappeared from Ken's version of paradise cinema before they got "old" for his particular tastes. Screen grabs of their faces would go out to other agencies and be posted on databases around the world. The Center for Missing & Exploited Children. The National Missing and Unidentified Persons System. Border Patrol. The Colorado Bureau of Investigation. The FBI. Interpol.

The videos in evidence covered six-and-a-half years. Did that mean there were no young women working for the Harrowsmiths before Sarah? Or no film of them? Or maybe Ken hadn't started his directing career yet?

"How are you planning to approach Mr. Harrowsmith?" Dani asked.

"I chose to interview Ken here instead of in Yuma," Jack said. "That's at least five hours round trip and would've taken the whole day."

The acting detective usually interviewed the suspect wherever he was being held. Bringing Ken to Denver was a judgment call on Jack's part.

"Who drove him?" Mike asked.

"Abbie."

"Nice." A grin broke across Mike's face.

Abbie Tapia was a young, pretty missing persons detective. In her late twenties but with no makeup could pass for a teenager, Ken's type.

"He talk to her?" Dani asked.

"Mostly a lot of whining and complaining," Jack said. "Although he made some interesting comments about how Ruth always chose the girls and for once he'd like a turn."

"He'll get a turn all right," Mike said.

"El-Tee, I thought I'd go to the Harrowsmith residence first and execute the warrant for the linens so the lab can get started matching fibers to what Lucia was wrapped in."

"How long do you think that'll take?" Dani asked.

"Coupla hours, maybe." It was almost four. Any hope Jack had of dinner, let alone sleep, was disappearing fast.

"How long has Mr. Harrowsmith been in holding?" Dani asked.

"Arrived an hour ago." Jack couldn't suppress disgust. "Had a headache when he woke up so they kept him for observation."

"All right," Dani said. "Get the linens and let him enjoy our hospitality for a few hours. What else have you got, Mike?"

"Have the Harrowsmiths under surveillance. Ruth went to the gym and church, left Stoney Gate at 9:30 with a young woman in, as the officer noted, 'Middle Eastern' clothes."

"Think that girl is Lucia's replacement?" Dani asked.

"Then Ken didn't get to choose," Jack said.

"Her life's gonna deteriorate fast," Mike said. "A gardener arrived at the Harrowsmiths' shortly after Ruth and went around back by the garages. The nephew, nut job or—what'd you call him?"

"Nishaat aka Bibi," Jack said. "High on my list of individuals to contact."

"Left at twelve-thirty and drove what appears to be a brand new Porsche to a Middle Eastern restaurant on Colorado Boulevard where he stayed an hour. Man, that's a sweet ride. Anyway, the restaurant is also named Bibi but with a Z—Bibi'z."

"Who owns it?" Dani asked.

"Mohamed Alzeshi is listed as the registered representative of the business, a DBA called FALNA Enterprises."

"Any idea what that stands for?" Dani asked.

"Negative," Mike said. "I ran some searches on Mohamed and couldn't find him in the DMV database, NCIC, or anywhere."

"Maybe he's not in the U.S.," Jack said. "I have an FBI contact I'll reach out to."

"Good." Dani nodded. "Ruth's from where...Jordan?"

"That's what she claims. The tattoo on Lucia's neck was in Arabic characters. Never thought I'd get to practice my little bit of Farsi on this job."

"Jack's proud of it, too."

"Mike's barely mastered one language," Jack shot back.

"I talked to Al," Dani said, "and Shores of Hope isn't on anyone's radar. He's agreed to be part of the task force and I've asked him to find out if 'Joy' is a known family."

Detective Al Gonzales was their "go to" source for all things trafficking and Jack was grateful to have him as a resource. Tattoos were often used as part of a trafficking organization or "family's" branding—and sometimes they did worse to mark their property, including actual branding.

"Serena's going to contact Heather Rattenberry," Jack said. "See if she can help identify these girls. Heather is Dustin's only alibi for Saturday night since he coincidentally sent his children away this morning to visit relatives."

Dani leaned back in her fancy leather office chair. "Interesting that Heather's avoiding giving us a statement."

"Literally ran into traffic to avoid Jack," Mike said.

Dani almost smiled. "I've heard that's become a thing, women avoiding Jack."

"Really, Lieutenant? You too?"

"You know it's like living in a small town." For a split second the El-Tee's teeth actually appeared. "I've authorized overtime and I'll put as many resources on this as I need to. A possible Muslim killer. There are demonstrators outside and Twitter's been crazy."

Protestors often showed up within minutes of an officer-involved shooting. Sometimes they seemed to arrive at homicides before the police themselves.

Dani gave Jack such an appraising onceover he wondered if his fly was unzipped. "I want you in the press conference later. Might as well put those good looks to *some* useful purpose."

Mike snorted and Jack groaned audibly.

"Swell."

CHAPTER THIRTY-THREE

"SINCE WHEN DO you summon me?" Sahir asked. "Not how it works."

"Unusual times," Dustin said. "You could say times of trouble. Cops have been at my church."

They were in Washington Park at Dustin's request. He wanted someplace public where the police couldn't listen and because he was never comfortable alone with Sahir. As if by prior agreement, they walked together down a path that looped around the small lake at the south end, not speaking until Sahir stopped in a grove of trees near the edge of the water where trash collected in scummy waves.

Before he could decide where to start Sahir said, "Let me see your phone."

Then snatched it from Dustin's hand and hurled it clear to the center of the lake where it disappeared with a small *plinking* sound.

"What the hell?" Dustin took an impotent step toward the filthy water.

Sahir reached inside his jacket and handed Dustin a new one.

"You can't just—" Dustin imagined the phone ringing underwater, going forever unanswered. "You know how many people have my number? It's posted at the church."

"Too dangerous. Cops are listening to all of us."

"Everything is too dangerous."

"Calm down."

Dustin fidgeted with the new phone for a minute. A fresh burner, Sahir's favorite. Life had been normal for so long he'd forgotten what he was up against. "Hard to be calm when cops are crawling all over my church, issuing subpoenas, and hunting my wife."

"Why I had a talk with her last night. Remind her how things work."

"Really? A talk? Tell me why I shouldn't bring you down?"

Sahir made a sound of, "Huh, huh, huh," not laughing, definitely scornful. "Man of God trying to sound tough."

"Heather's using again, thanks to you."

"Maybe she needs a vacation."

Code for rehab. "What possible good does it do to get her hooked again?"

Sahir stuck a cigarette in his mouth, cupped a hand to protect the flame as he lit it. "Best not to fight human nature. Better to work with it, use it to your advantage. What's the verse? Hard work keeps hands busy and mouths shut?"

Oh, man, not another lecture from this walking vermin on false motivation and marshalling base urges to one's advantage.

"Don't blaspheme. Turns out separation of church and state is a good idea. Weak minds aren't capable of discerning the Bible's truth."

Sahir moved in close. Impossible to see his eyes with the shades but Dustin knew he was always armed with at least one knife. Knew the rumors about what happened to the girls who worked for Ruth and Ken. He started to back away, put his hands up, to say, *Stop, I didn't mean it, I have information.*

Suddenly, surprising no one more than himself, he laughed instead. Sahir was so serious, wound so tight, in his own way so sanctimonious that he struck Dustin as the funniest person he'd ever met. Gales of laughter bordering on hysteria.

Sahir wasn't in on the joke. "Don't fucking laugh at me. You wanna die? What's wrong with you? Been smoking some of Princess's weed?"

Dustin forced himself to stop and stared right at his own reflection in Sahir's sunglasses, small and distorted, like a fun house mirror. Ticked off items on his fingers like he was teaching a sermon.

"One. You don't kill men. You only hurt helpless little girls. You're the one who might want to calm down. Two, you're not going to kill me in a public place. No witnesses, right? I've been paying more attention than you give me credit for. Three, I knew it was you all along that got Heather hooked whenever it served the devious purposes you concoct in that narrow mind of yours, only this time it's especially stupid."

Sahir tried to interrupt. "You don't know shit."

"Four." Dustin talked over him. "You're going to want to hear this next one so take a breath."

He waited. Watched. Sahir was so close he could smell stale tobacco breath combined with a sour, no doubt empty stomach. Ruth and Sahir were a pair, denying themselves earthly pleasure in the deluded belief it somehow made them stronger.

Dustin used his best pulpit voice. "Back up and give me some room."

Lo and behold, it worked. One step back, then two. From the thin line of his mouth to his tense posture Sahir was pissed, but no longer a threat.

"I paid Nicki a visit and she's a liability. She needs to be warned in a way that'll make an impression."

"What makes you think I don't already know all about that whore?"

"Then why haven't you done anything?"

"Because I don't work for you." Sahir bared his yellow teeth, a human snarl.

Dustin watched a leggy, spandex-clad redhead being pulled by a large Husky who lived on a different, saner planet.

"Nicki has a fondness for tall, dark, handsome detectives, much as my wife has for opioids. What we don't know is how much Heather told her bff. It's a serious exposure no matter who you work for, so deal with Nicki before she gets too chatty with her new police friend."

Sahir grunted. "Figures the cop'd go after the women. Closed a big case a while back, fucked the killer's wife. Word on the street he's hard to intimidate, thinks he has balls."

"I don't know where you pick up this garbage but for once your intel might be relevant."

"I find out what I need to," Sahir said. "Speaking of balls, didn't think you had any."

"You made the error of confusing love with weakness. Don't worry, it's a common mistake of narcissists."

"You telling me you love the Princess?"

All the Bible verses in the world couldn't explain love to Sahir. No one ever saw Heather's potential, including her. That was the deep, snarled taproot of Heather's problems: no self-esteem. Not that it mattered anymore.

It might be petty, seeking vengeance on Nicki, but she'd disrespected him for years, fed his wife cigarettes and alcohol, flouted every civil request he'd ever made. For once, he agreed with Sahir; Nicki was a whore. A man reaps what he sows and the verse held true for women, too.

Dustin held up his hand, fingers splayed. "Five. Admission of sin. Mine. Lucia was pregnant with my child. I'm sure you know because Ruth did, along with everyone in a three-state area except Heather."

Sahir, as usual, saw the profane angle. "Why should I

care who you fuck?"

"Think this through. Whether she hears it from the cops or from Nicki or figures it out on her own, how do you think Heather's going to take proof of my infidelity? Do you think she's going to be calm? Do you think she's going to be loyal? It's not going to go well for anyone."

"I used to have her under control."

"Drugs were your way of controlling her. I thought loving her would be even better."

Sahir called Heather a name Dustin hadn't heard for a long time. "You spoiled her."

"Yeah, well, it's been a nice run. Consider this your forewarning and the end of my obligations."

"What do you mean?"

That didn't credit an explanation. Dustin consulted his fingers. "Let me see. Is there anything else? Nope. I'm done. I'd say, go with God, but considering the circumstances you're on your own."

"Not so fast." Sahir still being the tough guy. "Where you going?"

Dustin savored the moment. "None of your damned business ever again."

CHAPTER THIRTY-FOUR

BIBI TROTTED DOWN the carpet runner covering his aunt's marble stairs and saw a man he didn't recognize standing in the hallway outside the dining room.

"Nishaat Alzeshi?" He was dressed in a suit and tie.

"Who the fuck are you?"

"Jack Fariel with Denver Homicide." He opened his jacket to reveal a badge. "Do you prefer Nishaat or Bibi?"

"I don't know who that is." Bibi spat the words in Farsi. "You ugly sack of camel shit."

"Moldy camel testes, how nice to say."

Bibi backed up a step. The man's Farsi was terrible but no one in Denver, certainly no Denver cop, spoke it at all.

"Who are you?"

"Lovely weather, nice day to drive your new car."

That part, the pleasantries, was flawless. Bibi wanted to run. And how did he know about the Porsche? "Aunt Ruth is here somewhere, I'll go find her."

He turned to leave and Farsi-speaking-maybe-cop stopped him. "Not Ruth. You, Bibi."

His eyes went to the man's gun. Couldn't outrun that. He shouldn't have come home but he needed a real shower with hot water. He'd also wanted a chance to apologize to the new girl, even if it wasn't allowed.

"I'm on my way to work," Bibi said.

The cop switched to English. "At the restaurant?"

"What?"

"I know your nickname is Bibi and there's a restaurant on Colorado Boulevard named Bibi'z, owned by a man named Mohamed Alzeshi. Is that your father? Nice they named it after you."

"Whatever." Always the fucking restaurant. He'd snuck out when Avi was distracted by a liquor delivery.

"I need to talk to you about Lucia Santiago."

Said her full name like Bibi wouldn't have known who he meant if he simply said, "Lucia."

"When was the last time you saw her?" Farsi-cop asked.

"Here."

"I didn't ask you where I asked you when, although thank you for being forthcoming. Maybe you're not comfortable with English? Do you need an interpreter?"

What a prick. "My English is better than your Farsi."

"I have no doubt that's true. I need to ask you some questions but I wonder if your aunt told you not to talk to me?"

Shit. What had she told him? Some crap about being a gentleman. And not asking for a lawyer.

"I might have had a few beers Saturday night."

"I'm not here about a DUI, either," Farsi-cop said. "Although your record doesn't inspire confidence. I sure hope you're careful with your new Porsche."

Whoever he was, dude was fucking smug. "Oh yeah? What do you care about?"

"You haven't answered my question about what time you were with Lucia Saturday night."

"Oh, um." Bibi licked his lips. "I was at the restaurant, like you said, and she came in. I tried to buy her a shot but she said no like always."

"Was she in the restaurant or the club?"

"Same thing, they're right next to each other."

"Right." The man sounded bored. "You were there for a

few hours and talked Lucia into driving home with you."

"She lived here."

"I've seen your texts to Lucia." Said with the same lack of interest as if he'd mentioned the weather.

Fucking caught again, outmaneuvered, outnumbered. Bibi was right back in that field, next to the metal rocket with the bully, about to be humiliated.

Farsi-cop droned on, oblivious. "And then maybe Lucia drove."

"What? Where?" Was he asking about when Ken asked Bibi to give Lucia a ride to the hotel? Or what?

"When the two of you came home together Saturday— or, rather, early Sunday—Lucia drove."

"Yeah." Bibi wasn't tracking but figured the less he said, the better.

The cop continued. "Anyway, I need you to come to homicide with me and give your statement."

Don't go anywhere with them. That part Bibi remembered. His right leg started to vibrate, like a spasm, his heel bouncing. He walked through the nearest doorway into the dining room which was set with three elaborate place settings and a huge centerpiece. Had he forgotten something? A holiday or someone's birthday? Bibi grabbed a shiny fork off of a napkin. There was cloth stacked on one end of the table and a second cop in a uniform appeared behind the one in the suit. He realized too late he'd trapped himself in a room with them.

"Lucia saw you were too drunk to drive," cop-in-a-suit said.

"Why do you think that?" Bibi played with the fork, pressed the tines into the heavily waxed wooden table, fascinated by the lines of dots. They made him think of coke and how badly he needed some. And then that made him wonder if there was any left in his room and if he'd get busted for it.

"Bibi, come on." Farsi-cop sounded like Sahir when he

was trying to get Bibi out of bed. "Let's get this over with and get your statement."

"I'm not going anywhere with you."

Suit exchanged smile with uniform. Bibi positioned himself behind the table like a shield.

Suit continued in the same smug tone, unfazed by Bibi's refusal. "Lucia lived with you, in this house along with your Aunt Ruth and Uncle Ken so it's natural that—"

Bibi interrupted. "He's not my uncle."

Farsi-cop slowed his speech like dealing with a moron. "Her room is downstairs, yours is upstairs; hers is neat and clean, yours requires a tetanus shot. But you both lived here and—"

"That's because my aunt wouldn't let her clean." Bibi let go of the fork and it skittered onto the floor. "Lucia wanted to, she was really nice."

"Okay. What happened after she drove you home that night?"

"Nothing." Bibi's eyes moved between suit and uniform, waited for the rest who were going to arrive and help beat him. Which one would hold his arms? Which one would bend him over? He almost wished for Sahir.

"Let's try this a different way. What did Lucia do when she got home?"

That was it. Relief as Bibi remembered what he was supposed to say. "I was drunk. It's a good thing she ran into me. I passed out and slept until noon. That's when I heard the news about Lucia, when my aunt got home from church."

"You're telling me the last time you saw Lucia alive was when you got home from the club at some unknown time—"

"It was late."

"Then you passed out, didn't see Lucia again, and found out from your aunt on Sunday that she was dead?"

"That's right." Bibi wiped his palms on his slacks.

"You didn't seem upset a few minutes ago when I told you I wanted to talk about Lucia."

Was this a trick? What was he supposed to have done? "So?"

"Are you upset about Lucia?"

"Oh. Yeah."

Farsi-cop fingered the linens, counted them. "How about your aunt?"

What could he say? Aunt Ruth had sighed. *"Now it's time to train a new one."* Even Bibi knew that sounded terrible.

Farsi-cop offered him a bully smile. "Come on, don't tell me you never put the moves on Lucia? Pretty girl like that you must have tried more than just texting."

The sudden subject change combined with the thought of sex with Lucia made Bibi dizzy.

"No, Lucia never came in my room." Stick to the script. "I don't remember much. I got home and passed out. Woke up at noon. Heard the news."

"At noon on Sunday?"

"Yeah, I've said it three times. Aunt Ruth talked to me after she got home from church."

"That's interesting." Asshole said it like it was nothing. "I was the one who made the notification to your aunt."

Bibi attempted attitude, an old, useless reflex. "I know what the word notification means."

"Your aunt didn't know Lucia was dead until I told her at three in the afternoon. Shortly after that time I conducted a search of the residence, including your room, and you weren't here. You still weren't here when I finished my search hours later."

Bibi had trouble following the times and the only conclusion he reached was that he'd fucked up. "My aunt already knew somehow. She knows everything."

After a beat, "What were you driving Saturday night?"

"I thought I told you. My Aunt's Range Rover because

it was snowing."

"The green one?"

Bibi didn't see the harm in agreeing.

"How about Lucia?"

Was Farsi-cop trying to make Bibi forget what he said five minutes ago? "She was in the Range Rover, too. I guess that's what you mean. She was driving I was a passenger."

"No, to the club. How did she get *to* the club?"

"Oh, Raven gave her a ride."

"Who's Raven?"

The enormity of his screw-up hit Bibi with such intensity his mouth dropped open. Shit. *Shit, shit, shit.*

"No, ah, I shouldn't have said that. I don't know for sure."

There was too much to remember, too many stupid rules. Bibi squeegeed his brow with the back of his hand. He'd deny it and no one would believe the police. Easy to blame them, to say they must have seen her on a camera or some surveillance shit, followed him or tapped his phone. Maybe that was why Sahir destroyed it. He wished they'd shoot him or lock him up, anything, just get it over with.

He gulped air like a fish, completely forgot he'd said he was headed to work. "I don't feel good. I wanna lie down."

Farsi-cop's face was hard. "How do I get ahold of Raven?"

"I don't know."

"You seem sorry to have mentioned her name."

"There you are." Aunt Ruth stood in the doorway. "You gave me such a fright."

How long had she been standing there? Had she heard? She rushed to Bibi and put her arms around him for a short second, a hug he was too startled to return.

"What's going on?" Farsi-cop asked.

Ruth placed a hand on her chest and acted it up for all she was worth. "Oh. Bibi's supposed to be at work and I got a call from the restaurant that he wasn't there and no one could find him."

"Why didn't you call me?" Bibi asked.

"I did try," Ruth said, "and got the recording that the call couldn't go through. My mind went dreadful places. What are you doing here anyway? Are you unwell?"

"I came home for a shower because—"

"Your face is shiny."

Bitch would point that out. Bibi was about to complain about Sahir but realized he couldn't do that in front of the cop. *Please*, he pleaded internally with an unnamed deity, *please don't ask her about Raven.*

His aunt lied smoothly and Bibi thought for a second she was going to cry. "After what happened to Lucia I've been quite nervous and when Bibi disappeared I thought the worst."

"I didn't disappear." Bibi's voice rose in protest. "I took a break. Don't I get to take a break like everyone else?"

"It wasn't gentlemanly of you to scare me."

The same word she used earlier when she told him how to act, a clear warning.

Farsi-cop said, "Ruth, if you don't mind, I have a few follow-up questions."

Her eyes were bright fake with tears. "I do mind. From now on I insist all communication take place in an official setting with our attorneys present. I can't take this kind of—of—disturbance. If you've located the items covered by your warrant I must ask you to leave the premises at once."

CHAPTER THIRTY-FIVE

⸻

"WHY ARE YOU being such a baby?" Raven was too stressed and in too much pain to be patient with the new girl.

Willow's cheeks were splotchy from crying. "I can't touch people, it's gross."

A customer waited on a table in the center treatment room. That's what they called it. Same way they performed holistic therapies for health and wellness. Total bullshit.

"No different from stuff you'd do with your boyfriend only this way you get paid for it." Raven spouted the line from habit and then regarded the young girl shrewdly. "You've never had a boyfriend, have you?"

"Sure I have. And I'm not a baby."

"Then no more crying, puhlease." Her hip throbbed and she didn't want to think what else Sahir would do if this little shit kept her from meeting her quota.

Raven pointed at a camera on the ceiling. "I know you're scared but you can't get me in trouble. They watch us all the time. All. The. Time. C'mon, get undressed."

She tried to smile as if it was all no big deal and shrugged out of her robe, a dark purple one bought with Sahir's last bonus. Miss Perkyprissy didn't budge, held her robe closed with both hands, and stared at the floor. Raven didn't get it; she'd been young when she started and never carried on this way.

Used another of Sahir's lines. "You have a nice body and it gives joy. Not everyone can do what we do, you should be proud."

"Of this? Yuck."

"Don't you want the tat so everyone'll know you're grown up?" Raven held up her own hair to show it off.

"When do you get that?"

"When you become one of us."

Truth was Raven didn't know because Sahir changed the rules constantly. Some magic combination of time, money, and customers and he took you to the tattoo place himself, like a proud daddy, and then out for a steak dinner as a reward. For her dinner he'd bought her an expensive dress and then ordered a glass of champagne so she could try it for the first time. Raven still guarded that dress like it was her child.

"The tat'll look cool on you." Raven forced another smile and Willow at least untied her robe. "Get a washcloth and a cup of water. Remember, that's not for us so don't drink it. And if they ask, how old are you?"

Willow answered in her childish voice. "Twelve-and-a-half."

"Nooo. We've practiced this. You're eighteen like me."

"No one'll believe that."

"What these men believe," Raven said, "is that we're into them. For as long as they pay for."

Her heart sank when she saw one of her regulars on his back on the table, a fat Russian who had trouble getting it up. He was ancient, like forty, with gray hair and lumpy brown moles.

He propped himself up on his elbows and stared. "Two for one? Sweet."

As if he could handle one of them. Raven stuck to Spanish with Willow in front of the customer. "Set down the water and take that robe off. *Vamos. Dame esa túnica.*"

Then leaned over the Russian so that her breasts were

in his face and let him knead her roughly for a minute. Ran her hands down his chest to his gigantic belly. "My goodness, darlin', I forgot how handsome you are. You weren't lying when you said you'd been working out."

He wriggled with pleasure on the table. "What's the little girl gonna do?"

"Willow has no experience with men," Raven whispered in the customer's ear. "She may even be a virgin."

He squinted at Willow. "That true, baby? You never been fucked?"

Raven smiled at him, hissed orders. *"No llorar."* *Don't you dare cry.* Asked the customer which parts were tight, already knowing the answer.

He put Raven's hand on his dick. "Lot of tension."

"That's because you're so muscular and work so hard. We'll give that area extra attention and Willow's gonna give you a scalp massage."

"There's other things I wish she'd rub." He grinned up at Willow as a tear slid down her cheek. "Don't worry baby, I'll break you in nice and gentle."

Raven wondered how anyone could cry so much. Sure, she had her bad times, but they were about real things like getting burned or having her friend die... No. She couldn't think about Lucia or she'd lose it, too.

Sahir told her to give the Russian ten minutes extra so she killed time by rubbing lotion into his arms and torso, keeping one eye on the clock on the wall. Out of spite, Raven wanted to make Willow work on his feet but knew that would be pushing things too far. They were hideous, with calluses and thick, yellow toenails.

Eventually, her hand grabbed his limp dick and started pumping.

"Yeah. Right there is very tight." But he leered up at Willow.

More hissed orders. "Stand closer. Look at him. *Míralo.*"

"What are you, thirteen?" The man reached up to feel

Willow's non-existent chest.

Willow shook her head, sniffled, but continued working her fingers up and down his jaw, using a technique Raven had shown her. The way the Russian focused on Willow he liked children, and Raven decided to use it, because if he didn't get off she'd be blamed.

"Willow, would you like to do this? I bet he'd love for you to touch him. Oh my, have you ever even touched a man before? You *are* a virgin aren't you? A big man like him would ruin you for anyone else if he was your first." Her stream of slutty talk had the desired effect and gave her hand something to work with.

Raven wondered how much Sahir would charge for Willow's virginity, real or not. At the beginning, Raven pretended to be a virgin all the time. Customers really got off on it and they'd even tried rigging up a thing with fake blood. Willow's crying would probably even be a turn-on. While her mind wandered Raven never forgot the clock; this job was all about timing. And when she got the Russian to finish right on schedule she felt, despite everything, a flicker of pride.

She made a motion with her hand to Willow. *You can stop.* "I always give them a minute, right after."

"Right after what?"

For God's sake. How could this idiot girl possibly not know what happened? "You're doing the next one. Give me the cloth."

Willow wiped her own hands off first and Raven's eyes went to the camera. "Nooo. Those are for customers. Get him a fresh one and warm it up."

"How?"

Raven snatched the cloth and stalked into the sitting area. She wet a new one in the sink and put it in the microwave. "Ten seconds. Shake it out and make sure it's not too hot."

Back in the room, she put the cloth in Willow's hand,

shoved her toward the table.

"Look, darlin', look who couldn't wait to touch you herself."

He opened one sleepy eye. "I'm gonna ask for you next time, little girl, would you like that?"

Willow giggled and jabbed at him tentatively with the cloth.

"You get extra time today for helping us train," Raven said. "So we're gonna give you hot stones."

"Sweet." With some effort, he turned over and his stomach fat spread across the table.

All of their supplies—the folding massage tables, the stones, the water dispenser—traveled with them. Sahir said they were leaving early, because of Lucia and all the cops wanting to deport them. Dottie would be pissed at the lost income but it served the bitch right.

"Take your time gettin' up, darlin'." With a flourish of tongue Raven whispered into the Russian's ear. That was something real massage therapists said, which she hoped to be one day.

Upstairs in the kitchen she wiped her palms against each other, as if brushing off crumbs. "Easy, right?"

"You don't..." Willow stared at the floor.

"Have sex with them? Depends on what service they bought." Raven tapped her phone. "Ten minutes. If we mess up the time we pay instead of the customer. It's important."

"How many customers are there?"

"You should hope we're busy because it means you're making money." And not getting burned or beaten.

"He was so old."

"You think young handsome men have to pay?"

"Do they ever try for more than what they paid for?"

"Sure." Raven said it dismissively. "That's why we have security."

Willow ran her toe along a ridge in the linoleum. "And

the tips?"

"So you're interested in money after all. Cash in while you're new, customers'll get tired of you fast, that's why we have to keep moving."

CHAPTER THIRTY-SIX

B IBI NEVER WENT to work. After the incident with the fake Farsi cop Ruth told him to go to his room and wait for further instructions. Like he was twelve. He'd noticed when he took his shower earlier that the room was clean and figured the new girl—what the hell was her name?—had done it. Still felt bad about her having to clean the bathroom but he'd taken it as a sign that they were going to treat him better.

He was wrong.

"Your aunt tells me you talked to the cops."

Sahir was in the doorway. Out of reflex Bibi reached in the nightstand for his vape. Stared stupidly at the empty drawer. Felt underneath.

"What'd you say to the detective?" Sahir asked.

"He wasn't even here for me. He was just here to get—"

With one hand, Sahir grabbed Bibi by the arm and slammed him against the wall. "You were alone with him. Ruth told me she came in on you chattering like a monkey."

"I didn't tell him shit. I'm not sure he's a real cop."

"Tell me why I shouldn't use this on you? Cut your fucking tongue out."

"My aunt won't let you." Bibi saw the knife and squeezed his eyes shut.

"Your aunt is suffering and you're making it worse."

But Sahir let go. Bibi opened his eyes and saw him next to the dresser holding Bibi's new phone. Obviously, Sahir had the code to unlock it. Obviously. Bibi's last text to Val was on the screen. *hey pls talk 2 me*

"Begging a girl." Sahir gave a disgusted whistle. "You must've really hurt Val, her feelings in addition to her body."

Bibi's stomach clenched as he took in the room and the truth sunk in; it was all gone. His scrips, his weed, his blow, everything. Not even a liquor bottle.

"Where is it?"

Sahir walked close. "Are you sure you don't know where Val is?"

"I told you."

"No," Sahir said. "You really didn't."

Bibi couldn't catch his breath and hated himself for gasping because it sounded like crying.

"I don't think you'd hurt anyone because you're a fucking coward," Sahir said. "Look at you quivering and whimpering. But the police don't know you're a pussy."

"Isn't that good?"

Sahir talked over him. "Val probably left Denver because of you and she'll talk. I need to know where you went with her Saturday and you'll tell me one way or another."

"Where is Aunt Ruth?"

"At a meeting for one of her charities."

"Aren't we going to have dinner?" Bibi's words rushed in a panicked torrent. "I saw the flowers on the table. Isn't it a special occasion?"

Sahir's smile was scary. "It's a special occasion all right. You and me are going to spend some quality time. And you haven't asked about him, but Ken's been arrested."

Bibi started shivering so violently he was sure Sahir could see. They were alone in the house. Except the new girl who didn't count. "I need to go to work."

Sahir snorted. "Since when do you wanna work?"

"Where's all my stuff?"

"Don't you care about your poor Uncle Ken being arrested?"

Of course he didn't care. And neither did Sahir so why was he pretending? Bibi licked chapped lips. "I need my stuff."

Sahir made a show of looking in the closet. "Everything seems to be in order."

"You know what I mean."

"What should be here is here. What shouldn't is not." Sahir consulted his own phone. "Time for *salah*."

"I don't do that anymore."

"You do now."

An app played the old, familiar sing-songy Arabic. Sahir walked to the door and locked it. Too late, Bibi noticed the new deadbolt, one that needed a key on each side.

"You're locking me in?"

"Think of it as a fresh start." Sahir made him stand at the correct angle, genuflect, chided him for not repeating the verses. "You forget where you came from?"

Maybe if Bibi played along Sahir would be satisfied. Muscle memory, like they say about riding a bike. In the old days at home he'd hear the call to prayer over the loudspeaker and jump out of bed without thinking. Fall back asleep right after.

Now, Bibi's stomach cramped and he barely made it through the last repetition. Ran to the bathroom and slammed—nothing. No door. Fresh white towels were on the rack. The hot water handle had been removed from the shower.

Sahir stood in the doorway and watched while he took a dump.

"Why are you doing this?" Bibi hunched, crossed his arms across his chest as if to fend off humiliation.

"There's more than one way to get the truth. Wash your hands when you're done."

Then made Bibi strip and went through his pockets.

"Found all your hiding places," Sahir said. "I know all the tricks. Air vents, electric outlets, pens."

The room spun around Bibi. The television was gone. A Quran on the nightstand.

"What am I supposed to do? It's dangerous to stop all of a sudden."

"I'll check on you. Wake you up for prayers."

"But what am I gonna *do*?" Bibi's voice rose in a wail.

"Drink lots of water."

Sahir took Bibi's phone. He heard the key turn in the new lock. Tried the door anyway, pounded on it, yelled. No one came. He stared unbelieving for a long time and then tore the room apart. Drawers dumped, hangars off the rod, containers pulled off shelves. Checked all of his shoes. Contents from under the bathroom sink swept with his arm onto the floor. Inside of the toilet tank. Nothing.

Nothing, nothing, nothing.

Sahir even found the fake shaving cream can and the hiding spot inside the curtain rod.

All this because of Val. No one understood how bad he felt, like they didn't get how hard things were for him. Bibi cringed every time he remembered his ruined date, the way they argued, the way Val threw his gift across the motel room. He should have taken her someplace nicer, but he was always having to sneak around behind his aunt's back, like he was still a teenager. Now Val's feelings were hurt and she was convinced he disrespected her and he couldn't do anything about it.

Suddenly exhausted, he crawled into bed and masturbated, only entertainment available. Pretended it was Val, that they'd made up and she was thanking him for the flowers he sent. That they were in her apartment. That he never had to see Sahir or his aunt again. Wondered if this was how Lucia and the others felt, prisoners in their rooms. Got up and checked the windows, discovered they had new locks, too.

He must have dozed off because strong hands pulled him out of bed. Bibi flailed, threw useless punches, felt himself dragged as easily as a rag doll.

"Time for Isha'a," Sahir said. Arabic droned from the phone.

"I need to take a piss."

"Good idea." Sahir paused the app. "Then I'll help with *wudu* since you've forgotten everything."

Sahir touched him and washed him like a child. Bibi wanted to cry from frustration, humiliation, fear. Prayed to whatever unknown deity there was that he didn't get turned on.

"My aunt won't let you do this."

"Her idea."

"I don't believe you." Bibi ran to the door and yelled for Ruth until Sahir pincered his shoulders and turned him toward Mecca. Knelt, stood, knelt again. Went through the motions. Mopped sweat from his brow.

When prayers were finished Sahir held up Bibi's phone, the same lame text on the screen.

"Val's not answering. What more proof do you need? What's it gonna take for you to let it go and stop causing trouble?"

"It's not my fault."

"Shit." Sahir shook his head. "Nothing's ever your fault. You have everything handed to you and you still fuck us over any chance you get."

"That's not true."

"I'll be back for Fajr which, in case you've forgotten, is 5:34 tomorrow."

"I'm hungry." Bibi hadn't eaten since that horrible forced breakfast with his aunt. It was seven at night and he couldn't possibly go that long with no food, or drugs, or anything to do.

Sahir looked him up and down. "Seems you could stand to miss a meal."

"But what am I supposed to do until morning?"

"Clean up. Here's a little motivation." A quick flash and Sahir pressed the tip of the knife into the soft underside of Bibi's chin. He felt a trickle of liquid run down his throat onto his chest. Stared helplessly at the mess he'd made earlier searching for his stuff. Heard the key turn in the lock. Started to shake.

CHAPTER THIRTY-SEVEN

IF RAVEN GAVE Lucia a ride to the club, it made sense to Jack that she was also the girl in the selfie. Bibi stopped talking after he used her name and appeared even more terrified when Ruth showed up. Until her arrival Bibi had barfed information without a trace of self-awareness, including the fact that Lucia drove him home in the Range Rover which fit nicely with Jack's early theory of Ken's jealousy.

The police now had ten additional tablecloths the same size and pattern as the one Lucia's body was wrapped in. All of the linens Jack saw in Ruth's cabinets were crisply ironed, folded with precision, and stacked in perfect white towers she no doubt verified with a laser level. It was likely Lucia had washed and ironed her own shroud and Tiffany was earning some of Dani's overtime, staying late to match fibers.

Being excused from cleaning Bibi's room was a small mercy, and Mike's ironic translation of his formal name, Nishaat, to "nut job" fit perfectly. Jack wished it was legal to bribe Bibi with cocaine; he'd have told them anything they wanted to know. He was an incoherent, sweaty disaster and Ruth wasn't going to be pleased when she saw the marks he'd made with the fork on her priceless Duncan Phyfe table.

One striking takeaway was Bibi's lack of emotionality in

regard to Lucia, as if he'd had human compassion trained out of him, most likely by Ruth-the-stoic who must have had some scary rigid upbringing of her own. Jack couldn't imagine tears being shed in that house over any of the girls. Of all the current suspects, Dustin had seemed the most torn up about Lucia—and that was setting a very low bar.

Jack made use of his task force by delegating the search for Raven, and prepped for his main event: Ken's interview. He had considerable circumstantial evidence—the threats, the porn, the pregnancy, the jewelry, the faux Muslim burial, the botched escape—but wished he had a primary crime scene and forensics. None of that would matter if he got a confession.

Ken Harrowsmith's right eye was twelve shades of purple and a dark blue train track of stiches curved from his temple up over his forehead to his hairline. Part of an eyebrow had been shaved, his lips looked swollen, and his right arm was in a sling. His left wrist was handcuffed and attached to a chain around his waist that was integrated with ankle shackles. Instead of one of his expensive suits he sported an orange prison jumpsuit.

Jack felt zero sympathy, was mostly surprised Ken was talking to him at all and hadn't asked for a lawyer.

"Are you on any medication?"

"They gave me extra-strength Tylenol."

That shouldn't be enough to alter anyone's comprehension. Jack placed a sheet of paper on the table in front of Ken. "You're in pain so I'll get right to it."

"I can't read that I'm afraid. My eye is injured."

"It's a transcript of your texts to Lucia from nine until midnight Saturday night."

Ken stared in the general direction of the paper. "I know it doesn't sound good."

Jack read the most pertinent one aloud, about strangling Lucia's pretty neck. "That's very specific."

"There are rules—ways of treating—" Ken licked his lips and started over. "I was good to Lucia and she misinterpreted my generosity."

Jack remembered Lucia on her knees in the closet and would have loved to point out that the generosity flowed a different direction. "Can you explain what you mean?"

"She'd begun to have an unfortunate attitude. Ungrateful, demanding."

"What was Lucia demanding Saturday night?"

An insulted tone entered Ken's voice. "She wanted me to drop what I was doing to be with her. If you read the texts you know this. I wasn't sure what to do about Lucia, to be perfectly honest."

Ken seemed to have become certain right before he dumped her in the alley. "When did you find out she was pregnant?"

Ken's shoulders slumped but he was clearly not surprised. "It's not mine."

Jack wasn't surprised, either, but stuck to his strategy. "I think I'd want to leave the country too, rather than tell Ruth that news."

"It was irrelevant. I had a vasectomy years ago."

Jack resisted snark about the inconvenience of safe sex. "Did Ruth ask you to do that?"

"How did you—" Ken frowned and winced, as if a stitch in his forehead caught. "She can't have children."

"If your wife couldn't get pregnant then why would you need a vasectomy?"

"You're a man. Do I have to explain? How is this relevant?"

Jack wasn't happy to be lumped in with Ken in any way, even by gender. "It's relevant because one of the young women you slept with was murdered."

"What do you mean, 'one of'?"

Jack intended to get there, and confront Ken with the porn, but not yet. "Apparently, in addition to not feeling you need to explain to me, you also didn't have to explain to Ruth. She knew you would cheat and, to eliminate unnecessary complications, the vasectomy was her idea."

"She didn't *know*."

"In fact, Ruth provided girls for you to sleep with. Housekeeper and girlfriend, two for the price of one."

"No, she didn't."

"But it sounds like she did." Jack kept his tone casual. "I've talked to a lot of people, including Dustin Rattenberry, your pastor, who told me he'd placed a number of young women in your employ and he always worked with Ruth."

"He's not my pastor."

This sleaze was contradicting himself all over the place and cherry picking which parts of questions he'd answer. That was okay by Jack; the more Ken tripped himself up the better.

"On the drive here from Yuma you were talking with the officer about how you wanted to pick the next one. Doesn't seem fair you never got a say if you were going to have a relationship with these"—Jack carefully chose his words—"With your own employees."

Ken hesitated. "Frankly, I'm not sure what I said in the car. I was in pain and they'd given me high doses of paracetamol."

It took Jack a second then he remembered Ken was British. "Right, the extra-strength Tylenol. Let's forget about the drive. I was surprised when I searched your residence to see that Lucia had been allowed to decorate her room. That seems above and beyond for a temporary employee."

"I wanted Lucia to be comfortable for the duration of her stay."

Words from the video ran through Jack's mind... *beautiful memories to take with you to paradise.* "You knew

Lucia wasn't going to be with you very long."

"No, of course she'd move on."

Jack couldn't help himself. "To paradise."

Ken shifted awkwardly in the chair. "I'm not sure what you mean."

"Paradise. Lucia's dead and isn't that where Muslims believe the virtuous go? Your version of heaven."

No answer. Jack continued. "Here's something I find troubling. Your behavior after Lucia was killed. Wrecking a car in a blizzard attempting to get out of state. Can you explain?"

"I was terribly upset when I heard about her on the news Sunday evening, that's why I drank myself legless. I don't ordinarily consume alcohol because of my religion and it hit me hard."

"You rented a car using your British passport and drove on country roads in a bad storm, at night, because the interstate was closed. That appears pretty desperate. What were you running from?"

Ken took a deep breath. "It wasn't the best judgment but I wouldn't categorize it as running, per se. As I said, I'd had far too much drink, and in my addled state thought perhaps I could get ahead of the storm, drive to Omaha or Kansas City and catch a flight from there. My meetings were important."

Jack offered a conspirator's smile. "Luckily for you I'm not interested in a DUI. I am trying to figure out why you even went to the airport Sunday morning when you knew your flight was canceled."

Ken cleared a blockage from his throat. "As I said, my meetings were critical, it was a terrible storm, I was upset about Lucia, everything was balls-up."

Brilliant, as they'd say in this dirtbag's homeland. Jack felt like smiling for real, but instead he frowned, as if confused. "Wait. You were upset about Lucia Sunday morning? You told me a few minutes ago you didn't know about Lucia until you saw it on the news in the evening."

This was the moment Jack was sure Ken would invoke, but for some bizarre reason he didn't.

"I also told you she'd acted rudely, which was quite out of character. It was unsettling for her to act that way. In fact"—Ken warmed to his story—"when I heard she'd died I was sad we'd never have a chance to put things right. She was a lovely young woman. Simply lovely."

Sack of shit pedophile sounded like he was writing Lucia's eulogy. Instead of encouraging more cringe-inducing declarations of admiration, Jack decided to further erode Ken's timeline and already lame excuses.

"I have a pretty good idea of your relationship with Lucia. What I'd like to do now is go over your activities that weekend. Take me through Saturday night. You went to a benefit with Ruth, correct? For the symphony?"

"Yes, that's right."

"Do you remember what vehicle you drove?"

"We took our green Range Rover due to the poor driving conditions."

Jack made a note to cover his jolt of excitement. Bibi, Ken and Ruth couldn't all have been driving the same car.

"You also own a black Jeep, correct?"

"No. That's a mistake." Ken seemed offended, as if a mere Jeep was beneath him.

Jack made another pretend note. "Got it. What time did you and Ruth return home in the Range Rover?"

"Around eleven. There was a late supper we didn't attend because of the dreadful weather and my flight the next morning. I always get up early for prayers, too."

"Fajr was shortly before six on Sunday."

"Are you Muslim?" Ken asked.

"Tell me what else you did."

"Ah—I'm a bit baffled, I'm afraid. Must be my bump on the head. Are we still discussing Saturday or have we moved on to Sunday? By then I was at the hotel by myself, my flight having been canceled. I was on the phone with the airline attempting to reschedule and ordered some dinner."

Was it Jack's imagination or did Ken seem eager to move on to the next day? "No, Saturday night, after you got home from the benefit, what else did you do?"

"Nothing. Ah, I mean, I went to bed."

"With Ruth?"

Ken's Adam's apple bobbed up and down. "May I get some water?"

Jack used the request as an excuse to leave for a few minutes and check in with Dani and Mike, who were watching on monitors in a nearby room.

Mike offered a sardonic smile. "You are the douchebag whisperer."

"Good to know I have a marketable skill."

"I can't believe he hasn't lawyered up."

"Don't jinx me." Jack turned to Dani. "Any suggestions?"

"I keep wondering, what's the catch? Why's Mr. Richie Rich talking to us?"

"The catch is maybe he didn't do it," Mike said.

"You did that with a straight face," Jack said. "Impressive."

"I'm serious. If he killed her do you think he'd be talking to you?"

"Or he thinks he's smart enough to go it alone."

"I've seen that mistake before." Dani shrugged. "If Ken's willing to talk you're willing to listen."

CHAPTER THIRTY-EIGHT

TWO PEOPLE, THE whore and a stocky man, arms pushed off his sides by muscles, were leaving an apartment building in the congested Capitol Hill neighborhood. Busy street, witnesses, maybe even cameras but it couldn't be helped. Each one of them would later tell a slightly different version of what happened.

This was a case of justice. Her crimes? Disrespect, disobedience, threats to the larger whole; offenses that often aren't taken as seriously as they should be. Sahir thought of the preacher's rules: Thou shalt not bear false witness. Thou shalt not lie or steal. She'd done that and more. While he didn't work for Dustin, they'd both reached the same conclusion independently. If any of Sahir's toys talked to the cops let alone behaved in a wanton manner to please a detective she'd be dead. Not possible in this case but that didn't mean there weren't other satisfying courses. Nicki was a whore and he figured he'd do what he never would with Raven: mark her so no man would desire her.

His own view was more prosaic and less flowery than the minister's. Promote right and discourage wrong. Simple. In a sense he was aiding in the fight for her soul, although right now this was all about business and Sahir fought sentiment at all costs.

Certainty was required, every why and how scrutinized

and put to rest. Knowing beyond righteousness that you had clear cause. One dozen, two dozen mental rehearsals until there was no hesitation, until you knew exactly where the cracks in the sidewalk would be, shadows cast by streetlights, nearest alley for escape and a dumpster.

He parked in a loading zone on a one-way street, left the door ajar, oblivious to horns or stares or dogs humping their backs in the stingy sharp strip of grass at the curb to relieve themselves. Tunnel vision. Eyes only for her.

She was wearing a jacket, fur, probably fake. High heels and heavy makeup. Laughed, tossed her hair, brushed it back with a scarlet-tipped hand. Lucia's lifeless face from Saturday night flashed in his mind, the garish stripe of lipstick, another ungrateful slut. Sahir forced himself into the present moment, the woman in front of him very much alive and in need of correction.

Discipline. Certainty. Not sentiment or fantasy.

Muscle man made a fatal pause, at least from her perspective, checked to make sure the front door was locked. The whore walked disrespectfully ahead of him. Bold harlot strides, white legs flashing from underneath the indecent skirt, head down as she worked her phone.

He blocked her path and struck the moment she lifted her head. It didn't take a second, a quick slice, up at an angle, left to right. No hesitation, practiced and confident. His weapon of choice meant the assault was intimate, if not prolonged. She staggered, surprise in her eyes, a hand to her cheek almost in wonderment. High heels sank as she veered like a drunk from sidewalk to grass, tried to get away, the stilettos impeding her flight.

Muscle man shouted, waved his arm, as if in a dream. Called the whore's name.

Sahir could have told her hysteria was pointless; one stroke only and there would be no pursuit. He could have told her women weren't equipped for battle regardless of footwear. But Sahir resisted words or any desire to watch.

There would be time to relish later. *Calm down.* The advice he gave everyone. Panic got you caught. Abrupt moves that broke the pattern and drew attention. His gaze fixed determinedly on the sidewalk as he returned to the car, even as people rushed past and jostled him. *"Did you see what happened?"* Hands in his pockets, shoulders hunched. *"She's been stabbed, don't let get him get away."* Still didn't break stride. *"Someone call 9-1-1."* One woman screamed, another was crying. Maybe the whore. He took deep breaths through his nose.

Then he was back behind the wheel, accelerating smoothly away from the curb as if he'd delivered a pizza. Most of the time, managing your own emotional response was all that was required for success. Like with Raven. Any time he felt soft toward her he forced himself to punish. Feelings got in the way. Sahir had a sense that Fariel could control himself, too, but pushed the thought aside. One problem at a time.

He kept his composure and no one interfered. All the witnesses tonight would tell a different story because they had an emotional reaction. They were much too interested in the young half-naked woman on the ground, the spreading blood, the gore, the excitement.

The whore wasn't dead but she'd never be the same person again. He'd be delusional to think he'd purified her, but perhaps he'd improved her. Only business. Only what was necessary. The weak soul at home was a different case entirely.

CHAPTER THIRTY-NINE

———

JACK RETURNED WITH water and shackled Ken bent awkwardly at the waist to drink.

"We were talking about Saturday night and your interactions with Lucia. When she disrespected you."

"I was angry," Ken said. "Shocked, in fact. I treated her so well, spoiled her to the extent it concerned my wife. Lucia's behavior was inexplicable."

"You know what strikes me as odd? You made no further attempt to contact Lucia after she was dead."

"What do you mean?"

Jack tapped the incriminating paper. "Right up until midnight practically nonstop texting. Then nothing."

"I told you, I went to bed."

"And still nothing the next morning."

"We lived in the same house, I didn't need to call."

"Except you didn't know where she was or who she was with. That's why you were so angry."

"I'm not sure what you're asking me," Ken said.

"Is that why you locked Lucia in her room? Because you didn't trust her?"

"That wasn't me."

"Ruth demonstrated the lock for me when I was there."

Ken bent forward for another drink. "It was for Lucia's safety and I didn't see any reason to argue with my wife."

Jack figured there were many other possibilities for

strife in the Harrowsmith household, from kiddie porn to religious differences. "The lock was Ruth's idea?"

"She has the best of intentions."

"You're exceptionally tolerant. Remember I told you I was at your house? I also saw Bibi's room. Yuck." Jack made a face and shuddered.

Ken didn't take the bait. "She's quite fond of her nephew."

"So was Lucia from what I hear." Jack casually lobbed that grenade but again didn't get a strong reaction. "Tell me more about Bibi."

"Such as?"

Why did people always do that? Worst evasion technique ever. "How do you get along? Where does he work? Does he have a girlfriend?"

"Ruth's family owns a restaurant on Colorado Boulevard. He works there and I think he's dating a waitress."

"Does the waitress have a name?" Jack asked.

"Valeria."

That seemed easy. "Bibi's got a record. Didn't that bother you? Having him in your house?"

"He's young."

"Here's what I think. Lucia was getting too close to Bibi and it infuriated you, all the money you spent on her, she shouldn't even look at another man. They were closer in age but you had a special relationship. I know if my girlfriend preferred Bibi it would make me crazy." Jack shook his head at the very idea of such an outlandish event.

Ken's free hand formed a fist. "I know what you're doing. It's the same thing she did, you're trying to make me jealous."

It seemed to be working. "Maybe you carried out your threat. You bought her jewelry worth tens of thousands of dollars and she disrespected you."

"Did you ask Bibi these questions?"

"I did. Bibi told me Lucia was at the club Saturday night with Raven. I don't know why she couldn't have just told you that. Women."

"Bibi said that?" Ken sounded strangely hopeful.

"Where does Raven work?"

A twitch started in Ken's cheek. "She does massage. Not the nice kind."

"The sexual kind you'd find online?"

"She might do, yes."

A valuable piece of information to give the task force. One step closer. "How did Lucia become friends with someone like Raven?"

"I'm sure I don't know," Ken said. "I was quite fond of Lucia. I need you to know that."

Yeah, that's what all perverts talked about, their fond, tender feelings for their victims. But it gave Jack a great lead-in. "That makes sense. After Lucia was dead, you wanted to give her a proper burial. A Muslim burial."

"I don't know what you mean."

"When we found Lucia, she was wrapped in white cloth. Positioned correctly in regard to Mecca. Stones in lieu of packed earth. I'm sure I don't have to tell you."

"Someone did that?" Ken asked.

"Someone who was fond of her." Jack waited a beat for his implication to sink in. "Who spoiled her, let her decorate her room, bought her jewelry."

"You're twisting my words."

"'Fond' was your exact word. In your text, you tell Lucia you'll take your gifts back and then strangle her. That's very specific. And why we didn't find a necklace on her body. Also why you didn't bother texting after midnight because you knew she was already dead."

"No," Ken said. "Don't you see? I'm being framed."

Still no mention of a lawyer, although Jack sensed he was on borrowed time. "It's why you got up early and went to the airport in a snowstorm for a cancelled—"

Ken interrupted. "I told you, for prayers."

"Lucia's murder wasn't on the news until later on Sunday when you were already at the airport and your response, instead of going home to check on your wife, or simply waiting for your flight, was to rent a car and try to escape."

"Well— I don't— I mean—" Ken started and stopped several sentences. "I know it seems a bit dodgy."

"Then you tried to make up for it, that's what I'm saying." Jack leaned forward. "That makes a difference, the way you tried to do right by Lucia at the end, to make things proper as a man, as a Muslim."

"But I didn't. I mean, I would have, but I didn't even know she was dead until I saw it on the news."

Jack decided it was time to show him pictures of Abigail and Dinah, screen grabs from less x-rated sections of the porn. "Okay. Let's change gears for a minute. Can you tell me who these girls are?"

Ken sucked in a loud breath. "Where did you get those?"

"I notice you aren't unsure who they are you only want to know how I got them." Victory mixed with disgust. Jack was close to putting this loathsome piece of garbage away but those girls—who were they really? Who loved them and missed them?

"Please," Ken said. "I don't want to see them."

Jack wished he could shove Ken's face into the laptop screen. "Guilt is a terrible burden. You know the Quran says killing is wrong, that the fate of murderers will be the first decided on the day of judgment. Tell me what happened. Maybe there's a reasonable explanation. Did they disrespect you like Lucia?"

"No."

"Then there's no reason not to identify them. There are families out there missing loved ones who need to know."

"I can't." Ken's voice keened with anguish. "I don't know, I can't, please don't make me look at them anymore."

"You seem like you feel remorse. That's important."

Ken stared. Jack continued. "Tell me what happened. Did they get pregnant, too? Did they betray you like Lucia?"

"No. Of course not."

Jack sat back. Calculated. What would piss off a Muslim man more than being cuckolded by a Christian?

"Did these girls also have a sexual relationship with Dustin?"

"What?" Ken's voice rose.

"Dustin Rattenberry. Placed all those girls with you. Or, rather with Ruth. You weren't upset about Lucia's pregnancy, which I found strange until I realized it was because you thought it was Bibi. Another Muslim man. A relative. But a Christian minister? That's a double betrayal."

Ken got much louder. "What are you telling me?"

"We've determined that Dustin is the father of Lucia's child."

"No." Ken bellowed like a wounded beast and pushed to his feet. "He's not. You're lying to trick me."

Even shackled, even with one incapacitated arm, Ken was a powerful man. His good hand grabbed the edge of the table and started to flip it. Jack lunged to his feet, too, and rescued his laptop as Mike and two uniformed officers entered the room.

"Sit down." Jack raised the volume. "Now."

"I want my lawyer."

"What you'll get is an electric shock through those ankle bracelets."

Ken roared as an officer took each of his arms. "They're hurting me. I'll bring charges. I'll sue the department. I demand to see a doctor."

Tough words from a man who still claimed entitlement.

Jack tried to explain his rights, to read the charges, but Ken wouldn't stop yelling.

"Do you know who I am? I demand to see my lawyer. Now. You can't do this to me, I have an alibi."

"Oh yeah?" Jack couldn't resist. "That why you talked to me? Because you were counting on Ruth? You might have wanted to get her cooperation first."

A feeling of grim vindication as Ken's belligerence collapsed into pure, unadulterated panic.

CHAPTER FORTY

———◆———

"*JOONAM*," SAHIR SAID. "You never come out here. Is everything all right?"

Ruth was in Sahir's room or, rather, cottage, a ten by sixteen gardening shed behind the garages she'd allowed him to convert for his personal use. He didn't need much. A metal rod for hanging his clothes, a narrow bed, a kerosene heater for warmth. Here he kept his large, hardcover Quran, open on a wooden stand oriented at an angle toward Mecca. A fringed rug covered the rough wooden floor and a stick of incense had burned to white ash in a bronze dish on a table, where Ruth stood looking at his small collection of photos.

"Do you think he's proud of me?" she asked.

"Who?"

By way of answer she showed him the small silver frame she held, a photograph of her father, Mohamed.

Ruth fixated on her dead father, always wondering if he'd approve of her actions. Believed all along she was more suited to run the business than her brother, also named Mohamed. Perhaps she was but it didn't matter because she was a woman. And perhaps that was unfair but very little, in Sahir's experience, had ever been fair.

"I'm certain he was," Sahir said. "Your father loved you unconditionally."

"And yet he left everything to my brother."

"That was the law, dear one. You took it far too personally."

Women could inherit under Sharia law, but daughters only received half as much as sons. In Ruth's view, her brother took everything from her and she refused to accept law as reality, which caused her additional suffering. Far better to acknowledge custom and be at peace.

She smiled at him. "I'm glad you don't mind my coming here unannounced."

"I stay here by your generosity."

"The generosity is yours. I don't know how I'd manage without you."

He mimed a shallow bow but in truth her expression, as well as her presence, alarmed him. "We need to find that girl. Valeria. Bibi didn't tell me where he took her even after—encouragement."

"You didn't hurt him, did you?"

Sahir hesitated. "I did what we discussed and cleared the house of drugs."

"Thank you. I never did have the stomach to discipline him."

"He'll find withdrawal unpleasant, but he'll be better off in the long run." Unpleasant enough that Bibi would be desperate for whatever Sahir gave him. Regaining control was viscerally satisfying, and he already had plans for expanding the operation, perhaps giving Raven more responsibility. There was, however, that one wrinkle still to be smoothed.

"We have to find Valeria. She's never at her apartment."

Ruth answered carelessly. "Perhaps she's left Denver. That would be good, wouldn't it?"

"It's an exposure, if the police find her. What if she talks out of spite? How do you know Ken isn't talking?"

"You look so tired," Ruth said. "Have a drink with me. I don't want to talk about my filthy husband and work can wait until morning."

Much too belatedly, Sahir noticed an ice bucket she must have brought, a bottle of champagne, two glasses.

"You know I don't drink," he said. "And I have to wake Bibi for Fajr."

"Prayers can be caught up and this is a special occasion. I dressed for you, I'm wearing your favorite blouse."

It wasn't. Sheer and off-white, the shirt was far too revealing, not that he'd ever correct her.

"Won't you open this?" She held up the wine, jewels on her hand and arm catching fire even in the dim light. No electricity in the shed but he had dozens of candles, some battery-operated, some real.

When Sahir didn't move, she set down the bottle and walked to him. Took each of his hands and kissed them in turn. Then the inside of his wrists.

She stared up at him. "We've waited for so long."

Then she leaned up and in to nuzzle his neck, along his jaw, to the corner of his mouth.

Instinctively, Sahir pulled away.

Her eyes widened with surprise. "What's wrong?"

"If I have behaved inappropriately, or misled you in any way, I most humbly apologize. Any confusion is mine alone. We've been in America too long, it's corrupted us."

"There's no confusion. I desire you. And I know you feel the same."

"No." Sahir said it much more emphatically than he meant to. She was only two years older, but he'd always looked up to her as a senior member of an elite family, utterly out of reach.

"Are you telling me what I feel? Or, are you claiming we both haven't been denying ourselves forever? Or, perhaps you don't find me attractive?" A trace of amusement as she said that, as if she knew it couldn't possibly be true.

"You are the most exquisite creature I've ever seen."

Sahir took a step back but she closed the gap. Put her palm flat on his cheek and raised up on her toes to try to kiss him again. "Not a creature. A flesh and blood woman."

It was pure instinct to back away again. Like a perverse dance.

"*Joonam,* we can't."

"Tell me one reason why."

There were a hundred reasons, going back generations. He worked for her family, his ancestors before him. They weren't equals. She was married. Did he really have to explain all of this to her?

Ruth took his silence for conquest. Moved to his bed and eyed him flirtatiously over her shoulder like a girl— like a spa girl. Began unbuttoning her blouse.

"Would you rather make love here?" She nodded toward the bed and smiled. "Or come inside and sleep upstairs in the master bedroom? Although, I can understand you'd prefer not to be surrounded by Ken's things."

Another button. He could see a flash of lace bra. Couldn't believe it, wouldn't believe it. "Stop, I beg you."

"What?" Shock replaced sultriness. Her hand froze on the next button.

"It's impossible." Sahir's voice was rough. "And you know it."

"I know you want me."

"I would never insult you." Sahir felt affection, devotion, nothing as common as desire.

"But, you kiss me." For the first time, Ruth sounded uncertain.

"Like a sister."

"Those are not chaste kisses."

"Again, I apologize. I meant only to show gratitude and respect."

"Respect?"

He ruined innocent young girls by the dozen, sold sex to men who were weak; he'd never be one of them. "You are far above me, in every way, and I could never sully you with animal behavior."

"Why not?" Her words became an urgent rush. "We're stronger together, I realize that now. Look how well we run the business. I made a mistake staying with Ken but it's not too late. We can fix everything. We can be happy."

Why now? What had changed? And was she talking divorce? Sharia law gave men the right to divorce at will, not women, and Ken would never agree. "Please. I don't want you to cause yourself future embarrassment."

"Do I repulse you because of—because of—" Her voice faded. "Being with other men."

"There are reasons you married Ken. I've always understood that."

"I understand he's a pig."

"He's of the same class and that's worth something."

"If that's what class does for me I don't want it."

"You don't mean that." Sahir struggled for words. "You're upset. Tell me what's happened and we'll work through it together."

"You have made it quite clear you don't want to be *together*."

"We'll forget this ever happened."

She flinched, like she'd been struck. "I don't want to forget."

"Dearest, what can I do to fix this? Tell me."

"Can you rewrite history so that no man's hands but yours have ever touched me? Then maybe you wouldn't find me loathsome."

"Far—joon—Ruth—" He sputtered. Words failed. He would fall on the floor at her feet. But never touch her, never use her like those men at the spa, like the other men in her life. Sleeping with her would be like pissing on a relic.

"Not history," Ruth said. "That was foolish. But we could have written the future."

"You're not foolish."

"I am cursed." Her voice was dark with tears. "Never to

be loved."

"That's not true. I love you with every fiber."

"Not as a woman."

She was crying. He'd made her cry. He'd rather stab himself in the heart. "It's unbearable to hurt you. Please, let's talk this through."

"No." Her tears flowed more freely than he'd ever seen. "I would not wish to risk either of us further embarrassment."

And then she was gone, candles flickering in her wake, in the breeze through the door she left open, her footfalls on the gravel path quickly retreating.

Run after her. Take her in your arms, kiss her like a lover. Sahir stood rooted like the trees that rustled all around the cottage. Too many years of tradition, ritual, discipline. Faith. To have denied himself for so long only to give in now was to have denied himself for nothing.

CHAPTER FORTY-ONE

A DRENALINE HANGOVERS WERE almost worse than the real thing. Jack sat with Mike at a restaurant near headquarters grabbing a quick, late dinner, and he recognized the sudden deflation, a slight disorientation, the feeling he could sleep for days.

"What a repulsive piece of shit."

Mike took a swig of beer. "Yeah, you mentioned that several times. We'll find those other girls."

"If they're alive."

"You don't know enough yet to come to that conclusion."

"You saw the same videos that I did."

"We don't have bodies," Mike said. "We don't have evidence of a crime, we don't even have missing persons reports. Where would we start?"

Mike somehow managed to distance himself emotionally, at least until they had more reality to work with. Jack needed to learn that trick.

"I was so close to getting him to confess. The way he reacted when I showed him those photos."

"Man, you're hard on yourself. You got him to admit he was escaping, caught him in more lies than I can count. And speaking of reactions, he was physically violent on camera when you presented the fact Lucia slept with Dustin—show that to a jury."

Jack's phone buzzed, alerting him to a voicemail. It was

from his neighbor, Ginger, asking him to stop by when he got home, no matter how late it was. Horrible timing but it was unlike Ginger to be dramatic, she must really need something.

He fought off a wave of exhaustion and sat forward. "It's interesting to me how all Ken cared about was where I got the videos. Didn't deny their meaning only wanted to know how I came to have them."

"Probably not significant."

"It's like—" Jack tapped his index finger against the neck of his beer bottle and stared into space. "He seemed to honestly be counting on Ruth. Why would he think she'd help him after the porn and all those girls?"

"Nothing honest about that sack of shit. Ken's going where he belongs."

Jack shared Mike's satisfaction that they'd been able to charge the self-important prick, although Dustin's involvement still nagged. Ken's multiple contradictions—cavalier attitude about Lucia's pregnancy, certainty it wasn't his, intense rage the baby was Dustin's—were a detective's dream. Sexual assault on a child, flight risk, public safety, false imprisonment—the list went on and on and on. Just not murder. Not yet.

Now that Ken had been charged the sense of urgency eased although Jack still had a case to build—possibly multiple cases—of first-degree murder. Or, in Ken's vernacular, one-way tickets to paradise.

Jack had done his photo op, straightened his tie, combed his hair and stood next to Dani and the Chief as they assured the citizenry they could rest easy now that Muslim Enemy Number One was behind bars. Protestors outside headquarters had seemed deflated by the police efficiency and the fact that they hadn't killed anyone in the process. Not that he was cynical or anything.

Mike cut through his brooding. "I found Raven online if you're interested."

"Yeah?" Jack started on his burger, with caramelized onions and blue cheese, and realized he was starving.

"Appears she was trafficked." Mike licked barbecue sauce off his fingers and brought up a website on his phone.

Jack leaned in to see the screen. "That's her all right."

Raven had a promoted ad, although Jack was pretty sure the breasts in the photo weren't hers. Or anyone human's.

"It's one of the sites that replaced *Backpage*," Mike said. "As far as we can tell the server for this one is somewhere in Asia."

Backpage at least used to be one stop shopping for trafficking victims. The backpage.com domain was operated by a company in Texas who cooperated with law enforcement. Shutting them down had only made criminals more creative.

Like a squalid hydra, the demise of one website gave birth to hundreds, and the online "adult entertainment" marketplace was a dizzying carnival of sexual hyperbole. Dollar signs, diamonds, hearts and promised expansive cup sizes: ♥DDDDD!♥ All age ranges from college students to a former NFL cheerleader to someone calling herself a "southern cougar." Awesome stuff like poinsettia oriental massage (which had nothing to do with Christmas), NURU (which was allegedly an urban myth), and showers unrelated to personal hygiene.

Everyone was new in town: fun, sexy, caring, sweet, and compassionate. In calls, outcalls, whatever you desired. In the mood for Chinese? Italian? Boriqua? No discrimination here. Unforgettable relaxation and pain relief. Plush bottoms, busty nurses, and what the hell was pine therapy?

"Jeez." Jack took another swig of beer. "I feel sheltered in homicide."

"Hopefully Raven's still in Denver and Lucia's murder didn't make her bolt."

"Or her keepers."

Mike held up his empty bottle and caught the server's attention. "Want another one?"

Jack stifled a yawn. "Can't. My neighbor has a crisis and I need to go check on her."

"The older lady?"

"Yeah. Asked me to stop by even if it was late."

"Good to be needed."

Jack laughed and reached for his wallet. "I could do with less in demand and more sleep."

He rapped on the old metal storm door thinking how out of character this request was for Ginger, who was usually practical and straightforward. Jack had believed it a perk of old age to be beyond drama, and he was expecting he'd have to break the door down and find her unconscious on the floor with a broken hip or something. Instead, she answered promptly, dressed in an unfussy sweatshirt and jeans, wide awake and seemingly healthy.

She led him to the kitchen with no preparation whatsoever.

"Hi, Jack."

"Hello, Corie."

For the second time that day Jack was ambushed. At least this time he wasn't holding a steaming-hot beverage. He noticed she was still wearing the same turquoise sweater from earlier.

"You're here alone?" Maybe it was because he was tired. Jack wanted to take the petty words back as soon as he spoke.

Ginger got him a glass and poured from a bottle of red. It was disconcerting to discover his neighbor was capable of subterfuge.

Corie, as usual, had a glass of white. "How are you?"

"Tired."

"Sit," Ginger said.

"I'm good." *Okay, time to stop the sulky teenager routine.*

"How long have you been in Denver?"

"I flew in the day before yesterday," Corie said. "A red eye to LA from Lihue."

That was the airport on Kauai which Jack knew from his obsessive use of Google maps.

"Those overnight flights are exhausting," Ginger said.

Corie visibly relaxed at her attempt at small talk. "Got into LAX so early Starbucks wasn't even open."

"Did the snow delay your flight?" Ginger asked.

"Not too bad."

Jack gave in to sarcasm, driven by hurt and confusion. "Air travel is *so* stressful these days. Hope they didn't lose your bags. And how 'bout them Broncos?"

"Jack."

Ginger's tone said, *take a breath, go easy.* He raised his hands in surrender, still trying to catch up with whatever the hell this was.

Ginger's expression could charitably be described as amused. "Sometimes it's best to chip away at the ice instead of diving in headfirst and breaking your neck."

Jack exhaled. "How long are you back for?" *And who's the dude you were having coffee with?*

"I'm not exactly back," Corie said.

"Okay." *Not back.* What did that mean?

"I had some legal stuff to deal with. I'm only here for a few days."

A few days plus the day before yesterday meant she was leaving tomorrow. Why a drive by? Why see him at all? He had to assume Corie was behind Ginger's strange, urgent request. Why couldn't she ask him directly?

Ginger still played perky mediator. "I'm delighted to see you and I'm sure he is, too."

Jack held Corie's blue gaze and remembered the several thousand reunion scenarios he'd fantasized. Not one of them involved a tense, artificial standoff at his eighty-year-old neighbor's kitchen table.

"Can I give you a hug?" He was sure she'd say no but she surprised him by standing and walking into his arms. It had to be enough to simply hold her and bury his face in her hair. After a few seconds he felt her relax in his embrace.

"I couldn't come to Denver and not see you," Corie said.

Me and coffee date guy. Jack willed his inner dialogue to stop. He decided she'd never, ever know about coffeegeddon.

"I'm sorry if I put you in the middle of something awkward," Corie said to Ginger.

"Pfft." Ginger waved a hand. "If your friends can't make a scene in your kitchen who can?"

Jack had no idea what the plan was. Corie stopped by for a glass of wine and to say hey? How exactly did that work? They weren't buds. They were in love, or at least he was. Were they going to try and resume their relationship or was it over? Anything other than yes, full stop, was a no.

He said, "Your hair's growing back." And took a hefty swallow of wine.

She reached up and ruffled it with her fingers. "For the first time in my life I'm low maintenance. Swim in the ocean, rinse off and let it do its thing. I might keep it short."

Corie used to have long, lush strawberry-blonde hair. In a fit of despair, shortly before she was injured, she'd cut it all off. Short hair, long hair, didn't matter; she'd be beautiful to him bald.

"How are you doing?" Corie asked.

"I'm all right," Jack said.

"I mean, with the—have you had any recurrences?"

Last year Jack had survived a bout of testicular cancer—the word everyone tiptoed around. He'd undergone surgery and radiation that made him insanely sick but had been clean so far in his follow up scans. Still, it was in the background waiting, like a loan that was going to come due. Plus, it wasn't like he'd been taking the most stellar care of himself the last couple of months. Jack realized at that moment how much he blamed Corie for that.

"All good so far with the cancer. How about you? How's the work going with the therapist?"

She'd gone to Hawaii to work with a counselor who specialized in PTSD. Jack knew Corie had suffered her share of trauma, although, in his worst moments, he couldn't help but think there had to be a qualified therapist less than three thousand miles away.

"It's going well, I think, although it's hard to quantify. There's no linear progression. I feel like I figure some things out and then take twenty steps backward." Corie reached for her glass. "I think it was a good decision to go someplace different, the change of perspective was healthy. And I can access my emotions with the therapist, so that's something."

"She sounds like she knows her stuff," Ginger said.

She meant well, and Jack adored her, but Ginger added an extra layer of awkwardness on top of what was already a difficult situation. Understatement.

"Hey, can we continue this next door? I'm beat and I'm sure Ginger's tired, too."

"Going to your house might not be the best idea." But Corie's smile told him she was considering it.

"I'd just like to change out of this suit and be able to relax. I have wine there, too."

"What do you think?" Corie asked Ginger.

"I think you're in good hands. And I'm right next door if he tries anything fresh."

Corie laughed and Jack chose to follow Ginger's lead and keep it light. "And don't let her diminutive size or age fool you. She could take me."

CHAPTER FORTY-TWO

———◆———

JACK WAS TRUE to his word. He changed into jeans and a T-shirt, did not throw Corie over his shoulder, carry her into the bedroom, and rip her clothes off. Noble, that was him. Instead, he opened a bottle of her favorite Chardonnay and they sat on the couch in his living room.

Corie asked again about his cancer.

"Everything was clear at my follow-up. Like I told you, there's nothing to report which is good. It's something I'll always have to think about, but for now you don't have to worry about me."

"Can I do it anyway?"

Jack held her gaze for a long moment. "As long as I can return the favor."

Corie broke eye contact and shrugged. "My recovery is taking longer than I would like but I'm getting there. And, Jack, I—"

She hesitated and he had a sixth sense what she was going to say. He was about to get the answer he thought he needed and suddenly wanted nothing more than to be lied to. He saw it was hard for her, that she wasn't casual or careless, and he also knew that much, if not all, of their shared past had meant suffering for her. That wasn't entirely his fault but it wasn't something he couldn't fix, either.

"You know you can say anything to me. I'm—" What

was he exactly? "I'm smart enough to recognize a happy ending's not on the table."

Corie got up off the couch and paced for a minute and then her words poured out in a rush. "I could sleep with you but it won't mean what you want it to mean. I didn't ghost because I don't want you sitting here in some agony of confusion. You want the truth, isn't that what you always say? The truth is I can't be what you want me to be, and I can't promise you anything, and I'm sick of other people writing their life story at my expense."

"I'm beginning to think the truth is overrated," Jack said.

"That isn't what I practiced in my head."

"Funny how that works." Corie wasn't the same girl he'd fallen in love with and he wasn't the same stupid eighteen-year-old boy. There was no way back to those people even if he wanted. "I hate the way people in your life have used you. I hope I haven't been one of them."

"You haven't. Ever." She rejoined him on the couch, one leg curled underneath her.

"I hope you're not saying that to make me feel better."

"Does it seem like anything I've said has been to make you feel better?"

Jack laughed, couldn't help it, and after a surprised second Corie joined in.

Then she spoke with renewed determination. "Everything that happened to me, you think you know what it was like, but you don't. I hope you never have to know. I wish no one did. I was thinking after all of this I might do something like be a victim's advocate."

"You'd be great at it." Jack's chest felt tight.

A small smile lit her eyes. "And, damn it, I'm still attracted to you. It's all mixed up in my head, in my psyche the therapist says. PTSD is tricky. That's a therapeutic term, 'tricky.' God, I'm not explaining this well and I really want to."

"You don't have to—"

"No, let me finish." She squared herself so she faced him directly. "There was a desire, at least on my part, to have a reboot, be seventeen again and brand new, as if all the other crap never existed. But that other crap did happen and it changed me whether I want that to be true or not. Sorry."

She swiped at her cheek and Jack's throat ached with his own uncried tears. He wanted to say, *"I saved you, doesn't that count for anything?"*

Corie continued. "I don't blame you. Or myself. I did the best I could, bad mother, father who left, blah, blah, blah. I'm working on it. The thing is and this is a good thing— now we have new chances. We're both still here, we're both still alive and trust me, I don't say that ironically anymore."

She reached for his hand. "I have to move forward and I want you to as well."

There it was. His truth. Her hand felt small and light in his and the metal band squeezing his chest let go. "I don't like giving up."

"No kidding. That's why you're good at what you do. But I have a feeling it hurts you."

He wanted to ask what the rules were going forward, because that's the way Jack's brain worked, but knew it wasn't a fair or necessary question.

"I should go," Corie said.

"Do you want to go?"

"No." Her voice had a desperate note. "That's the problem."

The problem was that she was too damned pretty, felt too good, smelled too good. That he couldn't have her this close and not kiss her. Despite everything. Knowing it was over, maybe because it was over.

She started to say, "Don't," but her body said something completely different. She leaned into him, her breath stuttered, her hand moved to his shoulder and then the back of his neck. He was greedier than he intended but she met him need for need, kissed him back, pulled even closer.

He made himself stop for a second to check in with her and immediately wished he hadn't.

"Jack, I'm not back. I'm not staying. It doesn't mean anything."

"Noted."

———————◆———————

He knew he was saying goodbye. With his mouth, with his hands, touching every inch of that beautiful, wounded body. He wanted to give pleasure, to make her forget pain if only for a few minutes. He undressed her slowly, the sweater first, his lips following the scar down her neck to the center of her chest. Injury number one, traumatic collapsed lung. It had been emergency surgery and they hadn't been especially careful. Corie told him once she didn't want to see a plastic surgeon, or make the scars disappear, because she'd earned them, like medals.

Jeans next, and Corie gasped as his lips traced the inside of her thigh, but he wasn't going to release her that fast. This wasn't the time to rush, or pounce, or be greedy. It was time to spin pleasure like strands of glass, stretch it to the breaking point; Jack wouldn't give in to impatience or desperation.

He kissed his way down both legs, to the shattered ankle, his heart breaking more, if that was possible, at the fresh scars, at the insults her body had endured. To the scar near her abdomen, from the bullet that nicked her liver. Wished he could fix all of it, make her whole again by sheer force of will.

His lips traced her shoulder, her collarbone, then he finally let himself crush her mouth, the way he'd fantasized. When he reached underneath her to unhook her bra, Corie arched her back and tried to help, but he held her slim wrist. "No. I'm not gonna hurry."

Her breath grew ragged and he lost himself in the taste of her. Felt her fingers in his hair, on his back, under his T-shirt. Struggled out of the rest, still fighting the urge to go too fast. Pushed thoughts of *last time* from his mind because he wouldn't succumb to self-pity. He couldn't see the visible reference points for her physical suffering and think about himself. He wanted her, but mostly he wanted to heal her.

She was so eager for him that lust and sensation threatened to obliterate any remaining shred of reserve. He stared into those blue eyes, almost to ground himself, and she touched his face. He lowered himself again, his lips moving on hers, her breasts against his chest, skin on skin. Explored those breasts properly with his tongue, pinched nipples to the edge of torment and followed with his mouth.

"Jack." He felt her hands on his shoulders.

"Am I hurting you?"

"No, you're torturing me."

"Yeah?" He smiled against her neck, nuzzled her, went in for another languorous kiss.

There was one item of clothing left and even then he took his time, ran a finger under the elastic, grazed the outside of the silky fabric, tempting, teasing.

"Jack. Oh, God." On a sob, high, breathless, urgent. "Please."

Then all the clothes were gone and he released her, finished his exploration, let his mouth visit the last place. She cried his name again and again, an endearment, a plea, a shout of satisfaction. He decided his name from her was the most amazing sound in the world, her voice molten like her body.

He had a fleeting thought of how perfect it felt, hard against soft, solid against liquid, and then everything changed from light, patient, exquisite to demanding, muscular, shattering, and there was no pain, no caution, no regret. Only Corie.

CHAPTER FORTY-THREE

———

SAHIR WAITED FOR a break in the vomiting. Arabic wailed from his phone.

"Please," Bibi collapsed onto the rim of the toilet, his prayer that this misery would end.

"Wash yourself." Sahir pulled him to his feet as if he weighed nothing and supervised the ritual cleansing. Stripped Bibi of everything.

His stomach hurt and his throat burned from the acid. His knees sank in the carpet and only Sahir's sharp hands kept him from collapsing.

"Don't hear you," Sahir said.

Words came of their own volition from deep in Bibi's memory. Genuflect. Stand. Kneel again. It was still dark and he struggled to remember which *salah* this was. Dawn. *Fajr.*

"Why are you doing this?"

"I'm done talking." Sahir blocked the door, knife in hand, and watched while Bibi picked up the room. Replaced drawers, put clothes back on hangers, even had to fix the curtain rod. He wept openly, not caring anymore, only wanting it over with.

"If you're gonna kill me just do it."

"I'll be back when it's time to go to work," Sahir said.

The key turned. Bibi was alone again.

CHAPTER FORTY-FOUR

JACK DIDN'T THINK he'd be able to sleep afterward, but he did, through his phone's super obnoxious ring tone, and through his alarm, which Corie must have turned off. Sunlight sliced the edges of the blackout shade and she was gone from the bed. Jack panicked, not about work, but because he was afraid she was gone.

On his phone he saw calls and texts from Mike, his Lieutenant, and a number he knew was homicide but all he focused on was finding Corie. He couldn't oversleep, not on the last morning, not the last time he'd maybe ever see her.

She came out of the bathroom like a vision, dressed in the now-familiar turquoise sweater, and Jack was so relieved he roughly pulled her into an embrace. "Thank God."

"Your phone's been going crazy. I didn't know what to do."

"I have to jump in the shower. Are you gonna—" He forced himself to say the words. "Will you still be here when I get out?"

"I'll make coffee. Something tells me you have a lot to do."

How was it almost nine? Jack stood under a shower as hot as he could stand, shaved too fast, and cut himself twice.

He pulled on a light blue dress shirt, buttoned it wrong, started over, yanked dry cleaning plastic off of a gray suit, and draped a tie around his neck to be knotted later. On his way out of the bedroom he mindlessly grabbed items off his dresser—a pen, coins, his wallet—and checked on the shaving wounds. Bits of tissue stuck to your face, always a good authoritative look.

His mind raced, fabricating excuses. *I took personal time, didn't that get communicated?* He couldn't be getting called out again, this was crazy; like a coward he messaged Dani and she dialed him back immediately.

"Where have you been?"

He mumbled something about an hour of personal time not seeming excessive after working forty-eight hours straight but whoever made up that saying about the best offensive hadn't ever worked for his Lieutenant. Jack held the phone away from his ear while Dani vented.

One of the texts he'd received was an address on Colfax and he read it back to her, hoping he was guessing correctly that was where he was supposed to be. "I'll be on scene in twenty."

"Keep me posted." She disconnected.

Damn it. Jack hated being caught off guard and even more than that, not getting five minutes to spend with Corie. He wasn't on call. This shouldn't be happening.

In the kitchen, she handed him a travel mug of coffee. Tried and failed not to laugh.

"I have to—" He shrugged with helpless apology, phone in one hand, coffee in the other. "This isn't how I wanted the morning to go."

She touched a wad of tissue still stuck to his jaw. "You're not gonna need stitches or anything are you?"

"Ugh. I was hoping to have time to talk to you, maybe have breakfast." He listened to a different message from Mike, all growly and pissed. Another dead girl, same tattoo as Lucia. ME on the way. Nicki in the hospital after an assault.

Corie noticed his expression change. "That looks serious."

Shit. Jack clipped the phone onto his belt. Another girl? When? And what the hell happened to Nicki? "What time are you leaving? Can I drive you to the airport?"

"Nope, it's covered. Go to work, that's the best thing you can do."

Whether or not that was true it's what he always did. "I don't want to say a hurried goodbye running out the door."

"You already said goodbye, quite nicely, I might add." She smiled up at him through her lashes. "Besides, I think it's better this way. You don't have time to agonize or obsess."

No, he'd do that at leisure later on. "I want to make sure you know that I get it. No guilt or obligation coming from me, okay?"

Before she answered someone pounded on the door. Police pounding—loud, fast, insistent.

"Oh good, you're alive." Mike stood on Jack's doorstep. His sunglasses made it impossible to fully read his expression but his wide-legged stance and posture telegraphed self-righteous outrage.

No way Jack would grovel. "I'm almost ready to leave."

From behind him Corie said, "Hi, Mike."

"Corie." Mike was civil but didn't step inside and didn't remove the shades. "How are you?"

"Fine, thanks. You?"

"Same. How long are you in town for?"

"I'm flying back to Hawaii tonight, actually."

The tension shimmering around Mike like an aura was so radioactive it could have cooked food.

"Mike, listen—"

"Jack, it's okay," Corie interrupted. "Do what you need to do."

He hadn't done anything wrong and Mike was being an asshole. "Give me one minute."

"Thirty seconds." Mike spoke like he was the cop and Jack was some drunk he'd picked up staggering in the street. "In the car or I'm leaving without you."

"Fuck you." Jack muttered under his breath as he slammed the door on Mike's stiff, retreating back.

With a resigned sigh, turned to Corie. "Apparently the world *has* fallen apart again."

The corners of her mouth twitched. "Well, then you *must* go and put it back together."

"Yeah, right. Can you do me a favor and make another to-go cup? Probably won't do any good but best not to approach Mike empty-handed."

Then he forced himself to take a breath and make sure he had everything he needed for what was shaping up to be another long day. Checked his gun, that he had an extra magazine, his phone, his notebook. That he was wearing pants. Everything was a blur when he wanted to freeze time.

Although. If last night was for being tortured—in both unpleasant and fun ways—this sunny, confused morning felt about the future. Albeit a future hurtling toward him much more rudely and insistently than he would have chosen. But maybe Corie was right. It was a rip-the-Band-Aid-off situation, no belabored goodbyes, no time for second-guessing.

He finished with his tie using the mirror next to the front door as Corie came back with coffee. One more thing he needed to do.

"Put that down for a second." Jack reached for her purposefully, felt the ribbed texture of the sweater, noted the ivory curve of her cheekbones, the deep pink of her lips, those amazing cobalt blue eyes. He kissed her like he had all the time in the world, no one waiting, no place he had to be, nothing he'd rather do.

When he let her go she was slightly breathless. "I'm pretty sure that was more than a second."

"If you ever need anything, anytime, doesn't matter what, you know where to find me."

She returned his smile. "You'll be right here, saving the world."

CHAPTER FORTY-FIVE

IT HAD TO have been a joke. Everyone always messed with Heather and she always fell for it. Dustin said it was cute how gullible she was. A tropical island. Was he kidding? Or a ski slope. He'd buy a plane and learn to fly it. Or they'd live on a boat, home school, sail around the world. Running made him silly happy, like one of the kids on a snow day. But they weren't really leaving Denver, were they?

Heather woke up that morning convinced it had all been a dream but before he left to go to work at church Dustin reminded her. The kids already had what they needed, he said; just pack two bags for themselves. Carry-ons. Travel light because they'd buy whatever they needed when they got there. Wherever there was.

With the kids gone, the house was way too quiet. Heather had nothing to do and everything to do. If they were really leaving. Summer clothes? Winter clothes? Fancy? Casual? What about her photo albums? Their TV? Her wedding dress? She didn't want to leave everything behind. She didn't want to join the witness protection program, change her name, never see family or friends again.

Frozen with indecision, she found herself on the couch watching TV, binging on cookies and diet soda. Breaking one of the biggest rules she'd walked to the convenience store on the corner and bought cigarettes. Who cared if she smoked in the house if they were leaving it? Dustin'd be pissed when he came home but Heather couldn't make herself care.

They had one of those video doorbells and, when it chimed, Heather saw an unfamiliar Black woman on the porch, nicely dressed, probably a Jehovah's Witness or something. Heather figured she'd pretend no one was home, but the woman kept pushing the button as if she knew. Maybe she heard the TV.

Pissed at the woman's pushiness, Heather yanked open the door and the words were out of her mouth before she noticed. "Look, you need to go away and quit ringing our doorbell before I call the police."

The woman was holding up a badge. "Heather Rattenberry?"

"I can't talk to you."

Heather started to close the door and the cop talked fast.

"Don't you want to know about your husband and Lucia?"

She gripped the edge of the door; didn't slam it, should have slammed it.

"You probably already know because a wife always senses these things intuitively." The cop removed her shades. "I'm Serena."

"I don't mean to be rude, but I don't care who you are."

"When did you find out Lucia was pregnant?"

"What?"

"We know it was Dustin's." The cop had soft brown eyes and a line formed between them as she frowned with sympathy. "Oh, I'm sorry, I can see you didn't know. I shouldn't have come right out with it like that."

Heather flashed to last night, down on her knees in front of Dustin but not for prayer. All his excited talk about sailing and flying and kickin' back on a beach.

She'd flat-out begged him to tell her the truth, made it as

easy for him as possible. Claimed she already knew. What was wrong with him? When exactly was he going to tell her? When Lucia had the brat? Heather remembered his line about Lucia demanding a "cut," the next line about Lucia spying for him, his tearful bullshit about getting her killed. How many lies could Dustin manufacture? It seemed there was no limit and Heather wondered if he'd ever been truthful.

Damn him. *God* damn him. Lord's name in vain and everything. Everyone deceived her including her so-called bestie Nicki, who'd assured Heather over and over that she could trust Dustin. Sahir was right; Nicki was a whore, like Lucia. Heather realized she was crying in front of the cop.

"I can see you're really upset." Serena's voice was soft, soothing. "There's nothing worse than being lied to by people you love."

"You're still a fucking cop." Which meant she couldn't be nice and she wasn't Heather's friend.

"It's not right that he didn't tell you, not at all. For a minister to act like that is especially wrong. I'll leave you be, you probably don't want to know all the rest of the details about him and Lucia anyway."

Like hell she didn't. Heather wanted to know every-fucking-thing and then she wanted to bury Dustin, would turn the key in the lock on his cell herself.

"No, wait." Heather opened the security door. "Come on in."

CHAPTER FORTY-SIX

IN THE CAR, Mike said, "Have fun with your neighbor's emergency?"

"For as tight as it is, you manage to talk out of your ass a lot." Jack took a sip of the coffee Corie had made, refused to either be intimidated or rushed out of his bliss. "When exactly did you get this righteous?"

"When did you become the kind of detective who turns off his phone and makes excuses?"

That one stung but Jack hadn't purposely blown off a direct responsibility. He hadn't known there was anything *to* blow off.

"Are you going to act like an officer or a girl I stood up?"

Mike gave the scantest of summaries. "Twenty-one-year-old female, Caucasian, found dead at oh-eight-hundred this morning."

"Message said she appears to have the same tat as Lucia."

"Affirmative."

"We have an ID?"

"Scalamandre caught it. Found some items in the motel room that were suspicious."

That wasn't terribly informative. "You plan to brief me or are we gonna play twenty questions?"

Mike clenched the steering wheel with both hands and stared straight ahead. "That depends."

On what? Jack promising to lay off Corie for life?

Holding up his hand and swearing eternal fealty to the DPD? Opening a vein to demonstrate his blood ran blue? "This victim have a name?"

"We found her ID."

Jack remembered the interview with Ken and, in a blind attempt at bursting Mike's smug superiority, threw out a name. "I don't know what your problem is but since you apparently want me to beg you for information I'm going to go out a limb and guess her name's Valeria."

Mike hesitated so long Jack prompted, his voice a snarl. "What?"

"Nothing."

"I'm right, aren't I? Bibi's girlfriend, the waitress."

"You don't have to look quite so proud of yourself."

Jack wasn't aware he looked any particular way at all. "When was she killed?"

"Don't know."

"How?"

"Undetermined."

"Ken implied she worked at Bibi'z. I'm assuming someone's confirmed that?"

"You're back amongst the living." Mike spoke as if amazed and then added, sheepishly, "Not yet."

"And here I thought you'd had this *long* productive morning. Corie and I got a lot resolved, actually, thanks for asking."

"Now who sounds like a girl?" But Mike's features relaxed from chiseled granite to something resembling human again. "Does that mean no more walking dead impersonations from you?"

"Good night's sleep'll do wonders. You on the other hand, might want to drink more of that coffee. Corie made it for you special."

Mike picked up his travel cup and eyed it. "Didn't poison it, did she?"

"Corie has no beef with you. You know that, right?"

"She looked good."

Having done his own very thorough examination, Jack could attest to the fact that Corie was in great shape, physically. "Mentally and emotionally it's still a challenge for her."

"That's always the hard part."

"You're discussing this with me? Talk about miracles. This might sound weird but I needed to know she was all right. Not that it's any of your business, but I got my answer and I also got that she's doing what she needs to for herself and I need to let her. You satisfied?"

It was a second before Mike answered. "That doesn't sound weird. In fact, for you, it sounds surprisingly sane."

———◆———

Dr. Greer Spahr, the forensic pathologist who'd done Lucia's autopsy, took in all of the suits crowding the small motel room. "How many detectives does it take to view one little body?"

Mike said, "This victim is possibly connected to the Lucia Santiago homicide."

Dr. Spahr's retort was good-natured. "Nice of you to join by lunchtime. When I said little, I meant that literally. I'd be surprised if she weighs 110."

No one had tucked this girl in, arranged her, or washed her. She was on her back in the soiled bed, eyes and mouth open, what appeared to be dried vomit on her chin. Her hair was light brown, fine, and straight; definitely not the smiling selfie girl with Lucia at the club.

Paul Scalamandre was the detective from homicide who'd caught the new case. "Manager wanted the girl out of the room and when she didn't answer repeated knocks on the door, contacted us for disposal."

Only a partial joke about using the police as a body disposal service. The motel manager probably had a running tab in her head of lost revenue as each hour ticked by.

The real transport guys stood ready with their gurney outside the door on the cement catwalk that ran along the rooms on the second level and overlooked a small parking lot. To the west there was a dramatic panorama of the mountains. Cheap motel with a million-dollar view.

Dr. Spahr said, "Here's what you're apparently dying to see, detective."

Jack groaned at the uncharacteristic pun. "That's bad, especially for you."

Valeria's thin body rolled with minimal effort. Cracked mouth open in a death grimace. Bare midriff streaked with yellowish green, like someone drew on her with a highlighter; the beginning of decomp. Dr. Spahr gently moved the victim's matted brown hair to one side.

And there it was. Even with lividity the now-familiar swooping characters.

"I meant to ask you yesterday, what's the tat say?" Dr. Spahr asked.

"It means joy."

"Hasn't lately."

Paul was circling fifty with remnants of blonde hair and seemed to own an infinite variety of eyeglasses, all metallic, stylish, vaguely Germanic. He took the pair he was wearing off and examined them. "Found a small zipper bag on the floor. Don't know that it wasn't a straightforward OD."

"A second girl with the same tattoo as Lucia," Jack said. "In Arabic characters. Sure, that happens all the time in Denver."

"Plus the purses," Mike said.

With an aggrieved sigh, Paul showed Jack a small, scuffed purse with a chain for a handle. The chain was plastic, painted to look gold, and large chunks of color had peeled off. Inside, a small wallet with a kitten charm containing eleven dollars and a license for Valeria

Monsour. Her address was on East Evans and the young face in the ID photo was shiny and hopeful, penciled brows and a pointed chin. Awfully quick trajectory to the girl on the bed.

"Haven't had a chance to go to her residence yet," Paul said. "Or had any luck finding an emergency contact or relative."

Jack didn't envy Dr. Spahr or Paul the task of making notifications. Parents of girls like this had screamed at him, cursed him out, ordered him to never call again. They were preferable, almost, to the ones who wept, who begged for reassurance and answers.

Your daughter was an emaciated junkie and prostitute who begged for food and tricks. Based on the fact she still had a length of plastic tubing around her upper arm I'm pretty sure she didn't have time to suffer. A detective couldn't say that.

Valeria was petite but not clearly emaciated. No drug paraphernalia in the room other than the baggie, and no track marks on her arms, also confirmed by Dr. Spahr. Or, in pathologist-speak, no apparent scarring of the antecubital fossa, which Jack had learned was a fancy term for the inside of your elbow.

"And this one is why I dragged you away from your busy morning." Paul showed Jack a much nicer second purse, real leather, fringed, pink.

From her spot near the bed Dr. Spahr said, "Wow, Gucci. That's at least a grand."

Not to mention incongruous inside a cheap motel room reeking of stale vomit, the ammonia twang of anonymous sex, and emptied bowels.

"Found items inside related to your case." Paul's tone remained ironic. "You know, clues."

First item was a laminated Colorado ID card. Lucia's ID.

Second, Lucia's birth certificate.

Third, a sickeningly familiar Stoney Gate prayer card with neat block printing on the back. Along with verses,

Dustin's note was so graphic it almost made Jack blush. No wonder Lucia wanted to keep it in her possession.

"If Ken's motive was jealousy…" Mike left the thought unfinished.

The Good Book wasn't ordinarily used to torment homicide detectives, and if Jack had to go back over five hundred years for entertainment he'd personally prefer Shakespeare. Or at least any entity that didn't claim Dustin as a representative.

Jack explained the meaning of the card. "Dead owner of the upscale purse, Lucia, had a stack of these in her bedside drawer."

"I wonder if Valeria was also a graduate of Shores of Hope?" Mike asked.

"That name gets more nauseating every time I hear it," Jack said.

"If so," Mike said, "they certainly have a high mortality rate."

Who was stupid enough to give one girl another girl's handbag without looking inside and removing the previous owner's personal items? Jack could think of one individual right off the top of his head. "Bibi is a fucking moron."

Mike pulled a small tube from the nice purse. "Lipstick."

This was obviously the handbag Lucia used most, where she kept her most valuable documents—if you counted Dustin's play-by-play for their next rendezvous as important. She would have guarded it closely. How did Bibi—or someone—get it?

Answering that question threatened to unravel the last forty-eight hours of Jack's professional life, because what else was the Venn diagram between Lucia and Valeria? Jack might be jumping to a conclusion, but Bibi, by Ken's admission, was dating Valeria, and lived with Lucia. With a jolt Jack realized there was a hole in his timeline: How did Lucia get to the hotel if Ken was with Ruth at the benefit? He racked his brain trying to remember if he saw the purse in the Rose Terrace video of Lucia leaving Saturday night. Couldn't do it. He'd have to go look at it again.

Paul adjusted his glasses, seemingly not a care in the world. "My money's on an OD. What are your thoughts, Greer?"

"You know I can't give you anything definitive at the scene." She sounded justifiably annoyed, being put on the spot.

"The vics could have been friends." Paul shrugged. "One left her purse behind, so what? Besides, these kind of girls always look beat up."

Paul might be correct but his cavalier attitude was offensive as shit. "We keeping you from something important?" Jack asked. Then turned to Dr. Spahr. "Any idea how long she's been dead? Ballpark."

"Rigor's already recessed so at least twenty-four but possibly as long as two or three days. Drugs—maybe—slight build, temp, unknown health, a whole lot of factors."

"Lucia was probably still using that purse Saturday night."

"Well that explains why the manager's panties are in a knot." Paul continued in his same glib manner. "Imagine how much business they've lost in three days."

"Find Valeria's phone?" Jack bit off the words.

"It's as dead as she is. Gonna have to take it back and let the lab do its magic."

"Do you know when Valeria was last seen alive or if people have been in and out of this room in the last few days?"

Paul regarded Jack archly as if wondering if he'd had a recent frontal lobotomy. "You know as well as I do how these places work. No one keeps track of who comes in and out, and it's not like they have regular housekeeping."

"I'll talk to the manager myself, thanks."

"Good luck with that. She's a real charmer."

"Paul, next time they offer cynical asshole training at the Academy I'm gonna recommend you as an instructor."

Jack was gratified to hear Dr. Spahr laugh as he stalked out of the room.

He swore it was the same manager as when he was on patrol years ago, or her clone. Same fantasy pink hair extensions interspersed with fried blonde and jet-black roots. Same skimpy tank top and truck-tire roll of fat above slashed jeans and flip-flops. Tats, piercings, chipped blue nail polish, chipped front tooth. One manager of a sleazy motel, please, personal hygiene and dental integrity optional.

A TV mounted and chained to the wall blared a Spanish-language channel and she didn't bother to drag her heavily made-up eyes away so Jack found himself addressing his questions to an awkward stud hanging from her right nostril, the stone too large to be a real anything. She might have seen the dead girl before. Might not. Bitch was supposed to be out of the room Sunday morning. Were the cops gonna pay for their lost income?

Jack asked if the room had been paid for in cash, which elicited an eye roll. Valeria had paid and the manager hadn't asked where the girl got the money. Not her job getting up in other people's business. Speaking of—eyes glued to the screen as a dark-haired actor peeled off his shirt—they were really busy and needed that room.

"At least change the sheets first." Jack made the futile request and left his card on the greasy counter next to a bell and a post-it with winning lottery numbers. Mike helped with a canvas of despair, accosting folks who abruptly emerged from their comas and moved with surprising speed toward cars or rooms or the sidewalk at their first glimpse of them. If Jack ever wanted to feel completely undesirable all he had to do was show up in a suit at the Silver Saddle Motel.

No one heard anything, saw anything, or was inclined to say anything. No one knew Valeria. No one remembered who she entered the room with or if anyone entered the room or if there even was a room. It was all an existential bewilderment, a drunk in a wheelchair told them, who knew if they were really anywhere at all? Jack showed Ken's picture, Bibi's, Dustin's, even, on a crazy whim, Ruth's. Nos and don't knows, blank stares, twitchy stares, incoherent muttering, and a fair number of very distinct fuck yous. The usual.

Back at the curb, one of the forensic imaging guys wordlessly offered a canister of antibacterial wipes from his white crime scene van. Traffic whizzed by on Colfax. Motel doors opened and closed and heads popped out at random intervals like a junkie cuckoo clock.

Mike watched a homeless man pushing a shopping cart. "Any bets on how long before this place is scraped for million-dollar condos?"

"In hours or minutes?" Jack said.

"Can I have one of those wipes?" Paul joined them near the van. "Lots of good warrants here for sure."

"There are security cameras across the street." The forensic photography guy pointed to a convenience store on the corner to the west of the motel. "We'll get working on obtaining the footage, assuming they work."

"Mind if Mike and I go to Valeria's apartment and have a look around?" Jack asked.

Technically, they all played on the same team, but Paul's mouth pursed, distaste or cynicism, it was hard to tell. "You mean I have choice?"

CHAPTER FORTY-SEVEN

———◆———

"DUSTIN SAID WE had to live modestly to set a good Christian example." Heather laughed, self-conscious at her stupidity. "You should see the piece of shit minivan I drive, kids' pudding and vomit and God knows what else in there, but I can't get a new one because we can't have anything too showy."

She and Serena were having a bitch session like friends, Heather giving full vent to her anger and frustration once she stopped sobbing. They sat at the kitchen table and tissues littered the floor.

"He's got all sorts of money stashed and we live like we've got nothing."

"Where is the money?" Serena asked.

"Dunno." Dustin always told her to let him worry about things like that. "Some offshore something while I can't even hire a cleaning service and have to do everything myself."

Serena fixated on the cash. "Did he ever say what country? A bank name? Would you recognize it if you heard it?"

Heather shook her head, tugged at a piece of hair to cover her face. "He said earlier, though, he was working on passports."

"He did? When was that?"

"Um, last night? When he told me we had to leave."

When she begged him to tell her the truth. "He wants us all to run away with him, no questions asked, leave the kids' school, our friends. It's so unfair."

"Mm mm mm." Serena made sympathetic murmurs.

"He told me I was too dumb to recognize lies from truth, and I guess it's true 'cause I fell for his shit."

"You sure you don't know where any of the bank accounts are?" Serena asked.

"Noooo. I'm the one who's taken a vow of poverty."

"Okay. Where did all that money come from?"

"Forget that. Tell me again, about him and Lucia." Heather decided it was like poking at a loose tooth, pain she couldn't resist.

"When they did Lucia's autopsy the doctor said she was about two months along."

"Can you tell." Another poke at the painful spot. "Is it— was it a boy or a girl?"

"We don't know that." Serena patted Heather's arm. "Only that it had to be Dustin's because Ken can't have children."

That made a weird kind of sense. Ruth had never been knocked up, never even talked about the possibility.

And it hit her. Dustin was surrounded all the time by young girls who adored him. He was their hero, their savior, from countries where priests were important. Who'd wanna leave that to sit on a beach with his frumpy wife? Lies, lies, lies; no tropical island, no sailing on a boat—at least not with her. Heather wondered who Lucia's replacement was and if that's who he was really getting a passport for.

She hugged herself. "I don't know what to do."

"I think—"

Serena hesitated and Heather prompted. "What?"

"I hate to talk trash about a man of God."

"Oh, please do."

"You're right, it's not fair how he treats you. He trusts

you to keep his secrets, he makes you live on the cheap, then leaves you holding the bag. Why isn't he here? Most of all, why'd he step out?"

"What if Lucia wasn't the first?" Heather shivered. "Am I in a lot of trouble?"

"You didn't decide to traffic young girls."

"No, but—" Heather wondered if she should talk about her own past, if it would help or hurt.

Serena sat forward. "I'm not gonna bullshit you, you've had enough of that. I'm a detective and my job is to find out how many individuals Dustin sold, where they are, whether or not they're okay. You help me and I'll do everything I can to protect you. Don't let him get away with it, Heather. Don't let him take all that money and leave you stuck here taking the fall."

She stared into Serena's soft brown eyes. It felt good to have someone to talk to, even if it was a cop. "I don't want to lose my kids."

"I'll make sure you don't."

"What do you want from me?"

"Anything we can use to find the young women he's placed, especially anyone who worked for the Harrowsmiths before Lucia."

Thinking about her kids made Heather start crying again. She couldn't trust a cop. She couldn't lose her kids, either. Eventually, she stood and led Serena down the basement stairs, moved a rolling clothes rack out of the way, and crouched down to open a fireproof safe.

Inside was a spiral-bound notebook and several bundles of cash. Heather placed her hand flat on the book for a moment, then pulled it out and closed the safe door; she'd keep the money for herself.

Presented the notebook without explanation and watched as Serena read. Dustin had told her he wasn't worried about the search warrant the police were getting because he had no intention of showing them the real records. Lying sack of shit.

"In that first column," Heather pointed. "Those are their original names, except for some reason Lucia got to keep hers."

"These are all immigrant girls?"

"Yeah. Well, mostly. I don't know for sure." She hadn't been. "Maybe some of them just ran away."

Serena opened the notebook flat on top of the dryer. "Explain to me exactly what I'm looking at."

"So the system is that families—well, not always families, um, sometimes businesses—need someone, you know, to work for them and they pay like a finder's fee." Now that Heather said it out loud it sounded really sketchy. "Dustin told me it was like you'd pay an employment agency only since these girls couldn't do that, because they're illegal or runaways or something, and because he was taking a big risk, he got more."

"A lot more."

She and Dustin had added entries together, watched the list grow, their future materializing in front of them like magic. Heather rationalized it wasn't that bad, what the girls went through. Hell, she should know.

Serena pointed at an entry for a girl named Manuela that they'd placed—sold—for twenty large. "This is her birth name?"

"Uh-huh. Oh, I remember her, she was before Lucia. See the rebirth name in the next column? She became Abigail."

"Rebirth? Like born again?"

"More like, you're going to have a new life filled with hope. Ugh, I get it now." The name of the charity that she'd never figured out.

Heather tapped her index finger on the last column where "priv" was written. "See, that means an individual or a family, "com" is short for commercial or a business."

Proud of herself for remembering the word

"commercial."

"What kind of businesses?" Serena asked.

"All kinds, even a spa."

"Like for massages and stuff?"

"Uh-huh."

Serena persisted. "What else can you tell me about the spa? Do they do hot stone massage?"

Heather's face heated to a thousand degrees and she stared at the cracked cement floor. Suddenly, she didn't want Serena to know she used to do that.

"Where is your husband right now?"

"At the church." Heather pictured Dustin impressing a new girl with scripture, writing out a note card, smiling with those blue eyes. Her heart pounded with fear, anger, and because it was breaking.

Serena typed on her phone, oblivious. "Are your kids someplace safe?"

"Uh-huh. They're out of town, staying with relatives."

"I need you to come with me to police headquarters."

A jolt of panic. "Am I under arrest?"

"No, hon, of course not. I need your help figuring this out and it'll be easier to do at my office where I have my computer and stuff." Heather hesitated and Serena added, in that same soft, understanding voice. "Do you want him walking in on us?"

Had her husband fucked all of the girls in that book, like part of their job interview? She really didn't want to see him again, ever. And couldn't imagine not seeing him. "I don't want to have to deal with that cute cop Nicki's screwing."

"What are you talking about?"

"He's tall, dark hair."

Serena frowned. "You mean Jack?"

"Whatever. I won't talk to him."

"I have one more question, although it's kind of weird." Serena touched the back of her own neck. "Do you have a tattoo right here? Like foreign characters?"

"Why would that matter?"

"Trust me, it's important."

Dustin made Heather wear her hair down. Not because he was ashamed, exactly, he just didn't like tats in general and the one on her neck meant bad memories.

Feeling trapped and hopeless, Heather turned and held up her hair.

CHAPTER FORTY-EIGHT

———

VALERIA'S APARTMENT BUILDING was two stories, sided with dingy, formerly-yellow, cracked stucco, and windows on the top floor barely visible inside a steep, shingled mansard roof. Some architect back in the day must have thought they were stylish but Jack had been inside enough of these old dumps to know those deeply recessed windows meant the interiors were dark and moldy.

"This place." He shuddered. "Her apartment on the second floor?"

Mike consulted his notes. "253. How'd you know?"

"Because I hate those stupid sloping roofs so it figured."

"I worked a suicide here once," Mike said, as they crossed the parking lot. "Also on the second floor."

"It's those roofs, man. Depressing." Inside, Jack bypassed the elevator and trotted up stairs covered in carpet worn to a matted sheen of grime.

Valeria's apartment was a long, dim rectangle, kitchen immediately on your right inside the front door, short hall, single bathroom and bedroom on your left, living room at the rear. Her bed was a mattress on the floor and a packing box served as a nightstand; the battered couch in the living room could have come from the curb. An antediluvian TV with rabbit ears on a wooden shipping pallet. No dining furniture at all and another box served as a makeshift coffee table.

Jack was hoping for prayer cards, a diary, a written confession—anything that provided a definitive link between Valeria and the rest of his case.

They had better luck next door. Apartment 255 was occupied by a young woman named Becky Moore who started sobbing at the news.

She said, "Was it him?"

Jack resisted looking at Mike. "Who do you mean?"

"Her boyfriend." The word twisted Becky's mouth with disgust. She pointed to her kitchen counter where three dozen roses were arranged in a vase with mylar balloons that said, "Get well soon," and a teddy bear on a stick. "Sent that shit. 'Get well,' as if she had the flu instead of bad taste in men."

Jack read the card. *Forgive me, I miss you, love Bibi.* Showed it to Mike. "Do you mind if we take this?"

"Please." Becky sounded emphatic. "Take the flowers, too, I don't want to look at them."

"When did they arrive?" Mike asked.

"Sunday night."

"You're sure?"

Becky was positive. When no one answered at Val's, the delivery person from the florist had brought them to her. Jack realized if that was true, Bibi was either being clever or didn't know Valeria was dead. The first option didn't seem likely.

"I was afraid of something like this," Becky said. "He did it, didn't he?"

"Why do you think that?" Jack, ever the master of subtlety.

"It's not the first time he hit her. Val met some bad people where she worked."

"At the restaurant," Jack said.

"Bibi'z. Named after him, the entitled shit. You couldn't talk to her about it. You know, you can't talk trash about someone's man 'cause they make up then you're the asshole."

"You said this wasn't the first time Bibi hit her," Jack said. "Did Valeria ever call the cops?"

"Nooo." Becky's tone implied that was the most bizarre idea ever.

"And she continued to date Bibi," Mike said.

"Unfortunately. He'd come see her at all hours, pound on the door. Didn't care about wakin' anybody up. Thought he could throw money around and make up for anything. One time—"

Her words tumbled over each other.

"One night, ugh, so pervy, I was coming home from work, you know, I work a car rental counter at DIA and it was late and I was wiped and I ran into them. She went to introduce me, you know, like normal, and he looked me up and down like I was a piece of meat and said 'maybe your friend would like a threesome.' As if. Offered me money. Can you believe that? He's short and he's gross and he probably has a tiny—"

Mike managed to interrupt with another question. "When was the last time you saw Valeria?"

Becky took an uneven breath. "Um. Saturday afternoon? Yeah, it was, around two, she came over to borrow my flat iron. Said she and Bibi were gonna hang out before work. Val liked the dinner shift on Saturday because she made good tips."

"Do you know where they were planning to go?" Jack asked.

"Uh-uh. Val said he was taking her someplace special. As if. Probably wanted an extra BJ."

Jack wished he could confirm her good instincts. If that cheap motel room was Bibi's idea of special, where did he take girls he didn't like? "Had he given her any gifts lately? Jewelry, clothing, purses, anything like that?"

"No. He pretty much did the flowers thing. Oh and—"

She hesitated and Mike filled in the blank. "Drugs."

"Yeah."

"You're not in trouble," Jack said. "We appreciate you helping us figure out who did this to Valeria."

"She was trying to clean up her act, she really was."

"What'd she like?" Mike asked.

"Weed, coke when she could get it, nothing bad, no needles ever."

Jack showed Lucia's photo. "Do you know this woman? Did you ever see her with Valeria?"

"Uh-uh." Becky shook her head. "He kill her, too?"

CHAPTER FORTY-NINE

"**H**EY!" RAVEN'S VOICE rose in outrage. "What are you doing here?"

Avi and Ruth were in the room. When did they get there? She'd been gone like ten minutes getting coffee.

Her few treasures were spread out on the bed, a special dress, the pieces of jewelry Lucia had lifted, a small photo of Raven's father. Avi climbed on a chair and removed the smoke detector.

"They have sprinklers," Raven said, stupidly.

Had Willow spilled? Sahir had forced her to share a room with the crybaby, but Willow couldn't possibly know Raven's hiding place, an empty soda can for small things, a ziploc for the dress, all tucked inside a filthy air vent.

"Those are my things."

Ruth held each piece of jewelry to the light, pretended to examine it. "These are yours?"

"This is my room."

"No," Ruth said. "The room is mine, these things are mine."

Hers? Sahir rented this room, same dump always in Denver, paid by the week in cash.

Ruth shook out the dress and Raven picked up a whiff of smoke, probably from the vent. You weren't supposed to smoke in the rooms but everyone did.

"Sahir gave that dress to me." She felt hot tears on her cheek and wiped at them impatiently. The deep blue velvet swam. She remembered how pretty she felt in it, special. She remembered—she remembered—

Ruth smoothed the dress. She'd brought a bag to pack things in and Raven noticed the closet door was open.

"What'd you do with my clothes?"

"Again," Ruth said. "Not yours."

"I need my clothes."

"No, in fact, you don't."

Avi smirked, made a gutteral *ha* sound.

Raven turned on him. "You prick. It's not bad enough you tell Sahir?"

Mistake. Ruth inclined her head, permission, and Avi backhanded her with a beefy paw, sent her sprawling.

"You'll keep a civil tone," Ruth said.

Raven pushed up onto her knees. Tried to catch her breath.

From above. "Don't ignore me."

Ruth's voice was filled with menace. She again gave Avi some kind of signal and he pulled Raven up roughly by one arm, twisted it savagely behind her back. She let out an involuntary shriek.

"Personally, I don't see it, but Sahir thinks she's special. I hear about you all the time, Raven, did you know that? Let's see if you can figure things out."

Special? What? Raven's words stuttered with pain. "I d-don't know what you want from me."

"You're like a wild animal with no manners so I'll explain this once. Yes, ma'am, yes, sir when you speak to your superiors. And everyone's your superior. Let's try it out."

The words clogged in her throat but she managed. "Yes, ma'am."

Ruth smiled in an understanding way that made Raven's stomach turn over.

"You and Lucia were saving up, stockpiling, so you'd be

able to make a fresh start."

It sounded at the same time reasonable and impossible. "What's wrong with that? Ma'am."

"If you were a decent girl I'd think you were smart. But you're only property."

"People can't be property."

The words were out before Raven thought and she braced for another blow, but Ruth put up her hand, signaling *stop*. "Of course they can. And you're mine, for as long as you turn a profit. After that, did you think you were going to have a life? How did you think this was all going to end? It isn't a career, despite what Sahir might have told you. There's no what would you call it? Upward mobility. When you're no longer marketable we dispose of you. Simple."

Ruth snapped her fingers. "I'm not surprised you'd steal but I am disappointed Sahir didn't take action. He's much too fond of you, fonder even than he is of me. Can you believe it?"

Through the horror of her situation, an odd thought gnawed at the back of Raven's mind. Ruth was jealous.

"Answer me."

"Yes, ma'am. I mean, no ma'am." What was the right answer to that question?

"How many times has he fornicated with you?" Ruth asked. "And don't lie."

"Never."

"I don't believe you."

Ruth looked at Avi again and Raven's words rushed fast and urgent.

"No, it's true, I swear. He burned me the other day because I went and talked to Avi without permission. Tell her. He never touches me, ever."

"True." Ruth snorted, pulled the blue velvet out of the suitcase. "You took what's mine, so I'm taking what's yours."

She'd come prepared. Held scissors out, handle first, for Raven to take. Handed a can to Avi. *Lighter fluid.* What? In the small kitchenette, Ruth ordered her to cut the dress into pieces, into the sink. Avi doused it with the lighter fluid.

"You'll set off the sprinklers." She felt heat as the fire surged.

Ruth added Raven's father's photo.

"No!" Raven lunged forward. "Not the picture, that *is* mine. He's dead and it's all I have."

She tried to snatch it, not caring about the flames, but Avi grabbed both arms from behind.

"Don't worry," Ruth said. "You don't need a picture because you'll be joining him soon enough."

Like when Sahir used the curling iron on her, Raven struggled in Avi's grasp, but it was no good. She was too weak, too stupid to see this coming, whatever this was. The picture caught, edges curled, her dad's smile disappeared. Her shoulder stabbed with matching fire and she wondered if Avi had pulled it out of the socket. When everything was ashes Ruth ran water onto the mess.

"Now you can focus on work. And you won't have time to steal and tempt good men like Sahir."

Tempt him? Sahir sold Raven, beat her, starved her. Ruth was bat-shit crazy and somehow, this was all because of Sahir. But what? Did Ruth honestly think he liked Raven?

Avi climbed on the chair to replace the smoke detector. Ruth set a can of scouring powder next to the sink.

"Clean this up. We don't want to pay a fine."

Ruth seemed to know about everything including their plan to escape. Maybe she killed Lucia, or had it done, and was going to kill Raven, too. Dispose of her.

Sahir couldn't—or wouldn't—defend her against Ruth and there was no one else who could help. Not for the first time, Raven knew she was completely on her own.

CHAPTER FIFTY

———◆———

BIBI'Z MIDDLE EASTERN restaurant was quickly becoming the center of a criminal universe and, based on the number of bodies crammed inside the small entry waiting for a table, it was also popular for lunch. Jack elbowed his way through the crowd and let the frazzled hostess see his badge. The dining room formed a large L with the short side along the front. All of the tables were full and two female servers, one blonde, one dark-haired, ran between them.

In stark contrast to the frenzied rush of the waitstaff, Bibi lounged behind the counter that separated the service bar from the back of the dining room. As Jack got closer, though, he saw the young man looked unwell, color greenish, sweating, and he wasn't lounging as much as collapsed onto the counter.

"Nice to see you," Jack said, in Farsi.

Bibi's eyes shifted left toward the swinging door into the kitchen. "I'm working."

Jack switched to English. "That what you call it."

The dark-haired server rushed the counter with a cry of frustration and slammed down her tray. "Bibi, what the hell. I need those orders for four and nine."

"I'm in the middle of something."

"Food's in the window." She pointed toward an opening into the kitchen. "You don't need your arms to talk."

Belatedly, her heavily made-up eyes absorbed Jack's suited presence and she slumped with annoyance and recognition. "Ugh. What'd he do now?"

"What's your name?" Jack asked.

"She's Lola."

"I didn't ask you, Bibi."

"We're down a server and people are stacked out the door." Lola motioned with her arms like she was directing a triple-seven to the gate. "Whatever he's done, can you talk later? Look at this place. He's useless but he's all we've got."

"I can't argue with the useless part." Jack made one of those split-second decisions that either turned out to be brilliant or to bite him in the ass.

"I'm here because I have bad news. Valeria Monsour was found dead this morning."

Lola went from animated to positively theatrical. Her hand flew to her mouth, she paced in a small circle, and she started to cry. "No." Her keening attracted the attention of nearby tables. "No, no, no, no, no."

Bibi stood up straight. "I knew you weren't a cop. What'd you do to her?"

"Me? What are you talking about?"

"Don't talk to him," Lola screeched.

"No one in Denver speaks Farsi." Bibi panted, as if he was out of breath. "He's just some cocksucker they hired to screw with me."

"You're a fucking idiot."

"You're a girl, you can't talk to me that way." Bibi's outrage made him even more breathless.

"He is so a cop. Look at him." Lola made some more dramatic arm gestures and repeated herself like an old record that skipped. "Don't talk to him, don't talk to him, don't talk to him."

Bibi's upper body convulsed, as if he was about to cry or vomit. "She's not dead it's a trick because I like Val."

"Like her?" If Lola's voice got any higher she'd shatter glass. "Screwing her, maybe."

"That's not true. I do like her. And not just for sex."

"You don't know women are good for anything else."

"And you don't know me so just shut up."

"Both of you shut up." Jack seriously regretted his approach. "I can assure you Valeria is quite dead and you need to tell me what you know."

Lola's voice dropped to a more human register. "I worked with her and I know she was stupid enough to hook up with Bibi, but that's it."

Bibi scrubbed at his face. "Sahir fucked with me all night and now this."

Lola gasped at the name. Turned and started pulling plates from the opening onto her tray.

"Who the hell's Sahir?" Jack asked.

"*Inshallah.*" Lola hoisted her tray onto a slim shoulder, visibly frightened, and walked away. Said something else in Arabic that struck Jack as a prayer for protection.

Bibi stared with big bloodshot spaniel eyes. "He did it to distract me so I'd forget about Val, which I wouldn't. Kept me up all night, starved me, like I'm a stupid slave with no feelings."

A slave who drove a brand new Porsche, blew a fortune up his nose, and gave a dead girl's purse to another dead girl. "Tell me about Sahir. Lola practically jumped out of her skin when you mentioned his name."

"I wanna know who you are. I know you're not a cop."

This was beyond tedious. "Yeah? Let me prove it. Downtown in an interview room like I should have done in the first place."

Bibi's gulped air. "So you can kill me too? I'm not going anywhere with you."

"Too? What are you talking about?"

Bibi grabbed another loaded plate and hurled it like a discus. Jack ducked but still got sprayed with something hot and greasy. Behind him, the plate hit a wall and exploded. The dining room silenced for a long second.

"What the fuck is wrong with you?"

Jack lunged and Bibi pushed through the swinging doors into the kitchen, had a momentary advantage in knowing the layout. The two men raced past startled line cooks chopping small mountains of onions, cucumber, and garlic. Steam rose from stockpots and sharp, spicy aromas filled the overheated air as Bibi wove through and pushed open a metal door onto the alley.

Jack was on him and had Bibi against the brick wall before it registered that something else had caught his attention.

Or, rather, someone.

"It figures." Bibi went limp.

Jack held him with one hand and the other went to his gun. A man leaned against the wall six feet away, stocky, about five-nine, having a smoke.

"This Sahir?" Jack's fingers bit into the pudge of Bibi's neck.

Mystery man's eyes narrowed in wishful menace, like all wannabe bad guys since time immemorial. "Who the fuck are you?"

"Took the words out of my mouth." Under Jack's grip Bibi squirmed but offered no serious resistance.

Man number two took a drag and watched with casual disinterest as if this was a sporting event where one team had run up the score and it was no longer a contest.

Jack let go of Bibi's neck and pulled his jacket open enough to display the badge clipped to his belt. His voice was a snarl. "Denver homicide. For real. And you would be?"

"That's cocksucker Avi," Bibi said. "Not Sahir or you'd already be dead."

"Bibi, you need to let people introduce themselves. Got a last name, Avi?"

But Bibi didn't follow directions at all. "He says Val is dead and I don't believe him because I've met him before and he's not a cop. All of you need to stay the fuck out of my life."

Avi remained motionless, his expression flat. "Hope not 'cause I'm sick of training waitresses."

Jack made another instinctive decision. "Bibi, go inside and wait for me."

"You can't tell me what to do."

"We have a difference of opinion on that." Jack reached for his neck again and Bibi let out a strangled squeak, backed up, and covered his face with chubby hands.

Jack repeated, "Inside," and Bibi oozed back through the kitchen door.

The interaction seemed to amuse Avi. "What a pathetic maggot."

Jack was only halfway sure he said maggot because Avi also spoke in Arabic. Could have been slug. Either word was appropriate and Jack considered whether it was worth the effort to pull his magic I-speak-Farsi-too trick again.

Decided it wasn't. "Let me see your ID and I'm not really asking."

Avi's eyebrows rose and he swiped with stubby fingers at his cheek. "You have some shit on your face."

Jack locked stares with Avi's opaque, brown, bovine eyes and took a step forward. Avi pushed away from the wall. Oh, good. First one lowlife hurled hummus at his head and now Jack was going to have to subdue two hundred pounds of suet in an alley. Instead, Avi held his hands up, palms out, and reached to toss his cigarette butt in a dumpster. "Bad to litter."

He was a completely different species; poised, confident, definitely no whimpering.

"ID." Jack growled the word. "Slowly."

According to his license, Aviram Ba'albaki had somehow

managed to reach the age of forty-one unscathed, although he did have a nifty scar that extended two inches from the left corner of a wide, flaccid mouth.

Jack radioed the pertinents and while he waited to hear back on what he expected to be a laundry list of outstanding warrants, thought about what to ask this idiot.

Decided to start simple. "Where were you yesterday afternoon and evening, Mr. Ba'albaki?"

If Avi was impressed Jack pronounced his name correctly he didn't let on. "Here."

"How about Saturday night?"

"Same. I'm the manager so I'm here all the time. Lots of people saw me, including cops."

Jack showed Lucia's picture on his phone. "Was this woman here Saturday night?"

"Don't recognize her."

Jack put his index finger to his lips, miming thoughtfulness. Eyes moved between the photo and at Avi. "Want to reconsider that answer?"

"Am I in trouble?"

"You tell me."

"If you're not here to arrest me then I have a lot of work to do."

Avi started toward the door and Jack blocked his path. *Bring it, asshole.* "Her name's Lucia but I'm sure you already know that. Same as we know she was here Saturday night. You said you're always here because you manage the place. Last chance to show a shred of intelligence."

"Lots of girls come here."

"Lots of girls don't wind up murdered."

Avi made a *tsking* sound. "Terrible. What's happening to our city?"

"Who was Lucia here with?"

"I didn't say she was here."

This was tiresome, especially since Jack already knew

the answer. They could play who's got the bigger pair all afternoon and while it might be fun to knock some of the arrogant wind out of this prick's ego it wouldn't get him anywhere.

However, Jack was human. "You don't know much, do you? Most people aren't as proud of their ignorance."

"I know I'm not telling you shit."

"Not even where can I find Raven?"

It took Avi at least three full seconds to wipe his face clean of shocked surprise. "Who?"

"Don't consider acting if this gig doesn't pan out. Where is she?"

"Dunno who that is."

"Were you born this good a liar or did it take practice?"

"Screw you."

"Not in this lifetime." Jack took a step closer and Avi's chin rose a belligerent notch. He held his ground and glared up like a short, frustrated bull. Garlic percolated off of him in nauseating waves. "If there's a brain inside that big ugly head you'll change your mind about talking to me. You sling hummus. Why do you want to get in the mix for two murders?"

"Somebody already slung hummus at your ugly face."

Not even creative enough to come up with his own insults. "Mr. Ba'albaki, when I find out what you're wanted for I'll be happy to escort you to jail myself. In the meantime, stay put."

"You can't tell me to do shit."

"You better hope Raven's still alive."

That got almost as scenic a reaction as the first mention of her name. Avi's retort was delayed but none the cleverer for having taken a moment. "Yah? You think you know but you don't."

CHAPTER FIFTY-ONE

——◆——

TEXT FROM THE spa: *Raven AWOL, customer aggro*
Shitty timing, with pissant preacher suddenly
deciding to be a tough guy, and cops crawling up their
ass. Raven, his best bitch, chose today to go dark.

Sahir found her at the motel, sprawled on the bed.

"What the fuck you doing? You don't stand up a
customer."

Started to yank her up onto her feet when he realized
she was weeping. "You never cry."

Motel room reeked of smoke and kerosene. Sahir
stalked to the kitchenette, doused a paper towel with cold
water. Saw bits of what looked like ash in the sink. Got a
story in confused fits and starts about Ruth, scissors, fire.

"My dress, all my other clothes, she was laughing! Said I
didn't need them. Why?"

"Gabi, stop crying. I'll buy you a new dress. I don't have
time for this shit." He called her by her real name when
they were alone, Gabriella, or Gabi. In fact, it suited her
much better than his invention: Raven.

"It's not just that. She burned my father's picture and it's
the only one I had. She said I'd be joining him."

That brought on a fresh flood of tears and Sahir
wondered why he couldn't have slept with Ruth, given
her the ego boost she so obviously craved. It wasn't hard
to have sex with a woman. Let her blow him if he couldn't

bring himself to do it any other way. Instead, more unexpected chaos.

He noticed the closet door was open, empty metal hangers. "Where are your things?"

"I told you! She made me cut things up and then she lit it on fire."

"When?"

"This morning."

An act of violence and aggression toward Raven was a display of passion. Of literal fire. He remembered Ruth's attempted seduction, undressing in his room, bringing him wine.

"She went after you because of me."

"Are you kidding?"

"You're young and beautiful." Hadn't been raped and humiliated by your family. Forced into a loveless marriage and trained to deny your feelings until your personality warped beyond recognition. Sahir could still remember Ruth from before, innocent, funny, vulnerable, all traits she now eschewed.

"She asked me how many times we—fornicated. I said never."

"See? You are smart."

"No. I've just become a world-class liar."

He rubbed the tears on Gabi's face with his thumb. Hadn't been lying when he said he wouldn't mark it; disfiguring her would be like taking a knife to the Mona Lisa.

"Fornication isn't what we do. It's a legal term invented by the church thousands of years ago."

"Ugh. Don't mention the church." She gave a little shake of her head. "And I still don't get it. You worship the ground Ruth walks on."

That was the problem. How much he was going to have to pay was the unknown. Then corrected himself. Young Ruth was who he idolized. A woman who no longer existed. Sahir saw hints of that lost girl in Gabi.

"This is my domain."

"Tell her," Raven said.

"The girls are off limits. Entire spa is off limits. Ruth isn't supposed to set foot." He fought to contain his growing rage. He might be a common pimp but it was still his operation to run his way. Sahir had very little and Ruth was stealing it, like she'd tried to take his dignity last night. Coming into his private place uninvited, coming to Raven's room like a thug. As if she was determined that no one in her orbit enjoyed a shred of comfort or security, let alone autonomy.

"She's going to kill me," Raven said. "I mean for real."

"I know what you meant and I won't let it happen. Where the hell was Avi?"

"He helped her. When she wanted a fire he poured lighter fluid like an obedient dog."

Ruth was throwing her weight around. Reminding him who worked for who and his exact place in the food chain. Whether it was revenge, jealousy, or an attack of paranoia didn't matter. Her mean power plays were reckless and dangerous.

"I'm moving up the circuit. You need to pack, we leave tonight."

With a harsh, high-pitched laugh, Raven waved in the direction of the empty closet. "Well, that'll be easy. I've got nothing left."

I'm sorry. The soft words were almost out before he caught himself. "Quit moping. I said I'd buy you another dress. Clean yourself up and I'll drive you to work. Tell Willow and the other bitches whatever you want, but not a word to Avi. We leave tonight but he's not going anywhere."

CHAPTER FIFTY-TWO

———▶———

"HOW MANY OUTFITS a day you gonna wear?" Mike asked.

Jack had stopped home for a quick change on his way to Denver Health to talk to Nicki. First coffee then greasy Middle Eastern shit that was probably never going come out of his suit. Add food fight to the list of skills they'd left out of Jack's job description. This day had gone from happy to crap with astonishing speed.

He gave Mike the briefest of explanations. "Bibi hurled a steaming hot plate of food at me before he took off and before he introduced me to a thug named Avi and dropped a new name, Sahir. Either of those ring a bell?"

"Negative."

It wasn't like Jack had much leisure time for either activity—changing clothes or visiting the hospital—but he felt somehow responsible. Nicki talked to him and next thing you know had her face slashed.

"Could be a coincidence," Mike said. "We don't know Nicki's attack has anything to do with Lucia's homicide."

Coincidence. Sure. "What do we know?"

"Call came in 22:10. She was transported and underwent surgery late last night. Lots of witnesses however in this case, quantity doesn't equal quality. All we could get a consensus on about the perp was white or possibly Asian or Hispanic."

"That's a consensus?"

Mike's eyebrows went up and down. "Definitely a male of the homo sapiens variety. Not tall but not short. Not fat but not thin."

"Stop. I'm already depressed. What about cameras?"

"HALO on a streetlight caught lovely video of his back and when he turned around he pulled his hood over his face and stared at the ground. He'd parked just out of camera range."

"Sounds professional."

"Yep. And Serena said she's tried multiple times to reach you." Mike held up his radio. "We need to get back to homicide as soon as we're done here."

A long chain of sutures, like the seam on a baseball, ran from the left corner of Nicki's mouth, up across her cheek at a diagonal, and angled under her eye toward her temple, maybe from dodging the blade.

Her friend Rob had been with her when she was cut and stood protectively hovering next to the bed, his hand on her shoulder.

"Doctor says she has great reaction time. Really lucky the way she turned her head because it saved her eye."

Those green eyes stared at Jack. "Lucky. That's me."

"They can do a lot now with scars and plastic surgery." Jack knew instantly how wrong a thing that was to say.

Rob joined the lame guy club. "I've been trying to tell her that. And that she's still pretty."

Still. Ouch.

"We'll find him," Mike said with his habitual certainty.

"Did he say anything?" Jack asked.

"Uh-huh. He knew who I was but I didn't recognize him." Nicki blinked furiously. "Can't cry. Gets in my stitches. You know, salt. Plus the plastic surgeon says to limit talking and moving my face."

"It was so quick," Rob said.

"Wicked fast," Nicki said. "Out of nowhere."

"I stopped for like one second to make sure the door was locked, heard shouting, and there was blood everywhere. I didn't try to go after him because I wanted to help Nicki."

Jack saw Rob felt guilty. "You did the right thing."

Nicki took a shaky breath. "He said my name and I looked at him and I didn't even realize at first what had happened. Someone screamed and I touched my face and my hand was bloody. Maybe I was the one who screamed."

"Anything else about him?" Jack asked. "Even a tiny detail could help."

"Um, bald, I think. He was wearing a hoodie. No beard. And he smiled. I'll always remember that smile."

"You think you could ID him?"

Nicki nodded and chewed her lip the way she had when he bought her a drink. Made him want to take her in his arms. Tell her it wouldn't matter to him and it wouldn't matter to a lot of guys. Another unhelpful comment he didn't make.

"Are you sure you don't know him from anywhere?" Mike asked. "Maybe the church? Your office? Think about it for a minute."

She didn't need a minute. "Uh-uh. Never saw him before. How does he know me? Why would somebody do this?"

Because you talked to me. Jack didn't say that, either. Didn't need her more frightened than she already was. "Either of you remember how he got away? On foot, car, bicycle?"

"Car." Rob answered fast then hesitated. "I think. I don't remember a bike and I didn't see anyone running."

"Do you remember anything about the car? SUV, sedan, pickup?"

Rob shook his head. "Sorry."

Nicki said, "Me either. I barely noticed him. Stupid."

Jack couldn't help himself. "You're not stupid. You're beautiful and you're being very brave."

———◆———

Heather sat in an interview room, evidence bags on the table in front of her along with her smartphone and a cheaper TracFone.

"Dustin bolted," Serena said with no preamble as soon as Jack arrived.

"When?"

"Unknown." Serena nodded in Heather's direction. "He left home at oh-eight-hundred for church like usual. They had a pair of burners, to be activated if they had to run."

"Only him, not us," Heather said. "Left me behind."

"There's kind of a code," Serena said. "He'd text her with a phrase claiming to be a relative and—"

Heather interrupted. "My Uncle Pete, retired in Mexico."

She held up the cheap phone and Jack read:

Hi honey. How's my favorite niece?

"Mexico? Dustin's on his way to Mexico?" It was one. Five hours. Juarez, closest point of entry, was about ten from Denver.

"We don't know that for sure," Serena said. "But that's where her uncle lives. Except he doesn't really exist."

"He sent fake cards on my birthday and everything," Heather said.

Serena attempted an explanation. "The burner phones were in a closet wrapped like presents. We collected wrapping paper and packaging from the trash."

Heather chimed in, "He said if we were robbed or something maybe they wouldn't take them if they couldn't see what they were. They were supposed to be a gift from Uncle Pete."

Jack looked between the two of them unsure how to parse this crazy story. "Do you even have an uncle?"

Heather shook her head. "They were like for a rainy

day."

"You need to stop speaking in code and tell me what this all means."

"A habit I must have picked up from my husband." Heather looked at Serena for reassurance. "He always speaks in parables. Anyway, Pete was a cover story. I don't have an uncle that I know of. It was Dustin's plan for if we had to leave in a hurry. He'd text my phone—well, not my real one, the burner—as Uncle Pete and tell me where to meet him, but he hasn't yet and we think he might be ditching me. He said when this happens it's going to be sudden so we've gotta be prepared."

Jack didn't find any of that especially clarifying. "What did Dustin mean by 'this'? Like he knew Lucia was going to die?"

Heather took a deep breath. "I don't think so. I mean, I guess he meant having to run, except I didn't know he'd opened the phones until after I showed Serena the ledger and we were leaving the house and I thought of it and looked in the closet. My burner was plugged in to charge and I guess he took the other one with him."

"Ledger?" Jack stared a question at his fellow detective.

Serena indicated one of the evidence bags. "There's a book. Heather gave it to me. Dozens, maybe hundreds of names of girls Dustin has sold. I'm getting it to the task force but wanted to show you first."

As if reacting to the mention of his name the TracFone on the table buzzed.

"Should I answer him?" Heather asked.

"Not yet," Jack said.

Having the original packaging from the prepaid phones meant serial numbers and EMEI numbers. Jack was skeptical Dustin was dumb enough to leave that behind. "We need to get started on a trace."

"Of course," Serena said. "But there are a couple of other things you need to know first, like Dustin's not driving his own car."

"I called the church looking for him." Heather sounded proud. "I've been helping Serena, cooperating. His associate pastor, ugh, this dude Eli—Elijah—who's holier than thou answered and he didn't want to tell me."

"Heather, could you get to the point?" To recap. Jack had a second dead woman, another woman with her face slashed, a runaway minister masquerading as a criminal mastermind and, now, a book with pages and pages of names of people who might be missing or dead. And that was this morning.

"Eli *finally* told me Dustin asked to borrow his car to run an errand," Heather said.

"What are you two talking about? Dustin's got a five-hour head start in a borrowed car on his way to Mexico pretending to be your uncle?"

"No, he doesn't," Heather said. "Eli doesn't start work until ten and he's always late although Dustin thinks he's wonderful."

"I've already put out an alert with a description of Elijah's car," Serena said. "I've been busy, too." Then she turned to Heather. "You need to show him, it's important."

Heather grunted with annoyance.

"We talked about this." Serena got all stern while Heather whined like a surly teenager.

"Do I have to?"

"Show me what?" Jack couldn't keep impatience out of his voice. "Heather, if you know something else about where Dustin might be—"

"Fine." Heather cut him off. Stood. Spun. Cocked a hip and lifted her hair revealing the goddamned Arabic characters adorning her neck. Clunkier, growing fuzzy with age, the dots weren't in color; they'd refined their tattoo techniques over the years. Then she spun back another 180 and glared at him.

"Satisfied? I feel like a fucking animal at the zoo."

"Thank you," Serena said. "I know this is hard."

"I was one of them." Heather spat the words at Jack. "Before I married Dustin and cleaned up my act I was one of them."

"There was no Shores of Hope yet when you met Dustin." Jack still felt a bit lost. Understatement. "Was there? Why do you have that tattoo?"

"Because it has nothing to do with Dustin." Heather's voice rose. "God. He hates tats. Grossed him out that I had one and that they did it to all the girls."

"Who's they?" Jack asked.

"Ruth. Sahir. It's some Middle Eastern thing."

"Joy." Jack felt emotions the opposite of that word. Dread and urgency leading the list. "Do you know a man named Sahir?"

"She worked for Sahir," Serena said. "Tell him."

"Ugh." Heather's face got blotchy. "I was a sex worker. Okay? You guys happy? And you don't get it, like, at all."

"What don't we get?" Jack asked.

"The spa," Serena prompted.

"It's not a spa like a building. They move around. I used to work out of an old motel on Colfax."

"The Silver Saddle?" Could it possibly be the same place Bibi took Val?

"Dunno," Heather said. "And not like I want to remember. And yes, Serena, you guessed earlier. They do hot stone massage."

Serena's voice was gentle. "That's why you were embarrassed."

"Of course I'm embarrassed. Wouldn't you be?"

"Serena, go get started tracing those phones. I want to talk to Heather alone for a few minutes."

That made Heather start to cry. He wasn't that scary, was he?

"All of this is incredibly helpful. I know this has got to

be rough on you and I appreciate you coming forward."

She appeared unconvinced by his attempt at empathy so he dove in with what he really wanted to ask.

"I just came from the hospital. Your friend Nicki had her face slashed last night."

Heather gasped. "Is she okay?"

"Who do you know that would do something like that? Is it something this man Sahir would do?"

"Oh, God, oh God." Heather buried her face in her hands. "It's my fault."

"What is?" Jack's feeling of dread intensified. Nicki talked to him and got cut up. Heather saw them having a drink together. She probably told Dustin and maybe he worked with Sahir on whatever insane trafficking operation this was turning out to be.

Right now he needed the semi-hysterical woman in front of him to answer questions.

"Look, you were upset when you saw me talking to Nicki at the hotel. It's natural you went home and told your husband. Plus, you were still in shock that day about Lucia."

"No." Heather stared at him wide-eyed. "I didn't go home. After I saw the two of you I was so upset I went to the restaurant."

"Bibi'z." It was, in fact, the center of a criminal universe. Kind of a superstore where you could order a side of hummus along with a child, a hit, a massage. None of which made any sense.

Heather's story poured out.

"I tried to have a drink but Sahir found me and locked me in his car. I was afraid of what he was gonna do to me so I told him about seeing the two of you together. I was more worried about myself and assuring him I hadn't said anything to you than about protecting my friend. I'm so sorry."

"You couldn't possibly have known what was going to happen to her."

"Oh." Heather grew deathly calm. "Oh yes, I could have known."

CHAPTER FIFTY-THREE

———

"IS IT TRUE?"

Bibi crashed through the back door, found Sahir, Raven, the little blonde, and a man he didn't recognize in Dottie's kitchen. Maybe a customer.

"Wait your turn," Sahir said.

"I'm not waiting. I want to know if it's true about Val."

Sahir turned to the strange man. "Next time you get a discount. Use my name."

The man smiled, he had terrible teeth. "Do I get both of 'em again?"

"Two for the price of one." Sahir smirked back, held the door open and ushered him out.

Turned on Bibi as soon as the man was gone. "You don't barge in like that. We have rules."

"That cocksucker who speaks Farsi was just at the restaurant and told me Val was dead. Did he kill her? Or did you?"

Sahir spun Bibi and pulled both his arms behind his back. Searing pain made him cry out. Willow screamed, too, and Sahir told Raven to get her out of there.

Bibi's cries came involuntarily. "Ow, that hurts. Stop it. Stop."

Sahir pinned him. Bent him over the counter. Bibi's head slammed into a cabinet.

"You need to calm down."

The pain needed to stop. "Okay, okay, let me go."

Sahir pulled harder. "That a yes?"

Bibi nodded. Not good enough. Sahir added a knee to his lower back, the metal edge of the counter dug into his balls

He screamed and, even to his own ears, sounded like a girl. "Yes."

Repeated it, *yes, yes, yes!* Almost like they were having sex and in a way, violence was sex, the way Bibi got turned on holding Raven. When Sahir let go he tried to move his right arm and couldn't. Started crying.

"Why don't you fight?"

"Because—you—I—couldn't."

"You're not turned on, are you?" Sahir reached and grabbed Bibi's crotch so hard he screamed again. "That's right, I forgot, you like it up the ass."

"Let me go." Unbearable pain. Bibi's cheeks were wet, his voice a girl's, his shame complete.

"Fucking sodomite."

Sahir released him and he dropped to the linoleum, only one functioning arm to break his fall. Buried his face against his knees.

Heard the flick of a lighter and smelled smoke. Sahir reached into a drawer above his head and got antacids.

"What I saw the other night." Sahir whistled in his way of signaling disgust. "Pretty girl and instead of having her like a man you want her to shove things up your butt. It would've still been fornicating but at least I would've known you were normal if you'd fucked the right way."

"That was—that was just—"

Bibi couldn't stop crying, even though he knew it was the worst thing he could do. He convulsed with weeping, his breath came in gasps, he started to shiver violently.

Sahir snorted. "You gonna tell me the stones were foreplay?"

In fact, that had been what Bibi thought it was. He liked

the feel of the warm rocks pushed into his body but now Sahir made it filthy and humiliating.

"You do it at the spa," Bibi managed.

"You're confusing what we do here with what you'd do with a decent girl? That's why no one likes you. Val was pretending because she thought you had money. Here."

Sahir held out a small plastic bag. "You're not strong enough for detox."

Bibi's mind knew it was a trick but his poor body practically sang with relief. He'd vomited for hours. After dawn prayers and cleaning the room, he'd finally fallen asleep only to have Sahir force him out of bed and drag him to work after a cold shower. It was unimaginable cruelty teasing him with drugs and Bibi expected Sahir to snatch the bag away the moment he reached for it.

He lurched to his feet. His mouth was so dry he had to try several times. "Wha—what—what is that?"

Sahir was a dark-eyed God with sour breath. He shoved the bag into Bibi's hand and closed fingers around it. "Take this somewhere and snort it out of my sight."

"Where will I go?"

"Not my problem."

———◆———

Bibi's Porsche was in the alley behind Dottie's, keys in the ignition. He blinked at it like a mirage, staggered and opened the driver's door with his left hand, his right still not quite working. Driving was hard, erratic, as if he was drunk, and he wondered if he'd get pulled over. Cars honked, someone flipped him off, once he hit the curb. Only place he could think to go was Val's, and Bibi was so relieved to manage it he didn't notice the unmarked car outside the apartment building. Hoped against hope she was alive. Fumbled at her door with his key, the one she'd given him. Sahir was wrong. Val really did like him. Wouldn't have given him a key otherwise.

Called her name again and again but no one answered. He collapsed onto the cheap sofa, something sharp jabbed him in the ribs. Wished he'd stopped and gotten some tequila, wished he at least had a good TV to watch.

He'd bought Val a nice flat screen once and his aunt jammed him up. Found the charge on his credit card and made him return it, even went to the store with him like he was twelve. She was all over his ass, counted every dime, he couldn't even grind on a pizza without her being up in his grill.

Bibi meant to look into prepaid cards, he did, but never had the time with work, or being beaten, or being forced to help while Sahir tortured someone. He'd never had a normal girlfriend, whatever that was, Sahir making him doubt himself and what he even wanted. He'd never rented an apartment, or gotten utilities, or even the plates for his own cars; his aunt took care of everything. Now, as he looked around Val's mostly empty crib, cardboard boxes for furniture for shit's sake, his frustration nearly choked him. Val worked really hard, she and Bibi both did, and they weren't allowed to be together like a normal couple. He'd only taken her to the cheap motel because he figured it was the one place neither his aunt nor prick Sahir would go.

Why couldn't he buy Val a car or give her one of his old ones? Why couldn't he take her out nice places? Why couldn't he so much as buy her a stupid television? Why couldn't he fight back, for shit's sake? Here, alone, he found his rage and his fist smashed into a wall, once, twice, three times. Cheap drywall gave easily, knuckles hit a stud, blood ran.

Pain siphoned off some of his fury, though, and he flexed the fingers on his injured hand. If Val were here she'd take care of him, she'd wash his hand and put medicine on it. Now, they'd taken her from him. Now, Bibi had no one.

Lying on her bed he masturbated with his good hand.

All he wanted was to get some relief and sleep. He wanted the easy life he was promised. He didn't want to work, he didn't want to beat anyone up, he didn't ever want to go back to Ruth's. *"Don't want to see you again,"* Sahir said. Maybe he could stay at Val's. Wondered how long she'd paid rent for.

Forgot for the moment that Avi and Sahir both knew her address

Fished the zipper bag out of his pocket and stared at it. *What the fuck?* An entire eight ball. Last night was what, fun for Sahir? Some kind of sick game?

Bibi rolled onto his side. Sahir also gave him drugs Saturday and now Val was dead. Was that how she died? No way of knowing.

He fingered the baggie, his nerve endings raw, screaming, begging. He needed this. But it might be poison. Bibi was in so much pain he was beyond caring.

"Don't have so much fun you're late for work." Sahir's smirking face floated in Bibi's mind. His black eyes. His unreal strength. All the cold showers, humiliation, forced meals. Then ridicule that his hair was greasy and he was fat.

Did Sahir kill Val? Or the other Farsi-speaking dude? Or someone else?

"Got you somethin' special, baby."

When Bibi showed her the baggie Saturday at the motel, Val jumped into his arms, legs around his waist. Exactly the reaction he was hoping for. So pretty, so happy to see him.

Until she looked inside the purse.

The plan was to do some bumps and have sex but Bibi needed to use the crapper first, which was disgusting. He heard shrieking and then Val was on him; she was small but she could hit. He'd barely finished taking a piss.

"You give me a gift from another girl? You fuck her too?"

"No, let me explain."

"What's to explain? Her stuff is still inside." Val swung the pink handbag at his head and then threw it across the room.

"That's because I didn't have a chance to clean it out yet." An explanation that didn't help.

"You give me another bitch's purse and expect to get laid? Get the fuck outta here."

"No, baby, look, I got you the good shit, and the purse is worth a lot of bank. Pawn it if you want then you can buy that flat screen. I was totally thinking about you."

"Get out get out get out."

Now she was dead and there was no making up, not ever. On her bed, he pulled a pillow over his face and tried to smell her. Val gave the best BJs, his cock looked so big going into her mouth. Bibi got turned on by BJs; that meant he was normal, didn't it?

With a groan he rolled onto his side and fished for his wallet.

Didn't care enough or have the energy to get up and find the small round mirror they usually used, the one where Val kept a candle when they weren't partying. Fished out his black card—the treacherous card his aunt got for him and used to spy. Did one bump off the card and it seemed okay, the familiar rush of coke along with a kind of thunder hitting his heart, rumbling, intense, beating stopped and started, but because he was feeling really crappy he did more as fast as he could, although his hands felt like bricks. Instead of relief his mind thickened like cotton, his mouth dried even more, his vision blistered. He spilled the rest because everything went off, ten, nine, nothing, like a light switch. Chasing and finally catching oblivion.

CHAPTER FIFTY-FOUR

———◆———

JACK JOINED SERENA and the task force detectives including Al Gonzales hunkered down in a conference room going through Dustin's ledger and doing math. The El-Tee hadn't been about to let a good task force go to waste and considering the latest developments, Jack was glad.

"Oh, thank God, food." He snagged one of the last bruschetta from a ravaged takeout container. Italian from a restaurant named Odyssey on Sixth Avenue. Jack personally might never be able to eat hummus again.

Mike was headed back to the hospital to see if Nicki could make an ID. Sahir Hassanzadeh was a nasty piece of work. Born in Iran, drug charges as well as violent offenses, most recently incarcerated in Limon, a high-security facility on the plains east of Denver, where he served a mandatory nickel for felony assault with a knife.

He was the "gardener" with the shaved head they'd seen going in and out of the Harrowsmiths', five foot ten, 150 pounds, brown eyes. His mean, angular face had also been captured on several security cameras from the three a.m. Sunday morning timeframe driving a black Jeep near the alley where Lucia was found. Sahir performing Lucia's ceremonial body dump/funeral made much more sense than Bibi. That careful scene—Lucia's body arranged, wrapped, oriented toward Mecca; if Bibi had disposed of

Lucia's body they'd have probably found a slice of leftover pizza in her hair.

Google maps showed Sahir's last recorded address wasn't a residence but a gas station on Federal. A call to his parole officer revealed many missed appointments and very little contrition at not performing what seemed, to Jack, minimal due diligence. Failure to check in with a parole officer was a technical violation and Sahir's name was on a list of individuals to follow up with as time and staffing allowed.

Jack intended to follow up with Sahir much, much sooner.

Serena had projected pages from the ledger onto the wall—hundreds of girls, staggering amounts of money. Unknown if any of them were also homicides.

"Has anyone counted?" Jack asked.

"I'm transcribing the names into a spreadsheet," Serena said. "So it'll be easier to search. I'll get the pages scanned too and cross-check the names with missing persons databases, and birth records, and social security indexes and—"

"Serena." Jack indicated one of the trafficking detectives. "We have a task force. Breathe. You spent a lot of time with Heather and I need to know what she said about our homicides, Lucia and Valeria."

"Nothing about Valeria but she sure didn't like Lucia. Although, she'd just found out from me her husband got Lucia pregnant."

"Nothing like a wronged spouse," Jack said.

"Don't I know it," Al added.

"You believe Heather didn't know?"

"I don't think she's that good an actress," Serena said.

Jack agreed. From what he'd seen, Heather was pretty transparent with no impulse control. "What about the other young women who worked for the Harrowsmiths? Heather have any idea what happened to them?"

"Nothing substantive, although she remembered Abigail was before Lucia and that they'd changed her name."

"Find Heather in the list."

Detectives gaped at Jack as Serena scrolled.

"You think Dustin bought his own wife?" Al asked.

There she was, at the top of the second page, born Amalia Valdez. Girls listed before that went for comparatively bargain prices, five hundred, a thousand.

Next to Heather's name, instead of a price tag, was a string of $$$$$. "Do all of the dollar signs mean Dustin thought she was priceless?" Jack said.

"That's some hard-core cynicism," Al said. "Especially coming from our resident romantic."

"Yes, this is certainly all about romance. How long have they been married?"

Serena answered. "Almost eleven years, right after Heather found out she was pregnant with Trysta. Is that important?"

"Helps build a timeline." Since Dustin hadn't been considerate enough to record dates or home countries with the names. "What's Dustin's last twenty-four look like? Before he bounced?"

"Heather said he was home last night and everything seemed fine." Serena consulted call reports on her laptop. "This is interesting. He drove downtown yesterday afternoon and talked to a young woman for a few minutes."

"We have a description of the woman?"

Serena scrolled. "No. I'll follow up with the officer who made that part of the report."

"Is the officer on shift? I want to talk to him or her now."

Serena got on the radio as Jack studied the whiteboard where they'd made notes about suspects. Dustin's list included:

Sells girls
Pathological liar
Father of Lucia's child
Gave her Prayer Cards
Jack added:
Bought wife
Met with mystery woman

Jack motioned impatiently at Al. "Find Raven in the book."

She was born Gabriella Niceta, fourteen when she was sold two years ago, private placement. By then, Dustin's prices had escalated and she went for $10,000.

Valeria was earlier in the book, five grand, no name change, commercial placement.

Heather had explained the system, such as it was, to Serena; sales to either families, individuals, or businesses, including the mobile spa.

Abigail began life as Manuela Cortolino. $20,000. Private.

A page-and-a-half before, Dinah. $10,000.

The Harrowsmith Girls, as Jack was beginning to think of them, sold for a premium. "Remind me, how much was Lucia?"

"Twenty-five," Serena said. "Dispatch is putting me through to the officer."

"Maybe prices went up because this a-hole Dustin knew they were being killed," Al said.

"And yet he kept sending them. Although it is perversely impressive they spent more than fifty grand so Ken could make bad porn."

"Shit, Jack, there're enough names here to keep me busy till retirement," Al said. "This organization is enormous. The commercial placements are possibly sex workers or at the restaurant, but who are all these families? Are they even in Colorado or did they get shipped to other states, other countries?"

"It doesn't help that some of the girls, like Raven, move around," Serena said. "She started off private."

"Why's everyone I question react like I hit them with a cattle prod when I mention her name?"

"Maybe she's moved up in the organization," Al said.

"I wonder if she ever worked for the Harrowsmiths," Jack said.

"You can ask her when you go for your *date*." Al made air quotes.

Jack had decided to approach Raven the old-fashioned way, the way they did it in the eighties—by going undercover as a customer.

"I'm getting responses from her or from someone. Not like I'm dealing with a legitimate business where they're going to deal straight. Serena, anything?"

"How much is that setting the department back?" Al asked.

"A lot. She was unavailable until I hit the right number. They're assuring me I won't be disappointed."

"I wonder if Dustin continues to get a cut after he's made a placement." Al made a note. "Serena, where's he keep all that money?"

"Heather said she didn't know. Said it was offshore and Dustin made vague comments about getting everyone passports."

"Well that narrows it down to the entire fucking world." Jack added *Hides/Launders money* to Dustin's list.

The officer who'd surveilled Dustin downtown finally responded and give a description of the woman he was seen with. Jack walked to the board, scratched out mystery woman, and wrote Nicki in red marker.

"Maybe he was trying to warn her?" Serena said.

"Just when I think you're becoming a top-notch detective you display this unfortunate optimistic streak. I think he was warning her all right, but in a less pastoral way."

"You think Dustin slashed Nicki?"

Serena sounded like she didn't buy it and neither did Jack. "Nah. I can't picture Dustin getting blood on his soft white hands. Sahir on the other hand went away for assault with a knife." If Nicki ID'd Sahir as her attacker that could be another link to Dustin. The minister's reference to scarlet lips in Lucia's note still bugged Jack.

"I think Dustin was trying to find out what Nicki told me. Serena, keep working with Heather. We need to see if we can bust Dustin's alibi for Saturday night. Right now all he's got is home with the wife and kids."

"You got it."

"Al, I need you to run searches against FALNA Enterprises." Jack explained that was the registered parent company for the club and restaurant.

"We already ran Avi," Al said. "Third degree assault, receiving stolen property, nothing useful."

"So disappointing he didn't have any good warrants."

Jack took a last look at the suspect board.

Under Bibi's name:

Lied about driving Range Rover
Admitted being with Lucia Saturday
Gave up Raven's name and panicked
Assaulted girlfriend
Girlfriend dead
Ran from restaurant/avoided interview

Jack wanted to add *assaulted an officer*, but wasn't sure hummus counted as a weapon.

Ken's list was impressive, mostly in regard to Lucia:

Multiple felony statutory rape
Child pornography

False Imprisonment
DUI
Attempting to flee country
Lousy/nonexistent alibi
Argued with Lucia/explicitly threatened Lucia

Ken was a sick fuck any way you analyzed it and good riddance. Jack should have no doubts about him whatsoever, regardless of scarlet lips.

"Serena, since you're our resident Bible expert see what else you can divine—pun intended—from Dustin's cards. One of you also needs to follow up with Paul or the ME on Valeria's autopsy.

"And pray for me, I'm headed to Stoney Gate."

CHAPTER FIFTY-FIVE

---

*H*I HONEY HOW'S *my favorite niece?*
    Their code phrase. When Dustin texted the burner it meant he was on the move and their escape plan was in motion. Pete, the gift-wrapped burners, the coded messages—all invented by Dustin. Every year on her birthday she got a card signed in an old man's shaky hand. Dustin had even photoshopped some pictures. Heather thought of all his careful planning wasted.

They asked her and asked her where he'd go, destinations he'd mentioned, names of associates. Over and over and over. Heather grew to really hate Jack. Even told him at one point, "I hate you," got up and pounded her head against the wall of the interview room while Serena tried to calm her down. Good cop bad cop was a real thing.

Maybe he was like Serena's boss or something, always telling her what to do, only Serena didn't seem to mind. And God, she might as well wear her hair up all the time now because all everyone wanted to see was the stupid tat.

What else could they get from her? They already had the phones, the ledger, the whole story about her fake uncle. Had searched her house, pawed through her trash, where they found the packaging from the burners; turned drawers upside down looking for the hidden messages underneath. Or whatever. All of her hatred for Dustin focused instead on the cops because they were there, front and center, right in front of her, stone-faced and disapproving. Except Serena, who was nice.

She wanted to scream at them, especially Jack when he sat all smug and knowing like men everywhere since the beginning of time, condescending like she was a stupid cunt who'd been used and taken advantage of and wasn't even smart enough to help herself.

He said that to her, arrogant prick, and Heather had to keep remembering her kids. She was doing this for them. Because she had to survive, stay out of jail, live without Dustin somehow.

What had Nicki seen in Jack? Maybe just the surface, square jaw, nice mouth, greenish-gray eyes. But God, he was stone cold, just like Sahir only in a different business. She'd learned to read men's faces. When Sahir's lips thinned and pressed together a certain way she knew she was gonna get beaten.

And man, she was using the Lord's name in vain all the time now, not even trying to stop herself.

"I don't know what Nicki saw in you." Heather yelled at Jack at one point. "You're awful and rude and insulting and—"

"We're not talking about me."

"Well maybe we should be." Which didn't make any sense even as Heather said it.

Then Jack would leave, and Heather would take a breath, and Serena would make sure she got Starbucks or a burger or a bathroom break, let her call her kids.

The cops asked all about the church. How they raised the funds for the building, how they were paid, where donations were deposited. Did they have a five-oh-one something? Who did their taxes? Could she show them the returns? How'd they make connections between girls at the charity and customers? Connections, like it was fucking online dating.

Don't know, don't know, don't know. All their questions revealed how truly ignorant Heather was, how meek and passive she'd been all along. Even she realized, as the interrogation proceeded, her astonishing lack of curiosity. Why didn't she know any of this? Why hadn't she asked?

Because she was usually getting high, then getting clean, then focusing on not getting high again. Or she was pregnant and sick and then nursing a finicky baby. All she could manage most days was to wash her hair and find clean clothes to wear, let alone worry about high finances and money laundering.

Even worse was when they wanted to know about her time as a sex worker for Sahir. Heather started to say it wasn't that bad. Realized with the force of shock how horrible her life had been in comparison with almost anyone else's. That it was that bad. That her mother had pimped her out for nothing and at least Sahir made it pay and at the ripe old age of sixteen she'd thought that was smart.

Worst of all was when she had to pretend with Dustin. They dictated stuff for her to text, fingers sticky and uncertain on the keys, expecting him to know it wasn't her, to stop replying, to accuse her of being a faithless harlot. If he called she was supposed to keep him talking and they'd even printed out a script for her to follow. All the while being scrutinized like a bug under a magnifying glass.

When was she going to burst into flames?

CHAPTER FIFTY-SIX

———◆———

JACK FELT FRESH disgust when he pulled into the parking lot and saw Dustin's abandoned car not thirty yards from a marked DPD cruiser. What a great job of surveillance that was. Dustin had to have walked right past the officers. Maybe he even waved or offered to pray for their incompetent souls.

Inside the church office, a skinny young man, associate pastor Elijah, confirmed that Dustin had borrowed his car to run a quick errand at ten thirty a.m.

"Oh, my gosh," Eli said. "I hope nothing happened to him. We had such a good talk before he left, pastor asked if I want to lead the service Wednesday night, which of course I do. He's wonderful to work for, just wonderful."

Eli was literally shiny, wide eyes, skin as white as his shirt, a blinding smile when he talked about the thrill of leading a service.

He was so bright he almost hurt Jack's eyes. "You said Dustin left here alone. Did he mention taking anyone with him, maybe having his wife join him?"

"No sir, just an errand. Are your sure pastor is all right? I've been calling hospitals."

"Tell me exactly what he said."

Eli's nod was as crisp as the crease in his khakis. "Pastor said his car had been making a strange sound and was shifting rough. He's so busy and works so hard he hadn't had a chance to have it looked at. When he asked if he could borrow mine of course I said yes."

"Did Dustin take anything with him?"

"A backpack and some papers."

"How about a laptop? That would fit in a backpack."

Eli considered the question a second then opened his pale blue eyes even wider. "You think pastor did something bad."

A trafficking operation had its headquarters across the parking lot. What did this man think about the nonstop parade of young girls?

"What's your involvement with the charity?" Jack asked.

"I'm not involved, that's pastor's domain. He loves his work just as much as he loves the Lord."

"How about you?" Jack asked.

"Of course I love the Lord."

"I meant, if you're not involved with the charity, what's your role?"

"Oh. I assist with services, church administration, and sometimes counsel parishioners."

"Did you ever counsel Lucia?"

Eli blinked rapidly, a blonde rabbit. "I know what happened to her but—no."

"Why not?"

"It's inappropriate for single men to be alone with single women."

"But for married men like Dustin anyone's fair game?"

"I don't mean to be disrespectful but you're misinterpreting, I think. Sir."

"I don't believe there's any misinterpreting the fact that Dustin was the father of Lucia's unborn child."

Jack wouldn't have thought it was possible for Eli to get whiter but he blanched to the point where his skin was nearly transparent.

"That can't be true."

"It is if you believe in science."

Jack surveyed Dustin's office, the very familiar oil painting mounted on a bronze tripod, the imposing desk. "I've seen that painting on the prayer cards Dustin gives out. You must have gotten some yourself."

"There would have been no reason."

Eli spoke as if Jack had asked something painfully obvious. "Enlighten me. Why is that?"

"Pastor said Christian men are made stronger by puzzling out problems on their own."

So much cynicism to suppress. "You mean only women received those cards from Dustin?"

"Yes. Men could of course receive counseling and attend Bible study."

"What were the women meant to do with the cards?"

"Study the verses pastor wrote addressing whatever issues the woman in question was experiencing. He told me wise women discern the true meaning and receive comfort."

"And if the woman isn't wise?" As in allowing herself to get knocked up.

"I don't know, I never thought of that. Where are you going with these questions?"

Nowhere, apparently. Jack showed Eli a picture of Nicki. "Do you know if this woman received any special counseling?"

Eli's mouth formed a thin line of distaste and he spoke with perhaps more intensity than he realized. "Not from me she didn't."

"Was that because she's single or because you don't like her?"

"I didn't say that."

"You didn't have to, it was clear from your expression. What does Nicki do that you disapprove of?"

No go. "I care and pray for each of our parishioners equally."

"Dustin visited Nicki at her office yesterday afternoon.

Do you know what that was about?"

"No, sir, I don't, but if he did there must have been a good reason."

"How about a woman named Valeria Monsour?"

"I don't know who that is." Eli answered with no hesitation. "If you'd like a list of parishioners I can provide that. Uh, if you get a warrant. Um, I'll have to check the procedure."

"You must have a safe for storing collection money. Can you open it for me?"

Eli repeated himself. "I'm pretty sure I shouldn't do that without a warrant."

Jack sort of lied. "That would be true if I was going to take anything but I'm not. I only want to look. I'm investigating the deaths of two young women and an assault on a third. I'm sure you're eager to clear Dustin's name."

Eli puffed his skinny chest, an offended Boy Scout. "It's horrible about the women, but pastor can't possibly be involved. Here, I'll show you."

He crouched and pressed on a section of wood paneling that popped open to reveal a heavy, metal, fireproof safe concealed behind.

An empty safe.

Jack felt zero surprise but Eli's mouth hung open. "I don't understand. There should be cash and checks from collections."

"You're sure Dustin didn't say anything else about his errand?"

"No. But he asked me if I'd like to lead the service tomorrow and if I'd learned—no. Oh, no."

"Learned what?"

"It's not possible."

Jack used his best impatient command voice. "What did Dustin say?"

Eli visibly deflated, sat down hard on the floor, back

against the wall. "He asked if I'd learned enough to run the church on my own."

"You're sure he didn't give any indication where he was going?"

Eli repeated, "It can't mean, it's not possible." Stared at Jack like he'd found out Jesus was caught butt-fucking the Easter Bunny.

Stated the obvious. "He's not coming back, is he?"

———————◆———————

Jack figured Dustin was unlikely to be as stupid as Ken and drive himself into a ditch. So many leads to follow, so little time. Then, as if the day couldn't get more complex or surprising, Ruth was waiting for him in the lobby at headquarters.

She stood when she saw him and extended a slim hand. Smiled. Dressed in shades of gray but younger somehow, softer. A long sweater over a short skirt, tights, boots. Her hair was curled and her makeup was muted. It was abnormal how normal she looked.

Ruth made a sound like humming. "Mmm. I thought perhaps I should wear a manteau and scarf. Very proper, very modest, you know, Iranian. Then I realized that would be foolish. You were born in the States and it'd be like wearing a costume."

He didn't respond to her stiff attempt at small talk and led her into an interview room. "I have a lot to do so if you could get right to the point of this visit I'd appreciate it."

She smiled again and tipped her head flirtatiously. "Of course. I came here because I felt there were a few things I could clear up for you."

More than a few, but no way he was falling for her warm, suddenly down-to-earth routine. This interview would be by the book. He had her state her name. Made it clear she was being recorded. Offered water. Gave her every opportunity to back out, reconsider, mention the dreaded L word.

Which, come to think of it, she had. "Are you now waiving your right to counsel? Because you were very clear when I was at your house executing warrants that any future communication was to be with your attorney present."

"Am I allowed to change my mind?"

"I need you to say specifically that you're here voluntarily and don't wish for a lawyer."

She did. "I think you may have found the way I acted earlier cold or strange."

"In what way?"

The point of a tongue swept her lips. "I have something to tell you that will clarify certain developments but it's extremely discomfiting and intensely personal."

Swell. He couldn't wait. She took a delicate sip of water in a way that struck him as decidedly feline, replaced the cap on the bottle, and set it back on the table in exactly the same spot. Her OCD behavior made his gut tighten but was also oddly riveting. He'd never watched anyone wield a water bottle with this much fascination.

Ruth grew serious. "It was comforting on Sunday to learn your mother's from Iran and that you're familiar with the culture, because what I have to tell you would shock most Westerners."

She paused for a long time and Jack fought his urgency, his desire to say "spit it out," and get back to the million things he had to do. But she'd come to him, not vice versa, and although he was driven to get this over with—whatever this was—he was also determined not to play the game by her rules. So he waited. It got so quiet he heard the fluorescent lights hum, footsteps crescendo and fade in the hallway, the big clock on the wall tick.

Then, with no introduction or disclaimer whatsoever: "I was genitally circumcised."

She enunciated clearly. There was no mistaking the

words. "When?"

"Many years ago. I'm sure you're aware that in our culture it used to be tradition for proper young girls."

Not any culture he was part of. "I'm aware it was barbaric and deserves to die out completely."

"I understood why it was necessary if—" She blinked back tears. "If what? Painful? Traumatic? There are no words. You see, I'd gotten pregnant. After I had the baby that's when—it happened."

He felt an involuntary pang of sympathy, but how the hell was this related to anyone's homicide? "How old were you?"

"Sixteen. My aunt accompanied me to Egypt where one could have the procedure performed by a doctor, all safe and sanitary. Not at all barbaric. But you care about now, as do I and—"

Jack cut her off. "Wait. Twenty-three years ago?"

"Yes."

Pieces fell into place. "Bibi."

"What about him?"

"He's twenty-three. Bibi's your son not your nephew." It explained a lot, her tolerance for the sloppy, destructive, chaotic disaster that was Bibi.

Ruth leaned forward, hands gripping the table, her breathing quickened. "Jack. You are by far the most intelligent man I've met in a long while. But you're guessing."

"I'm doing math and based on your reaction, correctly."

Another pause in which he heard the lights hum.

Then she said, "I must admit, you made this easier than I thought it would be, even though you're my sworn enemy."

"Which makes me wonder why you're here talking to me without a lawyer."

"Quid pro quo. An expression I know I won't need to explain to you. It seems I've been surrounded by imbeciles for so long who can't do simple arithmetic that I let my guard down."

"Why would you be"—Jack almost choked on the word—"circumcised. Because you had a child out of wedlock?"

There he was, talking like Heathcliff again; *wedlock,* Jesus. But she seemed to have that effect on him.

Ruth exhaled sharply. "I haven't told anyone, ever, outside of my immediate family but I need you to believe me, so I'll answer. I was sexually assaulted and, according to that same family, it was my fault. Perhaps with all pleasure removed I'd no longer have the irresistible urge to tempt decent men."

Her voice dripped acid and Jack couldn't blame her. Culturally, twenty odd years ago in the Middle East it was a sadly credible story.

Then her tone softened. "Do you find me a complete monster now or am I a tiny bit appealing? Sorry if that's a frivolous question."

She looked down shyly and his mother's words from Sunday night flashed in his mind. *Flatter her but be subtle.* "You know you're an attractive woman."

"I don't know that. And now that I've told you..." Her voice trailed off. "What must you think of me?"

Jack was trying hard not to reach conclusions about her as either a woman or a victim. "You claim that you're telling me this so I'll believe you. About what?"

"I know who killed Lucia."

"You're talking about Ken."

"Ken was a marriage of convenience, as I'm sure you realize. But there are accommodations, no, realities men from our culture understand, things that American men do not. That's why I feel I can talk to you."

A digression and an inaccurate one at that. "But I am American."

"You're not a typical American man, I can see your mother's influence. You have style, intelligence. Do you think you might have wanted to know me, personally, under different circumstances?"

For some reason, she seemed to care what he thought of her as an object of desire. Jack had murders to solve; playing to a suspect's ego, even if it made him feel phony and manipulated, went with the territory.

So he played. "Come on. You know you're good-looking with fantastic style of your own."

She held her arms away from her sides. "You like the outfit?"

"It shows you're in great shape as well as very beautiful." Jack forced a smile of his own, made eye contact, his eyebrows went up and down. All the while thinking, yes, and you've managed to somehow weaponize that beauty.

"Thank you," Ruth said. "My, um, pride has taken quite a beating."

"How so?"

"What Ken did with all those girls? My husband should have understood being from our—my culture, but he didn't. All sex, sex, sex; his needs. His rights. No concern for me or how difficult physical relations were." Ruth cleared her throat. "Why do you think I gave those videos to you despite the humiliation?"

Jack bit back the urge to say, *because I had a warrant?* Instead he said, "You hate your husband. That was pretty evident from day one."

"You make me sound like a teenager. I hate him, boo hoo."

"Not without good reason," Jack said. "But you have to see where this makes me suspicious. You have motive and then some to help put Ken away."

"I do. And I wish it were the answer. Let me explain. You were right, as usual, when you observed that I wouldn't marry out of my faith. Although, the first time Ken cheated, with a young woman named Eve, I certainly revisited that decision."

Jack frowned. Another name to add to the list? "When was that?"

"We moved here ten years ago and it started right after." Her mouth pursed as if she'd bitten into a lemon. "I tried to blame America as a corrupting influence but it seems unfair to blame a country for Ken's deviance. You've seen the videos?"

"I have."

"All that pathetic playacting. And before you ask—I know what happened because I installed cameras. I was blindsided the first time and wasn't going to be surprised again. After Bibi moved in surveillance became even more of a priority. Unfortunately, my nephew—my son—has similar weaknesses."

Watching those videos had made Jack wish he could bleach his brain, even without his spouse as a featured player. "Deplorable as Ken's behavior is, what does this have to do with Lucia's murder?"

"Right." She cocked a neatly groomed eyebrow. "This is work for you."

"What is it for you?"

"Honestly? A bit enjoyable. That sounds weird but after the company I've been keeping it's nice to talk to an intelligent, decent man."

"Lucia?" Jack prompted.

"I saw what happened on one of the videos. Are you sure you watched them all?"

"Why would Ken kill Lucia? Because she cheated on him and got pregnant?" What a bizarre concept; that Lucia, purchased for twenty-five thousand dollars and kept under lock and key, could have been "cheating" on the married man who owned her.

"No," Ruth said. "No, no, no. Not Ken. Although I wish it had been because then I'd have grounds in any religion to divorce him. It was a different individual, a man named Sahir."

"Who's Sahir?" Jack pretended not to know.

Ruth took another fastidious sip of water. "A colleague—no. An employee. Not an equal but someone I thought I could trust. His father worked for my father, going back years. I don't have words to describe the betrayal I feel. Not to mention I no longer feel safe. Can you arrest him? Do you need me to spell his name?"

"Let me get this straight. You're here accusing an employee of murder because he didn't know his place?" Jack was irritated, sure this whole performance was nothing but a time-wasting lie. But somehow he hit a bullseye and Ruth sounded amazed.

"In addition to doing Ken's bidding instead of mine, I discovered that Sahir's true allegiance is with a whore named Raven. I have a man in my home who frightens me."

Three people had now teed Sahir up for Jack's consideration. He may not be a nice guy but it all seemed way too good to be true. Plus, Ruth knew Raven?

"Tell me about Raven. I've heard her name several times."

"What's to tell? She's a sex worker." Ruth's eyes narrowed. "Sahir's favorite."

"How would you know a sex worker like Raven?"

Ruth answered easily. "From the charity. I met her at church."

"How did Sahir meet Raven?"

"Perhaps he paid for her services."

"This sounds like payback to me," Jack said.

"It's also true and I need you to take action. Sahir can no longer be relied upon and I don't know what he's likely to do next. I fear for my safety. I'll get a restraining order or whatever you advise."

Jack stated the most obvious flaw in her statement. "Lucia's murder isn't on any of the hard drives or memory devices I took into evidence."

"I can't explain that. I thought the security company stored everything. Contact my attorney again if you have any difficulty, I'll let him know I approve."

Ruth tucked a curl behind her ear. "Seriously. Men disgust me, except for the few decent ones like you. I honestly wish we could have gotten to know each other under different circumstances, without all this horror in our way."

Her attempts at flirtation were so stilted and awkward Jack almost wished for a head injury in his near future to erase the moment.

"Why should I believe you about Lucia's murder?"

"Quid pro quo. You now have information you could use to hurt me. As for Sahir's motives, I can only speculate he thought her death was what Ken wanted. It certainly did nothing for me other than require I go pick out another one and watch the cycle start again."

That comment conjured an image in Jack's mind of feeding mice to a snake. "You're telling me you weren't directly involved, you only saw Lucia's killing on a security video?"

"Yes." Said with a trace of impatience.

"Is what happened to Lucia what happened to Ken's previous companions? He got tired of them and Sahir or someone made them disappear?"

"I'm only here about Lucia. I assume you'll take appropriate steps?"

"An intelligent person would conclude this was a pattern and she wasn't the first."

"You're quite intelligent and I do enjoy talking to you, but no." Ruth pushed back her chair. "Are we finished?"

"You're not under arrest, you came to see me," Jack said. "One more question, before you go?"

"Of course."

"Other than being annoyed he went rogue, what did you feel about Sahir killing Lucia?"

"You are fond of therapy sessions." Ruth said it good naturedly. "Maybe we can do that over a drink sometime? Look, as I told you before, I didn't form a close attachment with Lucia so I didn't feel anything."

"That's cold, even for you."

"It's honest is what it is. You want to do therapy? After all the years of abuse I've suffered, I'm numb."

CHAPTER FIFTY-SEVEN

———◆———

DUSTIN'S VOICE RUMBLED from the phone. "I wasn't sure you'd answer. Can you talk?"

"Yes." True enough. While they hadn't let her leave, the cops had left her alone for once in the interview room. Even let her smoke.

"You didn't respond to my text so I wondered. Thought maybe the police had taken the phone. Are they giving you a rough time?"

Taken the phone. He knew the police had been to the house? How? Serena said there was no way Dustin could know she gave them the ledger unless she told him but he was good at reading her and getting information.

"They know you ran." Don't tell him anything else, she willed herself. Don't tell him. Crime was all it was and her husband—the father of her children—was a criminal.

"Is Eli okay?"

That jolted her. "How would I know?"

"I felt bad putting him in the middle."

"You care more about your associate pastor than you do about me?"

"Of course not. You know I love you."

"Then how could you leave without me?" This made her too nervous, playing games with her husband. Lying to him. Although, of course, he'd been lying to her for years.

"I didn't. I mean, that's why I texted you. I'm executing our plan. How are you doing?"

"How—" Heather stammered. How was she doing? Was he fucking kidding? Stuck with cops all day threatening her with jail and losing custody of her kids if she didn't cooperate and now her best friend was maybe dying. And her loving criminal husband had bounced leaving her to manage all of it.

All she could manage was a snarly "Fine."

"You don't sound fine."

"Nicki's in the hospital. Got her face slashed."

"They know who did it?" Dustin didn't sound the least bit surprised.

"I think you know who did it."

Heather jumped out of her chair when the interview room door opened. Jack. *Fuck.*

On the phone, Dustin started to deny knowing who hurt Nicki and she cut him off. "Save it."

"She gonna pull through?"

"Where are you anyway? On the way to Mexico?"

Jack's eyebrows went up. He made a motion with his hand, mouthed the words "keep him talking." That wasn't proving hard. Dustin seemed to want to talk except not about the things she needed him to talk about.

"Let's not get into that right now," Dustin said. "Tell me what happened to Nicki."

"Pete lives in Mexico so that's the plan, right? I'm not that dumb."

"Right now is not the time to—"

"Whatever. I have to ask you something and you need to tell me the truth. For real."

"Sure."

"Why'd you sleep with Lucia?"

In the room with her, Jack shook his head. *No.*

"I tried to warn you," Dustin said. "Remember, I asked if you had enough discernment? Cops'll tell you whatever they think will gain your cooperation. They make things sound real, say they have proof."

"You make things sound real when you're a dishonest prick." It had to be true, didn't it? About Lucia? Why would the cops make up a baby?

"They're lying to you," Dustin said. "We went over this. I tried to prepare you."

"I certainly am surrounded by lies."

She remembered the mother she had and the mother she wanted to be. Not a wasted flake who sold them out, even if it meant sacrificing her own happiness. Children needed their father, she should know better than anyone. Her life would have been so different, so much better, if her mother hadn't driven her real father away.

Why she wasted breath even now asking Dustin to tell the truth. If he did that, she'd do anything for him.

Her voice faded. "Please just be honest. Please."

Jack tapped the piece of paper with the script.

God, she hated him, hated all the cops. Felt crushing guilt about giving them the ledger and betraying her husband.

Betraying him. That was funny. She wasn't betraying Dustin. She hadn't slept around and gotten pregnant. She'd always done every single little thing he asked, life on the cheap, crappy minivan, giving up her old friends. She'd given him chance after chance after chance.

"Remember the Bible," Dustin said. "You assured me you could discern truth from falsehood."

Strange thing was she could. Heather started to cry and covered the phone, not wanting him to hear. Trysta and Ryan smiled back at her from the home screen of her real phone on the table. Ryan had been missing a tooth and she remembered sneaking into his room to leave money under the pillow. She had to hug them again, she had to hold them. They could not grow up without her. Would not.

"Please, Heather. I have to know we're still a family."

A voice, not her own, answered him. "Is that because you killed your other one?"

"No," Jack whispered, shoved the piece of paper with the shit she was supposed to say closer. But she wasn't following a script.

Dustin's voice turned cold, no longer pleading. "What have they told you?"

Heather couldn't help herself. "If that poor girl hadn't died I would've needed to plan a baby shower."

"Now it's 'poor girl'? You hated Lucia. You were always envious and insecure."

"Speaking of the Bible, you put away falsehood and tell the truth. I'll do anything for you, still, if you just come clean with me."

Jack looked like he was going to explode. Heather was afraid of him and knew she shouldn't say these things but she had to get Dustin to admit it. Had to. Only chance they had.

Instead, Dustin doubled down. "I have always been faithful to you. I thought I could trust you."

"Trust me?" She turned away from Jack. "You know about autopsies right? Since you're so smart. They did one on Lucia and found the fetus. Hard to lie about that."

"Wasn't mine."

Heather laughed, sniffled, wiped her nose. "Fuckin' save it."

And hung up.

"Heather, we went through this. Rehearsed it." Jack bit off the words. "Now you've tipped him off. Autopsy? He knows you're working with us."

"He just couldn't be honest," Heather said. "Unbelievable."

"You're unbelievable. And unreliable. Your husband sold children into sex work by the dozen."

"Dustin saved me." Heather still couldn't figure it out.

Jack could. "And he destroyed hundreds of others."

Serena opened the door and must have registered the expressions on both of their faces. Jack angry, Heather crying.

"You did great," Serena said. "We got him. He's pinging off a tower south of Santa Rosa, New Mexico."

Heather and Jack answered simultaneously, for once on the same page. "Good."

CHAPTER FIFTY-EIGHT

JACK WAS GETTING ready to head back to the hospital when Greer Spahr called with results from Valeria's autopsy.

She led off with, "You're not going to be happy."

"I'm already not happy."

"Valeria was an OD. Not exactly what you were expecting, huh?"

Jack was not exactly surprised. "On what?"

"Tox screens will take time, but there was foam in her lungs suggestive of opioid intoxication. And you don't sound at all disappointed."

"Her boyfriend OD'd too," Jack said. "In her apartment. But we found him in time to administer naloxone. It's possible he shared with Valeria, we have a witness who said coke was her drug of choice."

"Cocaine laced with fentanyl or carfentanyl would do it," Greer said. "For one example."

"Have you told Paul?"

"Called you first."

"It's his case."

"Ugh. I'm not sure I can deal with the gloating. You sure you don't want to do it? He sits right near you."

Jack glanced over at Paul, by all appearances working intently on his computer. Probably playing solitaire or fantasy football. "Positive. And do me a favor? I'm about to go interview the boyfriend back from the dead so wait fifteen minutes until I'm outta here?"

———————◆———————

"Look," Jack said, "it's Lazarus."

"Who?" Bibi was unsurprisingly confused.

"Except you haven't been dead three days. Valeria, on the other hand, that would be a miracle of biblical proportions."

Bibi was spending the night in the hospital. Like many individuals revived with Narcan, he'd been pissy, combative, and unappreciative of the first responders' efforts. Mike pulled out a chair and sat next to the bed. Jack preferred to stand and lean against the wall.

"You're lucky we came in and found you when we did," Jack said.

Bibi snorted. "Lucky."

"Lucky enough to OD in a dead girl's apartment."

"I have a key," Bibi said, as if that explained anything.

Mike assumed the proverbial good cop role—or, in this case, more like supernaturally patient cop. "Okay. A lot has happened. Let's break this down step by step. Tell us why you were there."

"Because I didn't want to go home."

"I specifically asked you to wait at the restaurant." Jack couldn't resist his pointless observation.

Mike said, "You went to Valeria's because it was a safe place. I get that. It was a way to feel close to her, maybe to say goodbye."

"Yeah." Bibi warmed to this benign line of questioning.

"And the way you relax is getting high. Don't worry about the drugs, we're not interested in that. We're interested in figuring out who's killing the girls in your employ, Lucia and now Valeria."

"Not my employ." Bibi, as usual, missed the salient point.

"You saw Valeria Saturday, right?" Mike asked.

"I took her to the motel and we were gonna, you know... but then she got mad."

"She got mad because you gave her Lucia's purse and weren't even smart enough to clean it out first." Although. In this particular instance Jack should be grateful for Bibi's stupidity.

Mike cut in. "I don't think you ever meant to hurt Valeria. In fact, one of her friends told us she liked coke. You guys worked together, sounds like you had a lot in common."

"We did." Bibi motioned at Jack "I tried to tell him I liked her."

"What I need to know is where you got the drugs you've been using," Mike said. "And who else you've shared with."

"Only Val." Bibi's pudgy finger pointed at Jack again. "And I told him where I got the shit, prick Sahir."

Jack wasn't remembering the same conversation. "Why would Sahir give you bad drugs?"

"I don't know."

Mike tried more explicit prompting. "Sahir gave you coke to use Saturday and Valeria OD'd. Then he gave you more and you OD'd."

Bibi frowned. This was a dawn that was exceptionally slow to break. "You guys think he knew?"

Mike nodded sagely. "We have to think he did."

"No, shit." Bibi looked between the two of them, not visibly angry. "Does my aunt know?"

"Which part?" Jack asked. "That you use and Sahir's your supplier? That you were technically dead? That Valeria's literally dead? You're going to have to be more specific."

"I was dead?" Bibi's voice held a tone of wonder. "Cool."

"No, not cool," Jack said. "You're looking at a murder charge for Valeria if you knew you were giving her poison."

"Not me, Sahir."

"Was it normal for Sahir to hook you up?" Mike asked.

"When it suited. Last night he pretended we were doing some kind of detox. Kept coming into my room and making me say prayers." Bibi's hand formed a fist.

Jack wondered if that was before, during, or after Sahir slashed Nicki. She'd been able to ID him when Mike showed her pictures. If so, why hadn't Sahir killed her? According to Ruth he killed Lucia. Bibi was claiming he knowingly provided lethal drugs that killed Valeria and almost killed Bibi. Why not finish Nicki off? Unless those weren't the instructions Sahir was given.

Ruth was a lot of things, but Jack had a hard time believing she'd order a hit on her own son. "Why would Sahir want to kill you?"

"You'll have to ask him."

"We'd love to," Jack said. "Where would you suggest we look?"

"He sleeps in a shed out back for appearances or some shit."

That surprised Jack enough he took a step away from the wall. He'd searched that goddamned residence. Or thought he had. "At your aunt's house?"

"He's on hand to do crap for her 24-7," Bibi said. "Mostly he tortures me."

Could Ruth have told him the truth? Jack debated how much to share with Bibi, and decided now wasn't the time to reveal his aunt was actually his mother. "Ruth told me today that Sahir killed Lucia."

"No shit," Bibi said, again.

"No shit that's true? No shit you're surprised? No shit that couldn't have happened?"

Busy few days for the mean piece of garbage and Jack could barely contain his frustration at coming so close to Sahir without realizing. It also appeared Sahir had no idea who Bibi really was.

Mike somehow maintained his calm, understanding

approach. "Bibi, look. We want to believe you. But this whole story is whacked. You need to take us through exactly what happened Saturday when you came home with Lucia."

"I can't." Bibi's voice faded and red splotches mottled his cheeks.

"Why is that?" Mike's voice was soft, edge-free. "Are you embarrassed about something?"

"Lucia rejected you," Jack said.

"No." Bibi wouldn't meet Jack's eyes.

"You know," Mike said. "Lucia was really pretty. Classy. Girls like that think they're better than us. Trust me, I've been shot down plenty of times."

Score one for dancing with douchebags.

"She was nice." Bibi sniffled. "A lot of the maids weren't."

"I think they all would've liked you if they had the chance," Mike said with a straight face. "Your aunt just worked them so hard and I'll bet she told them not to talk to you."

"That's true. Lucia wasn't allowed to clean my room. And you know, my aunt locked them in at night. There was this one girl...Sarah."

"Sarah" had been in the earliest porn videos.

Bibi gasped and Mike patted his arm. "Take your time."

"Her real name was Inez but I wasn't supposed to use it. She was my friend. For reals."

"Did Inez come from Shores of Hope?" Jack asked.

"They all do."

"Tell us more about Inez," Mike said. "You were friends? Ruth didn't keep you apart?"

Jack remembered Ruth's comment about Bibi having the same "weakness" as Ken.

"She tried," Bibi said. "I'd sneak downstairs at night after the bitch was asleep and sit outside Inez's room. She couldn't get out and I didn't have the code. One night, we stayed up so late I fell asleep on the floor in the hall. My aunt lost it."

Bibi squeezed his eyes shut as if unable to bear the memory. "She got special medicine from the Middle East for Inez to help her diet, but it made her sick, like really sick. I said she must be having a bad reaction and begged my aunt to let me take her to the doctor because by then I had my license. I begged and begged. Even though they were watching me I still went downstairs but Inez got so tired she slept all the time, although she told me she loved me right before—"

"Right before what?"

Mike's tone was soothing. Bibi opened his eyes. "Right before she disappeared."

Inez in particular would haunt Jack, her young body gaunt and waxy in her final video which still didn't stop Ken from sexually abusing her. Inez started out a pretty child, growing into a young woman, albeit in unspeakable circumstances. Then she aged in reverse; frail, listless, purple shadows under her eyes. By her final video she barely reacted to Ken, too tired to lift her head; it was watching a young girl die in slow motion.

Mike continued his patient coaching and Jack was happy to let him take the lead. "You were nice to Inez and I'll bet you were nice to Lucia, too. Tell us about Saturday."

Bibi stared at Mike. "No means no and everything, but she didn't say it. Lucia came on to me. It was her idea to drive me home."

"What happened once you got there?"

"I had some coke and some stones from the spa and we were gonna give each other massages. Lucia wanted to, we were making out in the car, she was into me I could tell. I didn't make her do anything."

"Sounds like you were having a good time. What happened next?"

Bibi squeezed his eyes shut again. "Everyone was still up in the living room."

"Who's everyone?" Mike asked.

"Ruth, Ken."

"Where was Sahir?"

"*Ch.* Lurking around. Like I said, he follows my aunt like a dog."

"Okay. What happened next?"

"Ken started complaining about how he liked this one and I always messed everything up. He slapped Lucia and she started screaming so I grabbed a decanter and locked myself in my room."

"You couldn't stand to stay and see what they did to Lucia," Mike said.

"I couldn't." Bibi's voice rose.

"Is there video surveillance in the living room?"

"My aunt says there isn't but she's a lying cunt."

"You didn't stay in your room though, did you?" Jack asked.

Bibi's eyes slid between the two detectives.

Mike prompted. "You'll feel better if you tell us everything."

"I did for a while but I was frustrated, you know, cock teased, thinking I was gonna fuck Lucia. I'm normal. I like girls. It got quiet so I went back downstairs but they weren't in the living room anymore, they were in the bathroom washing her."

"Who was?"

"My aunt and Sahir. He found the stones that we were gonna use and he was going on again about how I was a sodomite and he wanted to beat me."

"Why'd Sahir want to beat you? What had you done?"

"When I saw Lucia I started to cry. That's not bad is it?" Bibi stared imploringly at Mike.

Human emotion bad, Jack thought. Killing good. How things worked in Ruthworld. It was a wonder Bibi wasn't even more fucked up than he was.

"Lucia was already dead?" Mike asked.

Bibi nodded. "Sahir made me help wash her, which isn't the way it's done. My aunt should've done it because she's a girl. I never touched a dead body before. And then we wrapped her, and my aunt did the lipstick. She said Lucia was a whore and must be made up to look like one. Sahir said he'd do the burial because I couldn't be trusted and at that point I just wanted to get wasted so I went back to my room. I liked Lucia, I did."

"That's how Lucia wound up next to the dumpster," Mike said. "It wasn't your idea."

"It wasn't."

Jack said, "There were black stones found with Lucia's body. That doesn't look good for you."

Bibi's fist pounded on the bedspread again. "Oh ya, prick Sahir kept going on and on about them, proof of how sick I am, but Aunt Ruth said it was perfect, that we'd use them, that we must give the girl a proper burial this time."

Jack latched onto the words *this time*. "What does that mean?"

"Inez and all the other girls, Abigail, Dinah."

Jack exhaled. "Abigail was thirteen when she started working there, what could that helpless little girl have possibly done?"

Bibi mimicked Ruth. "They are all lazy and undisciplined and must learn to work hard." Then switched to his own voice.

"Abigail was cute at first, you know? I wanted to do her. Then she got fat."

"Like Inez," Mike said.

"That's why I started doing drugs, 'cause I was hungry all the time. My aunt doesn't have chips in the house or snacks or soda or anything and she only eats like a piece of lettuce a day."

"Did you ever ask where the girls went?"

"They'd say she went home, or quit, or didn't do a good

job. Then a new one would start and I'd be forbidden to mention the old one's name. Like now there's Esther."

"Esther?" Jack's stomach sank.

"She just started."

"Why don't they just let the girls go when they're done with them?" Mike asked.

"Ken doesn't like the idea that they'll be with someone else. And Sahir worries they'll talk to you guys."

"Tell us about Ken," Mike said. "He's the one who has sex with them and films them. Is he also the one who decides when they're done with a girl, or is it Sahir?"

"No." Bibi grew emphatic. "It's all her. Aunt Farah doesn't give a shit what Ken wants. She hates all the girls, even the ones at the spa."

Pieces snapped together. Girls at the spa, which included Raven. Jack exchanged a look with Mike and thought with disgust of Ruth's poor-me-I'm-so-abused act. And yet she had been, in the worst possible way, if Bibi was her son. "What did you call her?"

"Oh, right. In this country I'm supposed to call her Ruth. Bitch's name is really Farah."

Headline of the report Jack had received an hour ago from his FBI contact and hadn't had time yet to share with Mike: Mohamed Alzeshi, the ostensible owner of Bibi'z, died three years ago in Iran. The family ran a diversified, international empire that included trafficking, narcotics, and money laundering. Mohamed had been the focus of a multi-year criminal investigation and his death—from poisoning—was 100% verified with forensics.

He had one son, Nishaat, aka Bibi, and a sister who was about to turn forty.

Her name was Farah and Farah was Arabic for Joy.

But how much joy could come from being raped by your own brother?

CHAPTER FIFTY-NINE

———◆———

SPLIT SECOND DECISION, giving Bibi the drugs. Hearing that Val was dead and the cops had found her, the enormous exposure, the risk—everything destroyed for the miserable crying waste of space on the floor—it was too much.

Sahir left the spa and headed to Ruth's, wondered if he should simply keep going and leave Denver entirely. Except he couldn't let Ruth down, even after her bizarre behavior the night before. Maybe because of it. She was still his responsibility, even if lately he'd come to realize she wasn't as perfect and controlled as he'd long believed.

When he arrived at her house her behavior only confirmed his doubts. He found her in the living room, sitting in the dark. Bibi was one thing, he expected erratic behavior from that pissant, but not Ruth.

"*Joonam?*"

His tone was questioning and she snapped, "How dare you address me in that manner."

She'd never complained about the endearment before. "What shall I call you?"

"Ma'am will do."

"You're upset about last night," Sahir said. "I should have—" Should have what?

"No, you pointed out a home truth. I need to choose my companions from my same class."

She was dressed in a sweater that was much too tight and a skirt that was much too short. For a moment, he feared another seduction, then quickly realized she smoldered not with passion, but with rage.

Sahir took a deep breath. "A lot has happened and we have to talk. Make decisions."

Ruth snorted. "*Ma'am*. It's what I told Raven to call me. Sir, ma'am." With her voice she made one hard and the other soft. "They're not equal, are they? Men are offered much more dignity. Let me ask you, if tables were reversed, and I was a powerful man and you the subservient woman, the employee, would you have said no? You wouldn't have been able to. Right or wrong I would've had my way."

"I know you're—" He stopped himself short of using the word "hurt." "You have every right to be angry. I was out of line."

"You still are. Don't disrespect me with attributions like angry or upset like I'm a silly girl. Which I can assure you, I'm not."

"I know that." Sahir took another step into the room. "There are, however, developments we must discuss. Business developments."

"I'm your employer, your superior. We discuss what I say is important."

"Val has been found by the police. We must act."

"There's no 'we,' unless you're referring to you and your whore. Your beloved invention, Raven. You even named her. Made her exactly what you think a woman should be."

Where had she gotten these ideas? It was unfathomable that Ruth could feel threatened enough to behave as rashly as she'd done earlier at the motel. "Raven is product, nothing more, but she's my product and not yours to manage. I sell her body by the hour. She misbehaved and I burned her. Is that what you want? To be demeaned that way? Well, I won't do it."

"I saw the dress, I saw the jewelry. I thought it was only Ken who behaved like a besotted schoolboy."

"What jewelry?"

"Stop. Offer the simple respect of not lying.

"You know I respect you," Sahir said.

"But not Bibi."

"You asked me to help him get off the drugs."

Ruth gave Sahir an appraising look. "I underestimated how much you would enjoy it. It's true I thought Bibi needed more discipline and guidance than I could provide. But then, I never wanted to be a mother so it's no surprise I'm not very good at it."

Now Sahir was completely lost. It took him a minute before he answered, and he wondered if he'd heard correctly. "A what?"

"It's funny, because at the time, if it had been up to me Bibi would've never existed."

"What are you saying?"

She shook her head. "You *are* an imbecile. Let me explain so even you can grasp: Bibi is my son. The young man you have tormented and disrespected at every opportunity is my son."

Sahir was so stunned he said the first idiotic thing that popped into his head. "I was told you got rid of it, had an abortion, a procedure—"

She cut him off. "A what?"

"A procedure. That's why you went away."

Her laughter was bitter. "Oh, I had a procedure all right. And when Mohamed and that slut they bought for him to marry suddenly appeared with a baby? The timing didn't seem a bit odd?"

"I thought." Sahir licked his lips, his mind raced. "I wasn't sure, in truth, whether to believe you had an abortion. But then—I—so Mohamed raised the baby as his own?"

Her laughter intensified, hysterical, echoing off the

marble. "It's true what I told Jack about being surrounded by stupidity."

"Jack? The detective? What?" Sahir stepped close but the look on her face stopped him.

"He's much smarter than you, although that's not much of a challenge. He figured it out instantly."

"When did you talk to the police?"

"You don't question me. Mohamed is dead. I run the organization." She raised her chin. "Me and my son. It's time you realize your place."

She wanted to punish him; that much was clear. And he might have gone along and accepted any rebuke as just desserts except that he couldn't let everything fall apart. Bibi might be dead, Val was dead, and Ruth had apparently spilled her guts to the detective. Still, he couldn't abandon her, even if she wasn't who he always thought she was.

Sahir dropped to his knees at her feet. "Farah."

"Don't call me that, either."

"I'll call you whatever you wish. Madame Harrowsmith, Ruth, sir. But I need time to process this news. I need to know what you said to the police. And we have to leave Denver tonight, now, this instant. Be angry at me if you wish, insult me, correct me but it's still my job to protect you."

Her voice sliced the air. "Have you listened to one word I said?"

He reached for her hand which she jerked out of his grasp. "Why won't *you* listen? Val right after Lucia? No way cops'll let that go. We must leave."

"No." She coiled. It was as if the air pressure changed around her, a visible disturbance as she stood. Her words were measured and clear as ice. "You must pack your things and vacate the premises. You have two hours."

Sahir stared up at her from his knees, started to ask where he would go, what he would do, then realized his words, his posture were exactly like Bibi's earlier at the spa. What he'd done with physical violence she'd done with words.

Bibi. When Ruth found out she'd know it was him. "Answer one question, please. Did Bibi come home?"

"There will be no further discussion. Now get out of my sight."

Sahir pushed to his feet and ran for the stairs, heard her shout behind him ordering him to stop. Flung open the door to Bibi's room. Empty. Bathroom, closet same.

But he had nowhere else to go. Bibi had no friends, Ruth had always made sure of that. Still. Sahir texted Avi, asked if Bibi was at the restaurant. He wasn't.

Where? Not with family, not at work, he no longer had a girlfriend, not that Val was ever really—

"No." Sahir inadvertently said it out loud.

Ruth stood in the doorway. "Are you defying me? Do I need to call the authorities?"

Bibi wouldn't, couldn't be that stupid. And yet. It was Bibi.

Sahir brushed past her, down the stairs and headed for his car.

CHAPTER SIXTY

———

SHED. SMALL SQUARE building commonly used to house gardening implements. Not in this case. Men's clothes on a rack, a large book open on a pedestal, a sleeping bag on top of a narrow cot with a thin mattress. Windows covered with thick slabs of insulating foam. Homey.

"Looks like Sahir's been living out here," Mike said.

Didn't point out what seemed Jack's obvious failure, not looking inside a fourteen by sixteen building mere feet from a residence he had a warrant to search. Twice.

Jack pulled a shirt off the metal rack, pretended to examine it. Self-loathing, while distracting, wasn't helpful. He could berate himself later, when he had time.

Mike thumbed through the book. "A Quran. And don't beat yourself up that you didn't search this building. Why would you? We didn't even know Sahir existed until a few hours ago."

He was being reasonable but Jack wasn't interested in reason. "And now everyone is pointing their finger at him, including his landlady."

Several framed photos caught Jack's attention and as he picked one up, Ruth's voice lashed like a whip from the door.

"Don't touch those."

"What, this?" Jack bit back his first angry response,

along the lines of "I'll touch whatever the fuck I want to." Took his time scrutinizing all the pictures.

"What are you doing here?" Ruth continued in that same crack-the-whip tone. "You're trespassing."

She'd been a looker when she was a teenager, curvy, sensuous, smiled like she meant it. At least judging from a shot of her standing next to a young man Jack assumed was her brother.

He held up the photo. "This the dear, departed drug lord and rapist Mohamed?"

Ruth's eyes narrowed, her now familiar visible manifestation of rage. "I will not discuss—I demand you leave at once."

"Sore subject. I get it."

White hands clenched by her sides. "Why are you here?"

"We're attempting to contact a young woman named Esther," Mike said.

Ruth's head snapped in his direction. "And you are?"

"Where are my manners. I forgot you two hadn't had the pleasure. Allow me to introduce my associate, Detective Michael Delgado. We're here to do a wellness check."

Mike caught on to the fake formal tone. "If you'd be so kind as to show us to Esther."

"Why would she be out here?" Ruth's voice rose an octave. "This is unacceptable."

"Why would anyone be out here?" Jack answered smoothly. "Seems Sahir left in a hurry."

"I don't have to answer questions." Ruth sputtered. "I—this is completely—I'm going to call my attorney." She tapped on her phone.

"Great," Jack said. "Hopefully Tarek's got that new video ready for us. Maybe you can ask?"

Ruth glared, drew a ragged breath, lowered the phone. "What is it exactly you need?"

"I have to see with my own eyes that Esther's alive and healthy," Jack said.

"And what leads you to believe this woman is here with me?"

"Because I'm more intelligent than the people you ordinarily deal with. Or so you claimed when you came to see me."

She let that slide but made sure they left the shed in front of her. Secured a padlock on the barn-style door.

"Nice of you to provide room and board for your *gardener*," Jack said. "Earlier, you served him up on a plate. Interesting change of heart."

"I told you, I'm not answering anything else."

"That wasn't a question."

The young woman who responded to Ruth's summons couldn't have been fourteen. She was dressed in a long-sleeved gray coat down to her knees, leggings, and sneakers. Every inch of skin covered other than her face and hands, hair hidden under a scarf.

Ruth perched on the mile-long leather sofa in the living room like she had the first time Jack visited, only this time she wasn't still and composed. Her eyes darted to the door, she crossed and re-crossed her legs, twisted a heavy ring on her right hand. Esther stood in front of her on the dense carpet, visibly trembling.

Ruth's words from earlier played in his head, *I thought perhaps I should wear a manteau and scarf, very proper, very modest.* "Is she Iranian?"

"Of course not," Ruth said.

"Ah, right, another lucky Shores of Hope graduate, special delivery from pastor Dustin."

Esther jolted in recognition of the name and spoke fast Spanish.

Ruth clapped her hands and the girl stopped like a spigot. "Her English is fine. And as you can see, she's perfectly healthy. Now, if there's nothing else—"

"You clap at her like she's a dog? Why am I not surprised?"

Jack favored Esther with what he hoped was a friendly smile, shook his head and moved his eyes in Ruth's direction as if to say, she's a piece of work, isn't she? Esther had brown eyes and a crooked front tooth. She wasn't the least bit reassured by his lame attempt at miming commiseration. Basic Spanish. Jesus, he spoke French and Farsi but nothing useful. "*Como estas?*"

All he could remember. He looked at Mike who shrugged. Esther nodded furiously.

Jack tried again. "You're Esther? Si?"

"Si. Policia?"

Esther launched into another stream of Spanish, the gist of which seemed to be Jack was there to take her away.

"You're frightening her," Ruth said.

Really helpful. He could see that. How do you say, it's okay, I just want to make sure you're safe. Maybe it was like good in French. "*Bien?* Uh, *esta bien.*"

He added hand gestures because that always helped with translation. "I'm." A finger to his own chest. "Not here for you." Another head shake, a point in her direction.

She looked between Ruth and Jack, obviously confused. This was going really well.

"Esther." Ruth spoke so sweetly it set Jack's teeth on edge. "You're not in trouble. *Bien, muy bien.* Why don't you go lie down? *Abajo, por favor.*"

Esther started to leave the room and Jack made her wait. Forced her fingers to wrap around his card.

"My number. Mi nombre? Call anytime." Even mimed the universal gesture with his pinkie and thumb extended.

She disappeared toward the back of the house and Jack remembered the stairs from the kitchen descending to what he dubbed the servants' wing.'

"She's—" He hesitated. "She's in Lucia's room?"

"Where else would she sleep?"

"What's her real name?"

"I have no idea what you mean."

"Save it." Speaking of real names. Jack longed to say, *Save it, Farah*. Let her know the charade was over. But they hadn't built a case strong enough yet to allow them to arrest Ruth/Farah and withstand the siege of her high-priced attorneys. Close, but not quite.

Jack walked so near he could smell her expensive perfume, dark and syrupy. Leaned down, mouth inches from her bejeweled ear. "The way Esther is now? Fully functioning? Healthy, alive, all of her fingers and toes? That's how she's going to look when I come back tomorrow, and the next day, and the next."

He straightened. Ruth said, "Of course."

"A wellness check, huh?" Mike said when they were in the car. "Are you being creative or did someone actually call that in?"

"No more girls are dying on my watch."

"You made that very clear when you briefed the officers doing surveillance."

Jack had basically told them that if anyone got out of that house undetected he'd make sure the rest of their careers involved asking, would you like fries with that? Had made sure none of them were the same incompetent idiots who let Dustin drive right by them.

"I'm becoming more and more convinced that the earlier iterations of Lucia were also killed in that marble house-slash-mausoleum. I don't want Esther, or whoever she really is, joining them."

"If that's true," Mike said. "It could mean they each cleaned the remnants of their predecessor."

"Way to keep the help in line, right? See what happened to the girl before you who didn't do what we said?"

Jack could imagine Ruth supervising the cleanup. *You missed a drop of blood over there.*

"Reminds me," Mike said. "Serena did find a consistent

theme in the prayer cards. All of them contain a verse from the book of Ruth."

"Maybe it was a coded warning about her. But how was that supposed to help Lucia? And now we know Ruth isn't even her real name. Did Dustin know her identity?"

"Ask me, it was about Dustin easing his own conscience."

"We're going to need to go through all the videos and security feeds," Jack said. "Ruth—Farah—was pretty emphatic when she came to the station to ply her sad, poor me version of events, that video of Lucia's killing existed. Even said she'd authorize her attorney to work with us."

Mike let out a loud sigh. "Wow, can't wait to watch more of those."

"Why would Farah tell me Sahir killed Lucia? Just like that?"

"She's done with him? She's throwing you off track? It's true?"

"Truth. Yeah. Lotta that's been lobbed our way." Jack drummed his fingers on the steering wheel as they waited for a red at University and Hampden. "If I take Raven, assuming I actually get to meet her, hopefully that's enough to rattle Sahir's cage and make him surface. Plus, I'd love a real reason to arrest that walking rump roast who works for him."

"Avi's not important."

"I think of him as a bonus."

"Lots of 'I' all of a sudden. Sounds like it's getting personal."

"And that surprises you because…"

Mike laughed shortly and shook his head. "It's a fucking full-time job keeping you alive."

"Hey, it seems I've returned the favor a couple of times."

"Truth." Mike paused. "Let's get something to eat before you go undercover rousting bad guys, something decent."

"Not hungry."

"Not optional. You need to be on your game."

Mike was serious and he didn't say a lot of the things he could have—head out of your ass, Fariel. No guilt, no second guessing, no Corie; no anything other than being a cop and getting this right.

CHAPTER SIXTY-ONE

SAHIR WALKED, SUNK deep in his hoodie, to the front door of Val's apartment building as if he lived there. A uniformed cop stood near the front door and Sahir nodded to him. *S'up.*

Up the stairs, down the hall, knocked on her door. Too risky to let himself in this time. Pounded. Made so much noise a neighbor stuck her head out, the desired result.

"Shit. I thought you were another cop."

"Hey." Sahir evaluated her the way he did all girls, for their sales potential. Twenties, dark hair, dressed in workout clothes; too athletic. His customers skewed either to the extreme feminine, breasts, makeup, long curly hair, or the childlike. This bitch didn't fit either category.

"What's goin' on?" Sahir asked. "Why all the po po?"

"Oh. They took a dude out of there on a stretcher a while ago. I asked one of the EMTs and he said an OD. You a friend of Val's too?"

Sahir hewed close to the truth. "Her supervisor at the restaurant. Haven't been able to get a hold of her."

Bitch said, "Oh," again. Looked upset.

"You know where she is?"

"You haven't heard?"

If he'd heard why would he be asking? But Sahir kept up the act, dumb harmless manager. Just a guy. Stuffed his hands in his pockets and slouched. "Nah. Nobody tells me nothin'. Boss made me come down here in person to check."

Her eyes moved over his shoulder then to her right, checking to see who else was in the hall. "She died."

"Shit."

"Yeah."

"When?"

"Dunno. Ask one of them cops, they're everywhere. I'm thinking of moving, doesn't feel safe around here." She started to close the door.

"Hey. You said an OD. But that wasn't Val?"

"Uh-uh." Shook her head fast. "Her boyfriend."

The door closed and he heard her fasten the useless chain. EMTs, she said. Wouldn't be EMTs if Bibi was dead, would there?

Sahir left using a different door. Easily scaled the old, six-foot privacy fence in back of the property. Knew he should tell Ruth but couldn't bring himself to do it. They'd call her anyway; she was listed as Bibi's emergency contact.

Had to stay on foot now, was surprised he hadn't already spotted a tail when he drove to Ruth's, then Bibi'z, and then Val's apartment. His ability was to blend in was good—medium height, medium build, medium age—but he'd pushed his luck far enough.

Then he wondered where to go. No home, no position, no alliances. Sahir trusted structure, hierarchy, authority; without that he was in freefall. Either Bibi lived to run the organization into the ground or died, still first choice, and Sahir permanently burned any relationship with Ruth. Bibi's mother, if he was to believe her latest story. Sahir couldn't blame himself he never figured it out; Ruth wasn't the least bit maternal and everyone in her family maintained the fiction flawlessly.

Realized he had no interest in going back to the spa, like running a daycare full of whiny brats. *Except for Raven.*

Where that thought came from he wasn't sure, but once it struck he couldn't shake it. He'd told her he was moving up the circuit but, really, he couldn't care less about the other girls. Sex had to be controlled, either kept literally under wraps or merchandised. Simple. And why running the spa bored him senseless. Ruth had effectively fired him from a job he hated.

Only Raven didn't bore him. Gabi. He said she was product but he lied. Ruth was right when she called Gabi his creation. First time Sahir ever broke rank and demanded a favor. Burned a lot of cred taking Gabi for himself but she was worth it.

In the beginning, he dressed her. Curled her hair. Showed her how to put on makeup. She hadn't known how, fourteen, scared, and a virgin for real. He felt bad when he found that out firsthand, testing the product like he always did. Not for fun, never for pleasure, only business. He tried to explain that to Gabi but she wouldn't stop crying.

It's just a job, sweetheart.

Called her that, like he was her boyfriend, then beat her to stop her from crying and cure his own softness. Still, for weeks afterward he wouldn't sell her. Found all sorts of odd jobs for her to do to earn her keep and so he could save face.

It was a customer who finally broke the spell. Sahir said she wasn't available and the customer smirked. Peeled off a couple of hundreds from a big roll and said, I like virgins, only right I should pay extra. Sahir recognized a revenue opportunity when he saw one. He considered himself cured and Gabi got used to it, eventually. Got good at it. Almost too good. Bothered him a little that she might actually enjoy it, so sometimes he beat her as a preventative measure.

Don't get too comfortable.

He liked to think the beatings made her stronger. Girls

were like breaking a horse; you needed them to obey but not destroy their spirit. The good ones, anyway, which Gabi definitely was. She'd take her punishment stoically, smart enough not to complain. After she recovered he'd reward her, buy her clothes, take her out for dinner. Until the next time, when he caught her being a little too friendly, too flirty or affectionate with a john. They moved the operation constantly to stay ahead of the law but also so the girls didn't get dependent on regulars. Like he told Bibi and the other men—it's work. Don't lose control and don't get excited. No emotion.

He wondered now if he'd done too good a job of making Gabi hate him, then fantasized about how he'd make it up to her. For starters, he'd replace the dress Ruth burned. He'd been blinded by status, tradition, history; his father worked for Ruth's father, his grandfather for hers, and so on. No longer. Right then and there Gabi was off the market. He'd been patient and it was time for his reward; he didn't doubt for an instant that he could make her happy.

Gabi was smart and pretty with a gift for making men believe whatever she needed them to believe. He had cash and a talent for disappearing. Getting fake IDs was a cinch. She'd go with him because Gabi was rightly terrified of deportation. She'd go with him because he wouldn't tell her, at first, what he was planning. He'd let her think they were simply rotating on to the next city, Salt Lake after Denver, like they always did.

She'd go with him because he wouldn't give her a choice.

CHAPTER SIXTY-TWO

———◆———

AT ELEVEN, JACK approached a tidy brick ranch through the backyard as directed. Casement windows, neatly shoveled walk, yard enclosed by a chain link fence that didn't offer any obvious hiding places. What it did offer was easy access to Bibi'z, diagonally across the alley, and Jack heard music thumping as he hunched into his leather jacket—borrowed from Mike and three sizes too big. Under the coat he wore a team shirt, baggy jeans, and hiking shoes with thick wool socks. His plan was to get past any gatekeeper by acting like a sad, nerdy guy who couldn't get a date. Not that much of a stretch.

A woman in her seventies answered the door. She wore pantyhose with strappy high-heeled sandals and a parrot-green dress, way too short, made out of shiny material that bunched and stuck to her thighs. Bright fuchsia hair with color-coordinated lipstick and nails completed the Scary Hooker Grandma look.

"Hi honey, have an appointment?"

"Uh-huh." Jack rocked on the balls of his feet. "I'm here to see Raven?"

"What's your name?" The woman smiled revealing stains on her teeth.

"Oh, sorry, I'm Hank."

"You're right on time. I'm Dottie." She extended a crepey hand stained with so many liver spots it could've been giraffe skin.

"Text said to use the back door."

"Wouldn't want the neighbors to get funny ideas. Come on in before you freeze to death."

He followed her into a completely unrenovated 1960s tract home kitchen. Sink under a window overlooking the backyard. Four burner stove with electric coils. Linoleum floor and oak cabinets with warped doors and round button pulls.

"I'm really nervous, this is my first time." Nervous wasn't an act; Sahir was the textbook definition of armed and dangerous and if Avi showed up and saw Jack, this charade would be over real fast. So far as they knew from surveillance Avi tended to stay at the restaurant. Operational phrase "tended to."

"My, you're a tall one." Dottie put a hand flat on Jack's chest and pulled playfully at the zipper on his jacket. Her mascara clumped into thick spikes she attempted to flutter.

Instead of flinching, he leaned in and lowered his voice. "I'm getting divorced."

"Oh, how awful, honey."

Then he got to use one of his all-time favorite excuses. "I've never done anything like this before."

"Don't worry, Raven'll take good care of you."

As if on cue, a young woman opened the door opposite the back entrance. Raven, to Jack's surprise, was real and recognizable from her photos.

Sex workers, as Paul had cynically observed, usually looked like hell—dirty, bruised, scarred. But Raven, with ink-black curls, almond-shaped green eyes, and flawless pale skin, could've been a model. Her short robe was tied carelessly, offering a tease of thong, a glimpse of breasts the size of melons, her demeanor bored, world-weary.

Jack figured an insecure doofus like Hank would openly stare so he resisted his reflex to force his eyes to her face and even licked his lips. "Are you Raven?"

"Hold on." She wagged a finger. "First the rules."

"Oh, sure, of course." Jack blinked at Dottie. "I'm—uh—ah—just tell me what to do."

"Be nice to him, he's getting divorced." Dottie ran her spotted hand up and down Jack's arm.

"You can leave," Raven said.

"Don't you dare yell at me just because Sahir's not around. This is my house." She gave Jack one final pat and tottered unsteadily toward the front of the house on her heels.

"Who's Sahir?" Jack asked.

Raven ignored him and continued her spiel. "We run a clean operation. Only what you paid for. Don't try anything because we're not here by ourselves and you won't get away with it."

That last part was interesting. "We're not? What do you mean?"

"Nothing. Let's get ready for fun. Phones in the basket and coats over there." Raven spoke like a computer-generated telemarketer and motioned game-show style toward a round wicker container on the counter and pegs on the wall.

Jack had purposely worn his T-shirt tucked in and no belt a) because he thought it was nerdy and b) because it made it easier to see he wasn't carrying. Hopefully, they thought his baggy suburban Dad jeans and thick rag socks were uncool enough to let their guard down and miss his ankle holster. If it'd been summer he'd have worn socks with sandals.

"Empty your pockets." Flat-voiced Raven, reading from her script.

Jack pulled out fake ID, ChapStick, keys, and $100 in cash. "Some of that was a tip, um, you know, for you."

Raven's acrylic nails riffed the bills and she abruptly animated like a doll that got fresh batteries. "Come on, darlin', let's go downstairs."

"Downstairs?"

"That a problem?"

"Um, I don't know. Is there anyone else down there?" Jack rocked up onto the balls of his feet and squinted toward the stairs.

"Like who?"

"I don't know, someone to ambush me and take my kidney or something?" He figured that was the kind of lame-ass shit a guy like Hank would say. In reality, Jack hoped to meet someone very like Sahir and had felt sharp disappointment at Dottie's comment about him being gone.

Raven rolled her eyes and huffed out a loud sigh. "Do you want to have fun or not?"

Jack sniffled, blinked, scratched at his nose. He followed Raven down the stairs, every cell on high alert, relieved she didn't bolt the door at the top.

The basement was carpeted and he wondered if it was soundproof. There was a sitting area with a small loveseat, a gurgling fountain, and a big tank of water with pieces of fruit floating in it. A counter ran along one wall with stacks of plastic cups, neatly folded white washcloths, and a Crock-Pot. Jack saw three doors, all closed.

"Are you sure there's no one else here?"

"I'll show you." With a careless shrug Raven opened the doors. A massage table sat in the center of each covered with a white sheet. There didn't appear to be closets in the rooms. Or windows, which, for what it was worth, was a code violation. Then she slid off her robe in a brisk no-nonsense way that felt clinical. Right, Jack reminded himself; nothing about this was a seduction, merely a business transaction.

Hank would find naked Raven irresistible. Most straight men would. Long legs, flat stomach, and those breasts moved in a way that suggested they might actually be hers. Jack flipped a mental switch and appraised her as if he'd have to describe her from the witness stand. Her young body was far from perfect. Scratches, bruises she'd tried to cover with makeup, and a red, blistering welt that looked like a fresh burn.

"What happened to your hip?"

"You only have thirty minutes." Raven tapped her phone. "You wanna waste it talking?"

Jack fidgeted his nervous-Hank way toward the counter with the Crock-Pot. Instead of pot roast, black stones simmered inside. They were smooth and warm and mesmerizing. His hand played in the water, sorting and turning them.

"What are these for?" His fingers closed around one.

Raven sidled up to him. "You'll find out if you quit wasting time."

She started massaging his shoulders. "You're very tight."

She had to stand on her tiptoes to do it and he was much too aware of the pressure of her body from behind him.

"Could you—" He broke off, embarrassed.

Raven's mouth was close to his ear. "Could I what, darlin'?"

"Lift up your hair and turn around. I want to see you."

She stepped a few feet away and spun. With a coy smile over her shoulder, and a waggle of her butt, she raised her arms and lifted her hair. "Like it?"

The tattoo. The stones in the Crock-Pot. He'd arrived in evil's bullpen.

"Did you know what was going to happen to Lucia Saturday night?"

"What?"

"Lucia was your friend. I saw pictures of you at Bibi'z. You drove her there."

"You're not a customer."

Jack bore down on Raven. "Did Sahir tell you to drive her? Where is he? Are you in danger?"

"I don't know who that is." Raven's eyes flicked to the stairs.

Jack grabbed her robe off the peg and threw it at her. "Get dressed. I'm getting you out of here."

"Are you a fucking cop?"

"Lucia was your friend and I'll bet you didn't want her to die."

Raven didn't shriek. Instead, she said, "I want *ice cream*. Don't you want *ice cream*?"

She said it loud and clear and Jack could only assume it was their safe word.

CHAPTER SIXTY-THREE

———◆———

WILLOW CURLED INTO a ball on the floor of the motel room. Sahir kicked her in the ribs a second time, harder. "Where is she?"

"I told you, a customer." Willow protected her face, scooted as close as she could to the wall.

"She wasn't supposed to take any more customers. Was supposed to be ready to leave."

Gabi was right, Willow cried too damned much. He'd only hit her a couple of times, had done much worse to Gabi and she never got hysterical.

"Stop crying, I can't think." Drew back his leg as if to kick her again. She yelped and curled even tighter.

"Didn't she tell you to pack?" If she had, he saw no signs of it.

"Yeah." Willow peeked at him through her fingers.

"Do you know what time her customer was?"

Willow shook her head.

"How long? What kind of service? Anything useful?"

Another shake.

He lit a cigarette. Was it a problem Gabi took an unexpected customer? Must be a regular or offered to pay extra. Showed initiative. Except he'd told her not to, directly. He decided. When she worked, how much she worked, or, in this case, when he'd decided he didn't want her to work anymore at all.

Pacing near Willow's spot on the floor, the girl's pathetic squeaking and whimpering enraged him further, the way she flinched away from his foot and tried to hide. No fight in her whatsoever.

"Get up." He started to put out his cigarette on her bare shoulder. She jolted to her feet shrieking. Snot ran from her nose and her eyes were red. She put him in mind of a scrawny, unhealthy rat and he couldn't credit why he ever thought she was pretty.

Still had the nerve to complain. "You hurt me."

He backhanded her and she crashed into the dresser. "Keep mouthing off."

"Stop it." She cried harder, put the back of her hand against her lip and stared stupidly at the blood. "I thought you were nice."

"You sure you don't know anything else, you ignorant cunt?"

Her head shook fast and his arm arced of its own accord, slamming her against the dresser again. He longed to continue beating her simply for being stupid but Sahir stuck to his code: only what was necessary. You hurt someone to get intel, gain cooperation, send a message. He was getting nothing out of Willow and without a purpose he could easily edge into sadism. He reminded himself she was no longer his problem, he was no longer a pimp. She wasn't worth another moment's time or energy, especially now.

As he turned to leave he checked the feed on his phone out of habit. Saw a tall dark-haired man approach the back door and enter the kitchen. Knew who it was. Sound drained away for a moment before his pulse returned with a deafening roar. Blood ran icy hot, tingling in his veins. Sahir flexed the fingers of one hand, extending, clenching. *Mine.* No man touched Gabi without his permission and no other man was going to touch her ever again. Certainly no filthy cop.

Rage, betrayal, and years of pent-up frustration erupted in a bellow of pure pain that sent Willow scrabbling like a panicked crab trying to wedge herself under the bed.

"Get outta here," Sahir snarled and banged open the door. He had to get to the spa before it was too late.

She didn't move, remained on the floor, sobbing, useless. Gabi would never act that pathetic and his irritation at the girl erupted, his leg swung back, forward, no reserve as if she was a football. He felt the satisfying crack of bones and she sprawled facedown, finally quiet.

He spoke to her motionless back; dead, unconscious, didn't care. "If I ever see you again what I've done so far will feel like a spa treatment."

CHAPTER SIXTY-FOUR

———

THE DOOR AT the top of the stairs banged open and Avi trundled through running with a lumpy bow-legged stance down the stairs. Jack tried to get Raven behind him but clearly she didn't find him the good guy and scratched in the general direction of his eyes like a feral cat.

Girls fought dirty and Raven was no exception, kicking, clawing, tugging at his shirt. Operating on pure instinct Jack jabbed back at her with his elbow and connected with something in the general vicinity of her face. She yelped and he hoped it slowed her down for a few seconds but a girl who'd been cut and burned in the course of day-to-day business wasn't going to go away easily. He braced for her next onslaught as Avi moved in on Jack's right.

In the few seconds Raven was subdued, Jack backed against the counter, felt blindly for the Crock-Pot with his left hand and drew with his right.

"Police. Freeze. Both of you."

Avi's forward momentum stalled and his big, square head rocked from side to side in a way that seemed decidedly bovine. Jack was much more worried about Sahir, or any other reinforcements on the way, but hopefully they'd be his. All those cops supposedly listening and waiting were welcome to arrive any time.

"Freeze. Police. On the ground. Now." Jack yelled

the same things what felt like a dozen times while Avi demonstrated his ignorance of words and Raven continued to hone her already impressive street vocabulary. Basically neither of them froze and Jack was less than amped about the idea of firing his weapon in an enclosed space with moving targets, including an innocent girl—and boy was he visualizing quote marks around that word.

He was even less thrilled about dying so it was time to give up on subtlety. On her next lunge Jack's boot connected with Raven's solar plexus and launched her across the room. Yanked the electrical cord with his left hand and felt hot water on his arm. In the same moment the Crock-Pot launched, he registered Avi reaching inside his jacket and thought, swell, he'd be the cop remembered for bringing a kitchen appliance to a gunfight.

Somehow it worked. Round appliance connected with square head. "At least I didn't hit you anywhere that mattered."

"Fuck you, asshole."

Avi and Raven, practically in unison.

Adrenaline made Jack mouth off himself and say some things including what he'd thought when he was in the alley with Avi the first time. "Bring it."

An old lady's voice from the top of the stairs, high-pitched and quavering with outrage. "What's going on down there? You better not break anything."

"Ma'am I'm the police. Call 9-1-1."

Avi grabbed Raven, held her like a human shield with one thick arm, and trained his gun on Jack with the other hand.

"Hiding behind a girl, nice." Jack got a better grip on his weapon, ready to shoot.

Raven squirmed in Avi's grasp. "You always were useless."

"Shut up, bitch."

"Let me go."

The lump of suet did as asked, lifted Raven and hurled her at Jack as he simultaneously fired at Avi.

She landed against him with an angry shriek and he shoved her away with his right arm, barely registering an unpleasant tearing sensation in his shoulder, desperate to assess the situation. Relieved to find Avi down. Apparently, Jack could hit the broad side of an imbecile even under duress. He fended off yet another attack from Raven, this time using his right knee to shove her backward and then spinning to catch the slow, wounded bulk of Avi with the toe of his boot in his balls, assuming he had any.

This was street fighting at its worst: messy, close, unpredictable. And incredibly annoying. It made Jack long to simply shoot both of them, especially when Raven lunged yet again.

"Give it a fucking rest." Jack hated hitting women but it wasn't like she was giving him a choice. Gun in his right hand, his left closed around her wrist and he swung her out and back, face first, hard into the wall. Avi was on his hands and knees on the floor puking and dripping blood from an unfortunately non-fatal gunshot. Jack was about to attempt to handcuff the two of them together when he heard a familiar voice.

"You all right down there?" Mike, on the stairs, gun drawn.

"You have fucking terrible timing."

Jack's right shoulder began to throb like a son of a bitch and he instinctively switched the Glock to his left.

"You look awful." Uniformed officers moved down the stairs past Mike.

"You're supposed to announce yourself, didn't they teach you that in the academy?" Jack rubbed his cheek and his fingers came away sticky. "Shit. You got him?"

"Got who?"

"Sahir. Everyone raves about his big bad wolf act."

"Didn't see him," Mike said. "We found Betty Boop in the kitchen and were clearing the house when we heard a shot."

Jack holstered his gun as officers retrieved Avi's from where it landed when it flew out of his meaty paw. Noticed Raven was still naked.

"Raven, you're really starting to piss me off."

She gathered herself to spit even as an officer pulled her arms behind her back and blood streamed from her nose.

"Yeah, yeah. You're so tough. Avi needs an ambulance, Raven needs clothes along with some manners. And I need a tetanus shot."

"Got good news," Mike said when they were upstairs. "Guess what we found in the garage?"

"A black Jeep. Who's it registered to?"

"Betty Boop over there."

Jack saw Dottie, docile at the kitchen table, in handcuffs. "Where on earth did you come up with that?"

Mike shrugged. "Only old lady name I could think of."

"We manage to secure the Jeep or is Sahir driving it as his getaway car?"

"We secured the entire property and were coming to help you. All I can tell you is we didn't see him or anybody else."

"Maybe he has super powers." Jack attempted to circle his right shoulder which sent blinding hot pain strobing down his arm. "Ow."

"We'll have the EMTs check you out, too. No joke about the tetanus shot, she scratched the shit out of you."

"Awesome." At least he'd managed not to shoot her, for what that was worth.

"How'd you subdue Avi?" Mike asked.

"Crock-Pot. Then he used Raven to shoot himself with my gun."

Mike remained stoic. "You're buying the first round when I hear that story."

"Yeah, well, if you weren't always late... I'm gonna have a chat with 'Betty.'" Jack noticed shiny streaks in the thick powder Dottie wore. "Where is he?"

"Who?"

He slammed his good hand on the table so hard that a teacup jumped off its saucer and shattered onto the floor. "What are you, seventy, seventy-five and you're doing some Bonnie and Clyde shit or whatever to supplement your—"

She interrupted. "I'm sixty—"

"Shut up until I tell you to talk. Your friends assaulted an officer. You're running a trafficking operation out of your house. Your car was used in a homicide. So fucking tell me where Sahir goes and how you get in touch with him or I promise you'll die in jail, shuffling around a cell crapping into your adult diapers. Okay, now you can talk."

CHAPTER SIXTY-FIVE

—◆—

"**Y**OU BROKE MY nose."

Raven sported a bulky white bandage and Jack could tell from the bruising around it she'd look like a raccoon in twenty-four hours.

He pointed to his own butterfly bandage on his left cheek. "You assaulted an officer. Repeatedly. You have any interest in staying out of jail?"

She torqued her body sideways in the chair and tugged at her shirt. "These fucking clothes itch and I smell like an old lady."

Dottie had grabbed clothes before everyone was transported, so Raven, incongruously, wore a glittery pink angora sweater featuring kittens, and dark green sweatpants. Her attitude was anything but cute.

"I can only help if you come clean with me. Do you really want to serve time for Sahir? Hasn't he taken enough of your life?"

"I don't know shit."

"Right, cool, we're done here." Jack was in a significant amount of pain and felt entitled to sarcasm. His right arm was in a sling until an orthopedic doctor could evaluate his shoulder, he was catching up to Mike on sleep deprivation, and he couldn't take pain meds for fear they'd knock him out.

Avi was shining his beacon of stupid at the hospital.

Dottie had experienced shortness of breath and an irregular heartbeat and also been transported to Denver Health.

"Let me show you something." Jack displayed photos on his laptop—Lucia on the autopsy table with the Y incision, on her side with an investigator holding her hair out of the way, her wrapped body next to the dumpster.

Raven's mouth squinched up like she was chewing the inside of her cheek.

Jack continued. "You're not allowed to come and go as you please. You're not allowed to take Dottie's car without permission. If you're smart you'll realize Sahir couldn't care less if you live or die. Only how much money you make him."

"If you're smart you'll realize I'm not talking."

"How'd he burn you? Cigarette? Lighter? Iron?" Something in her eyes sparked at his last guess and he tweaked it. "Curling iron, nice. What'd you do to deserve that, smart girl? Does the punishment fit the crime?"

"Screw you, Hank, or whatever your name really is."

"Yes, let's use our real names, Gabriella. Your family know what you do for a living?"

She quickly forced her features back to sullen but for a split second he saw the young girl under the tough veneer and gentled his voice. "Two years is a long time to have someone hurt you and tell you lies."

"It feels like you've been talking that long already."

"Dottie's house has cameras. Did you think we couldn't get the footage? Did you think hundred-year-old Dottie wanted to go to jail? I can assure you she doesn't."

"That stupid old bitch."

"That old *woman* understood she could either cooperate with the Denver Police or die in jail. She grasped what seem to me very simple concepts. Maybe your mind has been so twisted you can't think right anymore. You'd rather go to jail, and if you're not too old and ugly when you get out, service twenty strangers a day until you wind up dead with a needle in your arm. Maybe it's worth it for a steak dinner now and then with your 'daddy.' Your call because I don't need you."

Jack built up an overwhelming rage as he spoke and was in no mood to finesse her. He was only partially bluffing about not needing her but mostly was too pissed and in too much pain to care. It wasn't acting when he stood, grabbed his laptop, and stalked to the door. What he wanted more than anything in that moment was a handful of the pills the EMT gave him and a tumbler of Scotch to wash them down with.

"Wait, that's it?" Raven's voice was high-pitched, reedy, and confused. "It's not fair you're gonna help that old bitch and not me. I know way more than her."

What do you know? Maybe finesse was overrated. He forced himself to take several deep breaths. He'd been in stressful, even painful situations before, so what was it about this girl that made him lose his temper? Was it the way she went after him in the basement?

But when he turned around she seemed defeated. She bit her lip and her face mottled in the way that suggested she was fighting tears. He saw her tug the fabric of her pants away from her hip, as if protecting the burn.

"We can get you a Band-Aid."

She didn't meet his eyes. Swallowed. Her fingers drummed nervously on the table and he noticed that several of her purple acrylic nails had ripped off, probably when she was scratching the shit out of his cheek.

When she spoke her voice had lost some of its edge. "You're just gonna deport me. Send me home to die."

"You can't be deported if you're a witness to a serious crime and trust me, this counts. If you cooperate for real we can write a letter of recommendation that helps with immigration."

Her chin lifted and he saw a flicker of hope. "Can I get

that in writing? About immigration?"

Jack wrote "NOT DEPORTED" in large letters on a yellow pad on the table and initialed it. "Would you like me to have this notarized?"

"Yes. And that letter thingy, too."

"What about 'Daddy' Sahir?"

"What about him?"

"Doesn't he bail you out?"

She seemed surprised by the suggestion. "No. Um, I mean, I'm sure he would, if he knew. It, um, doesn't usually..."

Some pimp. Didn't even take care of his product. Jack sat down again. "What happened Saturday night?"

"I finished with a customer at eleven thirty and had a short break so I went to Bibi'z for a pop. Lucia was there and we chatted for a few minutes until it was time for me to return to work. I was dressed in a comfortable top and skirt that offer freedom of movement and she was wearing a new dress and diamond necklace that Ken gave her."

Raven told her story in a rushed monotone, sprinkled with purposeful details, so clearly rehearsed that Jack couldn't help laughing. He held up a hand to stop her, wondering if someone had slipped one of those pills into his coffee without his knowledge.

"Pop? Really? Is it the 1950s?"

"Why are you laughing?"

"Sahir told you to say you drank 'pop' and 'chatted'?"

Raven got all huffy. "I don't know what you mean."

It was two a.m. He'd slammed her into a wall and busted her nose. He'd promised help with immigration and used the old cop trick of playing off one suspect against the other. What was it going to take for this girl to get real with him?

"This isn't much of a collaboration," Jack said. "If you don't tell me the truth."

"Collaboration." She snorted. "Fancy word for I'm screwed, like calling what I do the healing arts instead of prostitution."

Jack took another steadying breath. He'd interviewed gangbangers twice her age who weren't half as hard to connect with. "I know you don't know me, but I keep my word."

"You're a fucking cop."

"And you're a pro. What's your point?"

That actually elicited a thin smile from her. "I don't wanna be. You probably hear that all the time."

"I think you do what you need to do to survive. And right now, I'm your best shot at survival, whether you believe me or not."

He watched her process. Swipe angrily at tears. Put her head on her arms on the table like a child napping at their desk for so long he wondered if she'd fallen asleep.

She hadn't. "If you send me back I'm dead. And they're sending everyone back."

"I know. Tell me about Lucia. Give me something I can use, something that makes you valuable to the district attorney."

"She messed up."

"Lucia?"

A sniffle, a nod. "Uh-huh. We were leaving. Had it all arranged. I took Dottie's car, we had Lucia's jewelry to sell. I went to pick her up at the hotel and she forgot the fucking purse. Or lost it. Didn't know. I'm undocumented, but her ID was in the purse and we needed it."

Raven started crying in earnest. "I knew Sahir was gonna kill me for taking the car. If I got away I had to stay gone."

"Why he burned you?"

"And punched me."

"You were the one texting her all night."

"Yeah. Bibi drove her to the hotel so she figured she'd

left the purse in his car. We went back to the club and he told her he hadn't seen it so she had him take her home to look for it."

Jack knew where the purse wound up. "You were so close to getting away. That sucks."

Her eyes narrowed and he feared he'd pushed empathy a step too far. She was deeply suspicious of him, of anyone in law enforcement, and wasn't going to cave suddenly because of a few nice words. Best approach with a young woman who'd been abused like Raven was to play it straight.

"Okay. Here's what I need, what'll make you valuable. Anything that helps make the case for Lucia's killer. Anything that puts Sahir away for a long time. Information about the trafficking."

"What about the money laundering?"

"Yes. Absolutely."

Her crying stopped and she appeared, if not quite excited, a bit engaged. "The restaurant's a front but you probably already know that. It's great for moving cash."

"How about Avi? What's his role?"

She wrinkled her nose. "He's muscle. Fancies himself a playah and—"

Jack could guess what she'd been about to say. "Demands sexual favors but screws you over anyway."

"Yeah." She squinted at him. "How do you know so much?"

"He's such a stock character it's like he came from central casting." A reference Jack could see clearly confused her. "Who else is important?"

"Ruth."

"What's she do?"

"Plays God. Along with that cocksucker phony minister. You know about him, too?"

"Sure do. We're working to bring Dustin in right now."

Her eyebrows went up and down. "His little wifey? Sat

where I am not long ago."

"Heather was a sex worker?" Jack remembered the ledger, all the dollar signs next to her name.

"Uh-huh. Sahir's favorite moneymaker. Until Dustin decided he wanted her, wanted to do some kinda makeover like they were on a reality show."

"Tell me how Ruth plays God."

Raven mimicked. "You go here, you go there. She rates the newcomers."

"At the charity?"

That evoked a bitter laugh. "Huh. Ya. Charity. You know, back home we actually admire priests."

Jack had nothing reassuring to offer. He didn't think much of organized religion to start with. "Ruth decides if a young woman is going to be a private or commercial placement."

"And phony baloney minister is paid accordingly."

"I noticed private placements cost more."

"All Dustin cares about is bank. I tried to tell Lucia. I've seen preach turn away girls he thought were ugly. God knows what happens to them."

"Lucia had the tattoo even though she didn't work in the spa."

"Still made them a lot of bank."

"Them?"

"Right, deets. Sahir, Dustin, Ruth. Tat's supposed to be something about her, like her name, but that doesn't make sense."

It made sense to Jack. "Lucia trusted Dustin."

Raven's face clouded again. "She thought he'd be happy when she told him she was pregnant. I dunno, maybe she thought he'd leave his wife. But last Wednesday when she finally got a chance to talk to him he told her she had to get an abortion. To Lucia that was a sin. She was really religious, not like me. Or you."

Jack's eyebrows went up.

"I could tell. Anyway. Dustin rejected her, matter of time before Ken did away with her, no choice but to run."

"Did Ken know she was pregnant?" Jack asked.

Raven shook her head, exhaled. "She was gonna tell him but I managed to talk her out of it. He said he couldn't have kids but she didn't believe him."

Good instincts on Raven's part. Ken was insanely jealous, sent girls to their death rather than "have another's hands on them." Lucia had been on very borrowed time.

"Let's talk about placements," Jack said. "You were sold to Sahir."

"Not at first." Her mouth twisted. A smile, disgust, grief. "I went to the Harrowsmiths."

Jack hid his surprise. Raven hadn't been in any of the videos. "Did Ken ever film you?"

"Why am I not surprised you know about that? Man, Lucia hated making those. Ken never got that far with me 'cause of Sahir. Apparently there was grief over it."

"Over you?"

A shrug, an eyeroll. "Makes me soooo special. Way Sahir saw it they owed him and he called in a favor. Ruth didn't care. Plenty more where I came from."

She sagged in the chair. "I feel so guilty, though. It wouldn't have happened to Lucia, she wouldn't have wound up there. See, she and I were at the charity at the same time, same age, from the same place. I should have warned her."

"Wasn't like you had a lot of say. If it hadn't been her it would've been somebody else."

"But she was my friend, I know you don't believe me but she was."

"Tell me about your time at the Harrowsmiths'."

"Wasn't bad. I didn't stay over because Abigail was still there. She was supposed to train me, show me what to do, but she barely talked. I asked where she was going and she didn't say. Didn't know if they'd fired her or what. I figured she'd go back to the church."

"When was this?" Jack asked. "What time of year?"

"July I think, hot. Anyway, after a few days, they came for Lucia in the morning instead of me. Dunno why. I sat in that stupid church all day scared shitless, wondering how I screwed up, expecting ICE."

"Worse," Jack said. "Sahir."

"It was late when he came for me. Lucia hadn't come home so I guess she started staying with Ruth and Ken right away."

"What'd Sahir tell you had happened?"

"Nothing. To grab my shit and follow him. Not like we're worth explanations. By then it's nighttime and I used to be afraid of the dark. We drove for a while and he stopped at this field. Told me to stay in the car but I didn't wanna be left alone."

"Do you know where you were?"

"There was an old sign, I forced myself to memorize the letters even though I didn't understand it: *Bluefield*. You know what that is?"

Jack did; an old manufacturing site, deserted, perfect for discarding unwanted items. "What happened next?"

"I followed sounds, found Sahir and another man, never knew his name. Doesn't work for them anymore. Sahir was chewing him out, saying it should've already been done."

She got a faraway look in her eyes. Jack waited without prompting.

"They had shovels. They were digging. When Sahir saw me out of the car he was pissed. He said, 'Tell me why I shouldn't put you in here?' I tried to run but he caught me, knocked me down, beat me, kicked me. I kept waiting for him to use the shovel so I begged. I told him I'd do anything, that I hadn't seen a thing but I lied. They were digging a grave and there was something wrapped in white on the ground.

"When he finally stopped I hurt so bad I could hardly stand let alone run so I just laid there in the dirt. He finished with the hole and when he came to get me he laughed, like it was funny how scared I was. I peed blood for three days. He kept me locked in a room and when I was better laid out the rules."

She snapped back into the present, stared at Jack as if seeing him for the first time. "Tell you how stupid I was. I thought I was gonna be his maid."

"Did you ever find out what they were burying?" Jack felt chill certainty. Wrapped in white, five pieces for a woman. In July the ground wouldn't have been frozen.

"Here's the thing." Raven leaned forward, arms on the table, eyes blazing. "Lucia was given her room and all of Abigail's stuff was still there. Ruth said Lucia could take whatever she wanted and was to never mention the other girl again. If anyone, even Bibi, said her name they got hit. They made her disappear."

"Possible Abigail left in a hurry," Jack said. "Without her things."

"That's lame and you know it. Abigail." Raven paused, her voice softened. "Abigail. She had a name. She's in that hole. And I'm gonna be joining her."

"No, you aren't." Jack took the pad and turned to a fresh page. Wrote, *I'm going to keep you alive.* Signed it and handed it to her.

She took the paper. "This against Sahir? No offense, but you almost couldn't handle me and Sahir's the devil."

CHAPTER SIXTY-SIX

"**G**UN," HIS LIEUTENANT said, her hand out.

"I didn't even do it." Jack knew that sounded lame.

"You know the rules."

Crock-Pot-naked-girl-throwing-chaotic-mess that was the incident in Dottie's basement was still an officer-involved shooting. Even if it was only one shot. Even if the officer himself only felt tangentially involved.

Jack knew Aurora detectives were all over the old lady's basement. That was how it worked—Aurora investigated Denver's officer-involved shootings and Denver investigated theirs. Avi had a deadly weapon and Jack was pretty sure hurling a Crock-Pot didn't fall under the heading of excessive force. But you never knew what crap a shooting panel would come up with.

"Someone from firearms will be here with a replacement," Dani said.

"When will that be?" Low on the list of things Jack wanted to do was sit around for hours in the middle of the night while they woke someone up to come to headquarters and provide him with a temporary—and unfamiliar—weapon. Not to mention paperwork.

"I have other guns at home which is ten minutes away, less at this hour."

"Up to you." She didn't sound sure.

"I know how to pick up a tail, Mom, I'll be fine."

Her mouth curved in a smile. "You need to be in top form for your visitor tomorrow."

Despite his exhaustion, Jack grinned back and felt a jolt of energy. New Mexico had come through and taken Dustin into custody before he could cross the border. He'd put up no resistance although he had subjected the troopers to a mini-sermon on how mankind's feeble statutes had no dominion over God's warriors. Jack was going to present him with a very different viewpoint when Dustin arrived at headquarters.

"Wouldn't miss it. I'm looking forward to familiarizing Dustin with the laws of man."

Dani scrutinized him. "Seriously. Get some sleep and get that shoulder looked at. Man of God can wait."

There was also, as she had to remind him, an entire police force looking for Sahir. And Jack couldn't say sleep didn't sound fantastic. Wasn't sure he hadn't already started on the drive home. His right arm was immobilized in a sling and he had to go see an orthopoedic doctor for a follow-up on his shoulder. Possible torn rotator cuff, the EMT said. He felt fully depleted, mentally and physically exhausted. If a girl was going to fall on him he could imagine many more pleasant scenarios.

His garage clicker didn't work. He'd been meaning to replace the battery forever and, too wiped out to worry about it right then, found a spot to park in the alley. Eager to collapse into bed, lost in exhausted, rambling thoughts, it took him a slow second to register that the floodlight on a motion sensor above his back door didn't turn on, either. He snapped his fingers at it and no red light appeared meaning it wasn't merely a burned out bulb. Neighboring houses were mostly dark, considering the hour, but porch lamps and streetlights meant there was power. Weird.

He barely got inside his laundry room when a man spoke.

"You took something of mine."

Jack's heart galloped into a jerky, adrenaline fueled stampede. Gun. Only thing he could think, but they were safely locked in a cabinet. Groped for a light switch. Nothing.

Even in the dim light he was certain of the man's identity. Jack used his best command voice. "Drop the knife."

Sahir chuckled. "That's nice. You acting like you're still in charge."

Nothing woke you up like a knife-wielding psychopath in your kitchen at four a.m., a bad guy who'd been there long enough, Jack speculated, for his eyes to fully adjust to the dark.

No weapon. No vest. Only one working arm. Thoroughly screwed.

He did have his radio and managed, as Sahir lunged, to press the panic button on the top. That gave him what? Two, three minutes to play middle of the night ninja with this asshole before help arrived?

In keeping with his awesome new tactic of utilizing the most inappropriate weapons in lethal force situations, Jack threw the radio at Sahir's head and dove to the floor.

A blast of pain made him involuntarily cry out and reminded him how terrible an idea it was to drop and roll on his injured shoulder. Getting fileted was an even worse one.

He would've gone out the way he came in and run, Jack wasn't that heroic, but Sahir didn't give him a chance, moved like three men at once, a lethal blur.

Jack knew he had to get the goddamned sling off but all he could manage was another agonizing roll, then an awkward backwards scramble on the tile floor like a crab, dodging endless parries of the knife. It was one of those curved deals, meant for close battle, designed to kill.

Sahir was no Avi; no hesitation, no uncertainty.

No pausing for conversation or, seemingly, breath. Jack searched desperately for something better to throw. Famous last words to Dani, *I'll be fine*. His guns tantalizingly close but Sahir was, as Jack suspected he'd be, all business. *Hold on a second, Mr. Bad Guy, while I rearm*. Not gonna happen.

On the floor between the stove and the kitchen table, Jack groped blindly with his left hand until he felt the leg of a chair. In one quick movement, grateful for every crunch he'd ever done, he sat up and swung it. And connected. Sahir staggered backward, only for a second, but it was enough for Jack to wriggle out of the sling and regain his feet.

He blocked the next slash with both arms, back of his wrists facing outward, protecting the vulnerable interior with its veins and tendons. Grabbed Sahir's right wrist with his left hand and twisted while he pushed, kicked with his right leg, punched with his weakened right arm.

Avoid. Block. Disarm.

Yeah, that third part was turning out to be tricky. Jack practiced for situations like this including regular Krav Maga training, the Israeli self-defense system. He knew how to disarm individuals of knives, guns, and apparently even Crock-Pots. Krav, however, required strength and speed, neither of which he had in excess at the moment. It also required two arms.

His blocks were good and instinctive, but Jack knew that knife fights were fast, ugly, and you never walked away clean. His experience told him his arms were getting cut but damned if he could feel it; adrenaline was a wondrous thing. At least, he had some momentum on his side now, and he pushed Sahir back as they fought, got into the rhythm, was immensely gratified to see blood trickling from the asshole's nose.

Sahir gripped his weapon blade down, professional, dressed in dark clothes that made him hard to see even as Jack's eyes adjusted. Block, grab, kick and Sahir would slither like a wiry snake out of Jack's weakened grasp. Not even breathing hard.

Then Sahir changed it up, came straight at him instead of slashing, and the son of a bitch was laughing. Having a good time. Jack took one step backward, diagonally and to the side, blocked with the outside of his left arm and managed to land a punch with his right dead center of Sahir's throat followed by two quick kicks to the groin.

This had to end now. Jack's stronger left hand closed around Sahir's wrist again, torqued as hard as he could manage and pushed the arm close to Sahir's body so that if he stabbed anyone it would be himself in the armpit. All the while attacking with his right knee.

Sahir's eyes glittered. Jack held on with every bit of strength he had. Sahir released pressure so suddenly he pulled Jack forward, precipitating another searingly painful roll. He found himself by the door to the laundry room, braced with a hand on either side, and kicked Sahir with both feet. Not Krav by the book but it worked. Sahir landed hard, but kept his grip on the knife.

"I'm gonna kill you, asshole." Maybe Jack only thought it, because he was aware of conserving both breath and what little energy he possessed by not talking. Maybe Sahir read minds. At least he wasn't laughing anymore.

Slash. Upward stab. Downward stab. A series of repeated jabs that Jack blocked with the outside of his right forearm all the while hitting with his left. A second shot to Sahir's throat. A forceful palm to his chin that snapped his head back with a sickening crunch and would have finished off ninety-nine percent of the human race.

But.

In that fragment of time Sahir regrouped and shook his head. As if watching the scene in stop motion Jack saw each individual drop of sweat as it flew off Sahir's brow. Jack planted his left foot, regained a secure grip on Sahir's right wrist with his left hand, swung his right leg as the knife in Sahir's hand headed for Jack's eyes.

Boot connected soundly with knee and Jack felt the shockwaves in his own bones as Sahir went down with an unbelievably satisfying curse. The arm headed for Jack's face flailed harmlessly.

Jack maintained his grip and fell with him. Joints were the weakest links. Shoulders, ankles, wrists.

"Drop the knife."

"Fuck you."

Elbows. Heard the snap and the scream of agony as he landed, full weight on Sahir's hyperextended right arm. The knife flew away under the kitchen table. Sahir was human after all.

Jack kneeled over him and punched, pure blood lust now. His shoulder no longer mattered. Nothing mattered. Intoxicated so that he felt only insatiable greed, hunger to make this prick pay, to make him hurt, to make him suffer. In his memory, later, Jack would recall the lights being on, Sahir's face swelling like a blowfish, blood spraying. In reality Sahir was a dim blur.

"You come into my house?" Words punctuated with blows. "You. Piece. Of. Shit."

Neutralize the threat.

What every officer was trained to do. How many times do you shoot someone? As many as needed to neutralize the threat. No more, no less. Words civilians didn't understand. Words that finally penetrated the hot, adrenaline-saturated blood coursing through every cell of Jack's body. It felt like electricity, irresistible, instinctive, inevitable. Age-old, archetypal memory in his DNA from when men were warriors, our village or yours, our women and children or yours. My life or yours.

He stopped, backed off a few inches, watched. The threat wasn't fighting. It wasn't moving. It might not have still been breathing. It sure as hell wouldn't be using its right arm the same way ever again.

Out of habit, he handcuffed Sahir to one of the legs of the table. Secured the knife and barely registered the blood on it. Then moved to retrieve one of his guns.

But when Jack stood a wave of dizziness hit him, so bad he grabbed the edge of the counter for support. An area on the left side of his rib cage throbbed in a way that stood out from the other assorted variations of misery. He reached for a dish towel, pressed it to his side and a dark stain spread. When? How bad? It must be shallow because if the blade had slipped between two of his ribs he wouldn't be standing at all. Jack hadn't noticed in the heat of battle and it made him want to finish kicking Sahir to a pulp.

No. Enough. Sirens. Sounded close. He had to stay conscious, focus for a few more seconds. It was done. Sahir was dead or he wasn't, but it was done.

CHAPTER SIXTY-SEVEN

———

IT WAS A blustery day, cold but sunny, when they exhumed a mass grave in the middle of a suburban Denver neighborhood. Twelve acres and an abandoned, low-slung building, the former Bluefield manufacturing facility that for years contaminated adjacent houses so severely toxin levels exceeded government guidelines by a factor of hundreds.

From the air, the site resembled a grassy abstract dotted with patches of deteriorating cement and a few sickly trees. It was enclosed by easily breached chain link fencing; footpaths wove through the seemingly empty lot made by kids exploring, joggers wanting to escape traffic, murderers seeking to dispose of bodies.

Wind whipped sharply from the west, air forced up against the edge of the mountains, cycling upslope and back onto the plains and a city devoid of comfort. Like the morning when they found Lucia, Jack pointlessly tugged his collar up.

For days he stood at an arbitrary safe distance and watched technicians in hazmat suits painstakingly search with specialized geophysical devices, ground penetrating radar, and cadaver dogs. Then methodical, agonizingly slow excavation with probes, shovels, and trowels. Forensic anthropologists and medical examiners, including Dr. Greer Spahr, provided guidance. A priest stood by offering to sanctify what couldn't ever be explained.

Young women buried like garbage among dented drums of industrial solvent, metal scrap still marked with oil, and chunks of rusting equipment. As bodies were uncovered Jack realized how much he didn't want to be right. His certainty when he and Mike first watched the porn videos that those girls were dead—this was the worst kind of vindication. All of their fears had been realized and then some. They'd built a chronology and had names to match with remains. Families to notify. Closure built from despair.

Bibi and Heather had helped identify the first Harrowsmith girl, or, rather, girls because Farah acquired twins Sandra and Sylvia Quintana from Dustin's charity. Bibi especially acted glad it was finally over, relieved to be able to tell his story, cooperative. According to Bibi, Sandra disappeared first, ostensibly because Ken couldn't keep his hands off her and Farah wanted to send a firm message about molesting the help—a message Ken failed to receive.

Sylvia, renamed Adah, stayed for another two years before running. Bibi told them Farah and Sahir never "dealt" with her and were enraged by her unplanned departure. Score one for Sylvia if it was true she escaped. Once they completed exhumations, and had a final body count, maybe they'd be able to tell for sure.

After Sylvia broke out, also per Bibi's statement, Farah installed fancy locks on the doors and cameras in the rooms because Harrowsmith Girl number three Inez Gloriana Remirez, aka Sarah, had been both imprisoned and filmed.

During Inez's sentence—Jack couldn't think of it any other way—Farah made an extended trip to Tehran, allowing Bibi's relationship with Inez to flourish. While Farah was visiting, her brother Mohamed fell ill and died, and they knew from the intelligence reports provided by the FBI what he was poisoned with. If they were able to confirm they'd found Inez, testing would be done on her remains to see if they could identify a toxin and match it to what killed Mohamed.

To Jack the timing was beyond ominous, Mohamed poisoned while Farah was visiting. She certainly had motive, after a sexual assault that left her pregnant and subsequently mutilated. Then, not long after Farah's return to Denver, Inez fell sick and died an excruciating death taking the "special medicine" Farah provided. No way that was a coincidence.

Following Inez, Harrowsmith Girl number four was Dinah, birth name: Cristela Vigil, who lasted more than two years. That was a busy travel period for Ken which lightened her sentence somewhat and kept her fresh longer. By then, Farah had perfected surveillance and Bibi had no chance to bond with the help, being kept busy at the restaurant and spa.

Abigail was girl number five, born Manuela Cortolino, weeping and hanging onto Ken's trousers in her last video, on all fours while he whipped her with a riding crop, called her fat and slow. Bibi remembered quick turnover from Dinah to Abigail and again to Lucia; perhaps Farah concluded poison took too long, or by then preferred delegating to Sahir.

At least, that was Jack's first theory.

Harrowsmith Girl number six, Lucia Santiago.

Farah inadvertently told Jack the truth about one thing: there was video. She must have thought she destroyed it all, wiped hard drives and deleted files. Counted on it. But she didn't count on the cloud or police forensics.

The night of Lucia's death Farah and Ken were in the living room, still dressed up from their benefit. She had a small glass of what looked like brandy. He had a tall glass of soda. Lucia arrived with Bibi and visibly started when she saw Farah, hand to her throat as if hiding her necklace. Except it wasn't there. She'd been wearing it at the hotel and then must have given it to Raven for futile safekeeping.

In the video, Farah seemed glad to see them. "This is a happy accident."

"Oh shit, you're up," Bibi said.

Farah continued in the same pleasant, country club tone. "Lucia, are you sleeping with my nephew as well?"

Ken went on alert. "What do you mean 'as well'?"

"You haven't told him?" Farah gazed placidly at Lucia.

"Please, don't." Lucia wore the dress and fur coat Jack had seen on the hotel security video.

Bibi stood next to a heavy wooden sideboard with a marble top, hand on one of several decanters, about to pour.

Farah asked him to leave. "Drink in your room."

"That's not fair," Bibi said. "She came home with me."

Lucia pleaded, "No, Bibi tell them, it's not what you think."

"You were going to sleep with my nephew?" Ken thundered and Lucia denied.

Bibi whined, oblivious to Lucia's distress. "Why's it so hard for you to believe she might like me? Why don't I ever get to have any fun?"

"Bibi," Farah said, "take that whole decanter with you to your room. It's cognac."

"No, please don't leave," Lucia said. "Tell them. I just wanted to find my purse."

She grew increasingly frantic, begged Bibi repeatedly, and despite knowing the outcome, every time he viewed the video Jack willed Bibi to help her. Instead, Bibi grabbed the decanter and left.

Farah said, "My husband has very high standards. You should have informed him that you weren't a virgin. Your deception was unkind."

Lucia looked desperately between Farah and Ken. "I swear I was. You know I was."

"Bitch, what are you playing at?"

Ken bore down on Lucia as Farah spoke in that same honeyed voice.

"Hasn't Lucia told you the happy news?"

"No, please. I'll go away, I won't bother anyone."

"Our Lucia is expecting." Farah watched Ken with her teeth bared, couldn't call it a smile. "Pregnant. And it can't be yours."

She wielded Ken like a weapon, knew exactly what would provoke him enough to kill. Ken exploded. Lucia screamed, "No." Over and over. He demanded she tell him who she slept with. She wouldn't. Ken grabbed her, shook her, slapped her.

Big guy, a foot taller, outweighed Lucia by a hundred pounds. It was hard to watch. Her slender body jolted, as fragile in his hands as kindling. To the end she wouldn't give up the father's name, loyalty completely undeserved by Dustin.

"I'm so glad you met someone closer to your own age," Farah said. "Much more desirable than sleeping with an old man like my husband, I get it."

"You were mine," Ken shouted. "Only mine. No other man's hands."

Farah laughed. "Well, it seems there have been at least a few other hands. What are you going to do, *darling*? Are you going to let her disrespect you this way, let you believe she was a virgin when she wasn't?"

For a moment Ken hesitated. Looked between weeping, panicked Lucia and his calm, brittle wife.

Farah lit the final match. "It's a matter of honor."

Lucia backed against the sideboard and begged one final time for her life and that of her unborn child. "Let me go, please, I'll never tell anyone, please just let me leave."

Ken didn't. A big hand encircled each of her upper arms.

He pulled her forward as if into an embrace then slammed her back, hard, so that the base of her skull struck the beveled marble edge of the furniture.

Lucia went limp. Ken let her drop to the floor.

"I didn't think you had it in you." Farah sat on the couch as if watching a spectator sport. Lightly clapped her hands. "Bravo."

She took a sip of her drink, a perverse toast to a dying girl.

"Lucia?" Ken bent over, turned to Farah. Sounded uncertain. "What should we do?"

Farah got up, walked close, and put a hand on his shoulder. "You should go to bed. Tomorrow is a big travel day."

Ken stared down at Lucia. "Do you think—I mean—is she all right?"

"Stop." She caressed Ken's arm, tugged him away. "Go to bed. I'll deal with this and then join you."

"Shouldn't we get her a doctor?"

"You've had a terrible shock. You're not thinking clearly. Leave it all to me."

Ken left with disgustingly little argument. Farah never touched Lucia, never checked for a pulse, certainly didn't get a doctor. Simply returned to her spot on the couch and worked her phone. Twenty eternal minutes of video ticked by. Farah finished her drink and poured another, had to reach over Lucia to do it.

"I got here as fast as I could but with the weather—" Sahir took in the scene, bent down, put his fingers against the side of Lucia's throat. Closed her eyes.

"We must wash her." Farah started to leave the room. "Bring her to the bathtub. I'll get cloth to wrap her in."

Sahir touched a smear of blood on the edge of the marble. "Need to clean this up."

Farah turned back, casual, careless. "I'll let the new one do it."

"What happened?"

Her lips curved into a smile. "My husband surprised me."

We must give her a proper burial this time, Farah had said. By which she'd meant naked in an alley next to a dumpster in a snowstorm. A step up. For a beautiful, pregnant young woman who made the mistakes of wanting a better life and falling in love with a psychopathic preacher.

Dustin remained uncooperative, to date wouldn't reveal how many girls he placed with the Harrowsmiths or help locate individuals sold to other families. He concealed children with the intent to sell them, which qualified as kidnapping; kidnapping became a class one felony in Colorado if the person suffered bodily injury. Dustin's extreme disdain for the value of human life, in addition to being loathsome, fit the statute perfectly. Add on multiple counts of trafficking, sexual assault, money laundering, conspiracy—Dustin could go away for multiple lifetimes. Best case, he'd spend the rest of his days leading a prison ministry. No wonder he ran.

They might never prove how many people Sahir had killed on Farah's orders, how many were Ken's doing, and how many she took a more hands on approach to, like Inez and, allegedly, her brother. Farah was being held without bail after entering not guilty pleas; Jack fully expected her to work the battered spouse angle. Let her try.

Ken received a life sentence without the possibility of parole. In return for his assistance, Bibi received a plea deal that included some much-needed time in a mental health institution. Sahir survived to become someone's— or many someones'—one-armed bitch in prison. Very least that could happen to him.

Greer took a break from monitoring the exhumations and walked over to say hello. She pulled off her mask and nodded at the sling holding Jack's right arm snug against his side.

"What happened to you?"

It was the first time he'd talked to her since after Valeria's autopsy.

Additional injury to his right shoulder from the fight necessitated surgery and a long rehab, but he was alive. Also on the plus side, only four of his knife wounds required stitches and none had nicked anything important. He'd throw another punch, hold another woman in his arms, lift another drink. Nicki, with her parents' support and her friends helping her, was recovering fast. Heather had so far stayed clean and was reunited with her children.

Gabi and the other girls from the "spa" were safe, at least for the moment, in shelters where they'd receive medical and mental health services. They'd also be connected with legal assistance and educational opportunities. Deportation wasn't in Gabi's future if Jack had anything to say about it. He got her the promised letter for immigration and was helping her navigate a complex bureaucracy that he knew, despite her tough talk, completely intimidated her. Although she bombarded the assistant district attorney with questions every chance she got and was now convinced she wanted to be a lawyer. Gabi couldn't wait to go back to school, and the last time Jack saw her he almost didn't recognize her, she'd changed so much in a short time.

In addition to kidnapping, murder, and trafficking the charges against Farah, Dustin, and Sahir ran into the hundreds. Organized crime, keeping a place of child prostitution, pandering, sexual servitude, assault with a deadly weapon—the list went on and on. Deciphering it all could take years, providing Gabi ample time to earn permanent immigration status. With her help they'd also found a badly beaten young girl named Willow, real name Bonita, who'd run off after Sahir assaulted her.

But these girls in the ground. Not even coffins. Wrapped in the now familiar white cotton, deteriorated with time, moisture, contamination. A snippet from an old classic poem ran through Jack's mind, *"...Steal from the world, and not a stone tell where I lie..."*

For no reason he could figure other than spite.

To Greer he simply said, "A girl fell on me, and not in a good way."

She moved so she stood right next to him, strength in numbers. "I don't know how you make sense of it."

Jack knew she didn't expect him to answer which was good, because he didn't have any. He'd solved a lot of homicides. And he hadn't solved anything.

Slim, white shrouds were carefully placed on tarps on the ground, one next to the other, human cordwood.

He whispered names like a prayer: *Sylvia, Inez, Cristela, Manuela, Lucia.*

Greer touched Jack's arm and roused him from his morbid inventory. "Time for me to go back to work."

She stepped forward to supervise the handling of the bodies and Jack felt his first hint of relief. Here at last, at the very end, these girls had someone who would take good care of them.

RESOURCES

What is Human Trafficking?

Human Trafficking is a crime against humanity. It involves an act of recruiting, transporting, transferring, harboring or receiving a person through a use of force, coercion or other means, for the purpose of exploiting them. Every year, thousands of men, women and children fall into the hands of traffickers, in their own countries and abroad.

Trafficking is a lucrative industry. It has been identified as the fastest growing criminal industry in the world and is second only to drug trafficking as the most profitable illegal industry in the world.

In the United States, the most common venue or location of sex trafficking is illicit massage or spa businesses. According to Polaris Project, a leader in the fight to end human trafficking, there are more than 9,000 illicit massage businesses in the United States—compare that to 8,222 Starbucks.

———

To learn more:
https://thisishumantrafficking.com/

Polaris Project
https://polarisproject.org/

Polaris operates the National Human Trafficking Hotline
(NHTH) 1-888-373-7888 (TTY: 711)
https://humantraffickinghotline.org/
Or text "BeFree" to 233733

In April 2019, the Denver Police Department (DPD)
created a dedicated human trafficking enforcement team.
Learn more about the DPD at:
https://www.denvergov.org/Government/
Departments/Police-Department

(Denver-based) Laboratory to Combat Human
Trafficking (LCHT)
https://combathumantrafficking.org/
info@combathumantrafficking.org

Colorado Human Trafficking Council
https://sites.google.com/state.co.us/human-trafficking-
council

Human Trafficking Task Force of Southern Colorado
https://www.ht-colorado.org/

The FBI
https://www.fbi.gov/investigate/violent-crime/human-
trafficking

The United Nations Office on Drugs and Crime
https://www.unodc.org/unodc/en/data-and-analysis/
glotip.html

ABOUT THE AUTHOR

A NATIVE NEW YORKER, Merit Clark now writes from the Rocky Mountains. KILLING STREAK, the first mystery in the Jack Fariel series, won the Colorado Independent Publishers Association (CIPA) EVVY Book Award and was a quarter-finalist in the Amazon Breakthrough Novel contest.

Merit's short fiction has also won awards, most notably the high-velocity RESCUE, featured in the Blood & Gasoline anthology from Hex Publishers and singled out for notice by Kirkus Reviews, and an unsympathetic volunteer in HOSPICE, awarded fourth place (out of 18,000 entries) in the 74th Annual Writer's Digest Writing Competition.

You'd be correct in assuming this all sounds dark and extremely violent for mild-mannered software developer. In the course of research, Merit has been shot at by gang members, worn a bomb suit, and broken into a gangbanger's girlfriend's apartment. Not all at the same time.

For more about Merit including book news, links to purchase, blogs, and way too much information about serial killers, please visit www.meritclark.com

As well as the usual online haunts including:

Like on Facebook:
www.facebook.com/MeritClark
Follow on Twitter:
@MeritClark

Literary Crime on Pinterest:
www.pinterest.com/meritwriter/literarycrime/
Instagram:
@meritclarkauthor (less murder, more cute baby
wildlife photos)